Abou

Michelle Douglas has ...
since 2007, and belie ...
world. She's a sucker ...
have a secret stash of ...
how to laugh. She lives in Newcastle Australia with her
own romantic hero, a house full of dust and books, and
an eclectic collection of sixties and seventies vinyl. She
loves to hear from readers and can be contacted via her
website michelle-douglas.com

Beth Kery loves romance, and the more emotionally
laden, smart and sexy the romance, the better. She has
always been fascinated by human beings, their
motivations and emotions, so she earned an advanced
degree in the behavioural sciences. Her hope is that her
stories linger in the reader's mind long after the last
page is finished.

USA TODAY bestselling Author **Jules Bennett** has
penned more than fifty novels during her short career.
She's married to her high school sweetheart, has two
active girls, and is a former salon owner. Jules can be
found on Twitter, Facebook (Fan Page), and her website
julesbennett.com. She holds contests via these three
outlets with each release and loves to hear from readers!

Indecent Proposals

Indecent Proposals:
The Best Friend

MICHELLE DOUGLAS

BETH KERY

JULES BENNETT

MILLS & BOON

First Published in Great Britain 2022
By Mills & Boon, an imprint of HarperCollins*Publishers,* Ltd
1 London Bridge Street, London, SE1 9GF

www.harpercollins.co.uk

HarperCollins*Publishers*
1st Floor, Watermarque Building,
Ringsend Road, Dublin 4, Ireland

INDECENT PROPOSALS: THE BEST FRIEND © 2022 Harlequin
Enterprises ULC

First Comes Baby... © 2013 Michelle Douglas
The Soldier's Baby Bargain © 2012 Beth Kery
From Best Friend to Daddy © 2018 Jules Bennett

ISBN 978-0-263-30580-7

MIX
Paper | Supporting
responsible forestry
FSC™ C007454

This book is produced from independently certified FSC™ paper
to ensure responsible forest management.

For more information visit: www.harpercollins.co.uk/green

Printed and Bound in Spain using 100% Renewable electricity at
CPI Black Print, Barcelona

FIRST COMES BABY...

MICHELLE DOUGLAS

By Mills & Boon

To my editor, Sally Williamson, for her keen
editorial eye and all her support.

Many, many thanks.

CHAPTER ONE

'BEN, WOULD YOU consider being my sperm donor?'

Ben Sullivan's head rocked back at his best friend's question. He thrust his glass of wine to the coffee table before he spilled its contents all over the floor, and spun to face her. Meg held up her hand as if she expected him to interrupt her.

Interrupt her?

He coughed. Choked. He couldn't breathe, let alone interrupt her! When he'd demanded to know what was on her mind this wasn't what he'd been expecting. Not by a long shot. He'd thought it would be something to do Elsie or her father, but...

He collapsed onto the sofa and wedged himself in tight against the arm. Briefly, cravenly, he wished himself back in Mexico instead of here in Fingal Bay.

A sperm donor? Him?

A giant hand reached out to seize him around the chest, squeezing every last atom of air out of his lungs. A loud buzzing roared in his ears.

'Let me tell you first why I'd like you as my donor, and then what I see as your role in the baby's life.'

Her no-nonsense tone helped alleviate the pressure in his chest. The buzzing started to recede. He shot forward and stabbed a finger at her. 'Why in God's name do you need a sperm donor? Why are you pursuing IVF at all? You're not even thirty!' She was twenty-eight, like him. 'There's loads of time.'

'No, there's not.'

Everything inside him stilled.

She took a seat at the other end of the sofa and swallowed. He watched the bob of her throat and his hands clenched. She tried to smile but the effort it cost her hurt him.

'My doctor has told me I'm in danger of becoming infertile.'

Bile burned his throat. Meg had always wanted kids. She owned a childcare centre, for heaven's sake. She'd be a great mum. It took an enormous force of will to bite back the angry torrent that burned his throat. Railing at fate wouldn't help her.

'I'm booking in to have IVF so I can fall pregnant asap.'

Hence the reason she was asking him if he'd be her sperm donor. *Him*? He still couldn't get his head around it. But... 'You'll make a brilliant mum, Meg.'

'Thank you.' Her smile was a touch shy. It was the kind of smile that could turn the screws on a guy. 'Not everyone will be as understanding, I fear, but...' She leaned towards him, her blonde hair brushing her shoulders. 'I'm not scared of being a single mum, and financially I'm doing very well. I have no doubt of my ability to look after not only myself but whoever else should come along.'

Neither did he. He'd meant it when he'd said she'd be a great mother. She wouldn't be cold and aloof. She'd love her child. She'd fill his or her days with love and laughter, and it would never have a moment's doubt about how much it was cherished.

His chest burned. An ache started up behind his eyes. She'd give her child the kind of childhood they had both craved.

Meg straightened. 'Now, listen. For the record, if you hate the idea, if it makes you the slightest bit uncomfortable, then we just drop the subject, okay?'

His heart started to thud.

'Ben?'

She had her bossy-boots voice on and it almost made him smile. He gave a hard nod. 'Right.'

'Right.' Her hands twisted together and she dragged in a

deep breath. Her knuckles turned white. Ben's heart thumped harder.

'Ben, you're my dearest friend. I trust you with my life. So it somehow only seems right to trust you with another life—a life that will be so important to me.'

He closed his eyes and hauled in more air.

'You're healthy, fit and intelligent—everything I want for my child.'

He opened his eyes again.

She grinned. 'And, while you will never, ever get me to admit this in front of another living soul, there isn't another man whose genes I admire more.'

Behind the grin he sensed her sincerity. And, just like every other time he visited, Meg managed to melt the hardness that had grown in him while he'd been away jetting around the world.

'I want a baby so badly I ache with it.' Her smile faded. 'But having a baby like this—through IVF—there really isn't anyone else to share the journey with me. And an anonymous donor…' She glanced down at her hands. 'I don't know—it just seems a bit cold-blooded, that's all. But if that donor were you, knowing you were a part of it…'

She met his gaze. He read in her face how much this meant to her.

'Well, that wouldn't be so bad, you know? I mean, when my child eventually asks about its father I'll at least be able to answer his or her questions.'

Yeah, but *he'd* be that father. He ran a finger around the collar of his tee shirt 'What kind of questions?'

'Hair colour, eye colour. If you were fun, if you were kind.' She pulled in a breath. 'Look, let me make it clear that I know you have absolutely no desire to settle down, and I know you've never wanted kids. That's not what I'm asking of you. I'm not asking you for any kind of commitment. I see your role as favourite uncle and nothing more.'

She stared at him for a moment. 'I know you, Ben. I promise your name won't appear on the birth certificate unless you want to. I promise the child will never know your identity. Also,' she added, 'I would absolutely die if you were to offer me any kind of financial assistance.'

That made him smile. Meg was darn independent—he'd give her that. Independent *and* bossy. He suspected she probably thought she made more money than him too.

The fact was neither one of them was crying poor.

'I know that whether you agree to my proposition or not you'll love and support any child of mine the way you love and support me.'

That was true.

She stared at him in a way that suddenly made him want to fidget.

She curled her legs beneath her. 'I can see there's something you want to say. Please, I know this is a big ask so don't hold back.'

Her words didn't surprise him. There'd never been any games between him and Meg. Ben didn't rate family—not his mother, not his father and not his grandmother. Oh, he understood he owed his grandmother. Meg lectured him about it every time he was home, and she was right. Elsie had fed, clothed and housed him, had made sure he'd gone to school and visited the doctor when he was sick, but she'd done it all without any visible signs of pleasure. His visits now didn't seem to give her any pleasure either. They were merely a duty on both sides.

He'd make sure she never wanted for anything in her old age, but as far as he was concerned that was where his responsibility to her ended. He only visited her to make Meg happy.

He mightn't rate family, but he rated friendship—and Meg was the best friend he had. Megan Parrish had saved him. She'd taken one look at his ten-year-old self, newly abandoned on Elsie's doorstep, and had announced that from that day forth they were to be best friends for ever. She'd given his starved heart all the companionship, loyalty and love it had needed. She'd nurtured them both with fairytales about families who loved one another; and with the things they'd do, the adventures they'd have, when they grew up.

She'd jogged beside him when nothing else would ease the burn in his soul. He'd swum beside her when nothing else would do for her but to immerse herself in an underwater world—where she would swim for as long as she could before coming up for air.

And he'd watched more than once as she'd suffered the crippling agony of endometriosis. Nothing in all his life had ever made him feel so helpless as to witness her pain and be unable to ease it. His hands clenched. He hadn't realised she still suffered from it.

'Ben?'

'I'm concerned about your health.' Wouldn't her getting pregnant be an unnecessary risk at this point? 'That's what I want to talk about.'

He shifted on the sofa to survey her more fully. She held her glass out and he topped it up from the bottle of Chardonnay they'd opened during dinner. Her hand shook and something inside him clenched. He slammed the bottle to the coffee table. 'Are you okay?' he barked without preamble.

She eyed him over the glass as she took a sip. 'Yes.'

His tension eased. She wouldn't lie to him. 'But?'

'But it's a monthly problem.' She shrugged. 'You know that.'

But he'd thought she'd grown out of it!

Because that's what you wanted to think.

His hands fisted. 'Is there anything I can do?'

Her face softened in the dim light and he wanted to reach across and pull her into his arms and just hold her…breathe her in, press all of his good health and vitality into her body so she would never be sick again. 'No doubt Elsie's told you that I've had a couple of severe bouts of endometriosis over the last few months?'

His stomach rolled and roiled. He nodded. When he'd roared into town on his bike earlier in the day Meg had immediately sent him next door to duty-visit his grandmother, even though they all knew he only returned to Fingal Bay to visit Meg. Elsie's two topics of conversation had been Meg's health and Meg's father's health. The news had been chafing at him ever since.

'Is the endometriosis the reason you're in danger of becoming infertile?'

'Yes.' She sat back, but her knuckles had turned white again. 'Which is why I'm lusting after your genes and…'

'And?' His voice came out hoarse. How could fate do this to his best friend?

'I don't know what to call it. Maybe there isn't actually a term for it, but it seems somehow wrong to create a child with an anonymous person. So, I want your in-their-prime genes and your lack of anonymity.'

Holding her gaze, he rested his elbows on his knees. 'No fathering responsibilities at all?'

'God, no! If I thought for one moment you felt pressured in that direction I'd end this discussion now.'

And have a baby with an anonymous donor? He could see she would, but he could also see there'd always be a worry at the back of her mind. A fear of the unknown and what it could bring.

There was one very simple reason why Meg had turned to him—she trusted him. And he trusted her. She knew him, and knew how deftly he avoided commitment of any kind. She knew precisely what she was asking. And what she'd be getting if he went along with this scheme of hers.

If he agreed to be her sperm donor it would be him helping her become a mother. End of story. It wouldn't be his child. It would be Meg's.

Still, he knew Meg. He knew she'd risk her own health in an attempt to fall pregnant and then carry the child full term and give birth to it. Everything inside him wanted to weep at the thought of her never becoming a mother, but he couldn't be party to her risking her health further. He dragged a hand back through his hair and tried to find the words he needed.

'I will tell you something, though, that is far less admirable.' She sank back against the arm of the sofa and stretched her legs out until one of them touched his knee. 'I'm seriously looking forward to not having endometriosis.'

It took a moment for her words to reach him. He'd been too intent on studying the shape of her leg. And just like that he found himself transported to that moment ten years ago when he'd realised just how beautiful Meg had become. A moment that had started out as an attempt at comfort and turned passionate. In the blink of an eye.

The memory made him go cold all over. He'd thought he'd banished that memory from his mind for ever. That night he'd almost made the biggest mistake of his whole sorry life and risked destroying the only thing that meant anything to him—Meg's friendship. He shook his head, his heart suddenly pounding. It was stupid to remember it now. *Forget it!*

And then her words reached him. He leaned forward, careful not to touch her. 'What did you just say about the endometriosis?'

'You can't get endometriosis while you're pregnant. Pregnancy may even cure me of it.'

If he did what she asked, if he helped her get pregnant, she might never get endometriosis again.

He almost hollered out his assent before self-preservation kicked in. Not that he needed protecting from Meg, but he wanted them on the same page before he agreed to her plan.

'Let me just get this straight. I want to make sure we're working on the same assumptions here. If I agree to be your sperm donor I'd want to be completely anonymous. I wouldn't want anyone to know. I wouldn't want the child to ever know. Just like it wouldn't if you'd gone through a sperm bank.'

'Not all sperm banks are anonymous.' She shrugged. 'But I figured you'd want anonymity.'

She had that right. If the child knew who its father was it would have expectations. He didn't *do* expectations.

'And this is *your* baby, Meg. The only thing I'd be doing is donating sperm, right?'

'Absolutely.'

'I'd be Uncle Ben, nothing more?'

'Nothing more.'

He opened and closed his hands. Meg would be a brilliant mother and she deserved every opportunity of making that dream come true. She wasn't asking for more than he could give.

He stood. 'Yes,' he said. 'I'll help out any way I can.'

Meg leapt to her feet. Her heart pounded so hard and grew so big in her chest she thought she might take off into the air.

When she didn't, she leapt forward and threw her arms around all six-feet-three-inches of honed male muscle that was her dearest friend in the world. 'Thank you, Ben! Thank you!'

Dear, *dear* Ben.

She pulled back when his heat slammed into her, immediately reminded of the vitality and utter life contained by all that honed muscle and hot flesh. A reminder that hit her afresh during each and every one of Ben's brief visits.

Her pulse gave a funny little skip and she hugged herself. A baby!

Nevertheless, she made herself step back and swallow the excess of her excitement. 'Are you sure you don't want to take some time to think it over?' She had no intention of railroading him into a decision as important as this. She wanted—needed—him to be comfortable and at peace with this decision.

'He shook his head. 'I know everything I need to. Plus I

know you'll be a great mum. And you know everything you need to about me. If you're happy to be a single parent, then I'm happy to help you out.'

She hugged herself again. She knew her grin must be stupidly broad, but she couldn't help it. 'You don't know what this means to me.'

'Yes, I do.'

Yes, he probably did. His answering grin made her stomach soften, and the memory of their one illicit kiss stole through her—as it usually did when emotions ran high between the two of them. She bit back a sigh. She'd done her best to forget that kiss, but ten years had passed and still she remembered it.

She stiffened. Not that she wanted to repeat it!

Good Lord! If things had got out of control that night, as they'd almost threatened to, they'd—

She suppressed a shudder. Well, for one thing they wouldn't be having this conversation now. In fact she'd probably never have clapped eyes on Ben again.

She swallowed her sudden nausea. 'How's the jet lag?' She made her voice deliberately brisk.

He folded his arms and hitched up his chin. It emphasised the shadow on his jaw. Emphasised the disreputable bad-boy languor—the cocky swing to his shoulders and the loose-limbed ease of his hips. 'I keep telling you, I don't get jet lag. One day you'll believe me.'

He grinned the slow grin that had knocked more women than she could count off their feet.

But not her.

She shook her head. She had no idea how he managed to slip in and out of different time zones so easily. 'I made a cheese and fruit platter, if you're interested, and I know it's only spring, and still cool, but as it's nearly a full moon I thought we could sit out on the veranda and admire the view.'

He shrugged with lazy ease. 'Sounds good to me.'

They moved to the padded chairs on the veranda. In the

moonlight the arc of the bay glowed silver and the lights on the water winked and shimmered. Meg drew a breath of salt-laced air into her lungs. The night air cooled the overheated skin of her cheeks and neck, and eventually helped to slow the crazy racing of her pulse.

But her heart remained large and swollen in her chest. A baby!

'Elsie said your father's been ill?'

That brought her back to earth with a thump. She sliced off a piece of Camembert and nodded.

He frowned. The moonlight was brighter than the lamp-only light of the living room they'd just retired from, and she could see each and every one of his emotions clearly—primarily frustration and concern for her.

'Elsie said he'd had a kidney infection.'

Both she and Ben called his grandmother by her given name. Not Grandma, or Nanna, or even an honorary Aunt Elsie. It was what she preferred.

Meg bit back a sigh. 'It was awful.' It was pointless being anything other than honest with Ben, even as she tried to shield him from the worst of her father and Elsie. 'He became frail overnight. I moved back home to look after him for a bit.' She'd given up her apartment in Nelson Bay, but not her job as director of the childcare centre she owned, even if her second-in-command *had* had to step in and take charge for a week. Moving back home had only ever been meant as a temporary measure.

And it hadn't proved a very successful one. It hadn't drawn father and daughter closer. If anything her father had only retreated further. However, it had ensured he'd received three square meals a day and taken his medication.

'How is he now?'

'It took him a couple of months, but he's fit as a fiddle again. He's moved into a small apartment in Nelson Bay. He said he wanted to be closer to the amenities—the doctor, the shops, the bowling club.'

Nelson Bay was ten minutes away and the main metropolitan centre of Port Stephens. Fingal Bay crouched at Port Stephens' south-eastern edge—a small seaside community that was pretty and unspoilt. It was where she and Ben had grown up.

She loved it.

Ben didn't.

'Though I have a feeling that was just an excuse and he simply couldn't stand being in the same house as his only daughter any longer.'

Ben's glass halted halfway to his mouth and he swore at whatever he saw in her face. 'Hell, Meg, why do you have to take this stuff so much to heart?'

After all this time. She heard his unspoken rider. She rubbed her chest and stared out at the bay and waited for the ache to recede.

'Anyway—' his frown grew ferocious '—I bet he just didn't want you sacrificing your life to look after him.'

She laughed. Dear Ben. 'You're sure about that, are you?' Ever since Meg's mother had died when she was eight years old her father had…What? Gone missing in action? Given up? Forgotten he had a daughter? Oh, he'd been there physically. He'd continued to work hard and rake in the money. But he'd shut himself off emotionally—even from her, his only child.

When she glanced back at Ben she found him staring out at the bay, lips tight and eyes narrowed to slits. She had a feeling he wasn't taking in the view at all. The ache in her chest didn't go away. 'I don't get them, you know.'

'Me neither.' He didn't turn. 'The difference between you and me, Meg, is that I've given up trying to work them out. I've given up caring.'

She believed the first statement, but not the second. Not for a moment.

He swung to glare at her. 'I think it's time you stopped trying to understand them and caring so much about it all too.'

If only it were that easy. She shrugged and changed the topic. 'How was it today, with Elsie?'

His lip curled. 'The usual garrulous barrel of laughs.'

She winced. When she and Ben had been ten, his mother had dumped him with his grandmother. She'd never returned. She'd never phoned. Not once. Elsie, who had never exactly been lively, had become even less so. Meg couldn't never remember a single instance when Elsie had hugged Ben or showed him the smallest sign of affection. 'Something's going on with the both of them. They've become as thick as thieves.'

'Yeah, I got that feeling too.'

Her father had come to fatherhood late, Elsie had come to motherhood early, and her daughter—Ben's mother—had fallen pregnant young too. All of which made her father and Elsie contemporaries. She shook her head. They still seemed unlikely allies to her.

'But...' Ben shifted on his chair. 'Do we really care?'

Yes, unfortunately she did. Unlike her father, she couldn't turn her feelings off so easily. Unlike Ben, she couldn't bury them so deep they'd never see the light of day again.

Ben clenched a fist. 'You know what gets me? That you're now stuck looking after this monstrosity of a white elephant of a house.'

She stilled. Ben didn't know? 'I'm not precisely stuck with it, Ben. The house is now mine—he gifted it to me. He had the deeds transferred into my name before he left.'

His jaw slackened. 'He what? Why?'

She cut another slice of Camembert, popped it in her mouth and then shrugged. 'Search me.'

He leaned forward. 'And you accepted it?'

She had. And she refused to flinch at the incredulity in his voice. Some sixth sense had told her to, had warned her that something important hinged on her accepting this 'monstrosity of a white elephant of a house', as Ben called it.

'Why?'

She wasn't sure she'd be able to explain it to Ben, though. 'It seemed important to him.'

Dark blue eyes glared into hers. She knew their precise colour, even if she couldn't make it out in the moonlight.

'You're setting yourself up for more disappointment,' he growled.

'Maybe, but now nobody can argue that I don't have enough room to bring up a baby, because I most certainly do.'

He laughed. Just as she'd meant him to. 'Not when you're living in a five-bedroom mansion with a formal living room, a family room, a rumpus and a three car garage,' he agreed.

'But?'

'Hell, it must be a nightmare to clean.'

'It's not so bad.' She grinned. 'Confession time—I have a cleaning lady.'

'Give me a tent any day.'

A tent was definitely more Ben's style.

She straightened. 'You're home for a week, right?' Ben never stayed longer than a week. 'Do you mind if I make us an appointment with my doctor for Wednesday or Thursday?'

'While I'm in Fingal Bay, Meg, I'm yours to command.'

The thing was, he meant it. Her heart swelled even more. 'Thank you.' She stared at him and something inside her stirred. She shook it away and helped herself to more cheese, forced herself to stare out at the bay. 'Now, you've told me how you ended up in Mexico when I thought you were leading a tour group to Machu Picchu, but where are you heading to next?'

Ben led adventure tours all around the world. He worked on a contract basis for multiple tour companies. He was in demand too, which meant he got to pick and choose where he went and what he did.

'The ski fields of Canada.'

He outlined his upcoming travel plans and his face lit up. Meg wondered what he'd do once he'd seen everything. Start at the beginning again? 'Have you crewed on a yacht sailing around the world yet?'

'Not yet.'

It was the goal on his bucket list he most wanted to achieve. And she didn't doubt that he eventually would. 'It must take a while to sail around the world. You sure you could go that long without female company?'

'Haven't you heard of a girl in every port?'

She laughed. She couldn't help it. The problem was with Ben it probably wasn't a joke.

Ben never dated a woman for longer than two weeks. He was careful not to date any woman long enough for her to become bossy or possessive. She doubted he ever would. Ben injected brand-new life into the word footloose. She'd never met anyone so jealous of his freedom, who fought ties and commitment so fiercely—and not just in his love-life either.

Her stomach clenched, and then she smiled. It was the reason he was the perfect candidate.

She gripped her hands together. A baby!

CHAPTER TWO

I'M PREGNANT!!!

The words appeared in large type on Ben's computer screen and a grin wider than the Great St Bernard Pass spread across his face.

Brilliant news, he typed back. *Congratulations!!!*

He signed off as *Uncle Ben*. He frowned at that for a moment, and then hit 'send' with a shake of his head and another grin. It had been a month since his visit home, and now... Meg—a mum-to-be! He slumped in his chair and ran a hand back through his hair. He'd toast her in the bar tonight with the rest of the crew.

He went to switch off his computer but a new e-mail had hit his inbox: *FAVOURITE Uncle Ben! Love, M xxx*

He tried the words out loud. 'Favourite Uncle Ben.' He shook his head again, and with a grin set off into the ice and snow of a Canadian ski slope.

Over the next two months Ben started seeing pregnant women everywhere—in Whistler ski lodges, lazing on the beaches of the Pacific islands, where he'd led a diving expedition, on a layover in Singapore, and in New Zealand before *and* after he led a small team on a six day hike from the Bay of Islands down to Trounson Kauri Park.

Pregnant women were suddenly everywhere, and they filled his line of vision. A maternal baby bulge had taken on the same fascination for him as the deep-sea pearls he collected for himself, the rare species of coral he hunted for research purposes, and his rare sightings of Tasmanian devils in the ancient Tasmanian rainforest. He started striking up conversations with pregnant women—congratulating them on the upcoming addition to their family.

To a woman, each and every one of them beamed back at him, their excitement and the love they already felt for their unborn child a mirror of how he knew Meg would be feeling. Damn it! He needed to find a window in his schedule to get home and see her, to share in her excitement.

In the third month he started hearing horror stories.

He shot off to Africa to lead a three-week safari tour, clapping his hands over his ears and doing all he could to put those stories out of his mind. Meg was healthy. And she was strong too—both emotionally and physically. Not to mention smart. His hand clenched. She'd be fine. Nothing bad would happen to her or the baby.

It wouldn't!

'You want to tell me what's eating you?' Stefan, the director of the tour company Ben was contracted to, demanded of Ben on his second night in Lusaka, Zambia. 'You're as snarly as a lion with a thorn in its paw.'

Ben had worked for Stefan for over five years. They'd formed a friendship based on their shared love of adventure and the great outdoors, but it suddenly struck Ben that he knew nothing about the other man's personal life. 'Do you have any kids, Stefan?'

He hadn't known he'd meant to ask the question until it had shot out of his mouth. Stefan gave him plenty of opportunity to retract it, but Ben merely shoved his shoulders back and waited. That was when Stefan shifted on his bar stool.

'You got some girl knocked up, Ben?'

He hadn't. He rolled his shoulders. At least not in the way Stefan meant. 'My best friend at home is pregnant. She's ecstatic about it, and I've been thrilled for her, but I've started hearing ugly stories.'

'What kind of stories?'

Ben took a gulp of his beer. 'Stories involving morning sickness and how debilitating it can be. Fatigue.' Bile filled his mouth and he slammed his glass down. 'Miscarriages. High blood pressure. Diabetes. Sixty-hour labours!' He spat each word out with all the venom that gnawed at his soul.

His hand clenched. So help him God, if any of those things happened to Meg…

'Being a father is the best thing I've ever done with my life.'

Ben's head rocked up to meet Stefan's gaze. What he saw there made his blood start to pump faster. A crack opened up in his chest. 'How many?' he croaked.

Stefan held up three fingers and Ben's jaw dropped.

Stefan clapped him on the shoulder. 'Sure, mate, there are risks, but I bet you a hundred bucks your friend will be fine. If she's a friend of yours she won't be an airhead, so I bet you'll find she's gone into all this with her eyes wide open.'

Meg had, he suddenly realised. But had he? For a moment the roaring in his ears drowned out the noise of the rowdy bar. It downed out everything. Stefan's lips moved. It took an effort of will to focus on the words emerging from them.

'…and she'll have the hubby and the rest of her family to help her out and give her the support she'll need.'

Ben pinched the bridge of his nose and focused on his breathing. 'She's going to be a single mum.' She had no partner to help her, and as far as family went…Well, that had all gone to hell in a hand basket years ago. Meg's father and Elsie? Fat lot of good they'd be. Meg had no one to help her out, to offer her support. No one. Not even him—the man who'd helped get her pregnant.

A breath whistled out of Stefan. 'Man, that's tough.'

All the same, he found himself bristling on Meg's behalf. 'She'll cope just fine. She's smart and independent and—'

'I'm not talking about the mum-to-be, mate. I'm talking about the baby. I mean it's tough on the baby. A kid deserves to have a mother *and* a father.'

Ben found it suddenly hard to swallow. And breathe. Or speak. 'Why?' he croaked.

'Jeez, Ben, parenting is hard work. When one person hits the wall the other one can take over. When one gets sick, the other one's there. Besides, it means the kid gets exposed to two different views of the world—two different ways of doing things and two different ways of solving a problem. Having two parents opens up the world more for a child. From where I'm sitting, every kid deserves that.'

Ben's throat went desert-dry. He wanted to moisten it, to down the rest of his beer in one glorious gulp, but his hands had started to shake. He dragged them off the table and into his lap, clenched them. All he could see in his mind's eye was Meg, heavily pregnant with a child that had half his DNA.

When he'd agreed to help her out he hadn't known he'd feel this...*responsible.*

'But all that aside,' Stefan continued, 'a baby deserves to be loved unconditionally by the two people who created it. I know I'm talking about an ideal world, here, Ben, but...I just think every kid deserves that love.'

The kind of love he and Meg hadn't received.

The kind of love he was denying his child.

He swiped a hand in front of his face. No! *Her* child!

'You'll understand one day, when you have your own kids, mate.'

'I'm never—'

He couldn't finish the sentence. Because he *was*, wasn't he? He was about to become a father. And he knew in his bones with a clarity that stole his breath that Uncle Ben would never make up for the lack of a father in his child's life.

His child.

He turned back to Stefan. 'You're going to have to find

someone to replace me. I can't lead Thursday's safari.' Three weeks in the heart of Africa? He shook his head. He didn't have that kind of time to spare. He had to get home and make sure Meg was all right.

He had to get home and make sure the baby was all right.

CHAPTER THREE

A MOTORBIKE TURNED in at the end of the street. Meg glanced up from weeding the garden and listened. That motorbike sounded just like Ben's, though it couldn't be. He wasn't due back in the country for another seven weeks.

She pressed her hands into the small of her back and stretched as well as she could while still on her knees. This house that her father had given her took a lot of maintenance—more than her little apartment ever had. She'd blocked out Saturday mornings for gardening, but something was going to have to give before the baby came. She just wouldn't have time for the upkeep on this kind of garden then.

She glanced down at her very small baby bump and a thrill shot through her. She rested a hand against it—*her baby*—and all felt right with the world.

And then the motorbike stopped. Right outside her house.

She leapt up and charged around to the front of the house, a different kind of grin building inside her. Ben? One glance at the rangy broad-shouldered frame confirmed it.

Still straddling his bike, he pulled off his helmet and shook out his too-long blond-streaked hair. He stretched his neck first to the left and then to the right before catching sight of her. He stilled, and then the slow grin that hooked up one side of his face lit him up from the inside out and hit her with its impact.

Good Lord. She stumbled. No wonder so many women had fallen for him over the years—he was gorgeous! She knew him so well that his physical appearance barely registered with her these days.

Except...

Except when his smile slipped and she read the uncertainty in his face. Her heart flooded with warmth. This was the first time he'd seen her since she'd become pregnant. Was he worried she wouldn't keep her word? That she'd expect more from him than he was willing or able to give?

She stifled a snort. *As if!*

While she normally delighted in teasing him—and this was an opportunity almost too good to pass up—he had made this dream of hers possible. It was only fair to lay his fears to rest as soon as she could.

With mock-seductive slowness she pulled off her gardening gloves one finger at a time and tossed them over her shoulder, and then she sashayed down the garden path and out the gate to where he still straddled his bike. She pulled her T-shirt tight across her belly and turned side-on so he could view it in all its glory.

'Hello, *Uncle Ben*. I'd like you to meet *my baby* bump—affectionately known as the Munchkin.'

She emphasised the words 'Uncle Ben' and 'my', so he'd know everything remained the same—that she hadn't changed her mind and was now expecting more from him than he could give. He should have more faith in her. She knew him. *Really* knew him. But she forgave him his fears. Ben and family? That'd be the day.

He stared at her, frozen. He didn't say anything. She straightened and folded her arms. 'What you're supposed to say, *Uncle Ben*, is that you're very pleased to meet said baby bump. And then you should enquire after my health.'

His head jerked up at her words. 'How are—?' He blinked. His brows drew together until he was practically glaring at her. 'Hell, Meg, you look great! As in *really* great.'

'I feel great too.' Pregnancy agreed with her. Ben wasn't the only one to notice. She'd received a lot of compliments over the last couple of months. She stuck out a hip. 'What? Are you saying I was a right hag before?'

'Of course not, I—'

'Ha! Got you.'

But he didn't laugh. She leaned forward to peer into his face, took in the two days' worth of stubble and the dark circles under his eyes. Where on earth had he flown in from? 'How long since you had any sleep?' She shuddered at the thought of him riding on the freeway from Sydney on that bike of his. Ben took risks. He always had. But some of those risks were unnecessary.

His eyes had lowered to her abdomen again.

She tugged on his arm. 'C'mon, Ben. Shower and then sleep.'

'No.'

He didn't move. Beneath his leathers his arm flexed in rock-hardness. She let it go and stepped back. 'But you look a wreck.'

'I need to talk to you.'

His eyes hadn't lifted from her abdomen and she suddenly wanted to cover herself from his gaze. She brushed a hand across her eyes. *Get a grip. This is Ben.* The pregnancy hormones might have given her skin a lovely glow, but she was discovering they could make her emotionally weird at times too.

'Then surely talking over a cup of coffee makes more sense than standing out here and giving the neighbours something to talk about.'

Frankly, Meg didn't care what any of the neighbours thought, and she doubted any of them, except perhaps for Elsie, gave two hoots about her and Ben. She just wanted him off that bike.

'You look as if you could do with a hot breakfast,' she added as a tempter. A glance at the sun told her it would be a late breakfast.

Finally Ben lifted one leg over the bike and came to stand beside her. She slipped her arm through his and led him towards the front door. She quickly assessed her schedule for the following week—there was nothing she couldn't cancel. 'How long are you home for this time, Uncle Ben?' She kept her voice light because she could feel the tension in him.

'No!' The word growled out of him as he pulled out of her grasp.

She blinked. What had she said wrong?

'I can't do this, Meg.'

Couldn't do what?

He leaned down until his face was level with hers. The light in his eyes blazed out at her. 'Not Uncle Ben, Meg, but Dad. I'm that baby's father.' He reached out and laid a hand across her stomach. '*Its father*. That's what I've got to talk to you about, because father is the role I want to take in its life.'

The heat from his hand burned like a brand. She shoved it away. Stepped back.

He straightened. 'I'm sorry. I know it's not what I agreed to. But—'

'Its father?' she hissed at him, her back rigid and her heart surging and crashing in her chest. The ground beneath her feet was buckling like dangerous surf. 'Damn it, Ben, you collected some sperm in a cup. That doesn't make you a father!'

She reefed open the door and stormed inside. Ben followed hot on her heels. Hot. Heat. His heat beat at her like a living, breathing thing. She pressed a hand to her forehead and kept walking until she reached the kitchen. Sun poured in at all the windows and an ache started up behind her eyes.

She whirled around to him. 'A father? *You?*' She didn't laugh. She didn't want to hurt him. But Ben—a father? She'd never heard anything more ridiculous. She pressed one hand to her stomach and the other to her forehead again. 'Since when have you ever wanted to be a father?'

He stared back at her, his skin pallid and his gaze stony.

Damn it! How long since he'd slept?

She pushed the thought away. 'Ben, you don't have a single committed bone in your body.' What did he mean to do—hang around long enough to make the baby love him before dashing off to some far-flung corner of the globe? He would build her baby's hopes up just to dash them. He would do that again and again for all of its life—breezing in when it suited him and breezing back out when the idea of family started to suffocate him.

She pressed both hands to her stomach. It was her duty to protect this child. Even against her dearest friend. 'No.' Her voice rang clear in the sunny silence.

He shook his head, his mouth a determined line. 'This is one of the things you can't boss me about. I'm not giving way. I'm the father of the baby you're carrying. There's nothing you can do about that.'

Just for a moment wild hope lifted through her. Maybe they could make this work. In the next moment she shook it off. She'd thought that exact same thing once before—ten years ago, when they'd kissed. *Maybe they could make this work. Maybe she'd be the girl who'd make him stay. Maybe she'd be the girl to defeat his restlessness.* All silly schoolgirl nonsense, of course.

And so was this.

But the longer she stared at him the less she recognised the man in front of her. Her Ben was gone. Replaced by a lean, dark stranger with a hunger in his eyes. An answering hunger started to build through her. She snapped it away, breathing hard, her chest clenching and unclenching like a fist. A storm raged in her throat, blocking it.

'I am going to be a part of this baby's life.'

She whirled back. She would fight him with everything she had.

He leant towards her, his face twisted and dark. 'Don't make me fight you on this. Don't make me fight you for custody, Meg, because I will.'

She froze. For a moment it felt as if even her heart had stopped.

The last of the colour leached from Ben's face. 'Hell.' He backed up a step, and then he turned and bolted.

Meg sprang after him and grabbed his arm just before he reached the back door. She held on for dear life. 'Ben, don't.' She rested her forehead against his shoulder and tried to block a sob. 'Don't look like that. You are not your father.' The father who had—

She couldn't bear to finish that thought. She might not think Ben decent father material, but he wasn't his father either.

'And stop trying to shake me off like that.' She did her best to make her voice crisp and cross. 'If I fall I could hurt the baby.'

He glared. 'That's emotional blackmail.'

'Of the worst kind,' she agreed.

He rolled his eyes, but beneath her hands she felt some of the tension seep out of him. She patted his arm and then backed up a step, uncomfortably aware of his proximity.

'I panicked. You just landed me with a scenario I wouldn't have foreseen in a million years. And you…You don't look like you've slept in days. Neither one of us is precisely firing on all cylinders at the moment.'

He hesitated, but then he nodded, his eyes hooded. 'Okay.'

This wasn't the first time she and Ben had fought. Not by a long shot. One of their biggest had been seven years ago, when Ben had seduced her friend Suzie. Meg had begged him not to. She'd begged Suzie not to fall for Ben's charm. They'd both ignored her.

And, predictably, as soon as Ben had slept with Suzie he'd lost all interest and had been off chasing his next adventure. Suzie had been heartbroken. Suzie had blamed Meg. Man, had Meg bawled him out over *that* one. He'd stayed away from her girlfriends after that.

This fight felt bigger than that one.

Worse still, just like that moment ten years ago—when they'd kissed—it had the potential to destroy their friendship.

Instinct told her that. And Ben's friendship meant the world to her.

'So?'

She glanced up to find him studying her intently. 'So...' She straightened. 'You go catch up on some Zs and I'll—'

'Go for a walk along the spit.'

It was where she always went to clear her head. At low tide it was safe to walk all the way along Fingal Beach and across the sand spit to Fingal Island. It would take about sixty minutes there and back, and she had a feeling she would need every single one of those minutes plus more to get her head around Ben's bombshell.

Her hands opened and closed. She had to find out what had spooked him, and then she needed to un-spook him as quickly as she could. Then life could get back to normal and she could focus on her impending single motherhood.

Single. Solo. She'd sorted it all straight in her mind. She knew what she was doing and how she was going to do it. She would *not* let Ben mess with that.

'Take a water bottle and some fruit. You need to keep hydrated.'

'And you need to eat something halfway healthy before you hit the sack.'

'And we'll meet back here...?'

She glanced at her watch. 'Three o'clock.' That was five hours from now. Enough time for Ben to grab something to eat and catch up on some sleep.

He nodded and then shifted his feet. 'Are you going to make me go to Elsie's?'

She didn't have the energy for another fight. Not even a minor one. 'There are four guest bedrooms upstairs. Help yourself.'

They'd both started for their figurative separate corners when the doorbell rang. Meg could feel her shoulders literally sag.

Ben shot her a glance. 'I'll deal with it. I'll say you're not available and get rid of whoever it is asap.'

'Thanks.'

She half considered slipping out through the back door while he was gone and making her way down to the bay, but that seemed rude so she made herself remain in the kitchen, her fingers drumming against their opposite numbers.

Her mind whirled. *What on earth was Ben thinking*? She closed her eyes and swallowed. *How on earth was she going to make him see sense*?

'Uh, Meg?'

Her eyes sprang open as Ben returned, his eyes trying to send her some message.

And then Elsie and her father appeared behind him. It took an effort of will to check her surprise. Her father hadn't been in this house since he'd handed her the deeds. And Elsie? Had Elsie *ever* been inside?

Her father thrust out his jaw. 'We want to talk to you.'

She had to bite her lip to stop herself adding please. Her father would resent being corrected. She thrust her jaw out. Well, bad luck, because she resented being spoken to that way and—

'We brought morning tea,' Elsie offered, proffering a bakery bag.

It was so out of character—the whole idea of morning tea, let alone an offering of cake—that all coherent thought momentarily fled.

She hauled her jaw back into place. 'Thank you. Umm… lovely.' And she kicked herself forward to take the proffered bag.

She peeked inside to discover the most amazing sponge and cream concoction topped with rich pink icing. *Yum!* It was the last kind of cake she'd have expected Elsie to choose. It was so frivolous. She'd have pegged Elsie as more of a date roll kind of person, or a plain buttered scone. Not that Meg was complaining. No sirree. This cake was the bee's knees. Her mouth watered. Double *yum*.

She shook herself. 'I'll...um...go and put the percolator on.'

Ben moved towards the doorway. 'I'll make myself scarce.'

'No, Benjamin, it's fortunate you're here,' her father said. 'Elsie rang me when she heard you arrive. That's why we're here. What we have to say will affect you too.'

Ben glanced at Meg. She shrugged. All four of them in the kitchen made everything suddenly awkward. She thought fast. Her father would expect her to serve coffee in the formal lounge room. It was where he'd feel most comfortable.

It was the one room where Ben would feel least comfortable.

'Dad, why don't you and Elsie make yourselves comfortable in the family room? It's so lovely and sunny in there. I'll bring coffee and cake through in a moment.' Before her father could protest she turned to Ben. Getting stuck making small talk with her father and Elsie would be his worst nightmare. 'I'd appreciate it if you could set a tray for me.'

He immediately leapt into action. She turned away to set the percolator going. When she turned back her father and Elsie had moved into the family room.

'What's with them?' Ben murmured.

'I don't know, but I told you last time you were here that something was going down with them.'

They took the coffee and cake into the family room. Meg poured coffee, sliced cake and handed it around.

She took a sip of her decaf and lifted a morsel of cake to her mouth. 'This is *very* good.'

Her father and Elsie sat side by side on the sofa, stiff and formal. They didn't touch their coffee or their cake. They didn't appear to have a slouchy, comfortable bone between them. With a sigh, Meg set her fork on the side of her plate. If she'd been hoping the family room would loosen them up she was sorely disappointed.

She suddenly wanted to shake them! Neither one of them

had asked Ben how he was doing, where he'd been, or how long he'd been back. Her hand clenched around her mug. They gave off nothing but a great big blank.

She glanced at Ben. He lounged in the armchair opposite, staring at his cake and gulping coffee. She wanted to shake him too.

She thumped her mug and cake plate down on the coffee table and pasted her brightest smile to her face. She utterly refused to do *blank*. 'While it's lovely to see you both, I get the impression this isn't a social visit. You said there's something you wanted to tell us?'

'That's correct, Megan.'

Her father's name was Lawrence Samuel Parrish. If they didn't call him Mr Parrish—people, that was, colleagues and acquaintances—they called him Laurie. She stared at him and couldn't find even a glimpse of the happy-go-lucky ease that 'Laurie' suggested. Did he resent the familiarity of that casual moniker?

It wasn't the kind of question she could ever ask. They didn't have that kind of a relationship. In fact, when you got right down to brass tacks, she and her father didn't have any kind of relationship worth speaking of.

Her father didn't continue. Elsie didn't take up where he left off. In fact the older woman seemed to be studying the ceiling light fixture. Meg glanced up too, but as far as she could tell there didn't seem to be anything amiss—no ancient cobwebs or dust, and it didn't appear to be in imminent danger of dropping on their heads.

'Well!' She clapped her hands and then rubbed them together. 'We're positively agog with excitement—aren't we, Ben?'

He started. 'We are?'

If she'd been closer she'd have kicked him. 'Yes, of course we are.'

Not.

Hmm… Actually, maybe a bit. This visit really was un-precedented. It was just that this ritual of her doing her best to brisk them up and them steadfastly resisting had become old hat. And suddenly she felt too tired for it.

She stared at *Laurie* and Elsie. They stared back, but said nothing. With a shrug she picked up her mug again, settled back in her *easy* chair and took a sip. She turned to Ben to start a conversation. *Any* conversation.

'Which part of the world have you been jaunting around this time?'

He turned so his body was angled towards her, effectively excluding the older couple. 'On safari in Africa.'

'Lions and elephants?'

'More than you could count.'

'Elsie and I are getting married.'

Meg sprayed the space between her and Ben with coffee. Ben returned the favour. Elsie promptly rose and took their mugs from them as they coughed and coughed. Her father handed them paper napkins. It was the most animated she'd ever seen them. But then they sat side-by-side on the sofa again, as stiff and formal as before.

Meg's coughing eased. She knew she should excuse herself for such disgusting manners, but she didn't. For once she asked what was uppermost in her mind. 'Are you serious?'

Her father remained wooden. 'Yes.'

That was it. A single yes. No explanation. No declaration of love. Nothing.

She glanced at Ben. He was staring at them as if he'd never seen them before. He was staring at them with a kind of fas-cinated horror, as if they were a car wreck he couldn't drag his gaze from.

She inched forward on her seat, doing all she could to catch first her father's and then Elsie's eyes. 'I don't mean to be im-pertinent, but…*why*?'

'That *is* impertinent.' Her father's chin lifted. 'And none of your business.'

'If it's not my business then I don't know who else's it is,' she shot back, surprising herself. Normally she was the keeper of the peace, the smoother-over of awkward moments, doing all she could to make things easy for this pair who, it suddenly occurred to her, had never exactly made things easy for either her or Ben.

'I told you they wouldn't approve!' Elsie said.

'Oh, it's not that I don't approve,' Meg managed.

'I don't,' Ben growled.

She stared at him. 'Yeah, but you don't approve of marriage on principle.' She rolled her eyes. Did he seriously think he wanted to be a father?

Think about that later.

She turned back to the older couple. 'The thing is, I didn't even know you were dating. Why the secrecy? And…and… I mean…'

Her father glanced at Elsie and then at Meg. 'What?' he rapped out.

'Do you love each other?'

Elsie glanced away. Her father's mouth opened and closed but no sound came out.

'I mean, surely that's the only good reason to marry, isn't it?'

Nobody said anything. Her lips twisted. *Have a banana, Meg.* Was she the only person in this room who believed in love—good, old-fashioned, rumpy-pumpy love?

'Elsie and I have decided that we'll rub along quite nicely together.'

She started to roll her eyes at her father's pomposity, but then he did something extraordinary—he reached out and clasped Elsie's hand. Elsie held his hand on her lap and it didn't look odd or alien or wrong.

Meg stared at those linked hands and had to fight down a

sudden lump in her throat. 'In that case, congratulations.' She rose and kissed them both on the cheek.

Ben didn't join her.

She took her seat and sent him an uneasy glance. 'Ben?'

He shrugged. 'It's no business of mine.' He lolled in his chair with almost deliberate insolence. 'They're old enough to know what they want.'

'Precisely,' her father snapped.

She rubbed her forehead. No amount of smoothing would ease this awkward moment. She decided to move the moment forward instead. 'So, where will you live?'

'We'll live in my apartment at Nelson Bay.'

She turned to Elsie. 'What will you do with your house?'

Before he'd retired Meg's father had been a property developer. He still had a lot of contacts in the industry. Maybe they'd sell it. Maybe she'd end up with cheerful neighbours who'd wave whenever they saw her and have young children who'd develop lifelong friendships with her child.

'I'm going to give it to Ben.'

Ben shot upright to tower over all of them. 'I don't want it!'

Her father rose. 'That's an ungracious way to respond to such a generous gift.'

Ben glared at his grandmother. 'Is he railroading you into this?'

'Most certainly not!' She stood too. 'Meg's right. She's seen what you haven't—or what you can't. Not that I can blame you for that. But...but Laurie and I love each other. I understand how hard you might find that to believe after the way the two of us have been over the years, but I spent a lot of time with him when he was recuperating.' She shot Meg an almost apologetic glance that made Meg fidget. 'When you were at work, that is. We talked a lot. And we're hoping it's not too late for all of us to become a family,' she finished falteringly, her cheeks pink with self-consciousness.

It was one of the longest speeches Meg had ever heard her utter, but one glance at Ben and she winced.

'A family?' he bellowed.

'Sit!' Meg hollered.

Everyone sat, and then stared at her in varying degrees of astonishment. She marvelled at her own daring, and decided to bluff it out. 'Have you set a date for the wedding?'

Elsie darted a glance at Meg's father. 'We thought the thirtieth of next month.'

Next month? The end of March?

That was only six weeks away!

'We'll be married by a celebrant at the registry office. We'd like you both to be there.' Her father didn't look at her as he spoke.

'Of course.' Though heaven only knew how she'd get Ben there. He avoided weddings like the plague—as if he thought they might somehow be catching.

'And where have you settled on for your honeymoon?'

'I…' He frowned. 'We're too old for a honeymoon.'

She caught his eye. 'Dad, do you love Elsie?'

He swallowed and nodded. She'd never seen him look more vulnerable in his life.

She blinked and swallowed. 'Then you're not too old for a honeymoon.' She hauled in a breath. 'And, like Elsie, are you hoping to rebuild family ties?'

'I sincerely hope so, Megan. I mean, you have a baby on the way now.'

Correction—she'd never seen him look more vulnerable until *now*. He was proffering the olive branch she'd been praying for ever since she was eight years old, and she found all she wanted to do was run from the room. A great ball of hardness lodged in her stomach. Her father was willing to change for a grandchild, but not for *her*.

'Meg.'

She understood the implicit warning Ben sent her. He didn't

want her hurt or disappointed. *Again.* She understood then that the chasm between them all might be too wide ever to be breached.

She folded her arms, her brain whirling. Very slowly, out of the mists of confusion and befuddlement—and resentment—a plan started to form. She glanced at the happy couple. A plan perfect in its simplicity. She glanced at Ben. A plan devious in design. *A family, huh?* They'd see about that. All of them. Laurie and Elsie, and Ben too.

She stood and moved across to Ben's chair. 'You must allow Ben and I to throw you a wedding—a proper celebration to honour your public commitment to each other.'

'What the—?'

Ben broke off with a barely smothered curse when she surreptitiously pulled his hair.

'Oh, that's not necessary—' Elsie started.

'Of course it is!' Meg beamed at her. 'It will be our gift to you.'

Her father lumbered to his feet, panic racing across his face. Meg winked at Elsie before he could speak. 'Every woman deserves a wedding day, and my father knows the value of accepting generosity in the spirit it's given. Don't you, Dad?' *Family, huh?* Well, he'd have to prove it.

He stared at her, dumbfounded and just a little…afraid? That was when it hit her that all his pomposity and stiffness stemmed from nervousness. He was afraid that she'd reject him. The thought made her flinch. She pushed it away.

'We'll hold the wedding here,' she told them, lifting her chin. 'It'll be a quiet affair, but classy and elegant.'

'I…' Her father blinked.

Ben slouched down further in his chair.

Elsie studied the floor at her feet.

Meg met her father's gaze. 'I believe thank you is the phrase you're looking for.' She sat and lifted the knife. 'More cake, anyone?' She cut Ben another generous slice. 'Eat up, Ben. You're looking a bit peaky. I need you to keep your strength up.'

He glowered at her. But he demolished the cake. After the smallest hesitation, Elsie forked a sliver of cake into her mouth. Her eyes widened. Her head came up. She ate another tiny morsel. Watching her, Laurie did the same.

'What the hell do you think you're doing?' Ben rounded on her the instant the older couple left.

She folded her arms and nodded towards the staircase. 'You want to go take that nap?'

He thrust a finger under her nose. 'What kind of patsy do you take me for? I am *not* helping you organise some godforsaken wedding. You got that?'

Loud and clear.

'The day after tomorrow I'm out of here, and I won't be back for a good three months.'

Exactly what she'd expected.

'Do you hear me, Meg? Can I make myself any clearer?'

'The day after tomorrow, huh?'

'Yes.'

'And you won't be back until around May?'

'Precisely.' He set off towards the stairs.

She folded her arms even tighter. She waited until he'd placed his foot on the first riser. 'So you've given up on the idea of fatherhood, then?'

He froze. And then he swung around and let forth with a word so rude she clapped her hands across her stomach in an attempt to block her unborn baby's ears. *'Ben!'*

'You…' The finger he pointed at her shook.

'I *nothing*,' she shot back at him, her anger rising to match his. 'You can't just storm in here and demand all the rights and privileges of fatherhood unless you're prepared to put in the hard yards. Domesticity and commitment includes dealing with my father and your grandmother. It includes helping out

at the odd wedding, attending baptisms and neighbourhood
pool parties and all those other things you loathe.'

She strode across to stand directly in front of him. 'Nobody is asking you to put in those hard yards—least of all me.'

His eyes narrowed. 'I know exactly what you're up to.'

He probably did. That was what happened when someone
knew you so well.

'You think the idea of helping out at this wedding is going
to scare me off.'

She raised an eyebrow. Hadn't it?

'It won't work, Meg.'

They'd see about that. 'Believe me, Ben, a baby is a much
scarier proposition than a wedding. Even this wedding.'

'You don't think I'll stick it out?'

Not for a moment. 'If you can't stick the wedding out then
I can't see how you'll stick fatherhood out.' And she'd do everything she could to protect her child from that particular
heartache. 'End of story.'

The pulse at the base of his jaw thumped and his eyes
flashed blue fire. It was sexy as hell.

She blinked and then took a step back. Stupid pregnancy
hormones!

He thrust out his hand. 'You have yourself a deal, Meg, and
may the best man win.'

She refused to shake it. Her eyes stung. She swallowed a
lump the size of a Victorian sponge. 'This isn't some stupid
bet, Ben. This is my baby's life!'

His face softened but the fire in his eyes didn't dim. 'Wrong,
Meg. Our baby. It's *our* baby's life.'

He reached out and touched the backs of his fingers to her
cheek. And then he was gone.

'Oh, Ben,' she whispered after him, reaching up to touch
the spot on her cheek that burned from his touch. He had no
idea what he'd just let himself in for.

CHAPTER FOUR

BEN SLEPT IN one of Meg's spare bedrooms instead of next door at Elsie's.

He slept the sleep of the dead.

He slept for twenty straight hours.

When he finally woke and traipsed into the kitchen, the first thing he saw was Meg hunched over her laptop at the kitchen table. The sun poured in at the windows, haloing her in gold. She glanced up. She smiled. But it wasn't her regular wide, unguarded smile.

'I wondered when you'd surface.'

He rubbed the back of his neck. 'I can't remember the last time I slept that long.' *Or that well.*

'Where were you?'

He frowned and pointed. 'Your back bedroom.'

Her grin lit her entire face. 'I meant where exactly in Africa were you before you flew home to Australia?'

Oh, right. 'Zambia, to be exact.' He was supposed to be leading a safari.

She stared at him, but he couldn't tell what she was thinking. He remembered that conversation with Stefan, and the look of fulfilment that had spread across his friend's face when he'd spoken about his children. It had filled Ben with awe, and the sudden recognition of his responsibilities had changed everything.

He had to be a better father than his own had been. He had to or—

His stomach churned and he cut the thought off. It was too early in the day for such grim thoughts.

'Exciting,' she murmured.

He shifted his weight to the balls of his feet. 'Meg, are we okay—you and me?'

'Of course we are.' But she'd gone back to her laptop and she didn't look up as she spoke. When he didn't move she waved a hand towards the pantry. 'Look, we need to talk, but have something to eat first while I finish up these accounts. Then we'll do precisely that.'

He'd stormed in here yesterday and upended all of her plans. Meg liked her ducks in neat straight rows. She liked to know exactly where she was going and what she was working towards. He'd put paid to all of that, and he knew how much it rattled her when her plans went awry.

Awry? His lips twisted. He'd blown them to smithereens. The least he could do was submit to her request with grace, but...

'You're working on a Sunday?'

'I run my own business, Ben. I work when I have to work.'

He shut up after that. It struck him how much Meg stuck to things, and how much *he* never had. As soon as he grew bored with a job or a place he moved on to the next one, abuzz with the novelty and promise of a new experience. His restlessness had become legendary amongst his friends and colleagues. No wonder she didn't have any faith in his potential as a father.

All you did was collect sperm in a cup.

He flinched, spilling cereal all over the bench. With a muffled curse he cleaned it up and then stood, staring out of the kitchen window at the garden beyond while he ate.

You never planned to have a child.

He hadn't. He'd done everything in his power to avoid that

kind of commitment. Bile rose in his throat. So what the hell was he doing here?

He stared at the bowl he held and Stefan's face, words, rose in his mind. *A baby deserves both a mother and a father.* He pushed his shoulders back and rinsed his bowl. He might not have planned this, but he had no intention of walking away from his child. He couldn't.

He swung to Meg, but she didn't look up from her computer. He wasn't hungry but he made toast. He ate because he wanted his body clock to adjust to the time zone. He ate to stop himself from demanding that Meg stop what she was doing and talk to him right now.

After he'd washed and dried the dishes Meg turned off her computer and pushed it to one side. He poured two glasses of orange juice and sat down. 'You said we have to talk.' He pushed one of the glasses towards her.

She blinked. 'And you don't think that's necessary?'

'I said what I needed to say yesterday.' He eyed her for a moment. 'And I don't want to fight.'

She stared at him, as if waiting for more. When he remained silent she blew out a breath and shook her head.

He rolled his shoulders and fought a scowl. 'What?'

'You said yesterday that you want to be acknowledged as the baby's father.'

'I do.'

'And that you want to be a part of its life.'

He thrust out his jaw. 'That's right.'

'Then would you kindly outline the practicalities of that for me, please? What precisely are your intentions?'

He stared at her blankly. What was she talking about?

She shook her head again, her lips twisting. 'Does that mean you want to drop in and visit the baby once a week? Or does it mean you want the baby to live with you for two nights a week and every second weekend? Or are you after week-about parenting?' Her eyes suddenly blazed with scorn. 'Or do you mean to flit in and out of its life as you do now, only instead of calling you Uncle Ben the child gets the privilege of calling you Daddy?'

Her scorn almost burned the skin from his face.

She leaned towards him. 'Do you actually mean to settle down and help care for this baby?'

Settle down? His mouth went dry. He hadn't thought...

She drew back and folded her arms. 'Or do you mean to keep going on as you've always done?'

She stared at him, her blazing eyes and the tension in her folded arms demanding an answer. He had to say something. 'I...I haven't thought the nuts and bolts of the arrangements through.' It wasn't much to give her, but at least it was the truth.

'You can't have it both ways, Ben. You're either globe-trotting Uncle Ben or one hundred per cent involved Daddy. I won't settle for anything but the best for my child.'

He leapt out of his chair. 'You can't demand I change my entire life!'

She stared at him, her eyes shadowed. 'I'm not. I've never had any expectations of you. You're the one who stormed in here yesterday and said you wanted to be a father. And a true father is—'

'More than sperm in a cup.' He fell back into his seat.

She pressed her fingers to her eyes. 'I'm sorry. I put that very crudely yesterday.'

Her guilt raked at him. She hadn't done anything wrong. He was the one who'd waltzed in and overturned her carefully laid plans.

She lifted her head. 'A father is so much more than an uncle, Ben. Being a true father demands more commitment than your current lifestyle allows for. A father isn't just for fun and games. Being a father means staying up all night when your child is sick, running around to soccer and netball games, attending parent and teacher nights.'

His hands clenched. His stomach clenched tighter. He'd

stormed in here without really knowing what he was demanding. He still didn't know what he was demanding. He just knew he couldn't walk away.

'Ben, what do you even know about babies?'

Zilch. Other than the fact that they were miracles. And that they deserved all the best life had to give.

'Have you ever held one?'

Nope. Not even once.

'Do you even know how to nurture someone?'

He stiffened. *What the hell...?*

'I don't mean do you know how to lead a group safely and successfully down the Amazon, or to base camp at Everest, or make sure someone attaches the safety harness on their climbing equipment correctly. Do you know how to care for someone who is sick or who's just feeling a bit depressed?'

What kind of selfish sod did she think him?

His mouth dried. What kind of selfish sod *was* he?

'I'm not criticising you. Those things have probably never passed across your radar before.' Her brow furrowed. 'You have this amazing and exciting life. Do you really want to give it up for nappies, teething, car pools and trips to the dentist?'

He couldn't answer that.

'Do you *really* want to be a father, Ben?'

He stared at his hands. He curled his fingers against his palms, forming them into fists. 'I don't know what to do.' He searched Meg's eyes—eyes that had given him answers in the past. 'What should I do?' Did she think he had it in him to become a good father?

'No way!' She shot back in her chair. 'I am not going to tell you what to do. I am not going to make this decision for you. It's too important. This is something you have to work out for yourself, Ben.'

His mouth went drier than the Kalahari Desert. Meg meant to desert him?

Her face softened. 'If you don't want that level of involvement I will understand. You won't be letting me down. We'll carry on as we've always done and there'll be no hard feelings. At least not on my side.'

Or his!

'But if you do want to be a proper father it only seems fair to warn you that my expectations will be high.'

He swallowed. He didn't *do* expectations.

She reached out and touched his hand. He stared at it and suddenly realised how small it was.

'I'm so grateful to you, Ben. I can't tell you how much I'm looking forward to becoming a mother—how happy I am that I'm pregnant. You helped make that possible for me. If you do want to be a fully involved father I would never deny that to you.'

It was a tiny hand, and as he stared at it he suddenly remembered the fairytales she'd once spun about families—perfect mothers and fathers, beautiful children, loving homes—when the two of them had been nothing but children themselves. She'd had big dreams.

He couldn't walk away. She was carrying *his* child. But could he live up to her expectations of what a father should be? Could he live up to his own expectations? Could he do a better job than his father had done?

His heart thumped against his ribcage. It might be better for all concerned if he got up from this table right now and just walked away.

'I realise this isn't the kind of decision you can make over-night.'

Her voice hauled him back from the brink of an abyss.

'But, Ben, for the baby's sake...and for mine...could you please make your decision by the time the wedding rolls around?'

His head lifted. Six weeks? She was giving him six weeks? If he could cope with six weeks living in Fingal Bay, that was.

He swallowed. If he couldn't he supposed they'd have their answer.

'And speaking of weddings…' She rose and hitched her head towards the back door.

Weddings? He scowled.

'C'mon. I need your help measuring the back yard.'

'What the hell for—?'

He broke off on an expletive to catch the industrial tape measure she tossed him—an old one of her father's, no doubt—before it brained him. She disappeared outside.

Glowering, he slouched after her. 'What for?' he repeated.

'For the marquee. Elsie and my father can be married in the side garden by the rose bushes, weather permitting, and we'll set up a marquee out the back here for the meal and speeches and dancing.'

'Why the hell can't they get married in the registry office?'

She spun around, hands on hips. The sun hit her hair, her eyes, the shine on her lips. With her baby bump, she looked like a golden goddess of fertility. A *desirable* goddess. He blinked and took a step back.

'This is a wedding. It should be celebrated.'

'I have never met two people less likely to want to celebrate.'

'Precisely.'

He narrowed his eyes. 'What are you up to?'

'Shut up, Ben, and measure.'

They measured.

The sun shone, the sky was clear and salt scented the air, mingling with the myriad scents from Meg's garden. Given the sobering discussion they'd just had, he'd have thought it impossible to relax, but as he jotted down the measurements that was exactly what he found himself doing.

To his relief, Meg did too. He knew he'd freaked her out with his announcement yesterday—that he'd shocked and stressed her. He paused. And then stiffened. He'd *stressed* her. She was pregnant and he'd stressed her. He was an idiot! Couldn't he have found a less threatening and shocking way of blurting his intentions out?

His hands clenched. He was a tenfold idiot for not actually working out the nuts and bolts of those intentions prior to bursting in on her the way he had—for not setting before her a carefully thought-out plan that she could work with. She'd spend the next six weeks in a state of uncertainty—which for Meg translated into stress and worry and an endless circling litany of 'what-ifs'—until he made a decision. He bit back a curse. She'd dealt with him with more grace than he deserved.

He shot a quick glance in her direction. She didn't look stressed or fragile or the worse for wear at the moment. Her skin glowed with a health and vigour he'd never noticed before. Her hair shone in the sun and...

He rolled his shoulders and tried to keep his attention above neck level.

It was just... Her baby bump was small, but it was unmistakable. And it fascinated him.

'Shouldn't you be taking it easy?' he blurted out in the middle of some soliloquy she was giving him about round tables versus rectangular.

She broke off to blink at him, and then she laughed. 'I'm pregnant, not ill. I can keep doing all the things I was doing before I became pregnant.'

Yeah, but she was doing a lot—perhaps more than was good for her. She ran her own childcare centre—worked there five days a week and heaven only knew how many other hours she put into it. She had to maintain this enormous house and garden. And now she was organising a wedding.

He folded his arms. It was just as well he had come home. He could at least shoulder some of the burden and make sure she looked after herself. Regardless of any other decision he came to, he could at least do that.

She started talking again and his gaze drifted back towards her baby bump. But on the way down the intriguing shadow of cleavage in the vee of her shirt snagged his attention. His breath jammed in his throat and a pulse pounded at his groin. The soft cotton of her blouse seemed to enhance the sweet fullness of her breasts.

That pulse pounded harder as he imagined the weight of those breasts in his hands and the way the nipples would harden if he were to run his thumbs over them—back and forth, over and over, until her head dropped back and her lips parted and her eyes glazed with desire.

His mouth dried as he imagined slipping the buttons free and easing that blouse from her shoulders, gazing at those magnificent breasts in the sun and dipping his head to—

He snapped away. *Oh, hell!* That was *Meg* he was staring at, lusting after.

He raked both hands back through his hair and paced, keeping his eyes firmly fixed on the ground in front of him. Jet lag—that had to be it. Plus his brain was addled and emotions were running high after the conversation they'd had.

And she was pregnant with *his* child. Surely it was only natural he'd see her differently? He swallowed and kept pacing. Once he'd sorted it all out in his head, worked out what he was going to do, things would return to normal again. His hands unclenched, his breathing eased. Of course it would.

He came back to himself to find her shaking his arm. 'You haven't heard a word I've said, have you? What's wrong?'

Her lips looked plump and full and oh-so-kissable. He swallowed. 'I…uh…' They were measuring the back yard. That was right. 'Where are we going to find enough people to fill this tent of yours?'

'Marquee,' she corrected. 'And I'm going to need your help on that one.'

His help. *Focus on that—not on the way her bottom lip curves or the neckline of her shirt or—*

Keep your eyes above her neck!

'Help?' he croaked, suddenly parched.

'I want you to get the names of ten people Elsie would like to invite to the wedding.'

That snapped him to. 'Me?'

'I'll do the same for my father. I mean to invite some of my friends, along with the entire street. Let me know if there's anyone you'd like to invite too.'

'Dave Clements,' he said automatically. Dave had thrown Ben a lifeline when he'd most needed one. It would be great to catch up with him.

But then he focused on Meg's order again. Ten names from Elsie? She had to be joking right? 'Does she even *know* ten people?'

'She must do. She goes to Housie one afternoon a week.'

She did?

'Who knows? She might like to invite her chiropodist.'

Elsie had a chiropodist?

'But how am I going to get her to give me two names let alone ten?' He and his grandmother could barely manage a conversation about the weather, let alone anything more personal.

'That's your problem. You're supposed to be resourceful, aren't you? What do you do if wild hyenas invade your camp in Africa? Or if your rope starts to unravel when you're rock-climbing? Or your canoe overturns when you're white-water rafting? This should be a piece of cake in comparison.'

Piece of cake, his—

'Besides, I'm kicking you out of my spare room, so I expect you'll have plenty of time to work on her.'

He gaped at her. 'You're not going to let me stay?'

'Your place is over there.' She pointed across the fence. 'For heaven's sake, Ben, she's *giving* that house to you.'

'I don't want it.'

'Then you'd better find a more gracious way of refusing it than that.'

She stood there with hands on hips, eyes flashing, magnificent in the sunlight, and it suddenly occurred to him that moving out of her spare bedroom might be a very good plan. At least until his body clock adjusted.

She must have read the capitulation in his face because her shoulders lost their combativeness. She clasped her hands together and her gaze slid away. He wondered what she was up to now.

'I…um…' She glanced up at him again and swallowed. 'I want to ask you something, but I'm afraid it might offend you—which isn't my intention at all.'

He shrugged. 'Ask away, Meg.'

She bent down and pretended to study a nearby rosebush. He knew it was a pretence because he knew Meg. She glanced at him and then back at the rosebush. 'We're friends, right? Best friends. So that means it's okay to ask each other personal questions, don't you think?'

His curiosity grew. 'Sure.' For heaven's sake, they were having a baby together. How much more personal could it get?

'You really mean to stay in Fingal Bay for the next six weeks?'

'Yes.'

She straightened. 'Then I want to ask if you have enough money to see you through till then. Money isn't a problem for me, and if you need a loan…' She trailed off, swallowing. 'I've offended you, haven't I?'

He had to move away to sit on a nearby bench. Meg thought him some kind of freeloading loser? His stomach churned. He pinched the bridge of his nose. No wonder she questioned his ability to be any kind of decent father to their child.

'I'm not casting a slur on your life or your masculinity,' she mumbled, sitting beside him, 'but you live in the moment and go wherever the wind blows you. Financial security has never been important to you. Owning things has never been important to you.'

He lifted his head to survey the house behind her. 'And they are to you?' It wasn't the image he had of her in his mind. But her image of *him* was skewed. It was just possible they had each other completely wrong.

After all, how much time had they really spent in each other's company these last five to seven years?

She gave a tiny smile and an equally tiny shrug. 'With a baby on the way, financial security has become very important to me.'

'Is that why you let your father gift you this house?'

'No.'

'Then why?' He turned to face her more fully. 'I'd have thought you'd hate this place.' The same way he hated it.

She studied him for a long moment. 'Not all the associations are bad. This is where my mother came as a new bride. This is where I met my best friend.'

Him.

'Those memories are good. And look.' She grabbed his hand and tugged him around the side of the house to the front patio. 'Look at that view.'

She dropped his hand and a part of him wished she hadn't. The crazy mixed-up, jet lagged part.

'This has to be one of the most beautiful places in the world. Why wouldn't I want to wake up to that every day?'

He stared at the view.

'Besides, Fingal Bay is a nice little community. I think it's a great place to raise a child.'

He stared out at the view—at the roofs of the houses on the street below and the curving bay just beyond. The stretch of sand bordering the bay and leading out to the island gleamed gold in the sun. The water sparkled a magical green-blue. He stared at the boats on the water, listened to the cries of the seagulls, the laughter of children, and tried to see it all objectively.

He couldn't. Every rock and curve and bend was imbued with his childhood.

But...

He'd travelled all around the world and Meg was right. The picturesque bay in front of him rivalled any other sight he'd seen.

He turned to her. 'It's as simple as that? This is where you want to live so you accepted this house as a gift?'

A sigh whispered out of her, mingling with the sounds of the waves whooshing up onto the sand. 'It's a whole lot more complicated than that. It was as if…as if my father *needed* to give me this house.'

He leant towards her. 'Needed to?'

She shrugged, her teeth gnawing on her bottom teeth. 'I haven't got to the bottom of that yet, but…'

She gazed up at him, her hazel eyes steady and resolute, her chin at an angle, as if daring him to challenge her.

'I didn't have the heart to refuse him.'

'The same way you're hoping I won't refuse Elsie.'

'That's between you and her.'

'Don't you hold even the slightest grudge, Meg?'

'Don't you think it's time you let yours go?'

He swung away. Brilliant. Not only did she think him financially unsound, but she thought him irresponsible and immature on top of it.

At least he could answer one of those charges. 'Early in my working life I set up a financial security blanket, so to speak.' He'd invested in real estate. Quite a bit of it, actually.

Her eyes widened. 'You did?'

He had to grit his teeth at her incredulity. 'Yes.'

She pursed her lips and stared at him as if she'd never seen him before. 'That was very sensible of you.'

He ground his teeth harder. He'd watched Laurie Parrish for many years and, while he might not like the man, had learned a thing or two that he'd put into practice. Those wise investments had paid off.

'I have enough money to tide me over for the next six weeks.' And beyond. But he resisted the impulse to brag and tell her exactly how much money that financial security blanket of his held—that really would be immature.

'Okay.' She eyed him uncertainly. 'Good. I'm glad that's settled.'

'While we're on the subject of personal questions—' he rounded on her '—you want to tell me what you're trying to achieve with this godforsaken wedding?'

She hitched up her chin and stuck out a hip. 'I'm joying this "godforsaken wedding" up,' she told him. 'I'm going to *force* them to celebrate.'

He gaped at her. 'Why?'

'Because there was no joy when we were growing up.'

'They were never there for us, Meg. They don't deserve this—the effort you put in, the—'

'Everyone deserves the right to a little happiness. And if they truly want to mend bridges, then...'

'Then?'

'Then I only think it fair and right that we give them that opportunity.'

Ben's face closed up. Every single time he came home Meg cursed what his mother had done to him—abandoning him like she had with a woman who'd grown old before her time. Usually she would let a topic like this drop. Today she didn't. If Ben truly wanted to be a father, he needed to deal with his past.

She folded her arms, her heart pounding against the walls of her chest. 'When my mother died, my father just shut down, became a shell. Her death—it broke him. There was no room in his life for joy or celebration.'

Ben pushed his face in close to hers, his eyes flashing. 'He should've made an effort for you.'

Meg's hand slid across her stomach. She'd make every effort for *her* child, she couldn't imagine ever emotionally abandoning it, but maybe men were different—especially men of her father's generation.

She glanced at Ben. If a woman ever broke his heart, how would he react? She bit back a snigger. To break his heart a woman would have to get close to Ben, and he was never going to let that happen.

Ben's gaze lowered to where her hand rested against her stomach. His gaze had kept returning to her baby bump all morning. As if he couldn't get his fill. She swallowed. It was disconcerting, being the subject of his focus.

Not her, she corrected, the baby.

That didn't prevent the heat from rising in her cheeks or her breathing from becoming shallow and strained.

She tried to shake herself free from whatever weird and wacky pregnancy hormone currently gripped her. *Concentrate.*

'So,' she started, 'while my father went missing in action, your mother left you with Elsie and disappeared. She never rang or sent a letter or anything. Elsie must've been worried sick. She must've been afraid to love you.'

He snapped back. 'Afraid to—?'

'I mean, what if your mother came back and took you away and she never heard from either of you again? What if, when you grew up, you did exactly what your mother did and abandoned *her*?'

'My mother abandoned me, not Elsie.'

'She abandoned the both of you, Ben.'

His jaw dropped open.

Meg nodded. 'Yes, you're right. They both should've made a bigger effort for us. But at least we found each other. At least we both had one friend in the world we could totally depend upon. And whatever else you want to dispute, you can't deny that we didn't have fun together.'

He rolled his shoulders. 'I don't want to deny that.'

'Well, can't you see that my father and Elsie didn't even have that much? Life has left them crippled. But...' She swallowed. 'I demand joy in my life now, and I won't compromise on that. If they refuse to get into the swing of this wedding then I'll know those bridges—the distance between us—can never be mended. And I'll have my answer.'

She hauled in a breath. 'One last chance, Ben, that was what I'm giving them.' And that's what she wanted him to give them too.

Ben didn't say anything. She cast a sidelong glance at him and bit back a sigh. She wondered when Ben—*her* Ben, the Ben she knew, the Ben with an easy smile and a careless saunter, without a care in the world—would return. Ever since he'd pulled his bike to a halt out at the front of her house yesterday there'd been trouble in his eyes.

He turned to her, hands on hips. He had lean hips and a tall, rangy frame. With his blond-tipped hair he looked like a god. No wonder women fell for him left, right and centre.

Though if he'd had a little less in the charm and looks department maybe he'd have learned to treat those women with more sensitivity.

Then she considered his mother and thought maybe not.

'When was the last time *you* felt joyful?' she asked on impulse.

He scratched his chin. He still hadn't shaved. He should look scruffy, but the texture of his shadowed jaw spoke to some yearning deep inside her. The tips of her fingers tingled. She opened and closed her hands. If she reached out and—

She shook herself. Ben *did* look scruffy. Completely and utterly. He most certainly didn't look temptingly disreputable with all that bad-boy promise of his.

Her hands continued to open and close. She heaved back a sigh. Okay, we'll maybe he did. But that certainly wasn't the look she was into.

Normally.

She scowled. Darn pregnancy hormones. And then the memory of that long ago kiss hit her and all the hairs on her arms stood to attention.

Stop it! She and Ben would never travel down that road again. There was simply too much at stake to risk it. *Ever.*

She folded her arms and swallowed. 'It can't be that hard, can it?' she demanded when he remained silent. Ben was the last person who'd need lessons in joy, surely?

'There are just so many to choose from,' he drawled, with that lazy hit-you-in-the-knees grin.

The grin was too slow coming to make her heart beat faster. Her heart had already started to sink. Ben was lying and it knocked her sideways. She'd always thought his exciting, devil-may-care life of freedom gave him endless pleasure and joy.

'The most recent instance that comes to mind is when I bungee-jumped over the Zambezi River from the Victoria Falls Bridge. Amazing rush of adrenaline. I felt like a superhero.'

She scratched a hand back through her hair. What was she thinking? Of *course* Ben's life gave him pleasure. He did so many exciting things. Did he really think he could give that all up for bottles and nappies?

'What about you? When was the last time you felt joyful?'

She didn't even need to think. She placed a hand across her stomach. And even amid all her current confusion and, yes, fear a shaft of joy lifted her up. She smiled. 'The moment I found out I was pregnant.'

She was going to have a baby!

'And every single day after, just knowing I'm pregnant.' Ben had made that possible. She would never be able to thank him enough. Ever.

She set her shoulders. When he came to the conclusion she knew he would—that he wasn't cut out for domesticity—she would do everything in her power to make sure he felt neither guilty nor miserable about it.

Ben shaded his eyes and stared out at the perfect crescent of the bay. 'So you want to spread the joy, huh?'

'Absolutely.' Being pregnant had changed her perspective. In comparison to so many other people she was lucky. Very

lucky. 'We know how to do joy, Ben, but my father and Elsie—
well, they've either forgotten how or they never knew the secret in the first place.'

'It's not a secret, Meg.'

Tell her father and Elsie that.

'And if this scheme of yours doesn't work and they remain
as sour and distant as ever?'

'I'm not going to break my heart over it, if that's what you're
worried about. But at least I'll know I tried.'

He shifted his weight and shoved his hands into the pockets of his jeans, making them ride even lower on his hips. The
scent of leather slugged her in the stomach—which was odd,
because Ben wasn't wearing his leather jacket.

'And what if it does work? Have you considered that?'

She dragged her gaze from his hips and tried to focus. 'That
scenario could be the most challenging of all,' she agreed. 'The
four of us...five,' she amended, glancing down at her stomach,
'all trying to become a family after all this time. It'll be tricky.'

She wanted to add, *but not impossible*, but her throat had
closed over at the way he surveyed her stomach. Her chest
tightened at the intensity of his focus. The light in his eyes
made her thighs shake.

She cleared her throat and dragged in a breath. 'If it works
I'll get a warm and fuzzy feeling,' she declared. Warm and
fuzzy was preferable to hot and prickly. She rolled her shoulders. 'And perhaps you will too.'

Finally—*finally*—his gaze lifted to hers. 'More fairytales,
Meg?'

Did he still hold that much resentment about their less than
ideal childhood? 'You still want to punish them?'

'No.' Very slowly he shook his head. 'But I don't think they
deserve all your good efforts either. Especially when I'm far
from convinced anything either one of us does will make a
difference where they're concerned.'

'But what is it going to hurt to try?'

'I'm afraid it'll hurt *you*.'

He'd always looked out for her. She couldn't help but smile at him. 'I have a baby on the way. I'm on top of the world.'

He smiled suddenly too. A real smile—not one to trick or beguile. 'All right, Meg, I'm in. I'll do whatever I can to help.'

She let out a breath she hadn't even known she'd held.

'On one condition.'

She should've known. She folded her arms. 'Which is…?' She was *not* letting him sleep in her spare bedroom. He belonged next door. Besides… She swallowed. She needed her own space.

'You'll let me touch the baby.'

CHAPTER FIVE

MEG COULDN'T HELP her sudden grin. Lots of people had touched her baby bump—happy for her and awed by the miracle growing inside her. Why should Ben be any different?

Of course he'd be curious.

Of course he'd be invested.

He might never be Daddy but he'd always be Uncle Ben. *Favourite* Uncle Ben. Wanting to touch her baby bump was the most natural thing in the world.

She didn't try to temper her grin. 'Of course you can, Ben.'

She turned so she faced him front-on, offering her stomach to him, so to speak. His hands reached out, both of them strong and sure. They didn't waver. His hands curved around her abdomen—and just like that it stopped being the most natural thing in the world.

The pulse jammed in Meg's throat and she had to fight the urge to jolt away from him. Ben's hands suddenly didn't look like the hands of her best friend. They looked sensual and sure and knowing. They didn't feel like the hands of her best friend either.

Her breath hitched and her pulse skipped and spun like a kite-surfer in gale force winds. With excruciating thoroughness he explored every inch of her stomach through the thin cotton of her shirt. His fingers were hot and strong and surprisingly gentle.

And every part of her he touched he flooded with warmth and vigour.

She clenched her eyes shut. Her *best friend* had never looked at her with that possessive light in his eyes before. Not that it was aimed at her per se. Still, the baby was inside *her* abdomen.

He moved in closer and his heat swamped her. She opened her eyes and tried to focus on the quality of the light hitting the water of the bay below. But then his scent swirled around her—a mix of soap and leather and something darker and more illicit, like a fine Scotch whisky. She dragged in a shaky breath. Scotch wasn't Ben's drink. It was a crazy association. That thought, though, didn't make the scent go away.

Her heart all but stopped when he knelt down in front of her and pressed the left side of his face to her stomach, his arm going about her waist. She found her hand hovering above his head. She wanted to rest it there, but that would make them seem too much of a trio. Her throat thickened and tears stung her eyes. They weren't a trio. Even if by some miracle Ben stayed, they still wouldn't be a trio.

But he wouldn't stay.

And so her hand continued to hover awkwardly above his head.

'Hey, little baby,' he crooned. 'I'm your—'

'No!' She tried to move away but his grip about her tightened.

'I'm…I'm pleased to meet you,' he whispered against her stomach instead.

She closed her eyes and breathed hard.

When he climbed back to his feet their gazes clashed and locked. She'd never felt more confused in her entire life.

'Thank you.'

'You're welcome.'

Their gazes continued to battle until Ben finally took a step away and seemed to mentally shake himself. 'What's the plan for the rest of the day?'

The plan was to put as much distance between her and Ben as she could. Somewhere in the last day he'd become a stranger to her. A stranger who smelled good, who looked good, and who unnerved her.

This new Ben threatened more than her equilibrium. He threatened her unborn child's future and its happiness.

The Ben she knew would never do anything to hurt her. But this new Ben? She didn't trust him. She wanted to be away from him, to get her head back into some semblance of working order. She knew exactly how to accomplish that.

'I'm going into Nelson Bay to start on the wedding preparations.'

'Excellent plan. I'll come with you.'

She nearly choked. 'You'll what?'

'You said you wanted my help.' He lifted his arms. 'I'm yours to command.'

Why did that have to sound so suggestive?

'But—' She tried to think of something sensible to say. She couldn't, so she strode back around the side of the house.

'Time is a-wasting.' He kept perfect time beside her.

'It's really not necessary.' She tucked her hair back behind her ears, avoiding eye contact while she collected the tape measure along with the measurements he'd jotted down for her. 'You only got back from Africa yesterday. You are allowed a couple of days to catch your breath.'

'Are you trying to blow me off, Meg?'

Heat scorched her cheeks. 'Of course not.'

He grinned as if enjoying her discomfiture. 'Well, then...'

She blew out a breath. 'Have it your own way. But we're taking my car, not the bike, and I'm driving.'

'Whatever you say.'

He raised his hands in mock surrender, and suddenly he was her Ben again and it made her laugh. 'Be warned—I *will* make you buy me an ice cream cone. I cannot get enough of passionfruit ripple ice cream at the moment.'

He glanced at his watch. 'It's nearly lunchtime. I'll buy you a kilo of prawns from the co-op and we can stretch out on the beach and eat them.'

'You'll have to eat them on your own, then. And knowing how I feel about prawns, that'd be too cruel.'

He followed her into the house. 'They give you morning sickness?'

She patted her stomach. 'It has something to do with mercury levels in seafood. It could harm the baby. I'm afraid Camembert and salami are off the menu too.'

He stared at her, his jaw slack, and she could practically read his thoughts—shock that certain foods might harm the baby growing inside her—and his sudden confrontation with his own ignorance. Her natural impulse was to reassure him, but she stifled it. Ben was ignorant about babies and pregnancy, and it wasn't up to her to educate him. If he wanted to be a good father he would have to educate himself, exercising his own initiative, not because she prompted or nagged him to.

But she didn't want the stranger back, so she kept her voice light and added, 'Not to mention wine and coffee. All of my favourite things. Still, I seem to be finding ample consolation in passionfruit ripple ice cream.'

She washed her hands, dried them, stowed the measurements in her handbag and then lifted an eyebrow in Ben's direction. 'Ready?'

He still hadn't moved from his spot in the doorway, but at her words he strode across to the sink to pump the strawberry-scented hand-wash she kept on the window ledge into his hands. The scent only seemed to emphasise his masculinity. She watched him wash his hands and remembered the feel of them on her abdomen, their heat and their gentleness.

She jerked her gaze away.

'Ready.'

When she turned back he was drying his hands. And there was a new light in his eyes and a determined shape to his

mouth. Normally she would take the time to dust a little powder on her nose and slick on a coat of lipstick, but she wanted
to be out of the house and into the day. Right now!

She led the way to her car.

'Okay, the plan today is to hire a marquee for the big event—
along with the associated paraphernalia. Tables chairs and
whatnot,' she said as they drove the short distance to the neigh-
bouring town. 'And then we'll reward ourselves with lunch.'

'Do you mind if we do a bit of shopping afterwards? I need
to grab a few things.'

She glanced at him. Ben and shopping? She shook her head.
'Not at all.'

To Meg's utter surprise, Ben was a major help on the Great
Marquee Hunt. He zeroed in immediately on the marquee that
would best suit their purposes. The side panels could be rolled
up to allow a breeze to filter through the interior if the evening
proved warm. If the day was cool, however—and that wasn't
unheard of in late March—the view of the bay could still be
enjoyed through the clear panels that acted like windows in
the marquee walls.

Ben insisted on putting down the deposit himself.

Given the expression on his face earlier, when she'd asked
him about his financial circumstances, she decided it would
be the better part of valour not to argue with him.

Furniture was next on the list, and Meg chose round tables
and padded chairs. 'Round tables means the entire table can
talk together with ease.' Hopefully it would promote conversation.

Ben's lips twisted. 'And they'll make the marquee look
fuller, right?'

Exactly.

'What else?' he demanded.

'We need a long table for the wedding party.'

'There's only four of us. It won't need to be *that* long.'

'And tables for presents and the cake.'

Ben pointed out tables, the salesman made a note, and then they were done—all in under an hour.

Ben's hands went to his hips. 'What now?'

To see him so fully focused on the task made her smile. 'Now we congratulate ourselves on having made such excellent progress and reward ourselves with lunch.'

'That's it?'

She could tell he didn't believe her. 'It's one of the big things ticked off. It's all I had scheduled for today.'

'What are the other big things?'

'The catering, the cake, the invitations. And...' A grin tugged at her lips.

He leaned down to survey her face. His own lips twitched. 'And?'

'And shopping for Elsie's outfit.'

He shot away from her. 'Oh, no—no, no. You're *not* dragging me along on that.'

She choked back a laugh. 'Fat lot of use you'd be anyway. I'll let you off the hook if you buy me lunch.'

'Deal.'

They bought hot chips smothered in salt and vinegar, and dashed across the road to the beach. School had gone back several weeks ago, but it was the weekend and the weather was divine. The long crescent of sand that bordered the bay was lined with families enjoying the sunshine, sand and water. Children's laughter, the sounds of waves whooshing up onto the beach and the cries of seagulls greeted them. *Divine!* She lifted her face to the sun and breathed it all in.

They found a spare patch of sand and Meg stretched out her legs, relishing the warmth of the sun on the bare skin of her arms and legs. She glanced at Ben as he hunkered down beside her. He must be hot.

'You should've changed into shorts.'

He unwrapped the chips. 'I'm good.'

Yeah, but he'd look great in shorts, and—

She blinked. What on earth...? And then the scent of salt and vinegar hit her and her stomach grumbled and her mouth watered. With a grin he held the packet towards her.

They ate, not saying much, just listening to the familiar sounds of children at play and the splashing of the tiny waves that broke onshore. Nearby a moored yacht's rigging clanged in the breeze, making a pelican lift out of the water and wheel up into the air. It was summer in the bay—her favourite time of year and her favourite patch of paradise.

She wasn't sure when they both started to observe the family—just that at some stage the nearby mother, father and two small girls snagged their attention. One of the little girls dashed down the beach towards them, screaming with delight when her father chased after her. Seizing her securely around the waist, he lifted her off her feet to swing her above his head.

'Higher, Daddy, higher!' she squealed, laughing down at him, her face alive with delight.

The other little girl, smaller than the first, lurched across the sand on chubby, unsteady legs to fling her arms around her father's thigh. She grinned and chortled up at him.

Meg swallowed and her chest started to cramp. Both of those little girls literally glowed with their love for their father.

She tore her gaze away to stare directly out in front of her, letting the sunlight that glinted off the water to dazzle and half-blind her.

'More?' Ben's voice came out hoarse and strained as he held the chips out to her.

She shook her head. Her appetite had fled.

He scrunched the remaining chips and she was aware of every crackle the paper made. And how white his knuckles had turned. She went back to staring directly out in front of her, tracking a speedboat as it zoomed past.

But it didn't drown out the laughter of the two little girls.

'Did you ever consider what you were depriving your child of when you decided to go it alone, Meg?'

His voice exploded at her—tight and barely controlled. She stiffened. And then she rounded on him. 'Don't take that high moral tone with me, Ben Sullivan! Since when in your entire adult life, have you *ever* put another person's needs or wants above your own?'

He blinked. 'I—'

'I didn't twist your arm. You had some say in the matter, you know.'

Her venom took him off guard. It took her off guard too, but his question had sliced right into the core of her. She'd thought she'd considered that question. She'd thought it wouldn't matter. But after seeing that family—the girls with their father, their love and sense of belonging—she felt the doubt demons rise to plague her.

'Families come in all shapes and sizes,' she hissed, more for her own benefit than his. Her baby would want for nothing! 'As for depriving my child of a father? Well, I don't rate my father very highly, and I sure as heck don't rate yours. There are worse things than not having a father.'

Ben's head rocked back in shock. Meg's sentiment didn't surprise him, but the way she expressed it did.

He clenched his jaw so hard he thought he might break teeth. A weight pressed against his chest, making it difficult to breathe.

'Just like you don't rate me as a father, right?' he rasped out, acid burning his throat.

Eventually he turned to look at her. She immediately glanced away, but not before he recognised the scepticism stretching through her eyes. The weight in his chest grew heavier. If Meg didn't have any faith in him…

No, dammit! He clenched his hands. Meg didn't have all the answers.

He swore.

She flinched.

He kept his voice low. 'So I'm suitable as a sperm bank but not as anything more substantial?' Was *that* how she saw him?

She stared straight back out in front of her. 'That surprises you?'

'It does when that's your attitude, Meg.'

That made her turn to look at him.

Dammit it all to hell, she was supposed to *know* him!

A storm raged in the hazel depths of her eyes. He watched her swallow. She glanced down at her hands and then back up. 'How long have you wanted to be a father, Ben? A week?'

It was his turn to glance away.

'I've wanted to be a mother for as long as I can remember.'

'And you think that gives you more rights?'

'It means I know what to expect. It means I know I'm not going to change my mind next week. It means I know I'm committed to this child.' She slapped a hand to the sand. 'It means I know precisely what I'm getting into—that I've put plans into place in anticipation of the baby's arrival, and that I've adjusted my life so I can ensure my baby gets the very best care and has the very best life I can possibly give it. And now you turn up and think you have the right to tell me I'm selfish!'

She let out a harsh laugh that had his stomach churning.

'When have you ever committed to anybody or anything? You've never even taken a job on full-time. You've certainly never committed to a woman or what's left of your family. It's barely possible to get you to commit to dinner at the end of next week!'

'I'm committed to *you*.' The words burst out of him. 'If you'd ever needed me, Meg, I'd have come home.'

She smiled then, but there was an ache of sadness behind her eyes that he didn't understand. 'Yes, I believe you would've. But once I was back on my feet you'd have been off like a flash again, wouldn't you?'

He had no answer to that.

'The thing is, Ben, your trooping all over the world having adventures is fine in a best friend, but it's far from fine in a father.'

She had a point. He knew she did. And until he knew how involved he wanted to be he had no right to push her or judge her. 'I didn't mean to imply you were selfish. I think you'll be a great mum.'

But it didn't mean there wasn't room for him in the baby's life too.

She gestured to her right, to where that family now sat eating sandwiches, but she didn't look at them again. 'Is that what you really want?'

He stared at the picture of domestic bliss and had to repress a shudder. He wasn't doing marriage. Ever. He didn't believe in it. But… The way those little girls looked at their father— their faces so open and trusting. And loving. The thought of having someone look up to him like that both terrified and electrified him.

If he wanted to be a father—a proper father—his life would have to change. Drastically.

'Ben, I want a better father for my child than either one of us had.'

'Me too.' That at least was a no-brainer.

She eyed him for a moment. Whenever she was in the sun for any length of time the green flecks within the brown of her iris grew in intensity. They flashed and sparkled now, complementing the aqua water only a few feet away.

Aqua eyes.

A smattering of freckles across her nose.

Blonde hair that brushed her shoulders.

And she smelled like pineapple and coconuts.

She was a golden goddess, encapsulating all he most loved about summer.

'Ben!'

He snapped to. 'What?'

Her nostrils flared, drawing his attention back to her freckles. She glanced away and then back again. 'I said, you *do* know that I'm not anti-commitment the way you are, right?'

'Yeah, sure.'

His attention remained on those cute freckles, their duskiness highlighting the golden glow of her skin. He'd never noticed how cute they were before—cute and kind of cheeky. They were new to him. This conversation wasn't. Commitment versus freedom. They'd thrashed it out endless time. To her credit, though, Meg had never tried to change his mind. They'd simply agreed to disagree. Even that one stupid time they had kissed.

Damn it! He'd promised never to think about that again.

'Then you should also be aware that I don't expect to "*deprive*"—' she made quotation marks in the air with her fingers '—my child of a father for ever.'

He frowned, still distracted by those freckles, and then by the shine on her lips when she moistened them. 'Right.'

She hauled in a breath and let it out again. The movement wafted a slug of coconut infused pineapple his way. He drew it into his lungs slowly, the way he would breathe in a finely aged Chardonnay before bringing the glass to his lips and sipping it.

'Just because I've decided to have a baby it doesn't mean I've given up on the idea of falling in love and getting married, maybe having more kids if I'm lucky.'

It took a moment for the significance of her words to connect, but when they did they smashed into him with the force of that imaginary bottle of Chardonnay wielded at his head. The beach tilted. The world turned black and white. He shoved his hands into the sand and clenched them.

'I might be doing things slightly out of order, but…' She let her words trail off.

He stabbed a finger at her, showering her with sand. 'You are *not* letting another man raise my child!'

He shot to his feet and paced down to the water's edge, tried to get his breathing back under control before he hyperventilated.

Another man would get the laughter...and the fun...and the love.

He dragged a hand back through his hair. Of course this schmuck would also be getting hog-tied into marriage and would have to deal with school runs, parent and teacher interviews and eat-your-greens arguments. But...

'No!'

He swung around to find Meg standing directly behind him. 'Keep your voice down,' she ordered, glancing around. 'There are small children about.'

Why the hell didn't she just bar him from all child-friendly zones? She obviously didn't rate his parenting abilities at all. His hands clenched. But giving his child—*his child*—to another man to raise? No way!

He must have said it out loud, because she arched an eyebrow at him. 'You think you can prevent me from marrying whoever I want?'

'Whomever,' he said, knowing that correcting her grammar would set her teeth on edge.

Which it did. 'You and whose army, Ben?'

'You can marry *whomever* you damn well please,' he growled, 'but this baby only has one father.' He pounded a fist to his chest. 'And that's me.'

She folded her arms. 'You're telling me that you're giving up your free and easy lifestyle to settle in Port Stephens, get a regular job and trade your motorbike for a station wagon?'

'That's exactly what I'm saying.'

'Why?'

It was a genuine question, not a challenge. He didn't know how to articulate the determination or sense of purpose that had overtaken him. He only knew that this decision was the most important of his life.

And he had no intention of getting it wrong.

He knew that walking away from their baby would be wrong.

But...

It left the rest of his life in tatters.

Meg sighed when he remained silent. She didn't believe he meant it. It was evident in her face, in her body language, in the way she turned away. Her lack of faith in him stung, but he had no one else to blame for that but himself.

He would prove himself to her. He would set all her fears to rest. And he would be the best father on the planet.

When she turned back he could see her nose had started to turn pink. Her nose always went pink before she cried. He stared at the pinkness. He glanced away. Meg hardly ever cried.

He glanced back. Swallowed. It could be sunburn. They'd been out in the sun for a while now.

He closed his eyes. He ached to wrap her in his arms and tell her he would not let either her or the baby down. Words, though, were cheap. Meg would need more than verbal assurances. She'd need action.

'We should make tracks.' She shaded her eyes against the sun. 'You said you needed to do some shopping?'

He did. But he needed a timeout from Meg more. He needed to get his head around the realisation that he was back in Port Stephens for good.

He feigned interest in a sultry brunette, wearing nothing but a bikini, who was ambling along the beach towards them.

'Ben?'

He lifted one shoulder in a lazy shrug. 'The shopping can wait.' He deliberately followed the brunette's progress instead of looking at Meg. 'Look, why don't you head off? I might hang around for a while. I'll find my own way home.'

He knew exactly what interpretation Meg would put on that.

The twist of her lips told her she had. Without another word, she turned and left.

Clenching his hands, he set off down the beach, not even noticing the brunette when he passed her.

A baby deserves to have the unconditional love of the two people who created it. If he left, who would his child have in its day-to-day life? Meg, who'd be wonderful, and Uncle Ben who'd never be there. His hands clenched. Meg's father and Elsie could hardly be relied on to provide the baby with emotional support.

He shook his head. He could at least make sure this child knew it was loved and wanted by its father. Things like that—they did matter.

And this baby deserved only good things.

When he reached the end of the beach he turned and walked back and then headed for the shops. Meg should be home by now, and he meant to buy every damn book about pregnancy and babies he could get his hands on. He wanted to be prepared for the baby's arrival. He wanted to help Meg out in any way he could.

What he didn't need was her damn superiority, or her looking over his shoulder and raising a sceptical eyebrow at the books he selected. He had enough doubt of his own to deal with.

He turned back to stare at the beach, the bay, and the water. Back in Port Stephens for good?

Him?

Hell.

CHAPTER SIX

MEG SANG ALONG to her Madonna CD in full voice. She'd turned the volume up loud to disguise the fact she couldn't reach the high notes and in an attempt to drown out the chorus of voices that plagued her—a litany of 'what ifs' and 'what the hells' and 'no ways'. All circular and pointless. But persistent. Singing helped to quiet them.

She broke off to complete a complicated manoeuvre with her crochet needle. At least as far as she was concerned it was complicated. Her friend Ally assured her that by the time she finished this baby shawl she'd have this particular stitch combination down pat.

She caressed the delicate white wool and surveyed her work so far. It didn't seem like much, considering how long it had taken her, but she didn't begrudge a moment of that time. She'd have this finished in time for the baby's arrival. Maybe only just, but it would be finished. And then she could wrap her baby in this lovely soft shawl, its wool so delicate it wouldn't irritate newborn skin. She'd wrap her baby in this shawl and it would know how much it was loved.

She lifted it to her cheek and savoured its softness.

The song came to an end. She lowered the crocheting back to her lap and was about to resume when some sixth sense had her glancing towards the doorway.

Ben.

Her throat tightened. She swallowed once, twice. 'Hey,' she finally managed.

'I knocked.' He pointed back behind him.

She grabbed the remote, turned the music down and motioned for him to take a seat. 'With the music blaring like that there's not a chance I'd have heard you.'

He stood awkwardly in the doorway. She gripped the crochet needle until the metal bit into her fingers.

'Madonna, huh?' He grinned but it didn't hide his discomfort.

'Yup.' She grinned back but she doubted it hid her tension, her uneasiness either.

He glanced around. 'We never sat in here when we were growing up.'

'No.' When they'd been growing up this had definitely been adult territory. When indoors, they'd stuck to the kitchen and the family room. 'But this is my house now and I can sit where I please.'

He didn't look convinced. Tension kept his spine straight and his shoulders tight. Last week she'd have risen and led him through to the family room, where he'd feel more comfortable. This week...?

She lifted her chin. This week making Ben comfortable was the last thing on her agenda. That knowledge made her stomach churn and bile rise in her throat. It didn't mean she wanted to make him *un*comfortable, though.

She cleared her throat. 'Have a look out of the front window.'

After a momentary hesitation he did as she ordered.

'It has the most divine view of the bay. I find that peaceful. When the wind is up you can hear the waves breaking on shore.'

'And that's a sound you've always loved.' He settled on the pristine white leather sofa. 'And you can hear it best in here.'

And in the front bedroom. She didn't mention that, though.

Mentioning bedrooms to Ben didn't seem wise. Which was crazy. But...

She glanced at him and her pulse sped up and her skin prickled. *That* was what was crazy. He sprawled against the sofa with that easy, long-limbed grace of his, one arm resting along the back of the sofa as if in invitation. Her crochet needle trembled.

She dragged her gaze away and set her crochet work to one side. Her life was in turmoil. That was all this was—a reaction to all the changes happening in her life. The fact she had a baby on the way. The fact her father was marrying Elsie. The fact Ben claimed he wanted to be a father.

Ben nodded towards the wool. 'What are you doing?'

She had to moisten her lips before she could speak. 'I'm making a shawl for the baby.'

She laid the work out for him to see and he stared at it as if fascinated. When he glanced up at her, the warmth in those blue eyes caressed her.

'You can knit?'

She pretended to preen. 'Why, yes, I can, now that you mention it. Knitting clubs were more popular than book clubs around here for a while. But this isn't knitting—it's crochet, and I'm in the process of mastering the art.'

He frowned. And then he straightened. 'Why? Are you trying to save money?'

She folded her arms. That didn't deserve an answer.

His eyes narrowed. 'Or is this what your social life had descended to?'

If she could have kept a straight face she'd have let him go on believing that. It would be one seriously scary picture of life here in Fingal Bay for him to chew over. One he'd probably run from kicking and screaming. But she couldn't keep a straight face.

He leant back, his shoulders loosening, his grin hooking

up one side of his face in that slow, melt-a-woman-to-her-core way he had. 'Okay, just call me an idiot.'

If she's had any breath left in her lungs she might have done exactly that. Only that grin of his had knocked all the spare oxygen out of her body.

'Your social life is obviously full. I've barely clapped eyes on you these last few days.'

Had he wanted to? The thought made her heart skip and stutter a little faster.

Stop being stupid! 'It's full enough for me.' She didn't tell him that Monday night had been an antenatal class, or that last night she'd cooked dinner for Ally, who was recovering from knee surgery. Ben's social life consisted of partying hard and having a good time, not preparing for babies or looking after friends.

Ben's life revolved around adrenaline junkie thrills, drinking hard and chasing women. She wondered why he wasn't out with that sexy brunette this evening—the one he'd obviously had every intention of playing kiss chase with the other day—and then kicked herself. Sunday to Wednesday? Ben would count that a long-term relationship. And they both knew what he thought about those.

'So why?' He gestured to the wool.

He really didn't get it, did he? An ache pressed behind her eyes. What the hell was he doing here? She closed her eyes, dragged in a breath and then opened them again. She settled more comfortably in her chair.

'Once upon a time…' she started.

Ben eased back in his seat too, slouching slightly, his eyes alive with interest.

'Once upon a time,' she repeated, 'the Queen announced she was going to have a baby. There was much rejoicing in the kingdom.'

He grinned that grin of his. 'Of course there was.'

'To celebrate and honour the impending arrival of the royal

heir, the Queen fashioned a special shawl for the child to be wrapped in. It took an entire nine months to make, and every stitch was a marvel of delicate skill, awe-inspiring craftsmanship and love. All who saw it bowed down in awe.'

He snorted. 'Laying it on a bit thick, Meg. A shawl is never going to be a holy grail.'

She tossed her head. 'All who saw it bowed down in awe, recognising it as the symbol of maternal love that it was.'

The teasing in Ben's face vanished. He stared at her with an intensity that made her swallow.

'When the last stitch was finished, the Queen promptly gave birth. And it was said that whenever the royal child was wrapped in that shawl its crying stopped and it was immediately comforted.' She lifted her chin. 'The shawl became a valued family heirloom, passed down throughout the generations.'

He eyed the work spread in her lap. Was it her imagination or did he fully check her chest out on the way down? Her pulse pounded. Wind rushed in her ears.

'You want to give your baby something special.'

His words pulled her back from her ridiculous imaginings. 'Yes.' She wanted to fill her baby's life with love and all manner of special things. The one thing she didn't want to give it was a father who would let it down. She didn't say that out loud, though. Ben knew her feelings on the subject. Harping on it would only get his back up. He had to come to the conclusion that he wasn't father material in his own time.

She didn't want to talk about the baby with Ben any longer. She didn't have the heart for it.

'So, how's your week been so far?'

His lips twisted. 'How the hell do you deal with Elsie?'

Ah.

'The woman is a goddamn clam—a locked box. I'm never going to get those names for you Meg.'

She'd known it would be a tough test. But if Ben couldn't pass it he had no business hanging around in Fingal Bay.

His eyes flashed. 'Is it against the rules to help me out?'

She guessed not. He'd still have to do the hard work, but...

She didn't want to help him. She stared down at her hands. She wanted him to leave Fingal Bay and not come back for seven, eight...ten months.

He's your best friend!

And he was turning her whole life upside down. Not to mention her baby's.

She remembered the way she'd ached for her father to show some interest in her life, to be there for her. And she remembered the soul-deep disappointment, the crushing emptiness, the disillusionment and the shame when he'd continued to turn away from her. Nausea swirled in her stomach. She didn't want that for her child.

Did her baby need protecting from Ben? She closed her eyes. If she knew the answer to that...

'Why didn't you come over for dinner tonight? Elsie says you come to dinner every Wednesday night.'

She opened her eyes to find him leaning towards her. She shrugged. 'Except when you're home.'

His lips, which were normally relaxed and full of wicked promise, pressed into a thin line. 'And why's that?'

'I like to give you guys some space when you're home.'

'Is that all?'

Her automatic response was to open her mouth to tell him of course that was all. She stamped on it. Ben had changed everything when he'd burst in on Saturday. She wasn't sure she wanted to shield him any more. 'Precisely how much honesty do you want, Ben?'

His jaw slackened. 'I thought we were always honest.'

She pursed her lips. 'I'm about as honest as I can be when I see you for a total of three weeks in a year. Four if I'm lucky.'

His jaw clenched. His nostrils flared. 'Why didn't you come over to Elsie's tonight?'

Fine. She folded her arms. 'There are a couple of reasons.

The first: Elsie is hard work. You're home so you can deal with her. It's nice to have a night off.'

He sagged back as if she'd slugged him on the jaw.

'I make her cook dinner for me every Wednesday night. It's a bargain we struck up. I do her groceries and she cooks me dinner on Wednesday nights. But really it's so I can make sure she's still functioning—keep an eye on her fine motor skills and whatnot. See if I can pick up any early signs of illness or dementia.'

Which proved difficult as Elsie had absolutely no conversation in her. Until one night about a month ago, when Elsie had suddenly started chatting and Meg had fled. It shamed her now—her panic and sense of resentment and her cowardice. She could see now that Elsie had tried to open a door, and Meg had slammed it shut in her face.

Ben stared at her. He didn't say a word. It was probably why Elsie had reverted to being a clam around Ben now.

Still, it wasn't beyond Ben to make an overture too, was it? Meg bit her lip. If he truly wanted to be a father.

'Look, when you breeze in for an odd week here and a few days there, I do my best to make it fun and not to bore you with tedious domestic details. But if you mean to move back to Port Stephens for good then you can jolly well share some of the load.'

He'd gone pale, as if he might throw up on her pristine white carpet. 'What's the other reason you didn't come to dinner?' he finally asked.

She swallowed. Carpets could be cleaned. It was much harder to mend a child's broken heart. But...

'Meg?'

She lifted her chin and met his gaze head-on. 'I don't like seeing you and Elsie together. It's when I like you both least.'

He stared at her, his eyes dark. In one swift movement he rose. 'I should go.'

'Sit down, Ben.' She bit back a sigh. 'Do you mean to run

away every time we have a difficult conversation? What about if that difficult conversation is about the baby? Are you going to run away then too?'

The pulse at the base of his jaw pounded. 'Couldn't you at least offer a guy a beer before tearing his character to shreds?'

She stood. 'You're right. But not a beer. You drink too much.'

'Hell, Meg, don't hold back!'

She managed a smile. Somehow. 'I'm having a hot chocolate. I'm trying to make sure I get enough calcium. Would you like one too, or would you prefer tea or coffee?'

He didn't answer, and she led the way to the kitchen and set about making hot chocolate. She was aware of how closely Ben watched her—she'd have had to be blind not to. It should have made her clumsy, but it didn't. It made her feel powerful and…and beautiful.

Which didn't make sense.

She shook the thought off and handed Ben one of the steaming mugs. 'Besides,' she started, as if there hadn't been a long, silent pause in their conversation, 'I'm not shredding your character. You're my best friend and I love you.'

She pulled a stool out at the breakfast bar and sat. 'But c'mon, Ben, what's to like about hanging out with you and Elsie? She barely speaks and you turn back into a sullen ten-year-old. All the conversation is left to me. You don't help me out, and Elsie answers any questions directed to her in words of two syllables. Preferably one if she can get away with it. Great night out for a girl.' She said it all with a grin, wanting to chase the shadows from his eyes.

'I…' Ben slammed his mug down, pulled out the stool beside her and wrapped an arm about her shoulders in a rough hug. 'Hell, Meg, I'm sorry. I never looked at it that way before.'

'That's okay.' He smelled of leather and Scotch and her senses greedily drank him in. 'I didn't mind when your visits were so fleeting—they were like moments stolen from reality. They never seemed part of the real world.'

'Which will change if I become a permanent fixture in the area?'

Exactly. She reached for her mug again. Ben removed his arm. Even though it was a warm night she missed its weight and its strength.

'I deal with Elsie by telling her stories.'

He swung around so quickly he almost spilled his drink. 'Like our fairytales?'

She shook her head. No, not like those. They were just for her and Ben. 'I talk at her—telling her what I've been up to for the week, what child did what to another child at work, what I saw someone wearing on the boardwalk in Nelson Bay, what wonderful new dish I've recently tried cooking, what book I'm reading. Just...monologues.'

It should be a tedious, monotonous rendition—a chore— but in between enquiring if Elsie had won anything at Housie or the raffles and if she'd made her shopping list yet, to amuse herself Meg dramatised everything to the nth degree. It made the time pass more quickly.

'So I should tell her what I've been up to?'

She shrugged.

'But I haven't been doing anything since I got back.'

She made her voice tart. 'Then I suggest you start doing something before you turn into a vegetable.'

A laugh shot out of him. 'Like I said earlier, don't hold back.'

She had no intention of doing so, but... She glanced at the handsome profile beside her and an icy hand clamped around her heart and squeezed. Her chest constricted painfully. She didn't want to make Ben miserable. She didn't want him feeling bad about himself. She wanted him to be happy.

And living in Fingal Bay would never make him happy.

She dragged her gaze back to the mug she cradled in her hands. 'I already have the names of ten guests from my father.'

'How'd you manage that?'

'Deceit and emotional blackmail.'

He grinned. And then he threw his head back and laughed. Captured in the moment like that he looked so alive it momentarily robbed her of breath, of speech, and of coherent thought. She never felt so alive as when Ben was home. Yearning rose inside her. Yearning for…

He glanced at her, stilled, and his eyes darkened. It seemed as if the very air between them shimmered. They swayed towards each other.

And then they both snapped away. Meg grabbed their now empty mugs and bolted for the sink, desperately working on getting her breathing back under control. They'd promised one another that they would never go *there* again. They'd agreed their friendship was too important to risk. And that still held true.

In the reflection of the window she could see Ben pacing on the other side of the breakfast bar, his hands clenched. Eventually she wouldn't be able to pretend to be washing the cups any more.

Ben coughed and then stared up at the ceiling. 'Deceit and emotional blackmail?'

She closed her eyes, counted to three and turned off the tap. She turned back to him, praying—very hard—that she looked casual and unconcerned. 'I told him that Elsie would love a small party for a reception and that if he cared about Elsie's needs then he'd give me the names of ten people I could invite to the wedding.'

'It obviously worked.'

Like a charm. Her father and Elsie might not be particularly demonstrative, but Meg didn't doubt they cared deeply for each other. She remembered their linked hands, the fire in Elsie's eyes when she'd defended Laurie to Ben, and her father's vulnerability.

She glanced at Ben. He seemed completely unfazed by that

'moment'. The hot chocolate in her stomach curdled. Maybe she'd been the only one caught up in it.

She cleared her throat. 'It worked so well he actually gave me a dozen names.'

Ben rubbed his chin. 'If I did it in reverse...'

'Worth a try,' she agreed.

'Brilliant!' He slapped a hand down on the breakfast bar. 'Thanks, Meg.'

'Any time.'

But the words sounded wooden, even to her own ears. He opened the back door, hesitated, and then turned back. 'I didn't come back to make your life chaotic on purpose, Meg.'

She managed a smile. 'I know.'

'What night do you check up on your father?'

She should have known he'd make that connection. 'Tomorrow night. He refuses to cook, or to let me cook, so we have dinner at the RSL club.'

'Would it be all right if Elsie and I came along with you tomorrow night?'

What? Like a family? She frowned and scratched the back of her neck. Eventually she managed to clear her throat again. 'The more the merrier.'

'What time should we be ready?'

'He likes to eat early these days, so I'll be leaving here at six.'

With a nod, he was gone.

Ben stood in the dark garden, adrift between Meg's house and Elsie's.

He'd wandered over to Meg's tonight because he couldn't have stood another ten minutes in Elsie's company, but...

He scratched a hand back through his hair. He hadn't expected to be confronted with his own inadequacies. With his selfishness.

He threw his head back to glare at the stars. He dragged

cleansing breaths into his lungs. No wonder Meg didn't believe he'd see this fatherhood gig through.

He rested his hands against his knees and swore. He had to start pulling his weight. Meg was pregnant. She should be focussing on things like getting ready for the baby. Resting.

While he'd been off seeing the world Meg had been taking care of everyone. He straightened. Well, her days of being a drudge were over. He'd see to that.

He glanced at his grandmother's house. Shoving his shoulders back, he set off towards it.

He found Elsie at the kitchen table, playing Solitaire—just as she'd been doing when he'd left. The radio crooned songs from the 1950s.

'Drink?' he offered, going to the fridge.

'No, thank you.'

She didn't so much as glance at him. He grabbed a beer... stopped...set it back down again and seized a can of soda instead. The silence pressed down like a blanket of cold snow. He shot a glance towards the living room and the promised distraction of the television.

You turn back into a sullen ten-year-old.

He pulled out a chair and sat at the table with Elsie—something he hadn't done since he'd returned home—and watched as she finished her game. She glanced at him and then in the wink of an eye, almost as if she were afraid he'd change his mind, she dealt them both out seven cards each.

'Can you play rummy?'

'Sure I can.'

'Laurie taught me.'

His skin tightened. He rolled his shoulders. So far this was the longest conversation they'd had all week. 'I...uh...when he was recuperating and you visited?'

'That's right.'

He wanted to get up from the table and flee. It all felt so wrong. But he remembered Meg's crack about him reverting to a sullen ten-year-old and swallowed. 'When I was in Alaska I played a form of rummy with the guys off the fishing trawlers. Those guys were ruthless.'

But Elsie, it seemed, had clammed up again, and Ben wondered if it was something he'd said.

They played cards for a bit. Finally he broke the silence. 'Meg's looking great. Pregnancy obviously agrees with her.'

Nothing.

'She's crocheting this thing—a baby shawl, I think she said. Looks hard, and progress is looking slow.' He picked up the three of spades Elsie had discarded. She still didn't say anything. He ground back a sigh. 'Can you crochet?'

'Yep.'

She could? He stared at her for a moment, trying not to rock back on his chair. 'You should ask her to bring this shawl over to show you. In fact, you should make something for the baby too.'

She didn't look up from her cards. 'Me?'

He frowned. 'And so should I.'

'You?' A snort accompanied the single syllable.

He cracked his knuckles. 'I might not be able to knit or sew, but travelling in the remote parts of the world forces a guy to become pretty handy.'

Handy? *Ha!* He could fashion a makeshift compass, build a temporary shelter and sterilise water, but what on earth could he make for the baby that would be useful? And beautiful. Because he'd want it to be beautiful too. An heirloom.

'A crib.' As the idea occurred to him he said it out loud. He knew a bit about carpentry. 'I'll build a crib for the baby.' He laid out his trio of threes, a trio of jacks and placed his final card on Elsie's sevens. 'Gin.'

Elsie threw her cards down with a sniff.

'Best of three,' Ben announced. 'You're rusty. You need the practice. Though it's got to be said those Alaskan fisherman took no prisoners.'

Elsie picked up her second hand without a word. Ben mentally rolled his eyes. Meg was right. This was hard work. But he found a certain grim enjoyment in needling Elsie too.

As they played he found himself taking note of Elsie's movements. Her hands were steady and she held herself stiffly erect. No signs of a debilitating disease there as far as he could see. When she won the game in three moves he had to conclude that, while she didn't say much, her mind was razor-sharp.

'Gin!' There was no mistaking her triumph, but she still didn't crack a smile.

He snorted. 'I went easy on you.'

Her chin came up a notch. Her eyes narrowed.

'Oh, and by the way, we're having dinner with Meg and her father tomorrow evening at the club. I said we'd be ready at six.'

'Right.'

They played in silence for several moments, and then all in a rush it suddenly occurred to Ben that he might be cramping the older couple's style. He cleared his throat. It wasn't easy imagining Elsie and Mr Parrish wanting—needing—privacy. But that didn't change the fact that they were engaged.

'Do you mind me staying here while I'm in town?'

'No.'

'Look, if it's not convenient I can arrange alternative accommodation. I might be staying a bit longer than usual.'

'How long?'

'I'm not sure yet.'

Oh, he was sure, all right. He was staying for good. Meg should be the first to know that, though. 'I'd certainly understand it if you'd like me to find somewhere else to stay.'

'No.'

He stared at her. She didn't say any more. 'Did my mother really never contact you, not even once, after she left me here?'

The question shocked him as much as it probably shocked Elsie. He hadn't known it had been hovering on his lips, waiting to pounce. He hadn't known he still even cared what the answer to the damn question might be.

Elsie folded her cards up as tight as her face and dropped them to the table. 'No.'

Without another word she rose and left the room.

'Goodnight, Ben,' he muttered under his breath. 'Goodnight, Elsie,' he forced himself to call out. 'Thanks for the card game.'

Ben and Elsie strolled across to Meg's the next evening at six on the dot. At least Ben strolled. Elsie never did anything quite so relaxed as stroll. Her gait was midway between a trudge and a march.

They waited while Meg reversed her car—a perky blue station wagon—out of the garage, and then Ben leant forward and opened the front passenger door for Elsie.

'I insist,' he said with a sweep of his arm when she started to back away. He blocked her path. Her choices were to plough through him or to subside into the front seat. She chose the latter.

'Hey, Meg.' He settled into the back seat.

'Hey, Ben.' She glanced at Elsie. 'Hello, Elsie.'

'Hello.'

He didn't need to see Elsie to know the precise way she'd just folded her hands in her lap.

'How was work?' he asked Meg as she turned the car in the direction of Nelson Bay. He was determined to hold up his end of the conversation this evening.

'Hectic...Fun.' She told them a silly story about one of the children there and then flicked a glance at Elsie. 'How was your day?'

'Fine.'

'What did you get up to?'

'Nothing new.'

In the rear vision mirror she caught Ben's glance and rolled her eyes.

'Though I did come across a recipe that I thought I might try. It's Indian. I've not tried Indian before.'

Silence—a stunned and at a loss silence—filled the car. Meg cleared her throat. 'Sounds…uh…great.' She glanced in the mirror again and Ben could almost see her mental shrug. She swallowed. 'What did *you* do today, Ben?'

'I bought some wood.'

She blinked as she stared at the road in front of her. 'Wood?'

'That's right. But don't ask me what it's for. It's a surprise.'

She glanced at Elsie. 'What's he up to? Is he building you a veggie patch?'

'Unlikely. But if he does it'll be *his* veggie patch.'

In the mirror Meg raised an eyebrow at him and he could read her mind. They were having a conversation like normal people—him, her and Elsie. He couldn't blame her for wondering if the sky was falling in.

'I'll tell you something that's surprised the pants off of me,' he said, as smoothly as he could.

In the mirror he watched her swallow. 'Don't keep me in suspense.'

'Elsie plays a mean hand of rummy.'

Meg glanced at her. 'You play rummy?'

'Yes, your father taught me.'

Just for a moment Meg's shoulders tightened, but then she rolled them and shrugged. 'Rummy is fun, but I prefer poker. Dad plays a mean hand of poker too.'

Did he? Ben wondered if he'd ever played a hand or two with his daughter.

'So Elsie kicked your butt, huh?'

'We're a game apiece. The tie-break's tonight.'

'Well, now.' Meg pulled the car to a halt in the RSL Club's parking lot. 'I expect to hear all about it tomorrow.'

'If she beats me, I'm making it the best of five.'

Elsie snorted. 'If you come to dinner next Wednesday, Meg, you can join in the fun.'

He wasn't sure who was more stunned by that offer—him, Meg or Elsie.

'Uh, right,' Meg managed. 'I'll look forward to it.'

Elsie's efforts at hospitality and conversation had thrown him as much as they'd obviously thrown Meg, but as Ben climbed out of the car he couldn't help wondering when he'd fallen into being so monosyllabic around his grandmother. Especially as he prided himself on being good company everywhere else.

He frowned and shook his head. He'd *never* been anything but monosyllabic around Elsie. It was a habit. One he hadn't even considered breaking until Meg had sent out the challenge.

He glanced at the older woman. When had she got into the habit? Maybe nobody had ever challenged her, and—

Holy crap!

Ben's jaw dropped and his skin tightened when Meg rounded the car to join them. His chest expanded. It was as if he didn't fit his body properly any more.

Holy mackerel!

She wore a short blue skirt that stopped a good three inches above her knees and swished and danced about flirty thighs.

Man, Meg had great legs!

He managed to lift a hand to swipe it across his chin. No drool. He didn't do drool. Though, that said, until this week he'd have said he didn't do ogling Meg either.

Now it seemed he couldn't do anything else.

She had legs that went on for ever. The illusion was aided and abetted by the four-inch wedge heels she wore, the same caramel colour as her blouse. He toenails were painted a sparkly dark brown.

She nudged him in the ribs. 'What's with you?'

'I…um…' He coughed. Elsie raised an eyebrow and for the first time in his life he saw her actually smile. Oh, brilliant! She'd seen the lot and knew the effect Meg was having on him.

'I…um…' He cleared his throat and pointed to Meg's feet.

'Those shoes should come with a warning sign. Are you sure pregnant women are allowed to wear those things?'

She snorted. 'Just watch me, buster.'

He didn't have any other choice.

'I've given up caffeine, alcohol, salami and Camembert, but I'm not giving up my sexy sandals.'

She and Elsie set off for the club's entrance. He trailed after, mesmerised by the way Meg's hips swayed with hypnotic temptation.

How had he never noticed *that* before?

He swallowed. He had a feeling he was in for a long night.

CHAPTER SEVEN

MEG GLANCED AT Ben sitting at the table next to her in the club, and then away again before anyone could accuse her of having an unhealthy fixation with her best friend.

But tonight he'd amazed her. He not only made an effort to take part in the conversation, he actively promoted it. He quizzed her father on the key differences between five-card draw poker, stud poker and Texas hold 'em. She hadn't seen her father so animated in a long time. And Elsie listened in with a greedy avidity that made Meg blink.

The more she watched, the more she realised how good the older couple were for each other.

She bit her lip and glanced around the crowded dining room. She wanted to be happy for her father and Elsie. She gritted her teeth. She *was* happy for them. But their newfound vim made her chafe and burn. It made her hands clench.

Ben trailed a finger across one of her fists, leaving a burning path of awareness in his wake. She promptly unclenched it. He sent her a smile filled with so much understanding she wanted to lay her head on his shoulder and bawl her eyes out.

Pregnancy hormones.

Do you mean to use that as an excuse for every uncomfortable emotion that pummels you at the moment?

It might not explain her unexpected resentment towards the older couple, but it was absolutely positively the reason her pulse quickened and her skin prickled at the mere sight of

Ben. It had to be. And it was absolutely positively the reason her stomach clenched when his scent slugged into her—that peculiar but evocative mixture of leather and Scotch whisky.

For pity's sake, he wasn't even wearing leather or drinking whisky.

Her lips twisted. He couldn't help it. He smelled like a bad boy—all illicit temptation and promises he wouldn't keep. That grin and his free and easy swagger promised heaven. For one night. She didn't doubt for a moment that he'd deliver on *that* particular promise either.

And darn it all if she didn't want a piece of that!

She swallowed. She didn't just want it. She craved it. Her skin, her lungs, even her fingers ached with it.

Pregnancy hormones. *It had to be.*

Just her luck. Why couldn't she be like other women who became nauseous at the smell of frying bacon? That would be far preferable to feeling like *this* when Ben's scent hit her.

Her fingers curled into her palms. She had to find a way to resist all that seductive bad-boyness. For the sake of their friendship. And for the sake of her baby.

She dragged in a breath. She'd seen smart, sensible women make absolute fools of themselves over Ben and she had no intention of joining their ranks. She could *not* let lust deflect her from the important issue—ensuring her baby had the best possible life that she could give it. She could do that and save her friendship with Ben.

But not if she slept with him.

She ground her teeth together. Why had nobody warned her that being pregnant would make her…horny?

She shifted on her chair. Horny was the perfect description. There was nothing dignified and elegant or slow and easy in what she felt for Ben.

She risked a glance at him. Her blood Mexican-waved in her veins. Heat pounded through her and she squeezed her thighs tightly together. What she felt for Ben—*her best friend*—was hot and carnal, primal and urgent.

And it had to be denied.

She dragged her gaze away and fiddled with her cutlery.

Ben nudged her and she could have groaned out loud as a fresh wave of leather and whisky slammed into her. But it occurred to her then that she'd left the entire running of the conversation up to him so far. He probably thought she was doing it to punish him, or to prove some stupid point, when the real reason was she simply couldn't string two thoughts let alone two sentences together in a coherent fashion.

'Sorry, I was a million miles away.' She made herself smile around the table. 'My girlfriends have warned me about baby brain.'

Ben cocked an eyebrow. He grinned that slow and easy grin that could reduce a woman to the consistency of warm honey, inch by delicious inch.

She swallowed and forced her spine to straighten. 'Basically it means my brain will turn to mush and I won't be able to verbalise anything but nonsense for days at a time.'

She glanced at Elsie. 'Do you remember that when you were pregnant?'

Elsie drew back, paled, and Meg tried not to wince. She'd never asked Elsie about pregnancy or motherhood before and it was obviously a touchy subject. She hadn't meant to be insensitive.

In an effort to remove attention from Elsie, she swung to her father. 'Or can *you* remember Mum having baby brain when she was pregnant with me?'

An ugly red flushed his cheeks. As if she'd reached across and slapped him across the face. Twice.

Oh, great. Another no-go zone, huh?

She wanted nothing more than to lay her head on the table, close her eyes and rest for a while.

'And what a sterling example of baby brain in action,' Ben

murmured in her ear, and she found herself coughing back a laugh instead.

'I guess that's a no on both counts,' she managed, deciding to brazen it out, hoping it would make it less awkward all round. She glanced around the crowded dining room. 'There's a good crowd in but, man, I'm hungry. I wonder when our food will be ready?'

On cue, their table buzzer rang. Ben and her father shot to their feet. 'I'll get yours,' Ben told her, placing a hand on her shoulder to keep her in her seat.

Elsie watched as the two men walked towards the bistro counter where their plates waited. Meg made herself smile. 'Well, this is nice, isn't it?'

'You shouldn't have mentioned your mother.'

Meg blinked. 'Why ever not?'

Elsie pressed her lips primly together. 'He doesn't like to talk about her.'

Wasn't that the truth? 'And yet she was *my* mother and I do. Why should my needs be subordinate to his?'

'That's a selfish way to look at it.'

Interesting…Elsie was prepared to go into battle for her father. Something in Meg's heart lifted.

But something else didn't. 'Maybe I'm tired of stepping on eggshells and being self-sacrificing.'

Elsie paled. 'Meg, I—'

The men chose that moment to return with the food and Elsie broke off. Meg couldn't help but be relieved.

Ben glanced at Elsie and then whispered to Meg, 'More baby brain?'

'"Curiouser and curiouser," said Alice,' she returned.

He grinned. She grinned back. And for a moment everything was right again—she and Ben against the world…or at least against Elsie and Laurie, who'd been the world when she and Ben had been ten-year-olds.

They ate, and her father and Elsie reverted to their customary silence. Between them Meg and Ben managed to keep up a steady flow of chatter, but Meg couldn't help wondering if the older couple heard a word they said.

When they were finished, their plates removed and drinks replenished, Meg clapped her hands. 'Okay, I want to talk about the wedding for a moment.'

Her father scowled. 'I don't want a damn circus, Megan.'

'It's not going to be a circus. It's going to be a simple celebration. A celebration of the love you and Elsie share.' She folded her arms. 'And if you can't muster the courtesy to give each other that much respect then you shouldn't be getting married in the first place.'

Elsie and Laurie stared at her in shock. Ben let forth with a low whistle.

'Elsie—not this Saturday but the one after you and I are going shopping for your outfit.'

'Oh, but I don't need anything new.'

'Yes, you do. And so do I.' Her father had multiple suits, but… She turned to Ben. 'You'll need a suit.'

He saluted. 'I'm onto it.'

She turned back to the older couple. 'And you will both need an attendant. Who would you like as your bridesmaid and best man?'

Nobody said anything for a moment. She heaved back a sigh. 'Who were you going to have as your witnesses?'

'You and Ben,' her father muttered.

'Fine. I'll be your best man, but I'll be wearing a dress.'

'And I'll be bridesmaid in a suit,' Ben said to Elsie.

He said it without rancour and without wincing. He even said it with a grin on his face. Meg could have hugged him.

'Now, Elsie, do you want someone to give you away?'

'Of course not! Who on earth would I ask to do that?'

Meg leant back. She stared at the ceiling and counted to three. 'I'd have thought Ben would be the logical choice.'

The other woman's chin shot up. 'Ben? Do you really expect him to still be here in six weeks' time?'

'If he says he will, then, yes.'

'Give me away?' Her face darkened as she glared at Ben. 'Oh, you'd like that, wouldn't you? You'd love to give me away and be done with me for ever.'

Meg took one look at her best friend's ashen face and a scorching red-hot savagery shook through her. She leant forward, acid burning her throat and a rank taste filling her mouth. 'And who could blame him? I don't know why he even bothers with you at all. What the hell have you ever given him that he couldn't have got from strangers? You never show the slightest interest in his life, never show him the slightest affection—not even a tiny bit of warmth. You have no right to criticise him. *None!*'

'Meg.'

Ben's voice burned low but she couldn't stop. Even if she'd wanted to, she couldn't have. And she didn't want to. 'It was your job to show him love and security when he was just a little boy, but did you ever once hug him or tell him you were glad he'd come to stay with you? No, not once. Why not? He was a great kid and you…you're nothing but a—'

'Megan, that's enough! You will *not* speak to my intended like that.'

'Or what?' she shot straight back at her father. 'You'll never speak to me again? Well, seeing as you barely speak to me now, I can hardly see that'd be any great loss.'

Even as the words ripped out of her she couldn't believe she was uttering them. But she meant them. Every single one of them. And the red mist held her too much in its sway for her to regret them.

She might never regret them, but if she remained here she would say things she *would* regret—mean, bitter things just for the sake of it. She pushed out of her seat and walked away, walked right out of the club. She tramped the two blocks down to the water's edge to sit on a bench overlooking the bay as the sun sank in the west.

The walking had helped work off some of her anger. The warm air caressed the bare skin of her neck and legs, and the late evening light was as soothing as the ebb and flow of the water.

'Are you okay?'

Ben. And his voice was as soothing as the water too. But it made her eyes prickle and sting. She nodded.

'Do you mind if I join you?'

She shook her head and gestured for him to take the seat beside her.

'What happened back there?' he finally asked. 'Baby brain?'

She didn't know if he was trying to make her laugh or if he was as honest-to-God puzzled as he sounded. She dragged in a breath that made her whole body shudder. 'That was honest, true-blue emotion, not baby brain. I've never told either one of them how I feel about our childhoods.'

'Well, you left them in no doubt about your feelings on the subject tonight.'

She glanced at him. 'I don't particularly feel bad about it.' Did that make her an awful person? 'I don't want revenge, and I don't want to ruin their happiness, but neither one of them has the right to criticise you or me for being unsupportive. Especially when we're bending over backwards for them.'

He rested his elbows on his knees and then glanced up at her. 'You've bottled that up for a long time. Why spill it now?'

She stared out at the water. The sky was quickly darkening now that the sun had gone down. The burning started behind her eyes again. 'Now that I'm pregnant and expecting a child of my own, their emotional abandonment of us seems so much more unforgivable to me.'

He straightened and she turned to him.

'Ben, I can't imagine not making every effort for my child,

regardless of what else is happening in my life. I love it so much already and it makes me see…'

'What?'

She had to swallow. 'It makes me see that neither one of them loved us enough.'

'Oh, sweetheart.' He slipped an arm about her shoulders and she leant against him, soaking up his strength and his familiarity, his *Ben*-ness.

'You've never blown your top like that,' she murmured into his chest. And he had so much more to breathe fire about than her—not just Elsie, but his mother and father too. 'Why not?' It obviously hadn't been healthy for *her* to bottle her anger and hurt up for so long. If he was bottling it up—

'Meg, honey.' He gave a low laugh. 'I did it with actions rather than words. Don't you remember?'

She thought about it for a while and then nodded. 'You rebelled big-time.' He'd started teenage binge-drinking at sixteen, and staying out until the wee small hours, getting into the occasional fight—and, she suspected, making himself at home in older women's beds.

The police had brought him home on more than one occasion. He'd had a couple of fathers and one husband warn him off—violently. Yes. She nodded again. Ben had gone off the rails in a big way, and she could see it now for the thumbing of his nose at his family that it had been.

Still, he'd had the strength and the sense to pull out of that downward spiral. Dave Clements—a local tour operator—had offered him a part-time job and had taken him under his wing, had encouraged Ben to finish school. And Ben had, and now he led the kind of life most people could only dream of.

But was he happy?

She'd thought so, but…She glanced up into his face and recognised the shadows there. She straightened and slipped her hand into his, held it tight. 'I'm sorry if my outburst brought up bad stuff for you. I didn't mean—'

'For me?' He swung to her. 'Hell, Meg, you were magnificent! I just…'

She swallowed. 'What?'

He released her to rest his elbows on his knees again and drag both hands back through his hair. She wanted his arm resting back across her shoulders. She wanted not to have hurt him.

'Is it my coming home and turning your nicely ordered plans on their head? Did that have a bearing on your outburst tonight? I don't mean to be causing you stress.'

'No! That had nothing to do with it. That—' she waved back behind her '—was about me and them. Not about me and you.' She moistened her lips. 'It was about me and my father.' And about her anger at Elsie for not having shown Ben any love or affection. 'You had nothing to do with that except in…'

'What?'

'When I was busy doing what you were mostly doing tonight,' she started slowly, 'making sure the conversation flowed and that there weren't any awkward moments, I didn't have the time to feel those old hurts and resentments.'

'While I, at least whenever I've been home,' he said with a delicious twist of his lips, 'have been far too busy stewing on them.'

'But when you took on my role tonight I started to wonder why I was always so careful around them, and I realised what a lie it all seemed.'

'So you exploded.'

She slouched back against the bench. 'Why can't I just make it all go away and not matter any more? It all seems so pointless and self-defeating.' She couldn't change the past any more than she could change her father or Elsie. Her hands clenched. 'I should be able to just get over it.' She wasn't ten years old any more.

'It doesn't work like that.'

She knew he was right. She lifted her chin. 'It doesn't mean I have to let it blight the future, though. I don't have to continue mollycoddling my father or Elsie. At least not at the expense of myself.'

'No, you don't.'

He'd been telling her that for years. She'd never really seen what he meant till now.

'And I have a baby on the way.' She hugged herself. 'And that's incredibly exciting and it makes me happier than I have words for.'

He stared at her. He didn't smile. *They* had a baby on the way. *They.* She could read that in his face, but he didn't correct her.

She stared back out at the bay. The last scrap of light in the sky had faded and house lights and boat lights and street lights danced on the undulating water, turning it into a kind of fairyland.

Only this wasn't a fairytale. Ben said he wanted to be involved in their baby's life, but so far he hadn't shown any joy or excitement—only agitation and unease.

'So…?'

His word hung in the air. She didn't know what it referred to. She hauled in a breath and raised one shoulder. 'I don't much feel like going back to the club and dealing with my father and Elsie.'

'You don't have to. I asked your father if he'd see Elsie home.'

She swung back to him. 'I could kiss you!'

He grinned. A grin full of a slow burn that melted her insides and sent need hurtling through her. She started to reach for him, realised what she was doing, and turned the questing touch into a slap to his thigh before leaping to her feet.

'Feel like going for a walk?' She couldn't keep sitting here next to him and not give in to temptation.

Which was crazy.

Truly crazy.

Nonetheless, walking was a much safer option.

With a shrug he rose and they set off along the boardwalk in the direction of the Nelson Bay marina, where there was a lot of distraction—lights and people and noise. Meg swallowed. Down at this end of the beach it was dark and almost deserted. It would take ten minutes to reach the marina. And then they'd have to walk back this way. In the dark and the quiet.

Her feet slowed.

But by then—after all that distraction and the exercise of walking—she'd have found a way to get her stupid hormones back under control, right?

She went to speed up again, but Ben took her arm and led her across a strip of grass and down to the sand. He kicked off his shoes, and after a moment's hesitation she eased her feet out of her wedges.

They paddled without talking very much. The water was warm. She needed icy cold rather than this beguiling warmth that brought all her senses dancing to life. Paddling with Ben in all the warmth of a late summer evening, with the scent of a nearby frangipani drenching the air, was far too intimate. Even though they'd done this a thousand times and it had never felt intimate before.

Except that one time after her high school graduation, when he'd been her white knight and taken her to the prom.

Don't think about that!

She cleared her throat. 'Tell me again how magnificent I was.' Maybe teasing and banter would help her find her way back to a more comfortable place.

Ben turned and moved back towards her. He inadvertently flicked up a few drops of water that hit her mid-calf...and higher. They beaded and rolled down her legs with delicious promise.

He halted in front of her, reaching out and cupping her cheek. 'Meg, nobody has ever stood up for me the way you did tonight. Not ever.'

In the moonlight his eyes shimmered. 'Oh, Ben,' she whispered, reaching up to cover his hand with hers. He deserved to have so many more people in his life willing to go out on a limb for him.

'You made me feel as if I could fly.'

She smiled. 'You mean you can't?'

He laughed softly and pulled her in close for a hug. She clenched her eyes shut and gritted her teeth as she forced her arms around him to squeeze him back for a moment. She started to release him, but he didn't release her. She rested her cheek on his shoulder and bit her lip until she tasted blood. It took all her concentration to keep her hands where they ought to be.

And then his hand slid down her back and it wasn't a between-friends gesture. It was...

She drew back to glance into his face. The hunger and the need reflected in his eyes made her sway towards him. She planted her hands against his chest to keep her balance, to keep from falling against him. As soon as she regained her footing she meant to push him away.

Only, her hands, it seemed, had a different idea altogether. They slid across his shirt, completely ignoring the pleasant sensation of soft cotton to revel in the honed male flesh beneath it. Ben's chest had so much *definition*. And he was hot! His heat branded her through his shirt and his heart beat against her palm like a dark throbbing promise. The pulse in her throat quivered.

She swallowed and tried to catch her breath. She should move away.

But the longer she remained in the circle of Ben's arms, the more the strength and the will drained from her body and the harder it became to think clearly and logically.

And beneath her hands his body continued to beat at her like a wild thing—a tempting and tempestuous primal force, urging her to connect with something wild and elemental within herself.

She lifted her gaze to his. A light blazed from his eyes, revealing his need, an unchecked recklessness and his exaltation.

'I've been fighting this all night,' he rasped, 'but I'm not going to fight it any more.'

He tangled his hand in her hair and pulled it back until her lips lifted, angled just so to give him maximum access, and then his mouth came down on hers—hot, hungry, unchecked.

His lips laid waste to all her preconceptions. She'd thought he'd taste wickedly illicit and forbidden, but he didn't taste like whisky or leather or midnight. He tasted like summer and ripe strawberries and the tang of the ocean breeze. He tasted like freedom.

It was more intoxicating than anything she'd ever experienced.

Kissing Ben was like flying.

A swooping, swirling, tumbling-in-the-surf kind of flying.

He pulled her closer, positioned his body in such a way that it pressed against all the parts of her she most wanted touched—but it didn't appease her, only inflamed. His name ripped from her throat and he took advantage of it to deepen the kiss further. She followed his lead, drinking him in greedily. Her head swam. She fisted her hands in his shirt and dragged him closer. His strength was the only thing keeping them both upright.

She needed him *now*. Her body screamed for him. She pressed herself against him in the most shameless way she could—pelvis to pelvis, making it clear what she wanted. Demanding fulfilment.

His mouth lifted from hers. He dragged in air and then his teeth grazed her throat. She arched against him. 'Please, Ben. Please.' she sobbed.

With a growl, he scrunched her skirt in his hand. He traced the line of her panty elastic with one finger and she thought she might explode then and there.

His finger shifted, slid beneath the elastic.

Oh, please. Please.

A car horn blared, renting the air with discord, and Ben leapt away from her so fast she'd have fallen if he hadn't shot out an arm to steady her. When she regained her balance he released her with an oath that burned her ears.

'What the *hell* were you thinking?' His finger shook as he pointed it at her.

Same as you. Only she couldn't get her tongue to work properly and utter that remark out loud.

He wheeled away, dragging both hands back through his hair.

No, no, no, she wanted to wail. *Don't turn knight on me now—you're a bad boy!*

But when he swung back his face was tense and drawn, and she was grateful she hadn't said it out loud.

Because it would have been stupid.

And wrong.

Her flesh chilled. Trembling set in. She walked away from him and up the beach a little way to sit. She needed to think. And she couldn't think and walk at the same time because her limbs were boneless and it took all her concentration to remain upright. She pulled her skirt down as far as it would go and kept her legs flat out in front of her to reveal as little thigh as possible.

He strode up to her and punched a finger at her again. 'This is not on, Meg. You and me. It's never going to happen.'

'Don't use that tone with me.' She glared at him. 'You started it.'

'You could've said no!'

'You could've not kissed me in the first place!'

She expected him to stride away into the night, but he didn't. He paced for a bit and then eventually came back and sat beside her. But not too close.

'Are we still okay?' he growled.

'Sure we are.' But her throat was tight.

'I don't know what came over me.'

'It's been an emotional evening.' She swallowed. 'And when emotions run high you always seek a physical outlet.'

He nodded. There was a pause. 'It's not usually your style, though.'

She shifted, rolled her shoulders. 'Yeah, well, it seems that being pregnant has made me...itchy.'

He stared. And then he leaned slightly away from her. 'You're joking?'

'I wish I were.'

She had to stop looking at him. She forced her gaze back to the front—to the gently lapping water of the bay. Which wasn't precisely the mood she was after. She forced her gaze upwards. Stars. She heaved out a sigh and gave up.

'So you're feeling...? Umm...? All of the time?'

She pressed her hands to her cheeks and stared doggedly out at the water, desperately wishing for some of its calm to enter her soul. 'I expected to feel all maternal and Mother Earthy. Not sexy.'

'You know, it kind of makes sense,' he said after a bit. 'All those pregnancy hormones are making you look great.'

At the moment she'd take the haggard morning sickness look if it would get things between her and Ben on an even keel again.

'You sure we're okay?' he said again.

She bit back a sigh. 'I'm not going to fall for you, Ben, if that's what you're worried about.'

'No, I—'

'For a start, I don't like the way you treat women, and I'm sure as hell not going to let any man treat me like that.'

'I do not treat women badly,' he growled.

'Wham, bam, thank you, ma'am. That's your style.'

And as far as she was concerned it was appalling. She grimaced. Even if a short time ago she'd been begging for exactly that. She massaged her temples. She found her own behaviour this evening appalling too. She'd never acted like that before—so heedless and mindless. Not with any man.

'I haven't had any complaints.'

She snorted. 'Because you don't stick around long enough to hear them.'

'Hell, Meg.' He scowled. 'I show a woman a good time. I don't make promises.'

But he didn't care if a woman did read more into their encounter. He'd used that to his advantage on more than one occasion.

'Yeah, well, I want more than that from a relationship, and that's something I know you're not in the market for.' He grabbed her arm when she went to rise. She fell back to the sand, her shoulder jostling his. 'What?'

He let her go again. 'I'm glad we're on the same page, because…'

An ache started up behind her eyes. 'Because?'

'I've made a decision and we need to talk about it.'

She smoothed her skirt down towards her knees again. Ben was going to leave right after the wedding. That was what he wanted to tell her, wasn't it?

She pulled in a breath and readied herself for his news. It was good news, she told herself, straightening her spine and setting her shoulders. Things could get back to normal again.

'I've made the decision to stay in Port Stephens. I'll find work here and I'll find a place to live. I want to be a father to our baby, Meg. A *proper* father.'

CHAPTER EIGHT

THE WORLD TILTED to one side. Meg planted a hand against shifting sand. 'Staying?' Her voice wobbled.

Living here in Port Stephens, so close to Elsie and his childhood, would make Ben miserable. She closed her eyes. In less than six months he'd go stir crazy and flee in a trail of dust.

And where would that leave her baby and their friendship?

Depending on how much under the six-month mark Ben managed to hold on for, her baby might not even have been born. She opened her eyes. In which case it wouldn't have come to rely on Ben or to love him.

It wouldn't be hurt by his desertion.

But Ben would be. His failure to do this would destroy something essential in him.

And she didn't want to bear witness to that.

She turned to find him studying her. His shoulders were hitched in a way that told her he was waiting for her to say something hard and cruel.

And the memory of their kiss—that bone-crushing kiss—throbbed in all the spaces between them.

She moistened her lips. 'You haven't been back here a full week yet. This is a big decision—huge. It's life-changing. You don't have to rush it, or make a hasty choice, or—'

'When it comes down to brass tacks, Meg, the decision itself is remarkably simple.'

It was?

'Being a parent—a father—is the most important job in the world.'

Her heart pounded. He would hate himself—*hate*—when he found out he wasn't up to the task. Her heart burned, her eyes ached and her temples throbbed.

And at the back of her mind all she could think about was kissing him again. Kissing him had been a mistake. But that didn't stop her from wanting to repeat it.

And repeat it.

Over and over again.

But if they did it would destroy their friendship. She clenched her hands in her lap and battled the need to reach out and touch him again, kiss him again, as she hungered to do.

'Coming back home this time...' He glanced down at his hands. 'I've started to realise how shallow my life really is.'

Her jaw dropped.

'I know it looks exciting, and I guess it is. But it's shallow too. I've spent my whole life running away from responsibility. I'm starting to see I haven't achieved anything of real value at all.'

She straightened. 'That's not true. You help people achieve their dreams. You give them once-in-a-lifetime experiences—stories they can tell their children.'

'And who am I going to tell *my* stories to?'

Her heart started to thud.

'I've steered clear of any thoughts of children in my future, afraid I'd turn out like my parents.' His face grew grim but his chin lifted. 'That will only happen if I let it.'

He turned to her. *Stop thinking about kissing him!*

'What I really want to know is what you're scared of, Meg. Why does the thought of my coming home for good and being a father to our child freak you out?'

Because what if I never do manage to get my hormones back under control?

She snapped away at that thought. It was ludicrous. And unworthy. This should have nothing to do with her feelings and everything to do with her baby's. She couldn't let how she felt colour that reality.

'Meg?'

The notion of Ben coming home for good *did* freak her out. It scared her to the soles of her feet. He knew her too well for her to deny it. 'I don't want to hurt you,' she whispered.

He set his shoulders in a rigid line. 'Give it to me straight.'

She glanced at her hands. She hauled in a breath. 'I'm afraid you'll hang around just long enough for the baby to love you. I'm afraid the baby will come to love and rely on you but you won't be able to hack the monotony of domesticity. I'm afraid your restlessness will get the better of you and you'll leave. And if you do that, Ben, you will break my baby's heart.'

He flinched. The throbbing behind her eyes intensified.

'And if you do that, Ben...' she forced herself to continue '...I don't know if I could ever forgive you.'

And they would both lose the most important friendship of their lives.

He shot to his feet and strode down to the water's edge.

'And what's more,' she called after him, doing what she could to keep her voice strong, 'if that's the way this all plays out, I think you will hate yourself.'

There was so much to lose if he stayed.

He strode back to where she sat, planted his feet in front of her. 'I can't do anything about your fears, Meg. I'm sorry you feel the way you do. I know I have no one to blame but myself, and that only time will put your fears to rest.' He dragged a hand back through his hair. 'But when *our* baby is born I'm going to be there for it every step of the way. I want it to love me. I want it to rely on me. I'll be doing everything to make that happen.'

She shrank from him. 'But—'

'I mean to be the best father I can be. I mean to be the kind of father to my son or daughter that my father wasn't to me. I want our baby to have everything good in life, and I mean to stick around to make sure that happens.'

Meg covered her face with her hands. 'Oh, Ben, I'm sorry. I'm so, so sorry.'

Ben stared at Meg, with her head bowed and her shoulders slumped, and knelt down on the sand beside her, his heart burning. He pulled her hands from her face. 'What on earth are you sorry for?' She didn't have anything to be sorry about.

'I'm sorry I asked you to donate sperm. I'm sorry I've created such an upheaval in your life. I didn't mean for that to happen. I didn't mean to turn your life upside down.'

The darkness in her eyes, the guilt and sorrow swirling in their depths, speared into him. 'I know that.' He sat beside her again. 'When I agreed to be your sperm donor I had no idea I'd feel this way, and I'm sorry that's turned all your plans on their head.'

She pulled in a breath that made her whole body shudder. He wanted to wrap her in his arms. She moved away as if she'd read that thought in his face. It was only an inch, but it was enough. *All because of that stupid kiss.*

Why the hell had he kissed her? He clenched a hand. Ten years ago he'd promised he would never do that again. Ten years ago, when that jerk she'd been dating had dumped her. She'd been vulnerable then. She'd been vulnerable tonight too. And he'd taken advantage of that fact.

Meg wasn't the kind of girl a guy kissed and then walked away from. He might be staying in Port Stephens for good, but he wasn't changing his life *that* much. He had to stop sending her such mixed signals. They were friends. *Just* friends. *Best friends.*

He closed his eyes and gritted his teeth. Control—he needed to find control.

And he needed to forget how divine she'd felt in his arms

and how that kiss had made him feel like a superhero, shooting off into the sky.

She cleared her throat, snagging his attention again. 'Obviously neither one of us foresaw what would happen.'

Her sigh cut him to the quick. 'I know this is hard for you, Meg, but I do mean to be a true father to our child.'

She still didn't believe him. It was in her face. In the way she opened her hands and let the sand trickle out of them. In the way she turned to stare out at the water.

'And because I do want to be a better father than my own, I need to clear the air about that kiss.'

His body heated up in an instant as the impact of their kiss surged through him again. That kiss had been—

He fisted his hands and tried to cut the memory from his mind. He was not going to dwell on that kiss again. *Ever*. He couldn't. Not if he wanted to maintain his sanity. Not if he wanted to save their friendship.

Meg slapped her hands to the sides of her knees. 'You are nothing like your father.'

How could she be so sure of that?

'You would never, *ever* put a gun to anyone's head—let alone your own child's.'

Bile rose in his throat. That had happened nearly twenty years ago, but the day and all its horror was etched on his memory as if with indelible ink. His mother and father had undergone one of the most acrimonious divorces in the history of man. In the custody battle that had ensued they had used their only son to score as many points off one another as they could. At every available opportunity.

Their bitterness and their hate had turned them into people Ben hadn't been able to recognise. They'd pushed and pushed and pushed each other, until one day his father had shown up on the front doorstep with a shotgun.

Ben's heart pounded. He could still taste the fear in his mouth when he'd first caught sight of the gun—could still feel the grip of a hard hand on the back of his neck when he'd turned to run. He'd been convinced his father would kill them.

Ben pressed a hand to his forehead and drew oxygen into his lungs. Meg wrapped her arm through his. It helped anchor him back in the present moment, drawing him out of that awful one twenty years ago.

'My parents must've cared for each other once—maybe even loved each other—but marriage for them resulted in my father being in prison and my mother dumping me with Elsie and never being heard from again.'

'Not all marriages end like that, Ben.'

'True.'

But he had the same raging passions inside him that his parents had. He had no intention of setting them free. That was why he kept his interludes with women light and brief. It was safer all round.

Gently, he detached his arm from Meg's. 'Whatever else I do, though, marriage is something I'm never going to risk.'

She shook her head and went back to lifting sand and letting it trickle through her hand. 'This is one of those circular arguments that just go round and round without ending. We agreed to disagree about this years ago.'

He heard her unspoken question. *So why bring it up now?*

'Regardless of what you think, Meg, I do mean to be a good father. But that doesn't mean I've changed my mind about marriage.'

She stopped playing with the sand. 'And you think because I'm feeling a little sexy that I'm going to weave you into my fantasies and cast you in the role of handsome prince?' She snorted. 'Court jester, more like. It'd take more than a kiss for me to fall in love with you, Ben Sullivan. I may have baby brain, but that doesn't mean I've turned into a moron. Especially—' she shot to her feet '—when I don't believe you'll hang around long enough for anyone to fall in love with you anyway.'

He didn't argue the point any further. Only time would prove to her that he really did mean to stick around.

He scrambled to his feet. He just had to make sure he didn't kiss her again. Meg didn't do one-night stands—it wasn't how she was built inside. She got emotionally involved. He knew that. He'd always known that. He pushed his shoulders back and shoved his hands into the pockets of his shorts. He'd made a lot of mistakes in his sorry life, but he wasn't making that one.

He set off after Meg. 'What would you like me to do in relation to the wedding this week?'

She'd walked back to where they'd kicked off their shoes. He held her arm as she slid hers back on. He gritted his teeth in an effort to counter the warm temptation of her skin.

She blinked up at him as she slid a finger around the back of one of her sandals. She righted herself and moved out of his grasp. 'There's still a lot to do.' She glanced at him again. 'How busy are you this coming week?'

He'd be hard at work, casting around for employment opportunities, putting out feelers and sifting through a few preliminary ideas he'd had, but he'd find time to help her out with this blasted wedding. The days of leaving everything up to her were through. 'I have loads of time.'

'Well, for a start, I need those names from Elsie.'

'Right.'

They set off back towards the club and Meg's car. 'I don't suppose you'd organise the invitations, would you? I wasn't going to worry with anything too fancy. I was just going to grab a few packets of nice invitations from the newsagents and write them out myself. Calligraphy is unnecessary—they just need to be legible.'

'Leave it to me.'

'Thank you. That'll be a big help.'

'Anything else?'

'I would be very, very grateful if you could find me a gardener. I just don't have the spare time to keep on top of it at the moment. This wedding will be that garden's last hurrah, because I'm having all those high-maintenance annuals ripped out and replaced with easy-care natives.'

He nodded. 'Not a problem.'

They drove home in silence. When Meg turned in at her driveway and turned off the ignition she didn't invite him in for a drink and he didn't suggest it either. Instead, with a quick goodnight, he headed next door.

The first thing he saw when he entered the kitchen was Elsie, sitting at the table shuffling a deck of cards. Without a word, she dealt out a hand for rummy. Ben hesitated and then sat.

'How's Meg?'

'She's fine.'

'Good.'

He shifted. 'She'd feel a whole lot happier, though, if you'd give her a list of ten people she can invite to the wedding.'

Elsie snorted. He blinked again. Had that been a *laugh*?

'She said that although her father won't admit it, he'd like more than a registry office wedding.'

Elsie snorted again, and this time there was no mistaking it—it was definitely a laugh. 'I'll make a deal with you, Ben.'

Good Lord. The woman was practically garrulous. 'A deal?'

'For every hand you win, I'll give you a name.'

He straightened on his chair. 'You're on.'

Meg glanced around at a tap on the back door. And then froze. Ben stood there, looking devastatingly delicious, and a traitorous tremor weakened her knees.

With a gulp, she waved him in. Other than a couple of rushed conversations about the wedding, she hadn't seen much of him during the last two weeks. Work had been crazy, with two of her staff down with the flu, and whenever she had seen Ben and asked what he'd been up to he'd simply answered with a cryptic, 'I've been busy.' Long, leisurely conversations obviously hadn't been on either of their agendas.

Her gaze lowered to his lips. Lips that had caressed hers. Lips that had transported her to a place beyond herself and made her yearn for more. So much more. Lips that were moving now.

'Whatever it is you're cooking, Meg, no known man would be able to resist it.'

She snapped away and forced a smile.

'Cookies?'

Her smile became almost genuine at the hope in his voice. 'Chocolate chip,' she confirmed.

'Even better.' He glanced at her baking companions. 'Sounds like you guys have been having fun in here.'

Loss suddenly opened up inside her. He was her best friend. They had to find a way to overcome this horrid awkwardness.

She swallowed and hauled in a breath, gestured to the two children. 'This is Laura, who is ten, and Lochie, who is eight.'

'We're brother and sister,' Laura announced importantly.

'And Auntie Meg used to go to school with Mummy.'

'Felicity Strickland,' Meg said at his raised eyebrow. 'Laura and Lochie—this is my friend Ben from next door. He went to school with your mummy too. What do you think? Will we let him share our cookies?'

Lochie nodded immediately. 'That means there'll be another boy.'

In Lochie's mind another boy meant an ally, and Meg had a feeling he was heartily sick of being bossed by his sister.

Laura folded her arms. 'He'll have to work for them. It's only fair, because we've all worked.'

Meg choked back a laugh. She half expected Ben to make some excuse and back out through the door.

'What would I have to do?' he asked Laura instead. 'I'll do just about anything for choc-chip cookies. Especially ones that smell this good.'

Laura glanced up at Meg.

'How about Ben sets the table?'

'And pours the milk?'

She nodded. 'Sounds fair.'

Ben tackled setting the table and pouring out four glasses of milk while Meg pulled a second tray of cookies from the oven and set them to cool on the counter. She'd hoped that baking cookies would make her feel super-maternal, but one glance at Ben threw that theory out of the water.

She still felt—

Don't think about it!

Her hands shook as she placed the first batch of cookies on a plate and handed them to Laura, who took them over to the table.

They ate cookies and drank milk.

But even over the home-baked goodness of choc-chip cookies Meg caught a hint of leather and whisky. She tried to block it from her mind, tried to ignore the longing that burned through her veins.

The children regaled Ben with stories of their Christmas trip to Bali. Meg glanced at Ben and then glanced away again, biting her lip. It was no use telling herself this was just Ben. There was no *just* Ben about it—only a hard, persistent throb in her blood and an ache in her body.

When the phone rang she leapt to her feet, eager for distraction.

Ben's eyes zeroed in on her face the moment she returned to the kitchen. 'Problem?'

She clenched and unclenched her hands. 'The caterers I had lined up for the wedding have cancelled on me, the rotten—' she glanced at the children '—so-and-sos.'

She pressed her fingers to her temples and paced up and down on the other side of the breakfast bar. The wedding was three weeks away. Less than that. Two weeks and six days. Not that she was counting or anything.

Ben stood. 'What can I do?'

She glanced at him. She glanced at the children. A plan—devious, and perhaps a little unfair—slid beneath her guard. No, she couldn't.

Two weeks and six days.

She folded her arms. 'Are you up for a challenge, Ben Sullivan?'

He rocked back on his heels. 'What kind of challenge?'

She glanced at the children and then back at him, with enough meaning in her face that he couldn't possibly mistake her message.

He folded his arms too. 'Bring it on.'

'If you keep Laura and Lochie amused for an hour or two, it'll give me a chance to ring around and find a replacement caterer.'

He glanced at the television. 'Not a problem.'

She shook her head and glanced out of the kitchen window towards the back yard. There was no mistaking the panic that momentarily filled his eyes. 'I'll need peace and quiet.'

Did he even know the first thing about children and how much work they could sometimes be? Laura truly was the kind of child designed to test Ben's patience to the limit too. And when he found out the truth that being a father wasn't all beer and skittles—all fun and laughter at the beach and I-love-you-Daddy cuddles—how long before he left?

She did what she could to harden her heart, to stop it from sinking, to cut off its protests.

Lochie's face lit up. 'Can we go to the beach? Can we go swimming?'

Relief lit Ben's face too, but Meg shook her head. 'Your mum said no swimming.' Besides, she wanted them all here, right under her nose, where she could keep an eye on them.

Ben glared at her. 'Why not?'

She reached out and brushed a hand through Lochie's hair,

pulled him against her in a hug. 'Lochie's recovering from an ear infection.'

Ben shuffled his feet. 'I'm sorry to hear that, mate.'

Lochie straightened. 'We could play Uno. Laura remembered to bring it.'

'Because you *didn't*.' She rolled her eyes. 'You never do. Do you know how to play?' she demanded of Ben.

'No idea.'

'Then I'll teach you.' She took Ben's hand. 'Get the game, Lochie.'

'Please,' Ben corrected.

Laura blinked. So did Meg. 'Get the game, *please*, Lochie,' Laura amended, leading both males outside as she waxed lyrical about the importance of good manners.

Meg grimaced. Poor Ben. Laura was ten going on eighty. It hardly seemed fair to expect him to cope with her. She glanced down at her baby bump, rested her hand on it before glancing back out of the window. It was an hour. Two hours tops. She'd be nearby, and if he couldn't deal with Laura for that length of time then he had no right remaining here in Port Stephens at all.

Still, even with that decided Meg couldn't move from the window. She watched as the trio settled on the outdoor furniture, and as Ben listened while Laura explained the rules of the game in exhaustive detail. His patience touched her. Once the game started he kept both children giggling so hard she found herself wishing she could go outside and join them.

She shook her head. Two weeks and six days. She had a caterer to find.

It took Meg forty minutes' worth of phone calls before she found a replacement caterer. She glanced at her watch and winced. How on earth was Ben surviving? She raced into the family room to peer out through the glass sliding door that afforded an excellent view of the back yard and started to laugh.

Ben had set up an old slip 'n' slide of hers—one they'd played on when they were children—and the three of them were having the time of their lives. Laura giggled, Lochie chortled, and Ben's whole face had come alive. It shone.

She took a step towards the door, transfixed, her hand reaching out to rest against the glass as if reaching for...

Ben's face shone.

Her other hand moved to cover her stomach. What if Ben *did* stay? What if he kept his word and found fatherhood satisfying? What if he didn't run away?

Her heart thudded as she allowed the idea truly to sink in. The blood vessels in her hand pulsed against the glass. If Ben kept his word then her baby would have a father.

A real father.

She snatched her hand away. She backed up to the sofa. But she couldn't drag her gaze away from the happy trio in her back yard, watching in amazement as Ben effortlessly stepped in to prevent a spat between the children. He had them laughing again in no time. The man was a natural.

And he had a butt that—

She waved a hand in front of her face to shoo the thought away. She didn't have time for butts—not even butts as sublime as Ben's.

Or chests. She blinked and leaned forward. He really did have the most amazing body. He'd kept his shirt on, but it was now so wet it stuck to him like a second skin, outlining every delicious muscle and—

She promptly changed seats and placed her back to the door. She dragged in a breath and tried to control the crazy beating of her heart.

If Ben *did* overcome his wanderlust...

She swallowed. He'd never lied to her before. Why would he lie to her now? Especially about something as important as their child's happiness.

No! She shot to her feet. *Her* child!

She raced to the refrigerator to pour herself an ice-cold glass of water, but when she tipped her head back to drink it her eyes caught on the vivid blue of the water slide and the children's laughter filled her ears.

Slowly she righted her glass. This was their child. *Theirs*. She'd let fear cloud her judgement. Not fear for the baby, but fear for herself. Fear that this child might somehow damage her friendship with Ben. Fear that she might come to rely on him too heavily. Fear at having to share her child.

She abandoned her water to grip her hands together. She hadn't expected to share this baby. In her possessiveness, was she sabotaging Ben's efforts?

She moistened suddenly dry lips. It would be hard, relinquishing complete control and having to consider someone else's opinions and ideas about the baby, but behind that there would be a sense of relief too, and comfort. To know she wasn't in this on her own, that someone else would have her and the baby's backs.

She'd fully expected to be a single mum—had been prepared for it. But if she didn't have to go it alone…

If her baby could have a father…

Barely aware of what she was doing, Meg walked back to the double glass doors. Ben had a child under each arm and he was swinging them round and round until they shrieked with laughter. Laura broke away to grab the hose and aimed it directly at his chest. He clutched at the spot as if shot and fell down, feigning injury. Both children immediately pounced on him.

The longer Meg watched them the clearer the picture in her mind became. Her baby could have a mother *and* a father. Her baby could have it all!

Pictures formed in her mind—pictures of family picnics and trips to the beach, of happy rollicking Christmases, of shared meals and quiet times when the baby was put down and—

She snapped away. Heat rushed through her. *Get a grip!* Her baby might have a father, but that didn't mean she and Ben would form a cosy romantic bond and become the ideal picture-perfect family. That would never happen.

Her heart pounded so hard it almost hurt, and she had to close her eyes briefly until she could draw much needed breath into straining lungs.

Ben would never do family in the way she wanted or needed. That stupid kiss ten years ago and the way Ben had bolted from town afterwards had only reinforced what she'd always known—that he would never surrender to the unpredictability and raw emotion of romantic love, with all its attendant highs and lows. She might have baby brain and crazy hormones at the moment, but she'd better not forget that fact—not for a single, solitary moment.

Best friends.

She opened her eyes and nodded. They were best friends who happened to have a child together and they'd remain friends. They *could* make this work.

She rested her forehead against the glass, her breath fogging it so she saw the trio dimly, through a haze. If only she knew for certain that Ben wouldn't leave, that he wouldn't let them down. That he'd stay. She wanted a guarantee, but there weren't—

She froze.

She turned to press her back against the door. What did Ben want more than anything else in the world?

To be on the crew of a yacht that was sailing around the world.

Did he want that more than he wanted to be a father?

Her heart pounded. Her stomach churned. She pushed away from the door and made for the phone, dialling the number for Dave Clements' travel agency. 'Dave? Hi, it's Meg.'

'Hey, Meg. Winnie and I are really looking forward to the wedding. How are the preparations coming along?'

'Oh, God, don't ask.'

He laughed. 'If there's anything I can do?'

'Actually, I do need to come in and talk to you about organising a honeymoon trip for the happy couple.'

'Drop in any time and we'll put together something fabulous for them.'

'Thank you.' She swallowed. 'But that's not the reason I called.' Her mouth went dry. She had to swallow again. 'I've been racking my brain, trying to come up with a way to thank Ben. He's been such a help with the preparations and everything.'

'And?'

'Look,' she started in a rush, 'you know he's always wanted to crew on a round-the-world yacht expedition? I wondered if there was a way you could help me make that happen?'

A whistle travelled down the line. She picked up a pen and doodled furiously on the pad by the phone, concentrating on everything but her desire to retract her request.

'Are you sure that's what you want, Meg? When I spoke to him through the week it sounded like he was pretty set on staying in Port Stephens.'

She glanced out of the window at Ben and the children. Still laughing. Still having the time of their lives. 'It's something he's always wanted. I want him to at least have the opportunity to turn it down.'

But would he?

'Okay, leave it with me. I'll see what I can do.'

'Thanks, Dave.'

She replaced the receiver. If Ben turned the opportunity down she'd have her guarantee.

If he didn't?

She swallowed. Well, at least that would be an answer too.

CHAPTER NINE

BEN CRUISED THE road between Nelson Bay and Fingal Bay with the driver's window down, letting the breeze dance through the car and ruffle his hair. He put his foot down a centimetre and then grinned in satisfaction. This baby, unlike his motor-bike, barely responded.

Perfect.

The coastal forest and salt-hardy scrubland retreated as the road curved into the small township. On impulse he parked the car and considered the view.

As a kid, he'd loved the beach. He and Meg had spent more time down there than they had in their own homes. Maybe he'd taken it for granted. Or maybe he'd needed to leave it for a time to see some of the world's other beautiful places before he could come back and truly appreciate it.

Because Meg was right—for sheer beauty, Fingal Bay was hard to beat. The line of the beach, the rocky outcrop of Fin-gal Island directly opposite and the sand spit leading out to it formed a cradle that enclosed the bay on three of its sides. The unbelievably clear water revealed the sandy bottom of the bay, and the bottle-nosed dolphins that were almost daily visitors.

He'd fled this place as soon as he was of a legal age. Star-ing at it now, he felt as if it welcomed him back. He dragged in a breath of late-afternoon air—salt-scented and warm—then glanced at his watch and grinned. Meg should be home by now.

He drove to her house, pulled the car into her driveway

and blared the horn. He counted to five before her front door swung open.

Meg stood silhouetted in the light with the darkness of the house behind her and every skin cell he possessed tightened. Her baby bump had grown in the month he'd been home. He gazed at it hungrily. He gazed at *her* hungrily.

He gave himself a mental slap upside the head. He'd promised to stop thinking about Meg that way. He'd promised not to send her any more mixed messages. He would never be able to give her all the things a woman like her wanted and needed, and he valued their friendship too much to pretend otherwise.

If only it were as easy as it sounded.

With a twist of his lips, he vaulted out of the car.

When she saw him, her jaw dropped. She stumbled down the driveway to where he stood, her mouth opening and closing, her eyes widening. 'What on earth is that?'

He grinned and puffed out his chest. 'This—' he slapped the bonnet '—is my new car.' This would prove to her that he was a changed man, that he was capable of responsibility and stability. That he was capable of fatherhood.

He pushed his hands into the pockets of his jeans, his shoulders free and easy, while he waited for her to finish her survey of the car and then pat him on the back and meet his gaze with new respect in her eyes.

'You…' She swallowed. 'You've bought a station wagon?'

'I have.' His grin widened. He'd need room for kid stuff now. And this baby had plenty of room.

'You've gone and bought an ugly, boxy *white* station wagon?'

She stared at him as if he'd just broken out in green and purple spots. His shoulders froze in place. So did his grin. She planted her hands on her hips and glared. The sun picked out the golden highlights in her hair. Her eyes blazed, but her lips were the sweetest pink he'd ever seen.

Meg was hot. He shifted, adjusting his jeans. Not just pretty, but smokin' hot. Knock-a-man-off-his-feet hot. He needed something ice-cold to slake the heat rising through him or he'd—

'Where's your bike?' she demanded.

He moistened his lips. 'I traded it.' The icy sting of the cold current that visited the bay at this time of year might do the trick.

'You. Did. *What?*' Her voice rose on the last word. Her nostrils flared. She poked him in the shoulder. 'Have you gone mad? What on earth were you thinking?'

He leant towards her, all his easy self-satisfaction slaughtered. 'I was trying to prove to you that I've changed,' he ground out. 'This car is a symbol that I can be a good father.'

'It shows you've lost your mind!'

She dragged both hands back through her hair. She stared at him for a moment, before transferring her gaze back to the station wagon.

'Inside—now,' she ordered. 'I don't want to have this conversation on the street.'

He planted his feet. 'I'm not some child you can order about. If you want to talk to me, then you can ask me like a civilised person. I'm tired of you treating me like a second-class citizen.' Like someone who couldn't get one damn thing right.

He knew she was stressed about the wedding, about the baby, about him—about that damn kiss!—but he was through with taking this kind of abuse from her. Meg had always been a control freak, but she was getting worse and it was time she eased up.

He welcomed the shock in her eyes, but not the pain that followed swiftly on its heels. Meg was a part of him. Hurting her was like hurting himself.

She swallowed and nodded. 'Sorry, that really was very rude of me. It's just…I think we need to talk about that.' She gestured to his car. 'Would you come inside for coffee so we can discuss it?' When he didn't say anything she added, 'Please?'

He nodded and followed her into the house.

She glanced at the kitchen clock. 'Coffee or a beer?'

'Coffee, thanks.' Meg had been right about the drinking. Somewhere along the line, when he hadn't been paying attention, it had become a habit. He'd made an effort to cut back.

She made coffee for him and decaf for herself. He took in the tired lines around her eyes and mouth and the pallor of her skin where previously there'd been a golden glow and something snagged in his chest. 'What's wrong with the car?' he said, accepting the mug she handed him. 'I thought it would show you I'm serious about sticking around and being involved with the baby.'

'I think I've been unfair to you on that, Ben.'

She gestured to the family room sofas and he followed her in a daze.

She sat. She didn't tuck her legs beneath her like she normally did. She didn't lean back against the sofa's cushioned softness. She perched on the edge of the seat, looking weary and pale. Her mug sat on the coffee table, untouched. He wanted to ease her back into that seat and massage her shoulders…or her feet. Whichever would most help her to relax.

Except he had a no-touching-Meg rule. And he wasn't confident enough in his own strength to break it.

She glanced up, the green in her eyes subdued. 'You said you wanted to be an involved father and I automatically assumed…'

'That I was lying.'

'Not on purpose, no.' She frowned. 'But I didn't think you really knew what you were talking about. I didn't think you understood the reality of what you were planning to do.'

And why should she? The truth was he hadn't understood the reality at all. Not at first.

She glanced back at him and her gaze settled on his mouth for a beat too long. Blood rushed in his ears. When she realised her preoccupation she jerked away.

'I didn't think you knew your own mind.' She swallowed.

'That wasn't fair of me. I'm sorry for doubting you. And I'm sorry I haven't been more supportive of your decision.'

'Hell, don't apologise.' Coffee sloshed over the side of his mug and he mopped it up with the sleeve of his shirt. 'I needed your challenges to make me analyse what I was doing and what it is I want. I should be thanking you for forcing me to face facts.' For forcing him to grow up.

When he glanced back up he found her making a detailed inventory of his chest and shoulders. Her lips parted and fire licked along his veins.

Don't betray yourself, he tutored himself. *Don't!*

Her eyes searched his, and then the light in them dulled and she glanced away, biting her lip.

He had to close his eyes. 'You don't need to apologise about anything.'

He opened his eyes and almost groaned at the strain in her face. He made himself grin, wanting to wipe the tension away, wanting desperately for things to return to normal between them again.

'Though I have to say if I'd known that calling you on the way you've been treating me would change your thinking I'd have done it days ago.'

'Oh, it wasn't that.' She offered him a weak smile that didn't reach her eyes. 'It was watching you with Laura and Lochie last Saturday.'

He'd sensed that had been a test. He just hadn't known if he'd passed it or not.

'I had a ball.'

'I know. And so did they.'

'They're great kids.'

Just for a moment her eyes danced. 'Laura can be a challenge at times.'

'She just needs to loosen up a bit, that's all.' In the same way Meg needed to loosen up.

Who made sure Meg had fun these days? Who made sure

she didn't take herself too seriously? She'd said that the baby gave her joy, but it wasn't here yet. What else gave her joy? It seemed to him that at the moment Meg was too busy for joy, and that was no way to live a life.

He'd need to ponder that a bit more, but in the meantime…

'What's your beef with the car?'

That brought the life back to her cheeks. He sat back, intrigued.

'Could you have picked a more boring car if you'd tried?'

'*You* have a station wagon,' he pointed out.

'But at least mine is a sporty version and it's useful for work. And it's blue!'

'The colour doesn't matter.'

'Of course it does.' She leant to towards him. 'I understand you want to prove you're good father material, but that doesn't mean you have to become *beige*!'

'Beige' had been their teenage term for all things boring.

'I agree that with a baby you'll need a car. But you're allowed to buy a car you'll enjoy. A two-seat convertible may not be practical, but you're an action man, Ben, and you like speed. You could've bought some powerful V6 thing that you could open up on the freeway, or a four-wheel drive you could take off-road and drive on the beach—or anything other than that boring beige box sitting in my driveway.'

He considered her words.

'Do you think fatherhood is going to be beige?' she demanded.

'No!'

She closed her eyes and let out a breath. 'That's something, at least.'

He saw it then—the reason for her outburst. She'd started to believe in him, in his sense of purpose and determination, and then he'd turned up in that most conservative of conservative cars and he'd freaked her out.

Again.

He was determined to get things back on an even footing between them again. And he'd succeed. As long as he ignored the sweet temptation of her lips and the long clean line of her limbs. And the desire that flared in her green-flecked eyes.

'You don't have to change who you are, Ben. You might not be travelling around the globe any more, throwing yourself off mountains, negotiating the rapids of some huge river or trekking to base camp at Everest—but, for heaven's sake, it doesn't mean you have to give up your motorbike, does it?'

That—trading in his bike—had been darn hard. It was why it had taken him a full month of being back in Fingal Bay before he'd found the courage to do it. But he'd figured it was a symbol of his old life and therefore had to go. But if Meg was right...

'I want you to go back to that stupid car yard and buy it back.'

A weight lifted from his shoulders. He opened and closed his hands. 'You think I should?'

'Yes! Where else am I going to get my occasional pillion-passenger thrill? All that speed and power? And, while I know you can't literally feel the wind in your hair because of the helmet, that's exactly what it feels like. It's like flying.'

He had a vision of Meg on the back of his bike, her front pressed against his back and her arms wrapped around his waist. He shot to his feet. 'If I race back now I might catch the manager before he leaves for the day.' He had to get his bike back. 'He had a nice-looking four wheel drive in stock. That could be a bit of fun.' He rubbed at his jaw. 'I could take it for a test drive.'

Meg trailed after him to the front door. 'Good luck.'

Halfway down the path, he swung back. 'What are you doing Saturday?'

'Elsie and I are shopping for wedding outfits in the morning.' She grimaced. 'It's not like we've left it to the last minute or anything, but that grandmother of yours can be darn slippery when she wants to be.'

The wedding was a fortnight this Saturday. 'And in the afternoon?'

She shook her head and shrugged.

'Keep it free,' he ordered. Then he strode back, slipped a hand around the back of her head and pressed a kiss to her brow. 'Thanks, Meg.'

And then he left before he did something stupid, like kiss her for real. That wouldn't be getting their friendship back on track.

Meg glanced up at the tap on the back door. 'How did the shopping go?' Ben asked, stepping into the family room with the kind of grin designed to bring a grown woman to her knees.

Her heart swelled at the sight of him. *Don't drool. Smile. Don't forget to smile.*

The smiling was easy. Holding back a groan of pure need wasn't. 'The shopping? Oh, it went surprisingly well,' she managed. Elsie had been remarkably amiable and co-operative. 'We both now have outfits.'

They'd found a lovely lavender suit in shot silk for Elsie. Though she'd protested that it was too young for her, her protests had subsided once Meg had pronounced it perfect. Meg had settled on a deep purple satin halter dress with a chiffon overlay that hid her growing baby bulge. It made her feel like a princess.

'How are the wedding preparation coming along? What do you need me to do this week?'

Ben had, without murmur, executed to perfection whatever job she'd assigned to him. He'd been amazing.

She thought of the request she'd made of Dave and bit her lip. Perhaps she should call that off. Ben had settled into a routine here as if…almost as if he'd never been away. The thought of him leaving…

She shook herself. The wedding. They were talking about the wedding. 'You have a suit?'

'Yep.'

'Then there's not much else to be done. The marquee is being erected on the Friday afternoon prior, and the tables and chairs will all be set up then too.'

'I'll make sure I'm here in case there are any hitches.'

'Thank you.' He eyed her for a moment. It made her skin prickle. 'What?'

He shook himself. 'Have you managed to keep this afternoon free?'

'Uh-huh.' Something in her stomach shifted—a dark, dangerous thrill at the thought of spending a whole afternoon in Ben's company. 'What do you have planned?' If both of them were sensible it would be something practical and beige boring.

Ben's eyes—the way they danced and the way that grin hooked up the right side of his face—told her this afternoon's adventure, whatever it might be, was not going to be beige.

'It's a surprise.'

Her blood quickened. She should make an excuse and cry off, but...

Damn it all, this was Ben—*her best friend*—and that grin of his was irresistible. She glanced down at her sundress. 'Is what I'm wearing okay?'

'Absolutely not.' His grin widened. 'You're going to need a pair of swimmers, and something to put on over them to protect you from sunburn.'

Her bones heated up. She really, truly should make an excuse. 'And a hat, I suppose?' she said, moving in the direction of her bedroom to change.

'You get the picture,' he said.

Meg lifted her face into the breeze and let out a yell for the sheer fun of it. Ben had driven them into Nelson Bay in his brand new *red* four-wheel drive to hire a rubber dinghy with an outboard motor for the afternoon. They were zipping across the vast expanse of the bay as if they were flying.

Ben had given her the wind in her hair for real, and she couldn't remember the last time she'd had this much fun. She released the rope that ran around the dinghy's perimeter and flung her arms back, giving herself up to sheer exhilaration.

'Meg!'

She opened her eyes at Ben's shout, saw they were about to hit the wake from a speedboat, and grabbed the rope again for balance. They bounced over the waves, her knees cushioned by the buoyant softness of the rubber base.

Eventually Ben cut the motor and they drifted. She trailed her hand in the water, relishing its refreshing coolness as she dragged the scent of salt and summer into her lungs. Silver scales glittered in the sun when a fish jumped out of the water nearby. Three pelicans watched from a few metres away, and above them a flock of seagulls cried as they headed for the marina.

The pelicans set off after them, and Meg turned around and stretched her legs out. The dinghy was only small, but there was plenty of room for Meg and Ben to sit facing one another, with their legs stretched to the side. She savoured the way the dinghy rocked and swayed, making their legs press against each other's, the warm surge that shot through her at each contact.

Ever since that kiss she'd found herself craving to touch Ben—to test the firmness of his skin, to explore his muscled leanness and discover if it would unleash the heat that could rise in her without any warning.

It was dangerous, touching like this, but she couldn't stop herself. Besides, it was summer—the sun shone, the gulls wheeled and screeched, and water splashed against the sides of the dingy. For a moment it all made her feel young and reckless.

'This was a brilliant idea, Ben.'

He grinned. 'It's certainly had the desired effect.'

She reached up to adjust the brim of her sunhat. 'Which was?'

'To put the colour back in your cheeks.'

She stilled. It was strange to have someone looking out for her, looking after her. 'Thank you.' If Ben did stay—

She cut that thought off. Whether Ben stayed or not, it wasn't his job to look after her. He might fill her with heat, but that didn't mean they had any kind of future together.

Except as friends.

He shrugged. 'Besides, it's nice to have some buddy-time.'

She gritted her teeth. Buddy-time was excellent. It *was*!

She glanced at him and tried to decipher the emotions that tangled inside her, coiling her up tight.

She started to name them silently. One: desire. Her lips twisted. *Please God, let that pass.* Two: anger that he'd turned her nicely ordered world on its head. She shook her head. *Deal with it.* Three: love for her oldest, dearest friend, for all they'd been through together, for all they'd shared, and for all the support and friendship he'd given her over the years.

And there was another emotion there too—something that burned and chafed. A throbbing sore. It was…

Hurt.

That made her blink. Hurt? She swallowed and forced herself to examine the feeling. An ache started at her temples. Hurt that he'd stay in Port Stephens for their baby in a way he'd never have stayed for her.

Oh, that was petty. And nonsensical.

She rubbed her hands up and down her arms. She hadn't harboured hidden hopes that Ben would come back for her. *She hadn't!* But seeing him now on such a regular basis…not to mention that kiss on the beach…that devastating kiss…

'Cold?'

She shook her head and abruptly dropped her hands back to her lap. She dragged in a breath. She had to be careful. She couldn't go weaving Ben into her romantic fantasies. It would end in tears. It would wreck their friendship. And that would be the worst thing in the world. It was why she hadn't let herself get hooked on that kiss ten years ago. It was why she had to forget that kiss the other night.

A romantic relationship—even if Ben was willing—wasn't worth risking their friendship over.

Deep inside, a part of her started to weep. She swallowed. Hormones, that was all.

'I can still hardly believe that Elsie and your father are marrying.'

She nodded, prayed her voice would work properly, prayed she could hide her strain. 'It shows a remarkable optimism on both their parts.'

He surveyed her for a moment. 'How are you getting on with your father?'

'Same as usual.' She lifted her face to the sun to counter a sudden chill. 'Neither he nor Elsie have mentioned my outburst. It seems we're all back to pretending it never happened.' Not that she knew what else she'd been expecting. Or hoping for. 'It's the elephant in the room nobody mentions.'

'It's had a good effect on Elsie, though.'

She straightened from her slouch. 'No?'

'Yep.' He flicked water at her. 'She's less buttoned-up and more relaxed. She makes more of an effort at conversation too.'

'No?'

He flicked water at her again. 'Yep.'

'I'd say that's down to the effect of her romance with my father.'

'She's even knitting the baby some booties.'

Meg leant towards him, even though she was in danger of getting more water flicked at her. 'You're kidding me?'

He didn't flick more water at her, but she realised it had been a mistake to lean towards him when the scent of leather and whisky slugged into her, heating her up…tightening her up. Making her want forbidden things.

She sat back. Darn it all! How on earth could she be so

aware of his scent out here in the vast expanse of the bay? Surely the salt water and the sun should erase it, dilute it?

She scooped up a whole handful of water and threw it at him.

And then they had the kind of water fight that drenched them both and had her squealing and him laughing and them both breathing heavily from the exertion.

'How long since you've been out on the bay like this?' he demanded, subsiding back into his corner.

'Like this?' She readjusted her sunhat. 'Probably not since the last time we did it.'

'That has to be two years ago!'

'I've been out on a couple of dinner cruises, and I've swum more times than I can count.'

'What about kayaking?'

That was one of her favourite things—to take a kayak out in the early evening, when the shadows were long, the light dusky and the water calm. Paddling around the bay left her feeling at one with nature and the world. But when had she'd actually last done that?

She cocked her head to one side. She'd gone out a few times in December, but...

She hadn't been out once this year! 'I...I guess I've been busy.'

'You need to stop and smell the roses.'

He was right. This afternoon—full of sun, bay and a beat-up rubber dinghy—had proved that to her. She wanted to set her child a good example. She had no intention of turning into a distracted workaholic mother. She thought about her father and Elsie, how easily they'd fallen into unhealthy routines and habits.

She swallowed and glanced at Ben. He always took the time to smell the roses. Her lips twisted. Sometimes he breathed them in a little too deeply, and for a little too long, but nobody could accuse him of not living life to the full.

Would he still feel life was full after he'd been living in Port Stephens for a couple of years?

She glanced around. It was beautiful here. He was having fun, wasn't he?

For today.

But what would happen tomorrow, the day after that, and next week, next month, or even next year? *Please, God, don't let Ben be miserable.*

There was still so much that had to be settled. She leant back and swallowed. 'I agree it's important to slow down and to enjoy all the best that life has to offer, but you've still got some big decisions ahead of you, Ben.' And she doubted she'd be able to relax fully until he'd made them.

'Like?'

'Like what are you going to do with Elsie's house? Will you live there on your own after the wedding?'

'I haven't thought about it.'

'And what about a job? I'm not meaning to be nosy or pushy or anything, but…'

His lips twitched. 'But?'

'I figure you don't want to live off your savings for ever.'

'I have a couple of irons in the fire.'

He did? She opened her mouth but he held up a hand to forestall her.

'Once I have something concrete to report you'll be the first to know. I promise.'

She wanted to demand a timeframe on his promise, but she knew he'd scoff at that. And probably rightly so.

'Do you think I should move into Elsie's house?'

Her mouth dried. 'I…'

'If I do, I'll be paying her rent.' He scowled. 'I don't want her to give the darn thing to me. It's hers.'

She eyed him for a moment. 'What if she gifts it to the baby?'

His mouth opened and closed but no sound came out. It obviously wasn't a scenario he'd envisaged. 'I...' He didn't go on.

She glanced away, her stomach shrinking. The two of them had to have a serious conversation. But not today. They could save it for some other time.

'You better spit it out, Meg.'

She glared at the water. Ben knowing her so well could be darn inconvenient at times. She blew out a breath and turned to him. 'There are a few things I think we need to discuss in relation to the baby, but they can wait until after the wedding. It's such a glorious afternoon.'

And she didn't want to spoil it. Or ruin this easy-going camaraderie that should have been familiar to them but had been elusive these last few weeks.

'It could be the perfect afternoon for such a discussion,' he countered, gesturing to the sun, the bay and the holiday atmosphere of these last dog days of summer. 'When we're both relaxed.'

If she uttered the C-word he wouldn't remain relaxed. Still, she knew him well enough to know he wouldn't let it drop. She glanced around. Maybe he was right. Maybe she *should* lay a few things out there for him to mull over before Dave presented him with that dream offer. It only seemed fair.

She shivered, suddenly chilled, as if a cloud had passed over the sun. 'You won't like it,' she warned.

'I'm a big boy, Meg. I have broad shoulders.'

'You want to know if I think you should live in Elsie's house? That depends on...' She swallowed.

'On?'

'On what kind of access you want to have to the baby.'

He frowned. 'What do you mean?'

She wasn't going to be able to get away with not using the C-word. Dancing around it would only make matters worse.

'What I'm talking about, Ben, are our custody arrangements.'

* * *

Custody?

Ben flinched as the word ripped beneath his guard. His head was filled with the sound of shouting and screaming and abuse.

Custody?

'No!' He stabbed a finger at her. He swore. Once. Hard. Tried to quieten the racket in his head. He swore again, the storm raging inside him growing in strength. 'What the bloody hell are you talking about? *Custody?*' He spat the word out. 'No way! We don't need *custody* arrangements. We aren't like that. You and I can work it out like civilised people.'

Meg had gone white.

He realised he was shouting. Just like his mother had shouted. Just like his father had shouted. He couldn't stop. 'We're supposed to be friends.'

She swallowed and bile filled his mouth. Was she afraid of him? Wind rushed through his ears. No! She knew him well enough to know he'd never hut her. Didn't she?

His hands clenched. If she knew him well enough, she'd have never raised this issue in the first place.

'We're friends who are having a baby,' she said, her voice low. 'We need certain safeguards in place to ensure—'

'Garbage!' He slashed a hand through the air. 'We can keep going the way we have been—the way we've always done things. When you've had the baby I can come over any time and help, maybe take care of it some days while you're at work, and help you in the evenings with feeding and baths and—'

'So basically we'd live like a married couple but without the benefits?'

Her scorn almost blasted the flesh from his bones.

'No, Ben, that's *not* how it's going to be. Living like that— don't you think it would do our child's head in?' She stabbed a finger at him. 'Besides, I still believe in love and marriage. I am *so* not going to have you cramp my style like that.'

The storm inside him built to fever-pitch. 'You really mean to let another man help raise *my* child?'

'That's something you're going to have to learn to live with. Just like I will if you ever become serious about a woman.'

He went ice-cold then. 'You never wanted me as part of this picture, did you? I've ruined your pretty fantasy of domestic bliss and now you're trying to punish me.' He leaned towards her. 'You're hoping this will drive me away.'

The last of the colour bled from her face. 'That's not true.'

Wasn't it? His harsh laugh told her better than words could what he thought about that.

Her colour didn't return. She gripped her hands together in her lap. 'I want you to decide what you want the custody arrangements to be. Do you want fifty-fifty custody? A night through the week and every second weekend? Or...whatever? This is something we need to settle.'

Custody. The word stabbed through him, leaving a great gaping hole at the centre of his being. He wanted to cover his ears and hide under his bed as he had as a ten-year-old. The sense of helplessness, of his life spinning out of control, made him suddenly ferocious.

'What if I want full custody?' he snarled.

He wanted to frighten her. He wanted her to back down, to admit that this was all a mistake, that she was sorry and she didn't mean it.

He wanted her to acknowledge that he wasn't like his father!

Her chin shot up. 'You wouldn't get it.'

A savage laugh ripped from his throat. He should have known better. Meg would be well versed in her rights. She'd have made sure of them before bringing this subject up.

'I want the custody arrangements settled in black and white before the baby is born.'

That ice-cold remoteness settled over him again. She didn't trust him. 'Do you have to live your entire life by rules?'

Her throat bobbed as she swallowed. 'I'm sorry, Ben, but

in this instance I'm going to choose what's best for the baby, not what's best for you.'

She was choosing what was best for *her*. End of story. Acid burned his throat. Meg didn't even know who he was any more, and he sure as hell didn't know her. The pedestal he'd had her on for all these years had toppled and smashed.

'And as for you living next door in Elsie's house…' She shook her head. 'I think that's a very bad idea.'

He didn't say another word. He just started the dinghy's motor and headed for shore.

'How's Meg?'

Ben scowled as he reached for a beer. With a muttered oath he put it back and chose a can of lemon squash instead. He swung back to Elsie, the habit of a lifetime's loyalty preventing him from saying what he wanted to say—from howling out his rage.

'She's fine.'

Elsie sat at the kitchen table, knitting. It reminded him of Meg's baby shawl, and the almost completed crib he'd been working on in Elsie's garden shed.

'Is she okay with me taking her mother's place?'

Whoa! He reached out a hand to steady himself against the counter. Where on earth had that come from? He shook his head and counted to three. 'Let's get a couple of things straight. First of all, you won't be taking her mother's place. Meg is all grown-up.'

She might be grown-up, but she was also pedantic, anal and cruel.

He hauled in a breath. 'She doesn't need a mother any more. For heaven's sake, she's going to be a mother herself soon.'

He added controlling, jealous and possessive to his list. He adjusted his stance.

'Secondly, she won't be doing anything daft like calling you Mum.'

Elsie stared back at him. 'I meant taking her mother's place in her father's affections,' she finally said.

Oh. He frowned.

'Do you think she minds us marrying?'

Meg might be a lot of things he hadn't counted on, but she wasn't petty. 'She's throwing you a wedding. Doesn't that say it all?'

Elsie paused in her knitting. 'The thing is, she always was the kind of girl to put on a brave front.' She tapped a knitting needle against the table. 'You both were.'

He pulled out a chair and sat before he fell.

'Do *you* mind Laurie and I marrying?'

He shook his head. 'No.' And he realised he meant it.

'Good.' She nodded. 'Yes, that's good.' She stared at him for a bit, and then leaned towards him a fraction. 'Do you think Meg will let the baby call me Grandma?'

He didn't know what to say. 'I expect so. If that's what you want. You'll have to tell her that's what you'd prefer, though, rather than Elsie,' he couldn't resist adding.

Elsie set her knitting down. She took off her glasses and rubbed her eyes. Finally she looked at him again. 'After she left, I never heard from your mother, Ben. Not once.'

Ben's mouth went dry.

Elsie's hands shook. 'I waited and waited.'

Just for a moment the room, the table and Elsie receded. And then they came rushing back. 'But...?' he croaked.

Elsie shook her head, looking suddenly old. 'But...nothing. I can't tell you anything, though I wish to heaven I could. I don't know where she went. I don't know if she's alive or not. All I do know is it's been eighteen years.' A breath shuddered out of her. 'And that she knows how to get in contact with us, but to the best of my knowledge she's never tried to.'

He stared at her, trying to process what she'd said and how he felt about it.

'Your father broke something in her.'

He shook his head at that. 'No. The way they acted—they let hate and bitterness destroy them. She had a chance to pull back. They both did. But they chose not to. She was as much to blame as him.'

Elsie clenched her hand. 'All I know is that she left and I grieved. My only child…'

Ben thought about the child Meg carried and closed his eyes.

'When I came out of that fog I…we…me and you were set in our ways, our routines, our way of dealing with each other.'

Was it that simple? Elsie had been grief-stricken and just hadn't known how to deal with a young boy whose whole world had imploded.

'Your mother always said I suffocated her and that's why she went with your father. I failed her somehow—I still don't know how, can't find any explanation for it—and I just didn't want to go through all that again.'

He pulled in a breath. 'So you kept me at arm's length?'

'It was wrong of me, Ben, and I'm sorry.'

So much pain and misery. If his and Meg's child ever disappeared the way his mother had, could he honestly say he'd deal with it any better than Elsie had? He didn't know.

In the end he swallowed and nodded. 'Thank you for explaining it to me.'

'It was long overdue.'

He didn't know what to do, what to say.

'I'm grateful you had Meg.'

Meg. Her name burned through him. What would Meg want him to do now?

From somewhere he found a smile, and it didn't feel forced. 'I'm sure she'll be happy for the baby to call you Grandma.'

CHAPTER TEN

ON THE MORNING of the wedding Meg woke early. She leapt out of bed, pulled on a robe and raced downstairs, her mind throbbing with the million things that must need doing. And then she pulled to a halt in the kitchen and turned on the spot. Actually, what *was* there to do? Everything was pretty much done. She and Elsie had hair and make-up appointments later in the day, and her father was coming over mid-afternoon to get ready for the wedding, but till then her time was her own.

She made a cup of tea and let herself out through the glass sliding door. The garden looked lovely, and the marquee sat in the midst of it like a joyful jewel.

And then she saw Ben.

He stood a few feet away, a steaming mug of his own in hand, surveying the marquee too. He looked deliciously dishevelled and rumpled, as if he'd only just climbed out of bed. He didn't do designer stubble. Ben didn't do designer anything. There was nothing designed in the way he looked, but...

Her hand tightened about her mug. An ache burned in her abdomen. She'd barely seen him these last two weeks. He'd rung a few times, to check if there was anything she'd needed him to do, but he'd kept the calls brief and businesslike. He'd overseen the assembly of the marquee yesterday afternoon, but he'd disappeared back next door as soon as the workmen had left. He'd avoided her ever since she'd mentioned the C word.

'Morning, Meg.'

He didn't turn his head to look at her now either.

A cold fist closed about her heart. He was her best friend. He'd been an integral part of her life for eighteen years. She couldn't lose him. If she lost his friendship she would lose a part of herself.

The same way her father had lost a part of himself the day her mother had died.

The pressure in her chest grew until she thought it might split her in two.

'Lovely day for a wedding.'

He was talking to her about the weather. Everything in the garden blurred. She lifted her face to the sky and blinked, tried to draw breath into lungs that had cramped.

When she didn't speak, he turned to look at her. His eyes darkened and his face paled at whatever he saw in her face.

He shook his head. 'Don't look at me like that.'

She couldn't help it. 'Do you mean to resent me for ever? Do you mean to keep avoiding me? All because I want to do what's right for our baby?' The words tumbled out, tripping and falling over each other. 'Don't you trust me any more, Ben?'

His head snapped back. 'This is about your trust, not mine!' He stabbed a finger at her. 'You wouldn't need some third party to come in and organise custody arrangements if you trusted me.'

She flinched, but she held her ground. 'Have you considered the fact that it might be myself I don't trust?' She poured the rest of her now tepid tea onto the nearest rosebush. 'I already feel crazily possessive about this baby.'

She rested a hand against her rounded stomach. He followed the movement. She moistened her lips when he met her gaze again. 'I'm going to find it hard to share this child with anyone—even with you, Ben. It wasn't part of my grand plan.' As he well knew. 'I know that's far from noble, but I can't help the way I feel. I also know that you're this baby's father and you have a right to be a part of its life.'

But the first time their baby spent twenty-four full hours with Ben—twenty-four hours away from her—she'd cry her eyes out. She'd wander from room to room in her huge house, lost.

'Having everything down in black and white will protect your rights. Have you not considered that?'

One glance at his face told her he hadn't.

'I don't see why making everything clear—what we expect from each other and what our child can expect from us—is such a bad thing.'

He didn't say anything. He didn't even move.

'I understand that down the track things might change. We can discuss and adapt to those changes as and when we need to. I'm not locking us into a for ever contract. We can include a clause that says we'll renegotiate every two years, if you want.'

But she knew they needed something on paper that would set out their responsibilities and expectations and how they'd move forward.

For the sake of the baby.

And for the sake of their friendship.

'I know you love this baby, Ben.'

Dark eyes surveyed her.

'You wouldn't turn your whole life on its head for no good reason. You want to be a good father.'

He'd stay for the baby in a way he'd never have stayed for her, but she wanted him to stay. She wanted it so badly she could almost taste it.

'And you think agreeing to legalise our custody arrangements will prove I'll be a good father?'

She tried not to flinch at the scorn in his voice. She was asking him to face his greatest fear. Nobody did that without putting up a fight. And when he wanted to Ben could put up a hell of a fight.

She tipped up her chin. 'It'll make us better co-parents. So, yes—I think it *will* make me a better mother and you a better father.'

His jaw slackened.

She stared at him and then shook her head. Her throat tightened. She'd really started to believe that he'd stay, but now...

'I'm sorry,' she whispered. 'If I'd known five months ago what would come of asking you to be my sperm donor I'd never have asked.' She'd have left well alone and not put him through all this.

He stiffened. 'But I want this baby.'

Something inside her snapped then. 'Well, then, suck it up.' She tossed her mug to the soft grass at her feet and planted her hands on her hips. 'If you want this baby then man up to your responsibilities. If you can't do that—if they intimidate you that much—then run off back to Africa and go bungee-jump off a high bridge, or rappel down a cliff, or go deep-sea diving in the Atlantic, or any of those other things that aren't half as scary as fatherhood!'

He folded his arms and nodded. 'That's better. That meek and mild act doesn't suit you.'

Her hand clenched. She stared at her fist and then at his jaw.

'You're right. I do need to man up and face my responsibilities.'

Her hand promptly unclenched.

He ran a hand through his hair. 'Especially when they intimidate me, I expect.'

She stared, and then shook herself. 'Exactly at what point in the conversation did you come to that conclusion?'

'When you said how possessive you feel about the baby.'

Her nose started to curl. 'When you realised a custody agreement would protect your interests?'

'When I realised you weren't my mother.'

Everything inside her stilled.

'When I realised that, regardless of what happens, you will *never* become my mother. I know you will always put the baby's best interests first. That's when I realised I was fighting shadows—because regardless of what differences we might have in the future, Meg, we will never re-enact my parents' drama.'

She folded her arms.

'Are you going to tell me off now, for taking so long to come to that conclusion?'

'I'm going to tell you off for not telling me you'd already come to that conclusion. For letting me rabbit on and...' And abuse him.

'I needed a few moments to process the discovery.' He shifted his weight. 'And I wanted to razz you a bit until you stopped looking so damn fragile and depressed. That's not like you, Meg. What the hell is that all about?'

She glanced away.

'I want the truth.'

That made her smile. 'Have we ever been less than honest with each other?' They knew each other too well to lie effectively to the other. 'I've been feeling sick this past fortnight, worried that I've hurt our friendship. I want to do what's right for the baby. But hurting you kills me.'

He tossed his now-empty mug to the grass, as she had earlier. It rolled towards her mug, the two handles almost touching. At his sides, his hands clenched.

'The thing is, Ben, after this baby your friendship is the most important thing in the world to me. If I lost it...'

With a smothered oath, he closed the distance between them and pulled her in close, hugged her tightly. 'That's not going to happen, Meg. It will never happen.'

He held her tight, and yet she felt as if she was falling and falling without an end in sight. Even first thing in the morning he smelled of leather and whisky. She tried to focus on that instead of falling.

Eventually she disengaged herself. 'There's something else that's been bothering me.'

'What's that?'

'You keep saying you have no intention of forming a serious relationship with any woman.'

'I don't.'

'Well, I think you need to seriously rethink that philosophy of yours, because quite frankly it sucks.'

He gaped at her.

'You think fatherhood will be fulfilling, don't you?'

'Yes, but—'

'So can committing to one person and building a life with them.'

He glared. 'For you, perhaps.'

'And for you too. You're not exempt from the rest of the human race. No matter how much you'd like to think you are.'

He adjusted his stance, slammed his hands to his hips. 'What is it with you? You've never tried to change my mind on this before.'

That was true, but... 'I never thought you'd want fatherhood either, but I was obviously wrong about that. And I think *you're* wrong to discount a long-term romantic relationship.'

He shook his head. 'I'm not risking it.'

'You just admitted I'm not like your mother. There are other women—' the words tasted like acid on her tongue but she forced them out '—who aren't like your mother either.' She'd hate to see him with another woman, which didn't make a whole lot of sense. She closed her mind to the pictures that bombarded her.

'But I know you, Meg. I've known you for most of my life.'

'Then take the time to get to know someone else.'

His face shuttered closed. 'No.'

She refused to give up. 'I think you'll be a brilliant father. I think you deserve to have lots more children. Wouldn't you like that?'

He didn't say anything, and she couldn't read his face.

'I think you'd make a wonderful husband too.' She could

see it more clearly than she'd ever thought possible and it made her heart beat harder and faster. 'I think any woman would be lucky to have you in her life. And, Ben, I think it would make you happy.' And she wanted him happy with every fibre of her being.

He thrust out his jaw. 'I'm perfectly happy as I am.'

She wanted to call him a liar, except...

Except maybe he was right. The beguiling picture of Ben as a loving husband and doting father faded. Maybe the things that would make her happy would only make him miserable. The thought cut at her with a ferocity she couldn't account for.

She swallowed. 'I just want you to be happy,' she whispered.

He blew out a breath. 'I know.'

She wanted Ben to stay in Port Stephens. She *really* wanted that. If he fell in love with some woman...She shied away from the thought.

Her heart burned. She twisted her hands together. This evening Dave meant to offer Ben the chance to fulfil his dream—to offer him a place on that yacht.

'Can I hit you with another scary proposition?'

He squared his shoulders. 'You bet.'

Would it translate into emotional blackmail? Was it an attempt to make sure he did stay?

He leant down to peer into her face. 'Meg?'

She shook herself. It wasn't blackmail. It was her making sure Ben had all the options, knew his choices, that was all.

She swallowed. 'Would you like to be my birth partner? Would you like to be present at the birth of our child?'

He stilled.

'If you want to think about it—'

'I don't need to think about it.' Wonder filled his face. 'Yes, Meg. Yes. A thousand times yes.'

Finally she found she could smile again. What was a round-the-world yacht voyage compared to seeing his own child born? Behind her back, she crossed her fingers.

* * *

'Megan, I'm marrying Elsie because I care about her.' Laurie Parrish lifted his chin. 'Because I love her.'

Meg glanced up from fussing with her dress. In ten minutes he and she would walk out into the garden to meet Elsie and Ben and the ceremony would begin.

'I never doubted it for a moment.' She hesitated, and then leant across and took the liberty of straightening his tie.

He took her hand before she could move away again. 'Before I embark on my new life I want to apologise to you and acknowledge that I haven't been much of a father to you. I can't...' His voice grew gruff. 'I can't tell you how much I regret that.'

She stared at him and finally nodded. It was why he'd given her the house. She'd always sensed that. But it was nice to hear him acknowledge it out loud too. 'Okay, Dad, apology accepted.'

She tried to disengage her hand, but he refused to release it. 'I'm also aware that an apology and an expression of regret doesn't mean that we're suddenly going to have a great relationship.'

She blinked. *Wow!*

'But if it would be okay with you, if it won't make you uncomfortable or unhappy, I would like to try and build a relationship—a good, solid relationship—with you.'

Her initial scepticism turned to all-out shock.

'Would you have a problem with that?'

Slowly, she shook her head. She had absolutely no problem with that. It would be wonderful for her child to have grandparents who loved it, who wanted to be involved. Only...

She straightened. 'I'll need you to be a bit more enthusiastic and engaged. Not just in my life but in your own too.' She would need him to make some of the running instead of leaving it all up to her. But if he truly meant it...

Her heart lifted and the resentment that had built inside her these last few months started to abate. Unlike Ben, bitterness and anger hadn't crippled her during her teenage years. Sadness and yearning had. She couldn't erase that sadness and yearning now, and nor could her father. Nobody could. They would never get back those lost years, but she was willing to put effort into the future.

'Giving me the house was your way of saying sorry and trying to make amends, wasn't it?'

He nodded. 'I wanted your future secure. It seemed the least I could do.'

His admission touched her.

'But moving out of this house brought me to my senses about Elsie too. Missing her made me realise what she'd come to mean to me.'

So that had been the trigger—an illness, a recuperation, and then a change of address. Evidently romance worked in mysterious ways.

'I know this isn't going to change anything, Megan, but when you were growing up I thought you were spending so much time at Elsie's because she'd become a kind of surrogate mother to you. When I was recovering from my illness and Elsie was coming over to sit with me, I found out she'd thought Ben was spending that time here because I was providing the role of surrogate father. With each of us thinking that...' He pressed his fingers to his eyes. 'We just let things slide along the way they were.'

If they'd known differently, would he and Elsie have roused themselves from their depression? It was something they'd never know now.

She squeezed his hand. 'I think it's time to put the past behind us.' And as she said the words she realised she meant them. She had a baby on the way. She wanted to look towards the future, not back to the past.

'C'mon, I think it's time.'

'Is Ben going to do the right thing by you and the baby?'

She and Ben hadn't told a soul that he was the baby's father.

But her father and Elsie weren't stupid or blind. She pulled in a breath. 'Yes, he will. He always does what's best for me.'

She just wished she knew if that meant he was staying or if he was going. 'You have to understand, though, that what you think is best and what Ben and I think is best may be two very different things.' She didn't want the older couple hassling Ben, pressuring him.

'I understand.' Her father nodded heavily. 'I have no right to interfere. I just want to see you happy, Megan.'

'No,' she agreed, 'you're *not* allowed to interfere.' She took his arm and squeezed it. 'But you are allowed to care.'

She smiled up at him. He smiled back. 'C'mon—let's go get you married and then celebrate in style.'

The moment Meg stepped into the rose garden with her father Ben couldn't take his eyes from her.

'Are they there yet?' Elsie asked, her voice fretful, her fingers tapping against the kitchen table. 'They're late.'

He snapped to. 'They're exactly on time.' He kept his eyes on Meg for as long as he could as he backed away from the window. Swallowing, he turned to find Elsie alternately plucking at her skirt, her flowers and her hair. It was good to know she wasn't as cool and calm as she appeared or wanted everyone to think. 'Ready?'

She nodded. She looked lovelier than he'd ever seen her. He thought about what Meg would want him to say at this moment. 'Elsie?'

She glanced up at him.

'Mr Parrish is a very lucky man.'

'Oh!' Her cheeks turned pink.

He suddenly grinned. 'I expect he's going to take one look at you and want to drag you away from the celebrations at an indecently early hour.'

Her cheeks turned even redder and she pressed her hands

to them. The she reached out and swatted him with her bouquet. 'Don't talk such nonsense, Ben!'

He tucked her hand into the crock of his arm and led her through the house and out through the front door. 'It's not nonsense. Just you wait.'

Ben had meant to watch for the expression on Laurie's face the first moment he glimpsed Elsie, but one sidelong glance at Meg and Ben's attention was lost. Perspiration prickled his nape. He couldn't drag his gaze away.

Meg wore a deep purplish-blue dress, and in the sun it gleamed like a jewel. She stood there erect and proud, with her gently rounded stomach, looking out-of-this-world desirable. Like a Grecian goddess. He stared at her bare shoulders and all he could think of was pressing kisses to the beckoning golden skin. He could imagine their satin sun-kissed warmth. He sucked air into oxygen-starved lungs. A raging thirst built inside him.

A diamante brooch gathered the material of the dress between her breasts. Filmy material floated in the breeze and drifted down to her ankles. She'd be wearing sexy sandals and he wanted to look, really he did, but he found it impossible to drag his gaze from the lush curves of her breasts.

He moistened his lips. His heart thumped against his ribcage. His skin started to burn. Meg's dress did nothing to hide her new curves. Curves he could imagine in intimate detail— their softness, their weight in his hands, the way her nipples would peak under his hungry gaze as they were doing now. He imagined how they'd tauten further as he ran a thumb back and forth across them, the taste of them and their texture as he—

For Pete's sake!

He wrenched his gaze away, his mouth dry. A halfway decent guy did *not* turn his best friend into an object of lust. A halfway decent guy would not let her think even for a single second that there could ever be anything more between them than friendship.

He did his best to keep his gaze averted from all her golden promise, tried to focus on the ceremony. He wasn't equal to the task—not even when Elsie and Laurie surprised everyone by revealing they'd written their own vows. He was too busy concentrating on not staring at Meg, on not lusting after her, to catch what those vows were.

A quick glance at Meg—a super-quick glance—told him they'd been touching. Her eyes had grown bright with unshed tears, her smile soft, and her lips—

He dragged his gaze away again, his pulse thundering in his ears.

It seemed to take a hundred years, but finally Elsie and Laurie were pronounced husband and wife. And then Laurie kissed Elsie in a way that didn't help the pressure building in Ben's gut. There were cheers and congratulations all round. Four of Meg's girlfriends threw glittery confetti in the air. Gold and silver spangles settled in Meg's hair, on her cheek and shoulders, and one landed on the skin of her chest just above her—

He jerked his gaze heavenward.

Meg broke away from the group surrounding the newlyweds to slip her arm through his. 'We're going to have a ten-minute photoshoot with the photographer, and then it'll be party time.'

There was a photographer? He glanced around. He hadn't captured the way Ben had been ogling Meg, had he? Please, God.

'You scrub up real nice, Ben Sullivan.' She squeezed his arm. 'I don't think I've seen you in a suit since you stepped in to take me to my high school formal when Jason Prior dumped me to partner Rochelle Collins instead.'

He'd stepped in as a friend back then. He needed to find that same frame of mind, that same outlook, quick-smart.

Minus the kiss that had happened that night!

He dragged in a breath.

Don't think about it.

He'd been a sex-starved teenager back then, that's all.

And Meg had been beautiful.

She's more beautiful now.

'But I don't remember you filling out a suit half so well back then.'

He closed his eyes. Not just at her words, but at the husky tone in which they were uttered. The last thing he needed right now was for Meg to start feeling sexy. At least she had an excuse—pregnancy hormones. Him? He was just low life scum.

If he kissed Meg again it wouldn't stop at kisses. They both knew that. But one night would never be enough for Meg. And two nights was one night too many as far as he was concerned.

It would wreck their friendship. He couldn't risk that—not now they had a child to consider.

'You okay?'

He steeled himself and then glanced down. Her brow had creased, her eyes were wary. He swallowed and nodded.

She gestured towards the newlyweds. 'The service was lovely.'

'Yep.'

His tie tightened about his throat. Please God, don't let her ask him anything specific. He couldn't remember a damn thing about the ceremony.

She smiled, wide and broad. 'I have a good feeling about all of this.'

Just for a moment that made him smile too. 'Pollyanna,' he teased.

Her eyes danced, her lips shone, and hunger stretched through him.

If I lost your friendship, I don't know what I would do.

He swallowed the bile that burned his throat. He couldn't think of anything worse than losing Meg's friendship.

And yet...

He clenched his hands. Yet it wasn't enough to dampen his rising desire to seduce her.

Something in his face must have betrayed him because she

snapped away from him, pulling her arm from his. 'Stop looking at me like that!'

The colour had grown high in her cheeks. Her eyes blazed. Neither of those things dampened his libido. That said, he wasn't sure a slap to the face or a cold shower would have much of an effect either.

'Darn it, Ben. I should have known this was how you'd react to the wedding.'

She kept her voice low—bedroom-low—and—

He cut the thought off and tried to focus on her words. 'What are you talking about?'

'All this hearts and flowers stuff has made you want to beat your chest and revert to your usual caveman tactics just to prove you're not affected. That you're immune.'

'Caveman?' he spluttered. 'I'll have you know I have more finesse than that.'

They glared at each other.

'Besides, you're underestimating yourself.' He scowled. 'You look great in that dress.' With a superhuman effort he managed to maintain eye contact and slowly the tension between them lessened. 'Can we get these photos underway?' he growled.

He needed to be away from Meg asap with an ice-cold beer in his hand.

The reception went without a hitch.

The food was great. The music was great. The company was great. The speech Laurie made thanking Meg and Ben for the wedding and admitting what a lucky man he was, admitting that he'd found a new lease of life, touched even Ben.

The reception went without a hitch except throughout it all Ben was far too aware of Meg. Of the way she moved, the sound of her laughter, the warmth she gave out to all those around her. Of the sultry way she moved on the dance floor. He scowled. She certainly hadn't lacked for dance partners.

He'd made sure that he'd danced too. There were several beautiful women here, and three months ago he'd have done his best to hook up with one of them—go for a drink somewhere and then back to her place afterwards. It seemed like a damn fine plan except...

I don't like the way you treat women.

He'd stopped dancing after that.

His gaze lowered to the rounded curve of Meg's stomach and his throat tightened.

'Hey, buddy!' A clap on the shoulder brought him back.

Ben turned and then stood to shake hands. 'Dave, mate—great to see you here. Meg said you were coming. Have a seat.'

They sat and Dave surveyed him. 'It's been a great night.'

'Yeah.'

'Meg's told me what a help you've been with the wedding prep.'

She had? He shrugged. 'It was nothing.'

Dave glanced at Meg on the dance floor. 'That's not how she sees it.'

He bit back a groan. The last thing he needed was someone admiring Meg when he was doing his damnedest to concentrate on doing anything but.

Dave shifted on his chair to face him more fully. 'Something has popped up in my portfolio that I think will interest you.'

Anything that could keep his mind off Meg for any length of time was a welcome distraction. 'Tell me more.'

'If you want it, I can get you on the crew for a yacht that's setting off around the world. It leaves the week after next and expects to be gone five months.' He shrugged and sat back. 'I know it's something you've always wanted to do.'

Ben stared at the other man and waited for the rush of anticipation to hit him. This was something he'd always wanted—the last challenge on his adventure list. It would kill him to turn it down, but...

He waited and waited.

And kept right on waiting.

The anticipation didn't come. In fact he could barely manage a flicker of interest. He frowned and straightened.

'Mate, I appreciate the offer but...' His eyes sought out Meg on the dance floor, lowered to her baby bump. 'I have bigger fish to fry at the moment.'

Dave shrugged. 'Fair enough. I just wanted to run it by you.'

'And I appreciate it.' But what he wanted and who he was had crystallised in his mind in sharp relief. He was going to be a father and he wanted to be a *good* father—the best.

Dave clapped him on the back. 'I'll catch you later, Ben. It's time to drag that gorgeous wife of mine onto the dance floor.'

Ben waved in absent acknowledgment. A smile grew inside him. He was going to be a father. Nothing could shake him from wanting to be the best one he could be. His new sense of purpose held far more power than his old dreams ever had.

Her father and Elsie left at a relatively early hour, but the party in Meg's garden continued into the night. She danced with her girlfriends and made sure she spoke to everyone.

Everyone, that was, except Ben.

She stayed away from Ben. Tonight he was just too potent. He wore some gorgeous subtle aftershave that made her think of Omar Sharif and harems, but it didn't completely mask the scent of leather and whisky either, and the combination made her head whirl.

Some instinct warned her that if she gave in to the temptation he represented tonight she'd be lost.

'Meg?' Dave touched her arm and she blinked herself back inside the marquee. 'Winnie and I are heading off, but thanks for a great party. We had a ball.'

'I'm glad you enjoyed yourselves. I'll see you out.'

'No need.'

'Believe me, the fresh air will do me good.'

Keeping busy was the answer. Not remembering the way

Ben's eyes had practically devoured her earlier was key too. She swallowed. When he looked at her the way a man looked at a woman he found desirable he skyrocketed her temperature and had her pulse racing off the chart. He made her want to do wild reckless things.

She couldn't do wild and reckless things. She was about to become a mother.

And when he didn't look at her like that, when he gazed at her baby bump with his heart in his eyes—oh, it made her wish for other things. It made her wish they could be a family—a proper family.

But of course that way madness lay. And a broken heart.

She led Dave and Winnie through the rose garden, concentrating on keeping both her temperature and her pulse at even, moderate levels.

Just before they reached the front yard Dave said, 'I made Ben that offer you and I spoke about a while back.'

She stumbled to a halt. Her heart lurched. She had to lock her knees to stop herself from dropping to the ground. 'And…?' Her heart beat against her ribs.

'And I turned it down,' a voice drawled from behind her.

She swung around. *Ben!* And the way his eyes glittered dangerously in the moonlight told her he was less than impressed. She swallowed. In fact he looked downright furious.

'Have I caused any trouble?' Dave murmured.

'Not at all,' she denied, unable to keep the strain from her voice.

Winnie took her husband's arm. 'Thank you both for a lovely evening.' With a quick goodnight, the other couple beat a hasty retreat.

Meg swallowed and turned back to Ben. 'I…'

He raised an eyebrow and folded his arms. 'You can explain, right?'

Could she?

'Another test?' he spat out.

She nodded.

'My word wasn't good enough?'

It should've been, but...' She moistened suddenly parched lips. 'I wanted a guarantee,' she whispered.

He stabbed a finger at her. 'You of all people should know there's no such thing.'

Her heart beat like a panicked animal when he wheeled away from her. 'Please, Ben—'

He swung back. 'What exactly are you most afraid of, Meg? That I'll leave or that I'll stay?'

Then it hit her.

'Oh!'

She took a step away from him. The lock on her knees gave out and she plumped down to the soft grass in a tangle of satin and chiffon. She covered her mouth with one hand as she stared up at him.

Leaving. She was afraid of him leaving. Deathly afraid. Deep-down-in-her-bones afraid.

Break-her-heart afraid.

Because she'd gone and done the unthinkable—she'd fallen in love with Ben.

She'd fallen in love with her best friend. A man who didn't believe in love and marriage or commitment to any woman. She'd fallen in love with him and she didn't want him to leave. And yet by staying he would break her heart afresh every single day of her life to come.

And she would have to bear it.

Because Ben staying was what would be best for their baby.

CHAPTER ELEVEN

WITH HER DRESS mushroomed around her, her hair done up in a pretty knot and her golden shoulders drooping, Meg reminded Ben of a delicate orchid he'd once seen in a rainforest far from civilisation.

He swooped down and drew her back to her feet, his heart clenching at her expression. 'Don't look like that, Meg. We'll sort it out. I didn't mean to yell.'

He'd do anything to stop her from looking like that—as if the world had come to an end, as if there was no joy and laughter, dancing and champagne, warm summer nights and lazy kisses left in the world. As if all those things had been taken away from her.

'Meg?'

Finally she glanced up. He had to suck in a breath. Her pain burned a hole though his chest and thickened his throat. He dragged in a breath and blinked hard.

She lifted her chin and very gently moved out of his grasp. The abyss inside him grew.

'I'm sorry, Ben. What I asked Dave to do was unfair. I thought it would prove one way or the other whether you were ready for fatherhood.'

'I know you're worried. I can repeat over and over that I'm committed to all of this, but I know that won't allay your fears.' And he was sorrier than he could say about that.

'No.' She twisted her hands together. 'You've never lied to

me before. It shows an ungenerosity of spirit to keep testing you as I've done. Your word should be good enough for me. And it is. I do believe you. I do believe you'll stay.'

He eyed her for a moment. He wanted her to stop whipping herself into such a frenzy of guilt. This situation was so new to both of them. 'You don't need to apologise. You're trying to do what's best for the baby. There's no shame in that. Let's forget all about it— move forward and—'

'Forget about it? Ben, I *hurt* you! I can't tell you how sorry I am.'

She didn't have to. He could see it in her face.

'I let you down and I'm sorry.'

And how many times had he let *her* down over the years? Leaving her to deal with Laurie and Elsie on her own, expecting her to drop everything when he came home for a few days here and there, not ringing for her birthday.

'Although I don't think it's necessary, apology accepted.'

'Thank you.'

She smiled, but it didn't dispel the shadows in her eyes or the lines of strain about her mouth. His stomach dropped. *If I ever lost your friendship.* His hands clenched. It wouldn't happen. He wouldn't let it happen.

Music and laughter drifted down to them from the marquee. The lights spilling from it were festive and cheerful. Out here where he and Meg stood cloaked in the shadows of the garden, it was cool and the festivities seemed almost out of reach.

He swallowed and shifted his weight. 'You want to tell me what else is wrong?'

She glanced at him; took a step back. 'There's nothing.'

Acid filled his mouth. 'Don't lie to me, Meg.'

She glanced away. With her face in profile, her loveliness made his jaw ache. He stared at her, willing her to trust him, to share what troubled her so he could make it better. She was so lovely…and hurting so badly. He wanted—*needed*—to make things right for her.

She took another step away from him. 'Some things are better left unspoken.'

He wasn't having that. He took her arm and led her to a garden bench in the front yard. 'No more secrets, Meg. Full disclosure. We need to be completely open about anything that will affect our dealings with each other and the baby.' He leaned towards her. 'We're friends. Best friends. We can sort this out.'

She closed her eyes, her brow wrinkling and her breath catching.

'I promise we can get through anything.' He tried to impart his certainty to her, wanting it to buck her up and bring the colour back to her cheeks, the sparkle to her eyes. 'We really can.'

She opened her eyes and gazed out at the bay spread below them. 'If I share this particular truth with you, Ben, it will freak you out. It will freak you out more than anything I've ever said to you before. If I tell you, you will get up and walk out into the night without letting me finish, and I don't think I could stand that.'

She turned and met his gaze then and his stomach lurched. Some innate sense of self-preservation warned him to get up now and leave. Not just to walk away, but to run. He ignored it. This was Meg. She needed him. He would not let her down.

'I promise you I will not leave until the conversation has run its course.' His voice came out hoarse. 'I promise.'

Her face softened. 'You don't know how hard that promise will be to keep.'

'Another test, Meg?'

'No.'

She shook her head and he believed her.

Her hands twisted together in her lap. She glanced at him, glanced away, glanced down at her hands. 'I love you, Ben.'

'I love you too.' She had to know how much she meant to him.

She closed her eyes briefly before meeting his gaze again. She shook her head gently. 'I mean I've fallen in love with you.'

The words didn't make sense. He stared, unable to move.

'Actually, fallen is a rather apt description, because the sensation is far from comfortable.'

He snapped back, away from her. *I've fallen in love with you*. No! She—

'I didn't mean for it to happen. If I could make it unhappen I would. But I can't.'

'No!' He shot to his feet. He paced away from her, then remembered his promise and strode back. He thrust a finger at her. *'No!'*

She stared back at him with big, wounded eyes. She chafed her arms. He slipped his jacket off and settled it around her shoulders before falling back on the seat beside her.

'Why?' he finally croaked. He'd done his best to maintain a civilised distance ever since that kiss.

'I know.' She sighed. 'It should never have happened.'

Except…that kiss! That damn kiss on the beach. In the moonlight, no less. A moment of magic that neither one of them could forget, but…

'Maybe it's just pregnancy hormones?'

She pulled his jacket about her more tightly. 'That's what I've been telling myself, trying to will myself to believe. But I can't hide behind that as an excuse any longer.'

'Maybe it's just lust?'

She was silent for a long moment. 'Despite what you think, Ben, you have a lot more to offer a woman than just sex. I've been almost the sole focus of your attention this last month and a half and it's been addictive. But it's not just that. You've risen to every challenge I've thrown your way. You've been patient, understanding and kind. You've tried to make things easier for me. And I can see how much you already care for our child. You have amazed me, Ben, and I think you're amazing.'

His heart thumped against his ribs. If this were a movie he'd take her in his arms right now and declare his undying love. But this wasn't a movie. It was him and Meg on a garden bench. It was a nightmare!

His tie tightened about his throat. His mouth dried. He swallowed with difficulty. He might not be able to declare his undying love to her, but he could do the right thing by her.

'Would you like us to get married?'

'*No!*'

Ordinarily her horror would have made him laugh. He rolled his shoulders and frowned. 'Why not? I thought you said you love me?' Wasn't marriage and babies what women wanted?

'Too much to trap you into marriage! God, Ben, I know how you feel about marriage. The crazy thing is I would turn my nice, safe world upside down if it would make any difference. I'd follow you on your round-the-world yacht voyage, wait in some small village in Bhutan while you scaled a mountain, go with you on safari into deepest darkest Africa. But I know none of those things will make a difference. And, honestly, how happy do you think either one of us would be—you feeling trapped and suffocated and me knowing I'd made you feel that way?' She shook her head. 'A thousand times no.'

He rested his elbows on his knees and his head in his hands. His heart thudded in a sickening slow-quick rhythm in his chest. 'Would you like me to leave town? It'll be easier if you don't have to see me every day.'

'I expect you're right.'

He closed his eyes.

'But while that might be best for me, it's not what's best for the baby. Our baby's life will be significantly richer for having you as its father. So, no, Ben, I don't want you to leave.'

He stared. She'd told him he was amazing, but she was the amazing one. For a moment he couldn't speak. Eventually he managed to clear his throat. 'I don't know how to make things better or easier for you.'

She glanced down at her hands. 'For a start you can promise not to hate me for having made a hash of this, for changing things between us so significantly.'

He thrust his shoulders back. 'I will never hate you.' He and Meg were different from his parents. He lifted his chin. They would get their friendship back on track eventually.

'I expect I'll get over it sooner or later. I mean, people do, don't they?'

It had taken her father twenty years. He swallowed and nodded.

She turned to him. 'It's four months before the baby is due. Can we…? Can we have a time-out till then?'

She wanted him to stop coming round? She didn't want to see him for four months? He swallowed. It would be no different from setting off on one of his adventure tours. So why did darkness descend all around him? He wanted to rail and yell. But not at Meg.

He rose to his feet. 'I'll go play host for the rest of the evening. I'll help with the clean-up tomorrow and then I'll lock Elsie's house up and go.'

'I'm sorry,' she whispered.

'No need.'

'Thank you.'

He tried to say *you're welcome*, but he couldn't push the words out. 'If you want to retire for the night I'll take care of everything out here.'

'I'll take you up on that.'

She handed him back his jacket, not meeting his eyes, and his heart burned. She turned and strode towards the house. He watched her walk away and it felt as if all the lights had gone out in his world.

Ben moved into a unit in Nelson Bay. He should have moved further away—to the metropolis of Newcastle, an hour away and an easy enough commute—but he couldn't stand the thought of being that far from Meg. What if she needed help?

What if she needed something done before the baby came? She knew he was only a phone call or an e-mail away.

When he'd told her as much the day after the wedding she'd nodded and thanked him. And then she'd made him promise neither to ring nor e-mail her—not to contact her at all. He'd barely recognised the woman who'd asked that of him.

'It shouldn't be that hard,' she'd chided at whatever she'd seen in his face. 'In the past you've disappeared for months on end without so much as a phone call between visits.'

It was true.

But this time he didn't have the distraction of the next great adventure between him and home. Was this how Meg had felt when he'd left for each new trip? Worried about his safety and concerned for his health?

Always wondering if he were happy or not?

He threw himself into preparations for the big things he had planned for his future—things he'd only hinted to Meg about. Plans that would cement his financial future, and his child's, and integrate him into the community in Port Stephens.

But somewhere along the way his buzz and excitement had waned. When he couldn't share them with Meg, those plans didn't seem so big, or so bright and shining. He'd never re-alised how much he'd counted on her or how her friendship had kept him anchored.

Damn it all! She'd gone and wrecked everything—changed the rules and ruined a perfectly good friendship for something as stupid and ephemeral as love.

On the weekends he went out to nightclubs. He drank too much and searched for a woman to take his mind off Meg—a temporary respite, an attempt to get some balance back in his life. It didn't work.

I don't like the way you treat women.

Whenever he looked at a woman now, instead of good-time sass all he saw was vulnerability. He left the clubs early and returned home alone.

'Oh, you have it bad all right,' Dave laughed as they shared a beer one afternoon, a month after Ben had moved into his apartment in Nelson Bay.

Ben scowled. 'What are you talking about?' He'd hoped a beer with his friend would drag his mind from its worry about Meg and move it to more sensible and constructive areas, like fishing and boating.

'Mate, you can't be that clueless.'

He took a swig of his beer. 'I have no idea what you're talking about.' Did Dave think he was pining for greener pastures and new adventures? He shook his head. 'You've got it wrong. I'm happy to be back in Port Stephens, and I appreciate all your help over these last couple of months.'

Dave had tipped Ben off about a local eco-tourism adventure company that had come up for tender. There'd been several companies Ben had considered, but this one had ticked all the boxes. Contracts would be exchanged this coming week.

'This new direction I'm moving in is really exciting. I want to expand the range of tours offered, which means hiring new people.' He shrugged. 'But I've a lot of connections in the industry.' He meant to make his company the best. 'These are exciting times.'

Dave leant back. 'Then why aren't you erupting with enthusiasm? Why aren't you detailing every tour you mean to offer in minute detail to me this very minute and telling me how brilliant it's all going to be?'

Ben rolled his shoulders. 'I don't want to bore you.'

'Oh? And sitting there with a scowl on your face barely grunting at anything I say is designed to be entertaining, is it?'

His jaw dropped. 'I…' Was that what he'd been doing?

Dave leaned towards him. 'Listen, ever since you and Meg had that falling-out you've been moping around as if the world has come to an end.'

'I have not.'

Dave raised an eyebrow.

He thrust out his jaw. 'How many times do I have to tell you? We did not have a falling out.'

Dave eyed him over his beer. 'The two of you can't keep going on like this, you know? You have a baby on the way.'

Ben's head snapped back.

'It *is* yours, isn't it?' Dave said, his eyes serious.

Ben hesitated and then nodded.

'You need to sort it out.'

Ben stared down into his beer. The problem was they had sorted it out and this was the solution. He'd do what Meg needed him to do. Even if it killed him.

'Look, why don't you take the lady flowers and chocolates and just tell her you love her?'

Liquid sloshed over the sides of Ben's glass. 'I don't love her!' He slammed his glass to the table.

'Really?' Dave drawled. 'You're doing a damn fine impression of it, moping around like a lovesick idiot.'

'Remind me,' he growled. 'We *are* supposed to be mates, right?'

Dave ignored him. 'I saw the way you looked at her àt the wedding. You could barely drag your eyes from her.'

'That's just lust.' Even now her image fevered his dreams, had him waking in tangled sheets with an ache pulsing at his groin. It made him feel guilty, thinking about Meg that way, but it didn't make the ache go away.

Dave sat back. 'If it were any other woman I'd agree with you, but this is Meg we're talking about. Meg has never been just another woman to you.'

Ben slumped back.

'Tell me—when have you ever obsessed about a woman the way you've been obsessing about Meg?'

She was the mother of his child. She was his best friend. Of course he was concerned about her.

'Never, right?'

Bingo. But...

The beer garden spun.

And then everything stilled.

Bingo.

He stared at Dave, unable to utter a word. Dave drained the rest of his beer and clapped him on the shoulder. 'I'm off home to the wife and kiddies. You take care, Ben. We'll catch up again soon.'

Ben lifted a hand in acknowledgement, but all the time his mind whirled.

In love with Meg? *Him?*

It all finally fell into place.

Piece by glorious piece.

Him and Meg.

He shoved away from the table and raced out into the mid-afternoon sunshine. He powered down the arcade and marched into the nearest gourmet food shop.

'Can I help you, sir?'

'I'm after a box of chocolates. Your best chocolates.'

The sales assistant picked up a box. 'One can't go past Belgian, sir.'

He surveyed it. 'Do you have something bigger?'

'We have three sizes and—'

'I'll take the biggest box you have.'

It was huge. Tucking it under his arm, he strode into the florist across the way. He stared in bewilderment at bucket upon bucket of choice. So many different kinds of flowers...

'Good afternoon, son, what can I get for you?'

'Uh...I want some flowers.'

'What kind of flowers, laddie? You'll need to be more specific.'

'Something bright and cheerful. And beautiful.' Just like Meg.

'These gerberas are in their prime.'

The florist pointed to a bucket. The flowers were stunning in their vibrancy. Ben nodded. 'Perfect.'

He frowned, though, when the florist extracted a bunch. They seemed a little paltry. The florist eyed him for a moment. 'Perhaps you'd prefer two bunches?'

Ben's face unclouded. 'I'll take all of them.'

'All six bunches, laddie?'

He nodded and thrust money at the man—impatient to be away, impatient to be with Meg. He caught sight of a purple orchid by the till that brought him up short. A perfectly formed orchid that was beautiful in its fragility—its form, its colour and even its shape. It reminded him vividly of Meg on the night of the wedding.

He'd been such an idiot. He'd offered to marry her when he'd thought marriage was the last thing he wanted. He'd acknowledged that he and she were not his mother and father—their relationship would never descend to that kind of hatred and bitterness. He'd faced two of his biggest demons—for Meg—and still he hadn't made the connection.

Idiot!

Meg brought out the best in him, not the worst. She made him want to be a better man. All he could do was pray he hadn't left it too late.

The florist handed him the orchid, a gentle smile lighting his weathered face. 'On the house, sonny.'

Ben thanked him, collected up the armful of flowers and strode back in the direction of his car. His feet slowed as he passed an ice cream shop. Meg couldn't eat prawns or Camembert or salami, but she could have ice cream.

He strode inside and ordered a family-size tub of their finest. His arms were so full he had to ask the salesgirl to fish the money out of his jacket pocket. She put the tub of ice cream in a carrier bag and carefully hooked it around his free fingers.

She placed his change into his jacket pocket. 'She's a lucky lady.'

He shook his head. 'If I can pull this off, I'll be the lucky one.' He strode to his car, his stomach churning.

If he could pull this off. *If.*

He closed his eyes. *Please, God.*

CHAPTER TWELVE

MEG HEAVED A sigh and pulled yet more lids from the back of her kitchen cupboard. From her spot on the floor she could see there were still more in there. She had an assortment of lids that just didn't seem to belong to anything else she owned. She'd tossed another lid on the 'to-be-identified-and-hopefully-part-nered-up' pile when the doorbell rang.

She considered ignoring it, but with a quick shake of her head she rolled to her knees and lumbered upright. She would not turn into her father. She would not let heartbreak turn her into a hermit.

Pushing her hands into the small of her back, she started for the door. Sorting cupboards hadn't induced an early nesting instinct in her as she'd hoped—hadn't distracted her from the hole that had opened up in her world. A hole once filled by Ben.

Stop it!

Company—perhaps that would do the trick?

She opened the door with a ready smile, more than willing to be distracted by whoever might be on the other side, and then blinked at the blaze of colour that greeted her. Flowers almost completely obscured the person holding them. Flowers in every colour. Beautiful flowers.

Then she recognised the legs beneath all those flowers. And the scent of leather and whisky hit her, playing havoc with her senses.

That was definitely distracting.

Her pulse kicked. Her skin tingled. She swallowed. This kind of distraction had to be bad for her. *Very* bad.

She swallowed again. 'Ben?'

'Hey, Meg.'

And she couldn't help it. Her lips started to twitch. It probably had something to do with the surge of giddy joy the very sight of him sent spinning through her.

'Let me guess—you're opening a florist shop?'

'They're for you.'

For *her*? Her smile faded. An awkward pause opened up between them. Ben shuffled his feet. 'Take pity on a guy, won't you, Meg, and grab an armful?'

It was better than standing there like a landed fish. She moved forward and took several bunches of flowers out of his arms, burying her face in them in an attempt to drown out the much more beguiling scent of her best friend.

She led the way through to the kitchen and set the flowers in the sink, before taking the rest of the flowers from Ben and setting them in the sink too.

'Careful,' she murmured, pointing to the stacks of plastic containers littering the floor.

Every skin cell she possessed ached, screaming for her to throw herself into his arms. Her fingers tingled with the need to touch him. Ben had hugged her more times than she could count. He wouldn't protest if she hugged him now.

Her mouth dried. Her throat ached. The pulse points in her neck, her wrists, her ankles all throbbed.

She couldn't hug him. She wouldn't be hugging him as her best friend. She'd be hugging him as her dearest, darling Ben—the man she was in love with, the man she wanted to get downright dirty and naked with.

And he'd...

She closed her eyes. 'What are you doing here, Ben?'

When she opened them again she found him holding out a box of chocolates. 'For you.'

His voice came out low. The air between them crackled and sparked.

Or was that just her?

She took the chocolates in a daze. 'I...' She moistened her lips. 'Thank you.'

A silence stretched between them. She wanted to stare and stare at him, drink in her fill, but she wouldn't be able to keep the hunger from her eyes if she did. And she didn't want him to witness that. She didn't want his pity.

He started, and then held out a bag. 'I remembered you said you'd had a craving for ice cream.'

She set the chocolates on the bench and reached for the ice cream with both hands, her mouth watering at the label on the carrier bag—it bore the name of her favourite ice cream shop.

'What flavour?'

'Passionfruit ripple.'

He'd remembered.

She seized two spoons from the cutlery drawer, pulled off the lid and tucked straight in. She closed her eyes in bliss at the first mouthful. 'Oh, man, this is good.'

When she opened her eyes again she found him eyeing her hungrily, as if he wanted to devour her in exactly the same way she was devouring the ice cream.

She shook herself and swallowed. Maybe he did, but that didn't change anything between them. Sleeping with Ben wouldn't make him miraculously fall in love with her. Worst luck.

She pushed a spoon towards him. 'Tuck in.'

He didn't move. Standing so close to him was too much torture. She picked up the ice cream tub and moved to the kitchen table.

He'd brought her flowers. He'd brought her chocolates. And he'd brought her ice cream.

She sat. 'So, what's the sting in the tail?'

He started. 'What do you mean?'

She gestured. 'You've brought me the sweeteners, so what is it that needs sweetening?'

Her appetite promptly fled. She laid her spoon down. Was he leaving? Had he come to say goodbye?

She entertained that thought for all of five seconds before dismissing it. Ben wanted to be a part of their baby's life. He had no intention of running away.

She went to pick her spoon up again and then stopped. There was still another three months before the baby was due. Maybe he was leaving Port Stephens until then.

It shouldn't matter. After all, she hadn't clapped eyes on him for almost a month.

She deliberately unclenched her hands. *Get over yourself.* He'd only be a phone call away if she should need him.

Need him? She ached for him with every fibre of her being. And seeing him like this was too hard. She wanted to yell at him to go away, but the shadows beneath his eyes and the gaunt line of his cheeks stopped her.

She picked up her spoon and hoed back into her ice cream. She gestured with what she dearly hoped was a semblance of nonchalance to the chair opposite and drawled, 'Any time you'd like to join the party...'

He sat.

He fidgeted.

He jumped back up and put all the flowers into vases. She doggedly kept eating ice cream. It was delicious. At least she was pretty sure it was delicious. When he came back to the table, though, it was impossible to eat. The tension rose between them with every breath.

She set her spoon down, stared at all the flowers lined up on the kitchen bench, at the enormous box of chocolates—Belgian, no less—and then at the tub of ice cream. Her shoulders slumped. What did he have to tell her that could be so bad he needed to give her all these gifts first?

Flowers and chocolates—gifts for lovers. She brushed a hand across her eyes. Didn't he know what he was doing to her?

'I've missed you, Meg.'

And his voice...

'I needed to see you.'

She shoved her shoulders back. 'I thought we had an agreement?' He was supposed to stay away.

Was this a fight she would ever win? Her fingers shook as she pressed them to her temples. Would she ever stop needing to breathe him in, to feast her eyes on him, to wipe those haunted shadows from his eyes?

I love you!

Why couldn't that be enough?

She dragged her hands down into her lap and clenched them. 'Why?'

She might not be able to harden her heart against him, but she could make sure they didn't draw this interview out any longer than necessary.

'I realised something this afternoon.' The pulse at the base of his jaw pounded. 'And once I did I had to see you as soon as I could.'

Her heart slammed against her ribs. Just looking at him made a pulse start to throb inside her. She folded her arms. 'Are you going to enlighten me?'

He stared at her as if at an utter loss. 'I...uh...' He moistened his lips. 'I realised that I love you. That I'm *in love* with you.'

Three beats passed. Bam. Bam. Bam.

And then what he'd said collided with her grey matter. She shoved her chair back and wheeled away from him.

Typical! Ben had missed her and panicked. She got that. But in love with her? Fat chance!

She spun back and folded her arms. 'The Ben I know wouldn't have stopped to get flowers and chocolates if he'd had an epiphany like that. He'd have raced straight over here and blurted it out on the front doorstep the moment I opened the door.'

'Yeah, well, the guy I thought I was wouldn't have believed any of this possible.' He shot to his feet, his chair crashing to the floor behind him. 'The guy I thought I was didn't believe in love. The guy I thought I was would never have thought he could feel so awkward and at a loss around you, Meg!'

Her jaw dropped. She hitched it back up. 'None of that means you're in love with me. I accept that you miss me, but—'

'Then how about this?'

He strode around the table and shoved a finger under her nose. His scent slugged into her, swirling around her, playing havoc with her senses, playing havoc with her ability to remain upright.

'For the last month all I've been able to think about is you. I'm worried that you're hurting. I'm worried you're not eating properly and that you're working too hard. I'm worried there's no one around to make you laugh and to stop you from taking the world and yourself too seriously. Every waking moment,' he growled.

He planted his hands on his hips and started to pace. 'And then I worry that you might've found someone who makes you laugh and forget your troubles.' He wheeled back to her. 'Are you dating anyone?'

He all but shouted the question at her. For the first time a tiny ray broke through all her doubts. She tried to dispel it. This was about the baby, not her.

'Ben, no other man will ever take your place in our child's affections.'

'This isn't about the baby!' He paced harder. 'Every waking moment,' he growled. He spun and glared at her. 'And then, when I try to go to sleep, you plague my dreams. And, Meg—' He broke off with a low, mirthless laugh. 'The things I dream of doing to you—well, you don't want to know.'

Ooh, yes, she did.

'For these last two and a half months—eleven weeks—however long it's been—I've been feeling like some kind of sick pervert for thinking of you the way I have been. For having you star in my X-rated fantasies. I've struggled against it because you deserve better than that. So much better. It was only today that my brain finally caught up with my body. This is not just a case of out-and-out lust.'

He moved in close, crowding her with his heat and his scent.

'I want to make love to you until you are begging me for release.'

Her knees trembled at his low voice, rich with sin and promise. Heat pooled low in her abdomen. She couldn't have moved away from him if she'd wanted to.

'Because I love you.'

He hooked a hand behind her head and drew her mouth up to his, his lips crashing against hers in a hard kiss, as if trying to burn the truth of his words against her lips.

He broke away before she could respond, before she'd had enough...anywhere near enough.

He grabbed her hand and dragged her towards the back door. 'Where are we going?'

'There's something I want to show you.'

He pulled her all the way across to Elsie's yard, not stopping till they reached the garden shed. Flinging the door open, he bundled her inside.

In the middle of the floor sat a baby's crib. A wooden, hand-turned baby's crib. She sucked in a breath, marvelling at the beauty and craftsmanship in the simple lines. She knelt down to touch it. The wood was smooth against her palm.

'I've been coming here every day to finish it. I wait until you leave for work. I make sure I'm gone again before you get home.'

Her hand stilled. 'You made this?'

Drawing her back to her feet, he led her outside again. He gestured across to her garden. 'Who do you think is taking care of all that?'

For the first time in a month she suddenly realised how well kept the garden looked. She swallowed. It certainly wasn't her doing. She swung to him. 'You?'

'Tending your garden, making that crib for our baby—nothing has filled me with more satisfaction in my life before. Meg, you make me want to be a better man.'

He cradled her face in his hands. She'd never seen him more earnest or more determined.

'I want to build a life with you and our children—marriage, domesticity and a lifetime commitment. That's what I want.' His hands tightened about her face. 'But only with you. It's only ever been you. You're my destiny, Meg. You're the girl I always come home to. I just never saw it till now.'

For a moment everything blurred—Ben, the garden shed, the sky behind it.

'And if you don't believe me I mean to seduce you until you don't have a doubt left. And if you utter any doubts tomorrow I'll seduce you again, until you can't think straight and all you can think about is me. And I'll do that again and again until you do believe me.'

She lifted her hand to his mouth. 'And if I tell you that I *do* believe you?' She smiled. A smile that became a grin. She had to grin or the happiness swelling inside her might make her burst. 'Will you still seduce me?'

That slow, sinfully wicked grin of his hooked up the right side of his mouth. He traced a finger along her jaw and down her neck, making her breath hitch. 'Again and again and again,' he vowed, his fingers trailing a teasing path along the neckline of her shirt back and forth with delicious promise.

'Oh!' She caught his hand before he addled her brain completely.

'*Do* you believe me, Meg?' His lips travelled the same path his finger had, his tongue lapping at her skin and making her tremble.

'Yes.' She breathed the word into his mouth as his lips claimed hers.

The kiss transported her to a place she'd never been before—to a kingdom where all her fairytales had come true. She wrapped her arms about his neck, revelling in the lean hardness of his body, and kissed him back with everything she had.

It was a long time before they surfaced. Eventually they broke off to drag oxygen into starved lungs. She smiled up at him.

He grinned down at her. 'You love me, huh?'

'Yep, and you love me.'

Was it possible to die from happiness? She shifted against him, revelling in the way he sucked in a breath.

'You want to explain about the flowers and the chocolates?'

The fingers of his right hand walked down each vertebra of her spine to rest in the small of her back, raising gooseflesh on her arms. 'Dave said I should woo you with flowers and chocolates. I wanted to woo you right, Meg.'

She moved in closer. That hand splayed against her back. 'And the ice cream?'

'That was my own touch.'

'It was my favourite bit.'

His lips descended. 'Your favourite?'

'Second favourite,' she murmured, falling into his kiss, falling into Ben. *Her* Ben.

When he lifted his head again, many minutes later, she tried to catch her breath. 'Ben?'

'Hmm?'

'Do you think we can make our next baby the regular way?'

He grinned that grin. Her heart throbbed.

'You bet. And the one after that, and the one after that,' he promised.

* * * * *

THE SOLDIER'S
BABY BARGAIN

BETH KERY

My thanks to my editor, Susan Litman, for guiding me through this series with a sure hand and to Laura Bradford, my agent. As always, huge appreciation and a big hug to my husband for surviving yet another book with typical grace and patience.

Chapter One

Ryan Itani set down the magazine that he hadn't really been reading and glanced around the waiting room of the veterinarian's office. He wondered for the hundredth time if he shouldn't have tried to call Faith Holmes before surprising her while she was at work. If he were honest with himself, he'd have to admit he was worried that if he had called, she would have made an excuse not to see him.

Not that he blamed her. After what had happened last Christmas Eve, he technically couldn't hold it against Faith if she avoided him like the plague for the rest of her life. It would have been one thing if he'd stuck to his original mission that night three months ago—drive the twenty miles from Harbor Town to Faith's country house and pay his respects to his friend Jesse's widow. He'd been on three tours of duty with Jesse, both of them having served as pilots in the Air Force 28th Fighter Wing. He'd always respected Jesse's wife, Faith, always liked her openness and kind heart, appreciated her funny, warm letters to Jesse while they'd both been stationed in Afghanistan.

If he'd also thought Faith was one of the most stunning women he'd ever met, and that Jesse didn't deserve her, given his tendency for womanizing and infidelity, Ryan had kept that to himself.

Or at least he had until Christmas Eve.

Behind a partition, a dog barked loudly and a woman let out a shriek of alarm, bringing Ryan's straying thoughts back to the present moment. Another dog joined in the fracas. He heard a calm but authoritative woman's voice and went still. Faith had somehow passed him in the partitioned-off area of the waiting room where he sat. There must be another door leading from the exam rooms to the waiting area.

"Please put Knuckles's leash in the shortest, locked position, Mrs. Biddle." Faith's voice floated above the two dogs' loud barking. "You really shouldn't bring Sheba into the office without her container, Mr. Tanner. You can't blame Ivy and Knuckles for getting excited, seeing a cat unprotected like that. Jane, can you show Mr. Tanner and Sheba back to the examination room right away?"

"Sheba hates that container," a man grumbled. "*Sheba,* come back—"

"Wait, Knuckles! Oh, dear!" a woman moaned.

Ryan heard a sound like *omff* and sprung up from his chair. Rushing around the partition wall, he saw a gray, short-haired cat zooming across the room toward him. He bent and scooped it up into his arms without thinking before it had a chance to tear behind the receptionist's desk. When he straightened, he saw Faith in profile wearing a white lab coat, a skirt and pumps, her long, curling, dark hair rippling around her shoulders as she tried to restrain a scrambling Dalmatian puppy.

"Oh, no, Faith!" a short, blond-haired woman cried as she raced around the receptionist's desk. "Put him down. You shouldn't be holding a big dog like that in your condition."

"It's okay, I'm fine," Faith managed to get out as she soothed the squirming puppy.

"Here, I have the leash. Stupid of me, I somehow disconnected him when I was trying to restrain him by the collar," a frazzled-sounding, gray-haired woman in her fifties said as she grabbed Knuckles's collar. She reaffixed the leash, and Faith bent to deposit Knuckles on the floor.

Someone tapped on his forearm and Ryan pulled his glued gaze off the vision of Faith. What had the receptionist meant when she'd said *in your condition?* Was Faith ill? he wondered anxiously. He handed Sheba-the-cat to a husky black man in his twenties, nodding once distractedly when the man offered his thanks.

Faith was giving the gray-haired woman a weary smile. "Just remember—shortest, locked position for the leash for future office visits, Mrs. Biddle." She touched her belly as if to reassure herself.

It was a timeless gesture, and one Ryan immediately recognized.

Lightening-quick reflexes were an absolute must for a fighter pilot, and Ryan was known for being one of the fastest responders. In that moment, however, he uncharacteristically froze. An iron hand seemed to have clutched at his lungs, making breathing impossible. A thousand images and memories swept past his awareness as if he were a drowning man. One seemed to linger on the screen of his mind's eye: Faith answering the front door on Christmas Eve, her long, curling hair spilling around the snowy white robe she wore, her smile radiant, her large green eyes shining with emotion.

Ryan, I'm so happy you came.

Jesse would have wanted me to look in on you, make sure you were safe and sound.

He'd done more than just make sure Jesse's widow was safe and sound, though. A hell of a lot more.

Faith looked around and saw him standing in the waiting room. The stretched seconds collapsed.

"Ryan," she exclaimed in a shocked tone. The receptionist and all the patrons in the waiting room turned to gape at him. "What are you doing here?"

"I flew in for business," he said shortly, referring to the new charter airline business he'd begun after leaving the Air Force last December. His gaze flickered downward over Faith's belly before he met her stare again. He'd forgotten how vividly green her eyes were.

"I think we'd better talk," he said.

She bit at her lower lip anxiously and took a step toward him. All the color had left her cheeks.

"Yes. I think we'd better."

Faith took off her lab coat and hung it on the hook behind the door of her private office. She cast a nervous glance at herself in the mirror mounted on the wall.

She couldn't believe Ryan was *here.* And he knew. Somehow he'd guessed about the baby. She'd seen the stunned realization in his dark eyes as they'd stood there in the waiting room.

She tried to smooth her waving, curling tresses—hopeless cause. She sufficed by pulling the mass up onto her head and clipping it in place. It was probably better to look a little more…*professional* for this meeting anyway, she told herself as she pulled a few coiling strands down to frame her face.

Ridiculous, the idea of being professional. Her relationship with Ryan might be described as "nearly nonexistent" or perhaps as "friendly acquaintances" or perhaps *"odd"* but hardly "professional." Not after Christmas Eve. Seeing him standing there, so tall, so commanding, so intense—it'd brought it all back. How he must be regretting that impulsive, inexplicable moment of blazing lust now.

Afterward he'd suggested they'd acted out of the emotional turmoil of their shared remembrance of Jesse's death in a chopper accident a year before. He'd also worried that their impulsive tryst had ruined the chances of him being there for her. As a friend.

A dull ache flared in her breast at the memory. It'd hurt, having Ryan say those things. Maybe it was true, that the incredible heat between them had been generated from an emotional backfire. She couldn't be sure what had happened on that night.

True, he'd been grieving the loss of her husband, in more than the obvious sense. She'd learned in a particularly painful way just months before his death that Jesse had been unfaithful. Yes, she'd been grieving his death, but not in the same way a woman would be if she'd been in a happy, trusting marriage.

Another thought had haunted her after she and Ryan had started to come back to their senses that night. Perhaps *Ryan* was like a lot of top guns, craving the next female conquest in the same way he might hunger for the jolt of adrenaline that comes from a faster jet?

Maybe Ryan was like Jesse.

She straightened her spine. None of that mattered now, she thought as she touched her stomach. She had more important things to consider—like the future of her unborn child.

Anxious but determined, Faith walked into the waiting room. The first thing she saw upon opening the door was

Ryan. He sat facing her, his expression alert and stony. She met his gaze with effort.

His dark brown hair was short, but not military-short. It had started to grow out a bit since he'd become a civilian several months ago. His bangs fell onto his forehead, escaping the combed-back style. His lean jaw was dusted with whiskers. Although he looked entirely sober as he examined her, the lines that framed a firm, well-shaped mouth reminded her he was a man who liked to laugh.

When he wasn't still recovering from the shock of a lifetime, that is.

"Hi," Faith said shakily. She sensed an observant gaze and glanced behind the reception desk. Jane ducked her head and pretended to be utterly absorbed in the process of stuffing envelopes.

"We were able to clear about an hour and a half in my schedule, but I'm afraid we couldn't reach all of my patients' owners. I'm going to have to come back to work after we talk," she said nervously.

Ryan stood abruptly and came toward her. Funny— she'd only just left him in the waiting room forty-five minutes ago, but his height, his strength, his presence struck her anew. She found herself searching his features, trying to find some indication of what he was thinking or feeling. But Ryan wasn't known for being ice under pressure while performing complicated, dangerous flight maneuvers for nothing. Magnetically attractive and elementally male he might be, but she was learning he could be very difficult to read.

"Are you all right?" he asked tensely.

She blinked at the sound of his quiet, restrained tone. Perhaps he wasn't as impassive as she'd assumed.

"I'm fine. I'll explain everything." She waved toward the front door. She felt awkward and anxious. How did one go about telling a man that he was about to be a father? Not that the words really mattered. It was pretty clear to Faith that Ryan already guessed the result of that impulsive, foolish...*unforgettable* night.

"If we can just go somewhere private," Faith said.

He nodded once and touched her shoulder, encouraging her to go before him. Faith led him out the door. In a matter of days Holland, Michigan, would be blazing with color from its famous tulips and orchards, not to mention the brilliant sunsets over scenic Lake Michigan and Lake Macatawa. This afternoon, however, was a watered-down promise of what was to come. Weak sunlight fell on the budding trees and sprouting daffodils edging Faith's office building. She still felt the chill of winter in the mild breeze that touched her cheek.

"We can take my car," Ryan said, nodding toward a dark blue sedan in the nearly empty parking lot of her practice.

Faith's throat was too constricted with anxiety to respond. She said nothing as he opened the passenger-side door for her, although the very air between them seemed charged and electric with tension. They remained quiet as Ryan drove for a few minutes down the rural highway, and then pulled down a gravel lane that Faith knew led to a scenic lookout at Holland State Park. A moment later he stopped the car.

Both of them stared at the pale blue, rippling expanse of Lake Michigan and in the distance, the towering sand dune of Mount Pisgah. Faith struggled to find the right words, but nothing came. Nothing.

"You're pregnant," he said succinctly, breaking the silence.

"Yes."

A muscle jumped in his cheek and his hands tightened around the wheel. "Were you planning on telling me?"

"Of course," Faith said emphatically. She blinked back the tears that suddenly burned in her eyes and met his stare. "I was planning on calling you and telling you next week."

He closed his eyes. "So it *is* mine," he said in a choked voice.

"Yes," Faith whispered. "There isn't…there hasn't been anyone else."

"You told me on Christmas Eve that you were on the pill."

She swallowed convulsively. Here it was—her lie exposed.

"Ryan, I didn't want you to worry. I knew that if I told you we had unprotected sex that night—"

"That I wouldn't leave," he said abruptly. "And that was what you wanted the most, wasn't it, Faith? For me to vanish from your life?"

She closed her eyelids and a few tears spilled down her cheeks. "It was a mistake. All of it. You know that as well as I do."

His hands closed around the steering wheel in what looked like a death grip. "I don't know what the hell I thought it was," he said tensely. "I still hadn't gotten my bearings straight when you told me you didn't think we should see each other anymore."

"You told me you thought it'd been a sort of…emotional backfire, that we'd acted so impulsively because of Jesse's death. You were Jesse's good friend, a comrade in arms. I was—"

"His wife," he said.

"His widow," Faith corrected. *If he'd lived, I would have been his divorced wife by Christmas,* she added in her thoughts. Misery, anger and guilt swept through her—a potent, poison mixture of emotions with which she'd become all too familiar.

She wasn't sure how much Ryan knew about Jesse's affairs. Did they talk about them, perhaps share stories of sexual conquests, compare notes? Had Jesse confessed to him about his affair with Captain Melanie Shane? Melanie was a member of their wing, after all. She'd been the pilot and only survivor of the helicopter crash that had killed Jesse. Ryan might know that Melanie had contacted Faith and revealed her affair with Jesse months before the accident. He might already know Faith had filed for divorce at the time of Jesse's death.

Then again, he might not.

Most importantly, if Ryan had known about Jesse's infidelities, how much did that figure into what had happened between them at Christmas?

"When I said that thing about what happened between us being an emotional backfire, I was grabbing at straws," Ryan said in a low, vibrating voice. "I was looking for anything to help me understand how I could have taken advantage of a vulnerable woman—someone I care about. I returned to Michigan on Christmas Eve to offer support to my friend's widow. You know I always liked you...respected you, even if we'd only met a couple of times. What happened between us was the last thing I'd expected. I meant to make you feel better, but instead, I caused you harm," he said, wincing.

Her backbone stiffened. "You haven't *harmed* me. I'm thrilled about the baby, Ryan." He glanced at her, quick and wary, and she caught a glimpse beneath his stony, top-gun facade. For a brief second she saw the stark anxiety in his gaze. Her temporary irritation faded. She'd had three months to come to terms with the fact that her life was about to change forever. Ryan had had only an hour to absorb that mind-blowing reality.

"I don't expect you to be thrilled about it—at least not

right off the bat," she said quietly. "It's a shock. I know it's the last thing on earth you thought would happen."

Her hushed voice seemed to reverberate in the air between them.

"I want you to know I plan on sharing custody with you. I hope we can work together to make things as secure and comfortable for the baby as we can," she said, breaking the taut silence.

His face looked rigid as he turned and stared out at the great lake. Faith took the opportunity of his averted gaze to drink in her fill of the image of him. He had a great profile—a strong chin, straight, masculine nose; firm, well-shaped lips. *Hard.* That was the impression one got when they looked at Ryan. Tough as steel, honed, fast nerves, a brilliant mind. His body had been hard and honed as well, but also warm, sensitive, delightful for a woman to mold against…touch.

She inhaled sharply, willing her straying brain to come to order. His aftershave tickled her nose, the subtle, spicy, clean male scent triggering a wave of sensual memories. She knew from *that* night that the scent clung especially rich there at his nape at the edge of his hairline.

Her cheeks grew warm.

"I can't believe we're having this conversation," he said after a pause, forcing Faith to focus. "I can't believe you're going to have a baby."

"*We* are," she said softly. He turned his head and met her stare.

"Are you really happy about it?" he asked.

"I'll admit that at first I was pretty bowled over. It didn't take me long to get used to the idea…become excited," she said quietly, her fingers brushing against her abdomen instinctively. She paused when she noticed Ryan's stare on her hand. A warm, heavy feeling expanded in her belly and lowered. Her fingers seemed to burn beneath his gaze. How was it that he so effortlessly had this effect on her? She saw his strong throat convulse as he swallowed.

"So...you're about three months along?" he asked gruffly.

"I just started my second trimester."

"And the doctor says—"

"The baby is perfectly healthy. I've already had an ultrasound," she said, wonder filtering into her tone. Some of the miracle of that day came back to her unexpectedly. He was the father, after all, the cocreator of that tiny miracle she'd seen on the screen.

His expression looked flat. Faith realized she was witnessing a highly unlikely event firsthand—Major Ryan Itani in a state of shock.

"Ryan, are you all right?"

"Of course," he said. He blinked as if to clear the haze from his vision. "And you? You're healthy, as well?" he asked in a voice that struck her as strained.

She smiled reassuringly. "I'm fine. Completely healthy."

"What...what do you plan to do?" he asked after a moment.

"Do?" she asked bemusedly. "Well, have the baby, of course. Take care of it. Love it."

"All on your own?"

"I don't see why not. I have a good job. My practice is doing very well. I'm just as capable as any adult of taking care of a baby."

"Your parents moved to Florida a year ago," he said. "You don't have any other family remaining in the area, do you?"

"No, but that doesn't mean much. I doubt my parents would have been super excited to get involved anyway.

They're pretty involved with their own life. But I have good friends in town, like Jane."

"Your office manager?" he asked doubtfully.

She gave him a surprised glance. "Did you meet Jane while I was seeing patients?" she asked, referring to earlier, when he'd waited for her at her office.

He nodded distractedly. "She introduced herself. Besides, you talked about her on Christmas Eve, remember? You'd spent that evening with Jane's family."

"Oh, right."

An awkward silence settled. It struck her how bizarre this situation really was. She'd only met Ryan in person on two other occasions before Christmas Eve—at summer picnics for families of members of the 28th Wing while Jesse and Ryan had both been based in the Bay Area. She'd liked Ryan very much, and knew that Jesse's admiration for him bordered on worship. Ryan and she were both from Michigan, and Ryan had regularly spent his summers in nearby Harbor Town, so they'd had that in common. She'd enjoyed talking to him. She may have been married at the time, but she wasn't blind. Ryan was a very attractive man. Still, he'd never been in the forefront of her mind. Aside from those casual social events and constantly hearing his name mentioned by Jesse, Faith had known little else about him.

Christmas Eve had brought knowledge, of course, of the lightening strike of passion variety. But sharing a wild moment of lust with a man hardly qualified as true intimacy.

Now they were going to have a baby together. The strangeness of the whole thing was almost mind-numbing.

"You don't have enough people around you for support, Faith. I'm sure Jane is a good friend, but it's not the same as a family. We even talked about that very thing at Christmas."

Her mouth fell open. He'd been so approachable one

second, but now his serious tone sent a prickle of alarm through her. Surely he wasn't going to start dictating terms to her, was he? "I'll make do, Ryan. I'll figure things out."

"I'm all the way out on the West Coast."

"Well, I'm not moving."

He blinked, and she realized how emphatic she'd sounded. "Sorry—I know you weren't suggesting that, but well…please don't. Suggest it, I mean." She met his stare, hoping he'd understand. "I like my life here. I grew up in this area and think it'd be an ideal place to raise a child. I missed it during the years I traveled around with Jesse. Plus, I love my job. I'm proud of the practice I've built."

He studied his hands on the steering wheel. "You *should* be proud of it. You did it all on your own. Starting up this airline charter business, I know how much work that takes. How much dedication."

"Thank you for saying that," she said sincerely, some of her former tension draining out of her. "I don't blame Jesse for his job, or for the fact that it required him to be out of the country for a large chunk of our marriage. It forced me to be independent. I built my practice from nothing into something that's not only a thriving business, but an emotionally fulfilling one for me."

He studied her through a narrow-eyed gaze that she couldn't quite interpret. She avoided his laserlike stare, looking at her hands folded in her lap.

"I probably should get back to work," she said.

His hands slid along the steering will and he shifted the car into Reverse. He did a neat two-point turn and soon they were once again traversing the gravel drive.

"You mentioned being here on business." Faith attempted to bring the subject around to less charged topics. "How is your airline company going?"

"Really well. I've just been operating with the one plane,

with one other pilot besides myself, and an administrative assistant who does booking and some marketing work, but I'm about to expand," he said as he turned onto the highway.

"Really? That's wonderful, Ryan," Faith said enthusiastically. He'd mentioned to her casually while they talked at one of those Air Force picnics that he wanted to start up a charter airline business when he finally retired from the military. She'd been thrilled to hear when he paid her that unexpected Christmas Eve visit that he'd finally begun to live his dream. She was a little surprised at how gratifying it felt to her to know that Ryan was thriving and happy.

He gave her a sideways glance and smiled.

"Yeah. I've been flying a woman back and forth from this area to Lake Tahoe and San Francisco quite a bit— she has business to attend to in all those locations. Anyway, because I've been flying in and out of Tulip County Airport a lot because of this client, I've had my eye on a Cessna a man is selling there. I was going to make an offer on this visit. After I get a second plane, I'll be able to hire another pilot."

"That's great news," Faith said, even though her brain had gotten stuck on one thing that he'd said. "Tulip County Airport is so close."

"Yeah. Only a few minutes from here."

"So...you've been back to this area several times in the past few months?"

He glanced at her, doing a double take when he saw her expression. "Yeah," he admitted.

Her pulse began to thrum at her throat. "Why did you only come to visit me today?"

He stared straight ahead at the road, but she sensed the tension that leapt into his muscles. "You told me last Christmas you didn't think we should see each other again."

"Well, I know," she said awkwardly. "But you came anyway. I was just wondering—why today?"

His jaw tightened. He didn't immediately answer her, but focused on pulling into her office parking lot. Faith waited while he whipped the car concisely into a spot and put it into Park.

"I came because I'd hoped you'd had enough time to reconsider what you'd said that night," he said quietly. "Everything about what you told me today aside," he said, his gaze flickering down to her belly. "I was never convinced, like you seemed to be, that because of our...lapse, we should never see each other again. I came on that Christmas Eve to offer support to the widow of a good friend. Because it became more than that doesn't make it wrong."

Faith swallowed with difficulty, highly affected by the resonant timbre of his deep voice. An uneasy feeling settled in her belly. She shouldn't automatically assume that Ryan was like Jesse, but the only proof that she had was Jesse's joking, admiring references to the fact that Ryan could have just about any woman he wanted. He was in his mid to late thirties, and hadn't seemed to settle down into a monogamous relationship. After their all-too-brief encounter, she'd begun to wonder if he didn't consider sex in a similar vein to Jesse. Jesse and Ryan were both handsome, dashing pilots—the type of men that made female hearts flutter across the globe.

That was what had been behind her insistence that what had happened between them was a mistake.

That, and his references to their impulsive lovemaking ruining the potential *friendship* he wanted with her.

She hadn't changed her mind in the past three months. It seemed a lot more difficult to bolster her logic, however, sitting just feet away from Ryan and inhaling his spicy male scent. The last thing Faith needed was to get involved with another faithless man—not that Ryan was interested. Besides, she had the baby to think about now.

"Faith, what are you thinking?" Ryan asked. She realized he must have seen the turmoil on her face.

"I still think it was a mistake what happened between us. Just because a baby is going to come of it doesn't mean we should continue going down that wrong road. I know that when you showed up at my house on Christmas Eve, you weren't thinking about being strapped down with a woman and a baby."

"I'm not thinking of it as being *strapped down*," he said forcefully. "And just because I wasn't planning what happened doesn't automatically make it a mistake."

"I told you that I'm thrilled about the baby," she said sincerely. "It's a blessing to me. I've always wanted children. But the baby doesn't make it right for us to…*reconnect,* does it?"

He touched her jaw, the gesture in combination with his determined stare setting her off balance. His fingers felt warm and slightly calloused against her skin. She blinked in disorientation when he stroked the line of her jaw with his forefinger. "I think what's right is for us to spend more time together."

"Because of the baby?" she asked weakly.

His stare bored straight down into the core of her.

"No. Because I haven't been able to stop thinking about you since Christmas."

Chapter Two

Faith's pulse began to throb at her throat. She wanted to look away, but was ensnared by Ryan's eyes.

"Let me take you out to dinner tonight. We need to talk more," he said.

A battle waged in her breast. Part of her—the part that was getting breathless at the sensation of his skin touching her own—wanted very much to agree. Another part was wary, though. Her attraction for him could get her into a lot of trouble, and that was a potential heartache she'd already had enough of to last for three lifetimes.

Her practical side whispered to her that he only *couldn't stop thinking* about her since Christmas Eve because he felt guilty.

And yet she couldn't just ignore him. No matter how confused her feelings, Ryan was the father of her baby. Besides, she thought, breaking contact with his hand, there was a topic she really needed to broach with him.

"All right. As a matter of fact, there's something I want us to be on the same page about. It's about Jesse," she said.

He went still next to her, like a warrior suddenly sensing danger. "Okay," he replied slowly. "I suppose it's an inevitable topic, between us. Might as well face it head-on."

She gave him a puzzled glance.

"I just mean that Jesse's the common denominator between us." He hesitated. Faith had the impression he was choosing his words very carefully. "He must be on your mind a lot. That's understandable, especially now that…" He glanced briefly at her stomach and then out the front window. His jaw tightened.

Her heart went out to him. She knew from some of the things he'd said on Christmas Eve that he'd considered his actions to be the worst sort of treachery toward a friend. It didn't matter to him that Jesse had been dead for almost a year when they'd gotten together. Anger splintered through her at the thought. Jesse didn't deserve Ryan's show of loyalty. Not when Jesse himself had been so faithless.

"The baby has nothing to do with Jesse, Ryan," she said coolly, reaching for the door handle. "That's not what I wanted to talk to you about."

He put his hand on her shoulder, halting her exit. For a few seconds she thought he was going to demand that she tell him what she'd meant.

"I'll stop by your house tonight. Say six?" he said instead.

She nodded once, willfully ignoring her heart pounding in her ears, and stepped out of the car.

Ryan watched her through the window as she walked toward her office. Her figure still looked graceful and slender—from the back, anyway. He hadn't been able to stop himself from noticing as they sat in the car, however, that

her breasts appeared fuller than he recalled beneath the fitted, belted jacket she wore. His thoughts strayed to what
she'd felt like on that night—petal-soft, exquisitely sensitive skin sliding beneath his fingertips…his lips.

The sound of the office door shutting behind Faith made
him blink. His erotic memories scattered. What was he
doing, sitting here fantasizing about Faith when he'd just
gotten some of the most shocking, amazing news of his
life?

His mind went over their conversation. He'd wondered
incessantly if Faith knew about Jesse's womanizing. Something about her tension-filled reference to Jesse just now
had sent a warning bell going off in his head. Was Faith
planning to tell him that Jesse would forever be the love
of her life, that she deeply regretted their volatile, unexpected lovemaking?

Or was she going to tell him that she knew about Jesse's infidelities?

Damn.

He didn't know which possible truth pained him more.
He dreaded the possibility of hearing that Faith would eter-
nally be loyal to a man who was gone. He despised the idea
of how much Faith would have suffered at the knowledge
that Jesse had been unfaithful to her.

He took a moment to try to absorb everything that had
happened to him in the past few hours. No matter how hard
he tried, he couldn't do it.

Faith was going to have a baby, and he was the father.

She planned to raise the child here in Michigan, thousands of miles from where he worked and lived.

Being that far away suddenly become a reality he
couldn't bear.

It was bizarre to realize that just last Christmas, his
sister Mari had announced she was going to have another

baby. Until a few years ago Mari had been Ryan's only living family. Mari and her husband Marc Kavanaugh had had a daughter, and Ryan had felt blessed to add another name to the family list. Soon, he'd have another family member. It'd been amazing news to receive, even if there had been a hint of sadness mixing with his jubilation. He was thrilled for Mari, of course, but hearing about her pregnancy had made him wonder if he'd ever experience the same joy firsthand. Romance and women had come easily to him. Finding someone with whom he wanted to spend the rest of his life and build a family had proved to be much more elusive.

Strange, to consider in retrospect, that the same night Mari had announced she was going to have another baby, he'd driven the twenty miles from Harbor Town to Faith's house and done the unthinkable. He'd created his own.

He'd beaten himself up for losing control that night, but Faith had been so lovely, so fresh...so sweet. Had his admiration for her just been the surface of a much deeper attraction, feelings that had to be repressed given her marriage to his good friend?

He suspected that was the case. The only thing he knew for certain, Ryan thought grimly as he turned the ignition, was that there had been an inevitable quality to what they'd done on Christmas Eve. There was no changing it now. He wasn't sure he would, even if he could.

Instead of pulling out of the parking lot, he dialed a number on his cell phone.

"Deidre? It's Ryan," he said when Deidre Kavanaugh Malone, the client he'd flown to southwestern Michigan answered. Deidre was technically more than a client; she was extended family. Her brother Marc was married to Ryan's sister, Mari. He'd known Deidre since they were kids spending their idyllic summers in Harbor Town. Deidre had recently inherited a large fortune and was currently one of the wealthiest women in the country, but she remained the friendly, brave girl he'd always known.

Several months ago, Deidre and Nick Malone, the CEO of DuBois Enterprises, had set the business and social world ablaze with the news of their marriage. The financial world had assumed that Deidre and Nick, co-owner and leader of the DuBois conglomerate, would be natural adversaries. As an insider and friend to the couple, however, Ryan knew that immense wealth, media speculation and glitz and glamour aside, Deidre and Nick were deeply devoted to one another.

"Hi, what's up?" she asked.

"If it's all right with you, I'm going to have Scott fly in commercial to take you back to Lake Tahoe in a few days," he said, referring to Scott Mason, the other pilot that worked for his company, Eagle Air.

"That's fine with me," Deidre replied. "But is everything all right?"

"Yeah. I just got some news that is going to make it necessary to spend more time here in Michigan."

"Good or bad news?"

Ryan considered the question as he put the car in Reverse.

"Shocking...confusing...but good," he said. "Definitely good."

"I can't wait to hear about it."

"You will, eventually. It's not the kind of news that can stay a secret for long," he said dryly before he said his goodbye.

At six that evening Faith smoothed the black skirt over her hips and turned to examine herself in profile in the bathroom mirror. She hadn't gained a single pound so far with her pregnancy, something that her obstetrician insisted was perfectly normal for the end of the first trimester. Nevertheless her body weight seemed to be redistributing. There was a subtle curve to her once-flat belly and her breasts were starting to threaten to burst out of her bras. Faith kept having the strangest sensation that she was transforming…blooming like a flower.

She heard a knock at her front door. Topsy, her new puppy, began to yap loudly from the utility room. Her reflection in the mirror had previously been rosy-cheeked in anxious anticipation at going to dinner with Ryan. At the sound of his knock all of the color drained away.

She left the bathroom and hurried down the hallway to the front door. She couldn't help but relive racing toward the front door to greet him on Christmas Eve. Tonight's anxiety was worse, though. Much worse.

She swung open the front door. "Hi," she greeted upon seeing his tall, broad shouldered shadow on her stoop. "Come on in. I'm sorry about the racket."

"You got a dog?" Ryan asked, stepping into the foyer. Faith backed up, making room for him.

"Yes. A few weeks ago," she said, switching on the foyer light. For a split second they both examined each other. Faith blushed. Was he, too, recalling the other time he'd entered her house and they'd stood in this exact spot, inspecting each other with a sort of breathless curiosity? He looked fantastic—male and rugged, wearing a pair of jeans that emphasized his long legs and narrow hips, a white shirt and a worn dark brown leather flight jacket.

"You look great," he said.

"Thanks. You like nice, too," Faith murmured, feeling embarrassed. She'd worried she'd overdressed in the black skirt, leather boots and forest-green sweater. They weren't going on a *date,* after all. Despite that, she hadn't been able to stop herself from taking extra time with her grooming, even spending the ridiculous amount of time it took to straighten her hair with a flatiron.

She waved toward the interior of the house. "I just have to put Topsy in her crate, and I'll be ready to go."

"Topsy?" he asked, and she realized he was following her. She glanced over her shoulder.

"Yes, she was the runt of the litter from one of my oldest patients, a golden retriever named Erica," Faith explained breathlessly as they walked through the dining room and entered the kitchen. "All of Erica's purebred puppies went like hotcakes, but we had more trouble finding homes for this litter. Erica had an unexpected love affair with a local playboy—a spaniel-poodle mix. I was able to find homes for all of Topsy's brothers and sisters, but poor Topsy remained unclaimed."

"And so you couldn't resist adopting him…*her?*"

"Yes. Topsy's a she."

"You told me on Christmas Eve that you had a *strict* rule about pet adoption."

Faith paused next to the gaited entryway to the utility room. She blinked when she saw Ryan's mouth curved in a grin, his gaze warm on her face.

"If I took in every patient who needs a home that comes through my practice I'd be out of a home myself," she said.

Ryan didn't speak, just continued to study her with that knowing, sexy smile. Topsy yapped impatiently behind her.

Faith sighed and shrugged sheepishly. Ryan had her number, all right. "Well, I had a moment of weakness when I looked into Topsy's brown eyes. And like I told you," she said, her cheeks turning warmer even at the memory of their former meeting here in this house, "I had to take in Cleo—she's diabetic, and I couldn't convince anyone to do her injections every day. Smokey doesn't count, either, because who wouldn't give a home to a little thing like that?" Faith said, waving at the three-legged, pale gray cat that hobbled fleetly into the kitchen after them.

"There's no reason to be apologetic because you have a kind heart," he said quietly. He glanced down to his feet when Smokey brushed against his ankles. He bent and stroked the affectionate feline. Faith had been so offset by his candid compliment that she was glad for the interruption.

"Are you still serving as the president of the Animal Advocates Alliance?" he asked a moment later, standing.

"Oh, yes," Faith said enthusiastically, glad for a safer topic. Ryan knew about her charity work from Jesse. She'd been extremely touched when he'd made a generous donation to both the Armed Forces Foundation and the Animal Advocates Alliance in Jesse's name following the chopper crash that had killed him. She unhooked the gate that kept Topsy in the utility room. "The annual fundraiser ball is next week. I put a lot of hard work into it. Well?" she asked, glancing back at him. "Would you like to meet the Queen of Cute?"

"I can't wait," he said, walking toward her.

She started to open the gate wide enough for both of them to squeeze into the utility room without releasing the excited puppy, but noticed Ryan stared at her back door.

"What happened here?" he asked, pausing to look at the improvised "lock"—a thick piece of wood nailed to each side of the door. His eyebrows slanted in worry. "Nobody tried to break in, did they?"

"Oh, no. It's nothing. The old lock came loose, and I haven't had a chance to hire a locksmith to come and replace it yet." She shrugged. "It's not very pretty, but it'll keep things out. I've had a real rush of patients at my office as the weather warms up, and I just haven't had a chance to get it fixed."

"I'll come and put a lock on it tomorrow."

"Ryan, that's not necessary," she said, set off balance by his steadfast offer.

"It's not a big deal." Instead of waiting for her to inch back the gate—or to protest his offer—he just stepped over it.

"Hi, Topsy," he said.

Topsy wiggled in irrepressible excitement. She looked like a caramel-colored powder puff.

"I introduce you to Her Highness, Topsy-Turvy Blackwell."

"I was hoping she'd be a little bigger," he said.

"Oh, she'll still grow quite a bit."

"Yeah, but she doesn't look like she'll ever be much of a watchdog, does she?" he asked dubiously. He noticed her equally confused expression. "It is awfully isolated out here on this road."

He was obviously worried about the baby, Faith realized. "It's very safe here in the country, Ryan. I grew up in this house, and we've never had any problems. This area has one of the lowest crime rates in the state. It's quite safe and close to the population I serve, as well. Lots of my patients live on farms hereabouts."

Ryan didn't seem entirely convinced, but he refrained from disagreeing with her. Instead he bent his tall frame to pet the vibrating puppy. "How come you named her Topsy-Turvy *Blackwell?*"

"Oh. It's my maiden name. I plan to use it again, I just haven't gotten around to having it legally changed yet."

He looked up, his eyelids narrowing on her. She felt x-rayed. "I see," he said quietly, resuming petting Topsy.

"Do you?" Faith asked cautiously.

He didn't answer for a moment as he stroked the wriggling puppy. "I think I do. That's what you wanted to talk to me about tonight, isn't it?"

Faith swallowed thickly. A heavy sensation pressed down on her chest. Ryan knew that Jesse had been unfaithful to her. How else to explain his shuttered gaze and apparent discomfort? She experienced a wilting sensation. It was illogical and stupid, she knew, but it shamed her, to suspect he knew of Jesse's infidelities. No matter how much she rationally knew that Jesse had been in the wrong, she still felt vaguely substandard as a female, knowing he'd found other women more exciting than her, that she hadn't been sufficiently worth it for him to deny temptation and remain faithful.

"Yes, it is what I wanted to discuss with you. Among other things," she admitted, glancing away from his stare.

He nodded once and stood. "I guess we better get going, then."

She agreed. He helped her to put the squirming puppy into the crate.

"Topsy may not be ferocious, but you were right. She's the cutest thing I've ever laid eyes on," he observed a moment later as he opened the front door for her. Faith damned her pounding heart when he casually touched her waist as they walked together to his car.

"What are you hungry for?" she asked a few seconds later when he backed out of her driveway onto the rural road.

"I've already made reservations for dinner at Butch's Dry Dock, downtown." He glanced in her direction when she didn't immediately respond. "Is that all right?"

"Oh…yes," she said, flustered. "I love Butch's."

She couldn't tell him his response had set her off guard because he'd planned dinner with her at one of the nicest restaurants in the area. Despite her self-admonishments to remember that this was an opportunity to settle business with the father of her baby, the evening was, indeed, starting to feel more and more like a date.

An hour later Faith watched as Ryan leaned against the high-backed booth at Butch's, the remains of their delicious meal still on the table. Ryan had seemed intent on making her comfortable during their dinner, and his efforts were paying off. Her nervousness had slowly faded as the meal progressed and Ryan regaled her with some inevitable funny mistakes he'd made in starting up his business from scratch. It suddenly struck her that they hadn't yet landed on the topic of Jesse. She wondered if Ryan was avoiding the issue purposefully.

"Can I ask you a personal question?" Ryan asked, his eyes warm on her.

"It depends," she said, a smile flickering across her mouth.

"What's it been like for you? Being pregnant?"

"Oh," she said, her eyes going wide. "It's been...nice."

"You haven't been getting sick or anything?"

She nodded. "Yes, I got nauseous almost every day around the seven week mark, but believe it or not, I never threw up. It usually faded when I ate some crackers. I just had to make sure I didn't let my stomach get empty. It's gotten much better in the past week."

"And fatigue?"

Again, she nodded, this time more emphatically. She paused while a busboy came to clear their table. "That was probably the worst of it." She resumed when they were alone again. "Once I figured out why I felt like taking a nap by ten o'clock every morning, it seemed to help things, though."

"When did you find out? That you were pregnant?" he asked.

"When I was about five weeks along."

"I wish you would have called me."

The back of her neck prickled with awareness at the sound of his low, resonant voice.

"I meant to tell you all along, Ryan. Please believe that. I was going to tell you at the same time I told my parents."

"I believe you. You're much too honest to make me think otherwise."

She gave him a thankful smile. "I just wanted to get through my first trimester safely."

"I understand," he said. She searched his face. Seeing not a hint of anger, she sighed in relief.

"Ryan, there's something I want us to be on the same page about," she approached the topic cautiously after the waiter brought them coffee and tea. She sensed the tension that flew into his muscles.

"About Jesse?" he asked.

She nodded, took a deep breath for courage and blurted out the details of discovering Jesse's infidelities. She was learning to read him, she realized after a minute or two of talking almost nonstop. Most people would have called his flat expression impassive, but that slight widening of his eyes meant all-out shock on Ryan's face.

"I can't believe it," he said. "Melanie Shane *contacted* you, and told you about her affair with your husband?"

Faith nodded and poured hot water over her tea bag. The pain that went through her at the vivid memory was lessening now, altering from the stab of betrayal to the ache of regret. Mostly she was mad at herself for not facing the truth earlier. Jesse was charming and funny and dynamic, but he was *not* a one-woman man.

Nor a two-woman man, for that matter.

Sometimes it was just easier to be blind to the obvious.

"It was a few months before the crash. She found me through my veterinary practice's website," she said. She set down her spoon and met Ryan's stare. "I'm just thankful that I happened to open the emails that morning. Often, Jane does it before me."

Ryan shut his eyes briefly. Pain flickered across his hard face and was gone. "They had the most volatile relationship. Jesse and Melanie were either fighting like cats and dogs or they were—"

He stopped abruptly. Their stares held as she finished his sentence in her mind.

"When Melanie first wrote me, she was in quite a state," Faith said after a long pause. "Apparently she'd discovered that Jesse had slept with a lieutenant who trained airmen on computers at the airport. Melanie was pretty upset by it."

Ryan grimaced. "Damn. I can't believe Melanie did that." He exhaled heavily. "Strike that. I can. She'd get herself into a real state at times, when it came to Jesse. I suppose she had herself convinced she was doing you a favor by pouncing on you with the news?"

Faith nodded. "Bingo. You'd think we were blood sisters, both betrayed by the devil."

Ryan grunted. "When in reality, Melanie was feeling furious and rejected by what Jesse had done. She ran blabbing to you because she knew it would hurt Jesse. She never gave a thought or care about what she was doing to you. I'm sorry, Faith."

"It's not your fault. You have nothing to apologize for."

A muscle flickered subtly in his cheek. She shook her head sadly.

"You are *not* responsible for Jesse's actions," she stated the obvious.

"I'm responsible for my own."

Faith swallowed uneasily. Is that how he thought of her and the baby? A responsibility? A burden?

"What was Melanie like?" she asked shakily after a moment, trying to divert his attention.

Ryan shrugged and poured some cream into his coffee. "A good chopper pilot. Volatile. Bit of a daredevil. Feisty exterior with a vulnerable core," he mumbled succinctly.

"She was…pretty?"

He glanced up, pausing in the action of setting down the small pitcher. "Some men might have found her attractive," he said with what struck Faith as forced neutrality.

She stared at the snowy-white tablecloth. Much to her surprise, given the topic, she wasn't that upset. She'd suspected all along she wasn't as devastated by the news as she should have been that Jesse was unfaithful. She'd been hurt. Jesse had been her husband, after all, and she'd planned to spend the rest of her life with him—before she'd discovered his infidelities.

But deep down she knew that if Jessie'd been the love of her life, that email from Melanie—and Jesse's eventual admission that Melanie's accusations were valid—wouldn't have just been an unpleasant shock. It would have been a lancing, debilitating blow to her spirit.

Jesse had been so full of life. She'd often reflected after she'd learned of his infidelity that she didn't want to be Jesse's wife anymore, but she would have wished him well. Always. It hurt, to think of him not out there in the world somewhere…raising hell, warming someone with his smile and his jokes, hopefully finding the happiness she couldn't give him.

She became aware of Ryan's gaze on her—warm, concerned, wary. So, he *had* known all along about Jesse's womanizing. How did that knowledge factor into their impulsive, impassioned tryst on Christmas Eve? How would it play into the fact that they were going to have a baby together? It was becoming increasingly clear that Ryan felt some sort of misguided responsibility toward her.

"Don't pity me," she said.

"I don't pity you," he said, his eyebrows pinching together in apparent bewilderment at her quiet forcefulness.

"No?" she asked, calmly removing the chamomile teabag from her cup. "You don't have some kind of knight in shining armor syndrome going on for the scorned wife? You said that you visited me last Christmas Eve because you wanted to make sure I was okay…safe. Now that I'm pregnant, I don't want you feeling regretful, Ryan. I need a father for my baby, not a guilty lover. I don't want you to feel sorry for me."

The spoon he'd been using to stir his coffee fell several inches to the saucer with a loud clinking sound. "That's insulting."

She met his stare levelly, difficult though it was. His eyes blazed like black fire. "Then why did you act so guilty about Christmas Eve? I'm not the fragile victim you're imagining. If that was part of the appeal that night, you were misguided," she said quietly.

He placed his forearms on the table and leaned toward her, his nostrils slightly flared. "I didn't *know* whether or not you knew about Jesse and Melanie on Christmas Eve. For all I knew, you were still grieving the love of your life. I wanted you so much, I went ahead and did what I did anyway. So much for the idea that I'm *pitying* you."

The anger clinging thickly to Ryan's words didn't have quite the effect on her that she would have thought. For some reason, the memory of their fevered joining chose that moment to bombard her consciousness like rapid-fire bullets—Ryan's hands moving over her in carnal worship, his mouth closing over the tip of her breast and the answering sharp pain of longing in her womb, the feeling of him filling her until she was inundated by him, ready to burst with her desire.

By slow degrees she became aware that the blend of voices and clanking cutlery and china had become a distant buzz in her ears. Ryan blinked as if awakening from a trance and sat back in the booth.

"I am far from thinking that you're a weak victim." His gaze flickered up to meet hers. "I like you. I have from the first time Jesse ever read me one of your letters. I liked you even more when I finally met you. I respect the way you've built up your business and your life, even though you were a military wife and alone a lot of the time. I admired how you always managed to be so cheerful…convey so much warmth. I used to get resentful when Jesse didn't return your letters regularly. I used to get resentful toward Jesse for a lot of things," he mumbled under his breath, looking angry…*torn.*

"Can I bring you any dessert?"

Both of them blinked and stared at the waiter like he was an alien.

"Faith?" Ryan asked.

"No, nothing for me," Faith said.

Ryan also declined and the waiter left. Faith took a long drink of her ice water.

"That all still sounds like you're feeling sorry for me, Ryan," she said shakily.

"I don't pity you, but I do feel bad about some things that have happened," he said quietly. "I feel like a heel for barging in on you and laying you down on a couch and having unprotected sex with you after I'd been in your house for all of a half hour."

Her mouth fell open at his blunt words. Once again

the remembered images and sensations swamped her awareness.

"Let me get this straight," she said slowly. "You like me, and you respect me, but because you wanted to have sex with me that night, that's a problem. Is that because you usually don't like and respect the women you sleep with? Attraction and respect don't go together in your mind?"

"That's a hell of a thing to say."

"Jesse used to imply that you liked female companionship, but weren't much for a serious relationship with one woman."

Realization subtly settled on his features. His eyelids narrowed. Faith caught an edge of the diamond-hard focus that had made him such a valuable officer and pilot. "Are you implying I'm like Jesse?"

She tilted her chin up, refusing to be intimidated. "Maybe."

"Well I'm not," he stated flatly. "I'm not saying Christmas Eve was a mistake because I'm a womanizer. I'm saying it was a mistake because it was so abrupt…strange… irrational…"

Mind-blowing, Faith added in her private thoughts. His gaze flickered up to meet hers, as if she'd spoken aloud.

After a tense moment she exhaled and sagged in the seat. "I'm sorry. It's not my place to judge you one way or another. That part of your life is none of my business."

She glanced up in surprise when he reached across the table and grasped her hand.

"Just because I haven't found the right woman yet doesn't mean I haven't been looking. I don't thrive on conquest. Christmas Eve was *not* about that."

She couldn't look away from his eyes. His hand tightened on hers, his fingers brushing her wrist. She wondered distantly if he could feel the throb of her pulse.

"What was it about then?" she whispered.

Something flickered across his rugged features she couldn't quite identify. "I'm not entirely sure. It just felt… unstoppable. Like I said that night, all that emotion must have been building."

"You do hear about it happening after a tragic death," Faith admitted. "Stuff builds up and then…bang. A lightening strike."

They stared at each other across the table. Was he, like her, recalling what it'd been like as the electric desire blazed in their flesh, enlivened them, fused them?

"We're going to have a baby together," he said. "All of my life is your business now. Fate has seen to that. Whether we planned it or not, whether you like it or not, we're family now, Faith."

Chapter Three

When they walked out onto Eighth Street later, the sun was setting.

"How about a drive? There are a few things I'd still like to talk to you about," Ryan added when she gave him a doubtful sideways glance. He's sensed her wariness ever since he'd said that thing about them being family.

"Okay," Faith replied, although she looked uncertain.

He grabbed her hand and gave it a small squeeze as they walked toward his car. He waited for her to look at him.

"Why are you so uncomfortable around me? Is it just because of the baby?" he couldn't help but ask.

"You're not entirely comfortable around me, either, Ryan. I think we both know this situation is…unusual."

He grimaced slightly. He'd been more than a little confused about his feelings for Faith for a long time now. Finding out she was carrying his baby only amplified his bewilderment along with a lot of other emotions.

He'd never been able to tell anyone he had a sort of secret...*thing* for Jesse's wife for years now. It was too mild to be a crush. Ryan had secretly found his partiality for news about Faith or hearing her letters a little amusing in a self-deprecating sort of way. His feelings for her had never gone anywhere beyond admiration.

But as he drove through picturesque downtown Holland with Faith in the seat next to him, he'd have to admit it in hindsight that he'd been a little envious of Jesse for having a wife like Faith. It wasn't just that Faith was beautiful in the natural, girl-next-door, very sexy kind of way. He was drawn to her freshness, her intelligence, and most of all, her kindness.

He'd been highly irritated at Jesse for proving time and again that he didn't deserve her.

The fact of the matter was, until Christmas Eve, he'd never given his admiration for her much thought. She'd been off-limits for almost the entire time he'd known her. Maybe Jesse wasn't the ideal husband, and perhaps Ryan had questioned his judgment as an officer for getting involved with women during deployments, but Jesse had never done anything overtly to make Ryan question his ability to do his job. As a matter of fact Jesse had been a fine pilot, and in the friendship department at least, loyal to the bone.

The sun blazed bright orange, about to make its fiery plunge into the silvery waters of Lake Michigan when Ryan pulled the car into a lot at Laketown Beach. Because of the dunes, they were on a high vista. The beach itself was at the bottom of a long staircase. He shut off the ignition and glanced at Faith. He found the black leather, calf-hugging boots she wore extremely sexy, but wasn't so sure the heels were walking-friendly.

"There's a paved path along the bluff. Are you up for a walk?"

"Yes," she agreed.

She smiled at him a moment later when he came around the car to meet her. "I know you spent your summers in Harbor Town, but you seem very familiar with Holland, too."

He shrugged as he zipped up his jacket. There was a cool breeze coming off Lake Michigan. "My mom and dad used to bring us to Holland occasionally for dinner or a day at the beach."

"I think you said your parents have passed?" she asked softly. He recalled he'd mentioned to her that his parents were no longer living at one of those Air Force picnics, but hadn't given her any details.

"Yeah. They died while I was still at the Air Force Academy in Colorado. Dad used to like to explore the area when he'd come down on the weekends from Dearborn, so Mari—that's my sister—and I have seen pretty much every beach on the Michigan shoreline. I've done some exploring on my own in Holland for the past couple months, though," he said as he took her hand and they made their way down the sidewalk that trailed along the edge of the bluff. "When Deidre comes in for an overnight visit, I stay at a hotel near the airport."

"Deidre is the client you fly to this area?"

"Yeah, Deidre Kavanaugh Malone. When we were kids, the Kavanaughs lived on the same street as us in Harbor Town."

He glanced around in surprise when Faith suddenly came to an abrupt halt.

"Deidre's not *Brigit* Kavanaugh's daughter, is she?" Faith asked.

"Yeah. Faith?" he prompted, slightly alarmed when he saw her flattened expression.

"But that means…Ryan, was it your *parents* that were killed in that terrible car wreck all those years ago?"

Ryan inhaled slowly. "Yeah. How did you know?"

"I know Brigit Kavanaugh."

"How?"

"She's a member of the Southwestern Michigan's Women's Auxiliary. It's one of their missions to offer deployed military family members support. She came to visit me after Jesse died last year, and we've become friends." He saw Faith's throat tighten as she swallowed. Her face looked stricken. "She told me about her husband getting drunk and causing that accident. She told me that a couple had been killed that had lived just down the street from her. Oh, Ryan," she finished in a whisper. Tears filled her green eyes. "I'm so sorry. We heard about that crash here in Holland when I was a teenager, but I didn't recall any specific details. Brigit never mentioned names. I never realized…your *parents.*"

"It's okay, Faith," he said, concerned by her pale cheeks and obvious distress. He didn't have to think twice about taking her into his arms. She came willingly, hugging his waist as if to give him comfort. He lowered his head and pressed his mouth to her hair. He inhaled the achingly familiar scent of citrus and flowers. "It happened a long time ago," he murmured, lifting his head and willing her to look up at him. When she did, he used his thumb to gently wipe off several tears from her cheek.

"But you and your sister were so young. Did you have other family?"

"Only an aunt in San Francisco," Ryan murmured distractedly as he continued to touch her cheek. Her skin was incredibly smooth and soft. "She passed away a few years ago, though."

"I'm so sorry, Ryan," she said in a choked voice.

His heart squeezed a little in his chest. She seemed genuinely pained by the news that his parents had passed away almost seventeen years ago. He stopped drying her cheeks and palmed her delicate jaw.

"You're an amazingly nice woman, do you know that, Faith? Jesse never deserved you."

She blinked. Ryan realized how intense he'd just sounded. He hadn't meant to speak his thoughts out loud, but seeing Faith's lovely, troubled face and experiencing her compassion had caused the words to pop out of his throat. He regretted it when she released her hold on him and took a step back. A lake breeze whipped past them and Faith tightened the belt on her coat.

"Maybe we ought to skip the walk," Ryan said.

"No. No, let's walk over to that bench and watch the sunset," she said. "It's funny," she said a moment later as they sat side by side on the wooden bench next to the path. "I grew up watching these sunsets, but I never get tired of them."

"Kind of hard to get tired of something like that," Ryan agreed. For a few seconds they both watched silently as the ball of fire began to dip below the horizon, shades of magenta, pink and gold splashing across the sky in its wake.

"It's not too hard to believe you're pregnant," he said, studying her delicate, lovely face cast in the pink and gold shades of the sunset. Her face didn't "glow" like the stereotypical pregnant woman, but there was a sort of soft luminescence to her that he found compelling. "You've never looked so beautiful."

The pink in her cheeks wasn't caused by the sunset, he realized. Another breeze whipped past them, this one chillier. He leaned back on the bench and put his arm around her. Much to his satisfaction, she let her head rest on his shoulder. For several seconds they watched the sunset in silence. He felt entirely aware of her in those moments, of her firm, curving body, of her sweetness, the scent of her hair, the lock that fell just next to the pulse at her white throat. He brushed away the lock, stroking her skin in the process. Her shiver vibrated into his flesh. He braced himself for her reaction to what he was about to say.

"I can't leave you alone here, Faith," he said gruffly.

She lifted her head and studied him dazedly. "What do you mean?"

"I respect the fact that you want to raise the baby in Holland. It's your home. But I'm not comfortable with living three thousand miles away while my child is here."

Regret swept through him when he saw alarm flash into her eyes. She straightened, breaking the contact of their bodies.

"What do you plan to do?" she demanded.

"I'll move back to Michigan," he replied simply.

She blinked. "Ryan, you can't be serious. You've lived in San Francisco for years now. You started your new business out there. You can't expect to just pack up and move to Holland."

"It'll take some doing, I'll grant you that. But it'd be better to do it now, before the business grows any larger. I can even rent hangar space at Tulip County Airport. I've been giving it a lot of thought since this afternoon. It might be better for me to be centrally located versus on the West Coast, given the nature of my business. Actually, the beach area of Michigan is an ideal location to serve business people in Detroit and Chicago, and I've already make loads of contacts out west."

Faith stared at him like he was slightly mad as he spoke

his thoughts out loud. "Ryan, that seems so…sudden. Impulsive."

"Despite all the evidence against me from Christmas Eve, I'm not an impulsive person. But I do trust my instincts." He traced the line of her jaw with his forefinger.

She met his stare. He didn't bother to guard his desire for her. Her eyes widened slightly, and he knew she'd seen it. Was she, like him, thinking of those ecstatic moments when they'd both acted on glorious instinct? He hoped so. He wished like hell those memories had been permanently scored in her brain like they had been in his.

"I think we should talk about it more," she said in a voice barely above a whisper. "I'm not so sure instinct is the wise guiding principle for the future, given the fact that a baby is involved."

"I think it's the perfect principle."

"Why do you say that?"

"It got us here, didn't it?"

She stared at him in mute amazement.

Ryan scowled at the sound of voices in the distance. He turned his head and saw another couple approaching on the walk.

"Come on. It's almost dark," he said. "We can talk more in the car."

Faith's mind was a confused hodgepodge of thoughts, feelings and concerns as Ryan drove through the now dark streets of Holland. While they waited at a red light, Ryan turned toward her.

"You're vibrating with worry over there. Why don't you vent some of what you're thinking?"

She met his stare. His rugged features looked shadowed and compelling in the dim light.

"Are you really serious about moving back to Michigan?" she asked in a voice that sounded unnaturally high to her own ears.

"Is it really that unbelievable?"

"I just…I just hadn't expected that you might want to do that."

"Why not?" he asked, looking slightly puzzled. The stoplight turned green and he began to drive. "Did you really think I was going to be blasé about the fact that I was going to have a child?"

"I don't know," Faith stated honestly. "I guess I just assumed you'd…"

"Be satisfied seeing the baby a few times a month and on half the holidays?" Ryan asked when she faded off uncertainly.

"Well…you're a pilot," she said, as if that explained something.

"And?"

"Pilots are always on the go. One place is as much home as another. I just assumed you wouldn't consider the distance between Holland and San Francisco as significant as most people would."

He came to a stop at an intersection of a quiet residential neighborhood. "Family is very important to me, Faith. It always has been. That value was instilled into me a long time ago by my parents."

Her throat grew tight. "And then you lost them at such a young age," she whispered feelingly. Of course family was important to him.

"Besides, if I move back to Michigan, I'll be closer to my sister and her family. Mari is in Chicago. She's going to have another baby, too." He blinked as if in realization and gave her a small smile. Her heart seemed to throb as if in answer. "As a matter of fact, she's only a few months ahead of you."

"The baby will like having a cousin of the same age," Faith said, returning his smile.

The moment stretched as they sat there in the running car in the silent neighborhood, staring at one another and considering the future.

Ryan finally cleared his throat and resumed driving.

"You never told me if you knew the sex of the baby," he said.

She shook her head. "Not yet. I hadn't decided yet if I wanted to know or be surprised. Do you?" He glanced at her quickly. "Want to know?"

She watched as his expression went blank. He looked almost grim as he stared out the front window.

"I don't know," he said hoarsely after a moment. "One second, I think this whole thing has settled in, and the next I feel…"

"Overwhelmed?" she wondered.

He nodded once.

"I understand. It takes a while to fully absorb it," she said quietly. She studied his profile as he drove, wondering over the fact that she was sitting in the car with Ryan Itani—her former husband's good friend, the father of the child that grew in her womb…one of the most magnetically attractive and masculine men she'd ever encountered.

Maybe she was still overwhelmed, as well.

He pulled into her driveway a few minutes later. Faith studied her hands in her lap as he put the car in Park. She needed to banish this pervasive nervousness. She needed to get used to dealing with Ryan, with being around him.

"Would you like to come in and have a cup of coffee?"

"Yes." The bluntness of his reply made her head come up. In the dim dashboard lights, she could see him studying her. "But I'm going to say no, nevertheless," he added.

"Why?"

He abruptly turned in the seat as far as he could, given his big body and the confining space of the car. He took both of her hands in his. Spikes of pleasure prickled up her arms when he caressed her wrists with slightly calloused thumbs.

"I still want you, Faith. I think it's only fair to tell you that."

She started, shocked by his bold statement. She stared out the window to her neat, attractive ranch house, trying to gather her thoughts. It was hard with him stroking her skin and what he'd just said echoing around in her brain. She reached wildly for the threads of logic spinning around with a vortex of doubts and desire.

"You're just saying that because you're confused about the baby," she said.

"You said I was saying it last time because I was confused about Jesse's sudden death. When are you going to believe that I've always found you attractive, Faith?"

She looked at him in alarm.

"I never would have done anything while Jesse was alive. That's not my style. I know it's not yours, either," he said in a low, compelling voice. "The truth is, I didn't allow myself to think about it very much. You were another man's wife. Off-limits. I wouldn't even call my feelings toward you attraction. They were respect. Admiration. I liked you a lot."

She stared at him, her throat and chest feeling full—achy. She couldn't look away from his stark, handsome face.

"My feelings for you would have stayed in that holding pattern if circumstances hadn't changed. But they *did* change. You discovered Jesse wasn't faithful to you."

"I was filing for a divorce at the time he was killed," she said, shocking herself.

Ryan's expression tensed. His caressing fingers paused. "You were?"

She nodded. A tear spilled down her cheek. She was angry at Jesse for his infidelity. Furious. So why did guilt still rear its ugly head inside her when she thought of the fact that she'd been planning on leaving him when his life was cut unexpectedly short?

"I told him that I planned to divorce him when he admitted to his affairs with both Melanie and that other officer that worked at the airport. He was so upset about the divorce. He never told you?" she asked shakily, searching his face.

"He never said a word about you two breaking up," Ryan said. His flat expression told the absolute truth. Jesse had kept the impending end of their marriage to himself. Maybe he'd hoped she'd change her mind. He might have died with that secret. The realization caused a pain of regret to go through her. She shuddered. Damn these hormones. Since her pregnancy, she cried at the drop of a dime. Suddenly Ryan's arms were around her. She clutched on to his shoulders and wept.

"It's just...you knew Jesse. He was like a kid at times. I know he wasn't capable of being faithful. I know I wasn't meant to be his wife. But I cared about him."

"I understand," Ryan soothed, stroking her back. "Maybe he wasn't capable of being faithful to you, but I do know that Jesse cared about you, too."

"I hate to think of him dying, knowing that I was leaving him," Faith managed between bitter tears.

"I'm sure he was feeling regretful about having hurt you."

That made her sob harder.

"I'm sorry," he said, stroking her arms and back. "I shouldn't have said that."

"No. No, it's true. I suppose some people would feel vindicated that he felt guilty on the day he died, but I think it's just..."

"Terrible," Ryan finished for her. "I understand."

"Do you?" she asked wetly, leaning back slightly in order to see his face. His features looked like they'd been carved from rock in the dim lights emanating from the dashboard.

"Yeah. I think we both know that while Jesse might not have been ideal husband material, he was a good guy in a lot of other areas of life. It's got to be hard for you, thinking of him dying knowing that he'd done you wrong."

"Exactly," she whispered shakily.

"It's still not your fault, Faith. You didn't do anything wrong. You had every right to file for divorce once you learned he'd cheated on you, not once, but several times. It's just that life took a rotten turn in the interim, and Jesse was killed. You have absolutely nothing to feel guilty about."

"I know," she said weakly. She touched the side of his neck along his hairline. His hair was a pleasure to her fingertips—crisp and soft at once. "I'm always telling myself I didn't do anything wrong. I just wish I hadn't told him about the divorce when he was about to..."

Ryan shook his head, his face now rigid with compassion. "You're not all-seeing." He cradled her jaw gently. She went still, utterly aware of the intimate contact. "Death is the same way. You can't beat yourself up for things you don't have any control over. All we can do is take what we've been given and make the best of it."

His breath was warm and fragrant against her upturned lips and nose.

"I want to make the best of *this,* Faith—for whatever is happening between you and me," he said, his voice like a rough caress. "Part of me feels guilty for making love to you last Christmas Eve, but I'm tired of apologizing for it, sick of beating myself up about it. How can I apologize when it felt so damn good…so damn right?"

And suddenly his mouth was covering hers, warm, firm and once again, Faith was lost in the sensual storm that was Ryan.

Chapter Four

No one kissed like he did, Faith thought dazedly. His mouth felt like it was made to fit hers. He plucked at her with movements that struck her as languorous and demanding at once; he sandwiched her lower lip between his and bit at the sensitive flesh lightly, making her gasp. When she opened her mouth, he slid his tongue between her lips, a sleek, sensual invader. Ripples of pleasure cascaded down her spine.

He made a sound of male gratification as he tasted her, sweeping his tongue everywhere, exploring her...possessing her. Faith responded in the only way her muddled brain and buzzing body seemed to know how to respond to Ryan's sensual assaults—wholeheartedly. She tangled her tongue with his, absorbing his flavor, feeling their kiss in the very core of her being. She'd noticed that pregnancy had made her body extra sensitive, her sense of smell and taste more acute, her breasts plagued by a dull, not unpleasant ache.

Adding Ryan to the formula only seemed to amp up her sensitivities to a whole new level of feeling.

She tightened her hold on his hard shoulders, pulling herself toward him, pressing their upper bodies together. Feeling her breasts press against the solidness of his chest made her moan softly into his mouth. As if electrified by the sound, Ryan leaned into her further. His hands moved along the side of her body, molding his palms over her rib cage as if he wanted to feel her heartbeat. He touched the sides of her breasts and gave a low, tense moan, deepening their kiss. Pleasure rippled through her, the strength of it shocking her. Even through her coat and clothing, his caress had the power to make her forget her inhibitions and recall her elemental femininity all too well.

A shock went through his body. They broke apart. He cursed a second later when his thigh hit the gearshift.

"Are you all right?" Faith asked anxiously.

"Yeah. This just isn't an ideal location for this," he muttered, trying to arrange his long body in the seat. What *this* actually meant penetrated Faith's lust-befuddled consciousness.

"It's not the ideal *situation* for it, either," she said starkly, leaning back, breaking their contact. She stared out the front window, letting her arms fall to her sides, regretting the loss of Ryan's hard male body almost as much as she did the feeling of his hands sliding off her torso. She breathed deeply, trying to find some sanity. One second they'd been pressed together too tight to slip a match between them, and the next, they were separate…

…alone.

She suffered through a tense moment of silence before he spoke.

"Just because the situation is unusual doesn't mean it's wrong."

She couldn't help but give a bark of hysterical laughter. "*Unusual?* Don't you think you're stating it a bit mildly? I'm pregnant with my dead husband's friend's baby, whom I hardly know. I'd say that's a bit more than unusual. Ryan? What are you doing?" she asked in amazement when he unfastened his seat belt and reached for the door handle.

"I'm walking you to the front door. We'll talk about this more tomorrow."

"Tomorrow?" she asked, eyes wide.

"Yeah," he said, pulling the latch. He glanced back at her. She saw that his features were tight with regret. "I didn't mean to upset you. I don't know how many times I can say that without sounding like a fool or a liar."

Faith shut her eyelids and took a deep breath to restore her calm. "I'm okay, Ryan. I'm not upset." She opened her eyes and regarded him. "You have to admit, though…this whole thing is awfully strange."

"Strange, maybe," he conceded, swinging his long legs onto the driveway. "Not awful, though. Far from awful."

Later that night Faith lay in bed wide awake, her hand curved protectively over her belly, staring blankly at the ceiling. What was she going to do about Ryan's decision to move to the area? Did she have a right to do or say anything? Didn't he have a right to be near his own child, if he chose?

What was she going to do about him *period*?

Despite her anxious thoughts, her errant brain kept returning to that kiss in the car. She'd learned at Christmas that logic and kissing Ryan did not go hand in hand. For the past three months thoughts of that night would sneak up to plague her during the dark, quiet hours when she had nothing else to distract her from them. In the interim of Ryan's absence she'd almost convinced herself that what had happened on that night was an aberration of memory. Surely Ryan's kiss couldn't be that wonderful, his touch that powerful.

But now he'd kissed her again, and she could no longer deny the truth.

The first part of that visit on Christmas Eve had gone reasonably well, Faith recalled. At first she'd been aware of a certain tension in the air upon seeing Ryan so unexpectedly for the first time in two years. He hadn't been given a leave of absence to attend Jesse's funeral, so she hadn't seen him then. Every time she'd met with him before, it'd been within the safety of a large gathering…within the security of her marriage.

Faith hadn't fully realized until later that evening, however, that the thick tension between them on Christmas Eve had been of the sexual variety.

Perhaps she shouldn't have served him a glass of her spiked Christmas punch? It'd be convenient to blame what happened later that night on alcohol consumption, but Faith suspected very strongly that Ryan had been right when he'd said the experience felt unstoppable, Christmas punch or no.

She vividly recalled how stunned and pleased she'd been when he'd called that night and said he was nearby.

"This is wonderful," Faith said when he entered the house, bringing a brief blast of cold winter air with him. "What are you doing back in Michigan?"

"I'm visiting my sister, Mari," Ryan said, his gaze dropping over her robe-covered figure regretfully. "I'm sorry it's so late. I should come back tomorrow."

"Don't be ridiculous! Come with me to the kitchen. I have some punch left over. I'll get us a cup and we'll talk."

"Jesse used to say your punch had more juice than an F-15."

"The way he used to drink it, he was right," she said, smiling as she glanced back at him.

He chuckled. "I don't want to be any bother. I'll stop by another time...if that's all right," he added cautiously.

"Of course it's all right, but you're not a bother now. I was only going to bed because I didn't have anything better to do."

"Were you here alone?" he asked when she flipped on the kitchen light. She did a double take when she saw the concerned expression on his face.

"I wasn't alone. I went over to a friend's house—she's my office manager, actually."

"Oh, yeah. Jane, right?"

She paused, stunned. "How do you know about Jane?"

He shrugged. "Jesse used to read me your letters."

She blushed and glanced away.

"Not...not all of them, just portions," he hurried to say. "I hope you don't mind. Entertainment on a deployment is kind of scarce, but warmth and affection from a loved one is an even rarer commodity."

"So you shared some of Jesse's?" she murmured.

"Not in a weird way or anything," he said, looking a little uncomfortable.

She laughed softly. "Don't worry, I don't take offense. There was nothing in my letters that couldn't have been read on the base announcement system, anyway. I just tend to ramble on in my letters like a crazy woman."

"I liked them. You're a good writer. You could get published, telling all those stories about your practice. Some *of them were really funny. I could sense your personality through your words."*

"Thanks," she said, both flustered and flattered.

"So...you were with Jane tonight?"

"Yes," she said, swinging open the refrigerator. "She has a huge family. Half the people there assumed I was a long lost cousin. It was nice," she said, pulling out the plastic-covered large bowl she'd used to transport the punch.

"Really?" he asked pointedly.

"What do you mean?" she asked, twisting her chin to look over her shoulder.

"I was at a family gathering tonight, where I was the outsider," he admitted, stepping closer and closing the refrigerator door for her. "I was at my sister's in-laws' family gathering in Harbor Town. I'm glad you felt like you belonged. Personally, I felt the urge to run a couple times, but I was there at my sister's request."

She paused in the action of removing two cups from the cabinet. "Well...maybe I did exaggerate my comfort level with Jane's family a little bit. Still, it's nice not to be alone. On Christmas."

"Yeah. Now we can not be alone together," he said, smiling.

Their gazes stuck. She realized she'd frozen in her task. She hurried to fill their glasses.

Ryan's eyebrows shot up a moment later when he took a drink.

"Jesse wasn't exaggerating. Now I get why they call it punch," he said, blinking.

She laughed. "We'll keep it to one glass, but we could use some Christmas cheer, right?"

"Right."

She smiled and turned and replaced the bowl in the refrigerator.

"Merry Christmas," she said when she rejoined Ryan a moment later, holding up her glass.

"Merry Christmas." They watched each other over the rims of their glasses as they drank.

"I'm sure you have plans for Christmas," she said after they talked a while. "But I hope you'll consider yourself invited here, if you have any free time. I'll make a nice lunch or dinner for us. And your sister and her family are invited, too, if they'd like to come."

"That's very generous," he said slowly. "I guess I shouldn't be surprised."

"What do you mean?" she asked.

"Jesse used to say you didn't know a stranger."

"You're not a stranger," she said, smiling. "I feel like I know you as well as some people that I see every day of my life." The full awareness of what she'd just said—of how much she'd meant it—seemed to soak into her brain slowly. When it fully penetrated, she'd looked at Ryan cautiously, her breath stuck in her lungs.

He stared at her. Black lashes emphasized eyes that were so dark brown they verged on black. She would have thought eyes that color would be cold in appearance, but Ryan's shone with warmth.

With heat?

She spilled a little of her punch on her robe when she stood too abruptly. Ryan sprung up almost as rapidly. She laughed awkwardly as she wiped away the red liquid with her hand.

"Clumsy," she muttered under her breath. Now her hand was all sticky. "Uh, excuse me...I just need to..."

"Faith?" he called when she rushed over to the kitchen sink and turned on the water.

"Yes?" she asked, glancing around to see he'd followed her and set his half-empty glass on the counter.

"You don't feel like a stranger to me, either."

She stared, her mouth partially opened in amazement at his stark declaration.

His deep voice seemed to ring in her head three months later as she lay in bed. Faith kept telling herself to stop remembering—reliving—every detail of that night. She told herself to forget.

The problem was, part of her rebelled against that very idea. Part of her clung on to the memories of feeling so alive…so cherished. He'd made her feel so special, made her so aware of her femininity, made her prize again what Jesse had found replaceable.

Part of her treasured the memories of Ryan, and that part was only growing since he'd come back into her life. That realization worried Faith.

It worried her a lot.

She was in the process of doing Saturday morning chores when she heard a car door slam. Her heart lurched against her breastbone when she peeked out the window and saw Ryan's car in the driveway. He'd said that he'd stop by again today, but she hadn't expected him so early.

She dropped the curtain and glanced at herself in the vanity mirror. She'd washed her hair this morning, but hadn't styled it. It'd dried into a wild riot of curls, which she'd restrained in a low ponytail at her neck. She wore an old pair of low-rise jeans and a simple white T-shirt. The shirt was a lot tighter than she ever remembered it being before, and the jeans kept slipping down her hips while she worked, resulting in her newly expanding belly protruding over the waistband.

A brisk knock resounded down the hallway. Topsy charged to the front door, yipping ferociously the entire time. Panicked, Faith flung open her closet and grabbed an old flannel shirt. She hurriedly slipped it on, and then hitched up her uncooperative jeans. She grabbed Topsy before she opened the front door.

Ryan stood there in the sunshine holding a toolbox. His dark hair fluttered in the spring breeze. He wore a pair of well-fitted jeans, brown work boots and a dark blue thermal shirt with a T-shirt beneath it. He pretty much epitomized the sexy tool man that every female with a healthy pulse on the planet would love to invite into her house.

She mentally rolled her eyes at the errant, ridiculous thought and opened the screen door for him.

"Is this a good time?" Ryan asked.

"Er…a good time for what?" she wondered, her gaze running over the line of his slightly whiskered jaw and well-shaped mouth.

His lips tilted ever so slightly.

"To fix your back door. Unless you had something else in mind. I'm flexible."

Faith realized his gaze had dropped. She'd tried to close the flannel shirt over the revealing T-shirt, but Topsy had wiggled her way into the opening, parting the material. Her nipples prickled beneath Ryan's warm glance. Heat rushed into her cheeks.

"Fixing the back door would be great. If you're sure you don't mind?" she asked, flustered. She tried to tug the flannel shirt closed over the strip of bare skin above her jeans. She backed up so that he could enter. If he were just a few inches taller, he'd have to duck his head to not hit the doorframe. As soon as the door was closed, she set down Topsy, who yipped and frolicked on Ryan's boots and around his ankles. The puppy wagged her entire bottom, not just her tail, as he bent to pet her.

"Am I interrupting anything?" Ryan asked after he'd stood.

"No," she said, leading him to the kitchen, hurriedly buttoning the flannel shirt. "I was just doing some cleaning, and I have to attack the den later."

"Attack?" he asked. She heard the smile in his voice before she glanced back to see it. His wind-ruffled dark hair fell attractively on his forehead. "Sounds pretty hardcore."

"I keep procrastinating on it," Faith said as she watched him set down his toolbox next to the back door. She realized she was staring at his rear end as he bent over and glanced away, blushing.

"What's the hurry?" Ryan asked, flipping open the lid on the metal box.

"Well, the baby coming, I guess."

He paused at that, his head swinging around. She felt herself being examined by his incisive stare.

She gave him a weak smile. "The den is going to be the nursery. I have to clear it all out before I can start to decorate and buy the furniture."

She saw the color wash out of his face beneath his tan. He just stood there, holding a hammer and looking stunned.

"Ryan? Are you okay?"

After a second he nodded. He stepped toward the door. "It's really going to happen, isn't it?" he said after a moment. "You're actually going to have a baby."

She nodded, giving him a quizzical glance. He shook his head slightly, as if to clear it. "I woke up this morning, wondering if it had all been a dream," she heard him mutter as he lifted the claw of the hammer to loosen the piece of plywood.

"Like I said, it takes a while to set in. It seems a little surreal to me all over again, with you being here," she admitted.

For a stretched second they looked at one another. Then Ryan inhaled and returned to his task. "I'll come and help you with the den after I finish here. Do me a favor?"

"What?" Faith asked.

"Don't lift anything heavy or overexert yourself."

She crossed her arms at her waist. "You make it sound like pregnancy is a frailty. I'm very healthy."

He arched his eyebrows at her defiance, his mouth twitching in a grin. "I agree. I'd just like to keep it that way."

She couldn't help returning his small smile. It was difficult to get miffed at him when he was so charming. Still, she wouldn't want to set a precedent with him for allowing heavy-handedness.

"I'm perfectly capable of taking care of myself. And the baby," she said, quietly but firmly.

"There's no doubt about that. But I'm the baby's father, and I want to help. No reason for me not to do the heavy jobs," he said, pulling on the hammer and prying the nails out of her back door like it was made of butter instead of wood. He gave her a sideways glance. "*I'm* capable, too, Faith. And willing."

Faith couldn't argue with that. He was, indeed, capable…at many things. She wasn't sure how to respond to that knowing look in his eyes when he'd admitted to being *willing,* as well. She felt her cheeks heating and figured it was best to retreat for now.

"Would you like me to make you some coffee?"

He shook his head, his attention now so entirely on his task she might have imagined the heat in his eyes right now. "I'm good."

"Then I'll be in the den."

"I'll be there in a while," Ryan replied briskly.

True to his word, he joined her in the den a little less than an hour later. Faith glanced up when he entered the room and towered over where she sat on the floor next to her old hope chest.

"All finished in the kitchen," he said, glancing around the room. His gaze stuck on an old Holland High School booster banner tacked on the bulletin board. "I thought you said this was the den. It looks like your old bedroom."

"It was," Faith admitted. "When I bought the house from Mom and Dad, it sort of became a combination den and storage room. I have another guest bedroom for visitors, and I moved into the master suite. This room gets the best morning sunlight, though, so I thought it'd be ideal for the nursery."

She held up the high school report card she'd found in the trunk. "I can't believe my mother saved some of this junk," she said before she started to throw the card into a plastic garbage bag. Ryan halted her with a hand at her wrist. She glanced up in surprise when he took the report card from her. He stood there, examining it, an amused expression lighting his carved features.

"Straight A's in trigonometry, chemistry, AP English and economics." His eyebrows went up. "A C minus in gym class?"

Faith blinked in embarrassment and stretched to snatch the card out of his hand. She tossed it into the garbage bag and gave him a rueful glance.

"We had softball that quarter. I can't hit a ball for anything. Let's hope the baby gets your athletic abilities and reflexes, and not mine," she mumbled, smiling grudgingly. She looked up in amazement at the sound of his deep laughter. He knelt on the carpet next to her, still chuckling. Her grin widened. She went still when he leaned toward her and picked up a curl that had fallen over her shoulder. She didn't move as he rubbed the coil of hair between his fingers, his expression growing thoughtful.

"I hope the baby gets your curls." He met her stare. "And your smile."

She stared at him, wide-eyed. Suddenly, the space between them seemed very small. The air itself seemed to grow heavy, like a pocket had just been formed around them and was shrinking by the second. She couldn't think of what to say.

She couldn't think, period.

"Can I ask you a favor?" he asked in a subdued, serious tone.

She just nodded, her lips falling open. He met her gaze solemnly.

"Can I touch our baby?"

Chapter Five

When she didn't speak immediately, she saw his muscular throat tighten as he swallowed. "It's just that it's been really hard for me to absorb this. It might help me. It might make it more real somehow…"

He trailed off when she just continued to stare at him. He tightened his hands on his thighs.

"Never mind," he said gruffly. "I'm sorry I mentioned it."

"No," Faith said quickly, regret filtering through her entrancement. His request was incredibly intimate, but not in the sexual sense. It was as if her brain didn't quite know how to interpret his question. "I'm sorry. You just took me by surprise," she said, coming up on her knees and facing him. She smiled nervously. "I understand about finding it hard to accept. I didn't really start to soak it in until I saw the ultrasound."

"What was it like?"

"Incredible. You could see the heart beating," she said in a hushed voice.

"Wow." A strained silence followed as they just looked at each other. "Do you think I could come? For the next ultrasound?"

She nodded.

"Thanks."

"I have a picture of the baby, Ryan. I'll show it to you."

"That'd be great."

She told herself to stand and get the ultrasound photo, but instead she remained kneeling there. Her heart went out to him. How difficult it must be for him. She had the baby with her every second of every day—a warm, wonderful secret growing within her very flesh. It seemed so unfair, to keep him separate from that awesome experience.

Slowly she began to unbutton the flannel shirt. He went utterly still, the only exception being his dark-eyed gaze flickering downward, following the path of her fingers.

Faith hesitated when she saw that the thin T-shirt had again wormed its way up over the nearly insubstantial bump in her belly, while her low-riding jeans had gone in the opposite direction. She willfully ignored the heat that rushed into her cheeks, however. Hadn't Ryan just asked if he could come to the next ultrasound? She might as well get used to allowing him to see her naked stomach.

She opened the flaps of the flannel shirt and glanced up with effort. Her hands trembled slightly as she held the fabric when she saw that his dark eyes weren't trained on her belly, but on her breasts pressing tightly against the white cotton. The silence seemed to take on weight. His gaze lingered, and then lowered over her.

Had she just thought that his request was intimate, but not sexual? She'd been wrong, Faith realized as her heartbeat began to throb in her ears and he stared at her belly. It was both.

In spades.

Her mouth went dry when he reached with one hand, and gently pulled up the T-shirt to her waist. She held her breath until it burned in her lungs when he placed his hand over her abdomen. She knew from experience that her belly felt taut and smooth. His hand looked dark next to her pale skin, his fingers long and strong. He nearly encompassed her width. A warm pressure spread at her core, making her ache.

She glanced up at him, her curiosity overcoming her embarrassment. His face looked rapt. When his gaze flickered upward, she gave him a shaky smile.

"Pretty awesome, huh?" she said softly.

"Amazing," he agreed, looking like he meant it in the literal, not everyday usage of the word. He moved his hand. His palm was warm against her bare skin.

"Can you feel the baby moving yet?" he asked.

She shook her head. In his leaned-over position, his face was very close to hers. She could smell his spicy, clean scent. They'd taken to talking in hushed tones, as if they were conversing at a sacred event. Which they were, Faith supposed.

"The doctor says I should at around sixteen to twenty-two weeks. Maybe later, since it's my first pregnancy."

"So this *is* your first pregnancy."

She blinked in surprise, but then caught what he'd meant. It was possible that she'd gotten pregnant before, and lost the baby. "Yes. I've never been pregnant until now. Jesse wasn't interested in having children," she said gently.

He didn't say anything, just glanced back down to his hand on her stomach. He moved it slightly, spiking tendrils of pleasure through her flesh.

"Ryan?" she asked quietly. He looked up at her, his expression solemn.

"Did you? Want a child? Someday, I mean?" she clarified.

"Yes."

She gave a tremulous smile. The conviction in his voice had been absolute.

"Well...even if the timing and circumstances weren't what you might have wanted, I'm glad that your wish came true," she whispered.

"Thank you. For making it come true," he said quietly.

Her lips parted, but she couldn't speak. She was caught in his stare. Neither of them spoke when he lifted his hand. Somehow she knew what he was about to do. She didn't protest when he gently cupped her right breast. The heavy, pleasurable ache at her center amplified to a slow burn.

"You're changing here, too," he said gruffly.

She stifled a gasp when his fingers moved, ever so slightly, grazing a sensitive nipple. "Yes."

"Are you planning on breast-feeding?" he asked.

When she didn't immediately respond, his gaze flashed up to her face. She nodded, her throat too tight with emotion to speak. His nostrils flared. He seemed to come to himself. He dropped his hand and stood. Faith looked up at him helplessly. His face was rigid and difficult to read, but his tense muscles and hard body betrayed his arousal.

He excused himself and walked out of the room, leaving her spinning in confusion and desire.

After taking a few minutes to compose himself, Ryan returned to the den. Regret hit him when he saw Faith glance up at him from where she still sat on the floor, her face looking pale, her eyes huge. She'd rebuttoned the flannel shirt, which amplified his guilt, but also gladdened him. All in all, he thought it was best for the time being that she cover herself from his greedy gaze. The last thing he wanted to do was to alienate her, but seeing the subtle transformation of her lovely body had moved him deeply.

It had also been one of the most erotic experiences he could ever imagine—touching her. If that had been true on Christmas Eve, it was even more so now that his child grew inside of her.

A child.

Their baby.

And people said miracles didn't happen anymore. Couldn't they see they occurred every day, right in front of their eyes?

"What should I tackle first?" he asked, forcing his mind to the mundane and glancing around the room. He was glad to see the tension seep out of her face.

"Oh, well I suppose you could start with the closet? Pretty much everything in there is stuff that I've already gone through and want to throw away."

"What about all this furniture?" he asked, inspecting the large cherry desk, bureau and full-size bed.

"I was planning on hiring movers to do that. I'm going to donate the bed and bureau to the Salvation Army. They said they'd come and pick it up with their truck if I got the items out into the driveway. As for the desk, I'm moving that to the guest bedroom," she said, standing.

Ryan nodded, assessing the items. "I can do it today. I'll run into town and rent a hand truck, then stop by the Salvation Army and ask them to pick up the bed and bureau later this afternoon." He noticed Faith's amazed expression. "But if you'd rather I worked on the closet instead, that's fine, too."

"No, I just hadn't expected that it all could be taken

care of so quickly by one person. Are you sure? It seems like such a big job."

"Not if I have the right tools to do it with," Ryan said. He caught her gaze and gave her a smile. He hoped she recognized it as an apology for pawing her earlier. Not that he'd considered it pawing, by any means. More like carnal worship, but he couldn't really tell Faith that without making more of a fool of himself than he already had.

"I'll be back in less than an hour. How about if I bring us back some lunch, too?"

"That'd be great." She gave him a shaky smile, and he thought he might have been forgiven.

He hoped so, anyway.

When he returned with the rented hand truck, he taped all the drawers together on the desk and moved it into the spare bedroom. Afterward, they took a break. He got everything ready for their lunch while Faith admired her newly fixed back door, complete with not just one, but two sturdy-looking brass locks. She opened it and gazed at the back yard. Topsy was almost immediately there, panting to get outside. Faith laughed and let the puppy run into the yard.

"This is great. I used to have to take her out the front and go around the house to let her into the fenced-in area. Thank you for fixing it, Ryan," she said, coming toward him and accepting the sandwich and salad he offered her, along with a carton of skim milk.

"My pleasure," Ryan said, watching Topsy through the window over the sink. She zipped from place to place, sniffing every bush and new bloom avidly. He laughed. Faith looked over and smiled. She really liked his deep, booming laugh. "She's like a hyperactive bee out there sniffing those bushes," he said.

"I didn't call her Topsy-Turvy for nothing," Faith said wryly, setting out napkins and forks for them. "Are you a mind reader?" she asked a few seconds later as she sat at the breakfast nook and unwrapped her sandwich. "This is my favorite from the City Deli," she said, grinning and picking up the vegetarian sandwich. "How did you know?"

"I just asked the lady behind the counter if she knew you and what you liked. She did, apparently," he said, watching her as she took a healthy bite.

"That's Celia," Faith said after she'd swallowed. "One of the many advantages of living in a small town. The townsfolk know all your habits and secrets, both bad and good. I'll bet Celia was very interested in getting you whatever you wanted," she said with wry amusement before she took another bite. Celia was a kind, attractive woman in her late thirties who had never made a secret about her open admiration for the male of the species. Since Ryan was a prime example of that, she knew for a fact he'd been the target of Celia's earthy flirtation. Jesse had certainly seemed to be the object of it whenever he came to Holland. Jesse had soaked up Celia's attentions, Faith recalled.

"I think Celia was more interested in the fact that I wanted to know exactly what *you* wanted," Ryan said after he'd swallowed his first bite of his roast beef and Swiss.

Faith gave him a surprised glance. She had to hand it to him. That was the perfect response to silence her vague uneasiness.

As if she had a right to get miffed at the thought of him flirting with another woman, she thought, mentally rolling her eyes at herself. Jesse had really done a number on her, for her to get this paranoid.

She forked her salad slowly, steeling herself for bringing up a potentially dicey topic when she and Ryan were getting along so well together.

"Did you give any more thought about what you said last night…about moving to Michigan, I mean?"

He nodded as he chewed, waiting until he swallowed. He took a swig of ice water. "Yeah, I did. I called my sister, Mari, late last night and had a conversation with her about it."

Faith set down her fork, shocked. This was not the response she'd expected. She'd thought maybe he'd had time to reconsider his impulsive decision to relocate his home and business—his entire life. "You had a conversation with her about moving to Michigan?"

"Yes, and about the baby." Her mouth fell open in amazement. "I hope that's okay. Mari and I are really close. And like you said earlier, it's really big news. Talking to her helped me get my bearings a little bit. Faith?" he asked, his dark eyebrows pinching together as he looked at her. "Is that okay?"

She blinked. "Yes. Of course. Like I said, I'll be telling my parents soon. And Jane knows already. Of course you wanted to tell your sister." She picked up her fork again. "How did Mari take it?"

"She was floored."

"Naturally," Faith muttered, suddenly feeling nervous for some reason. Was she worried about what Mari would think of her? Would Ryan's sister perhaps disapprove of the unusual circumstances?

Ryan gave her a warm glance. "But then she really started to get excited." He seemed to hesitate for a second, and then took a bite out of his sandwich.

"Ryan, what is it?" Faith asked, sensing he was holding back. He took several seconds to respond.

"It's just…Mari wants to come to Michigan to visit tomorrow." He gave her a fleeting glance, and Faith realized he seemed uncomfortable. "She…um…wants to meet you."

"Oh."

He set down his sandwich. "You don't have to, if you don't want to."

"I do want to," Faith said breathlessly. "It's just…"

"What?"

"It all seems so…*serious.*"

They just looked at each other for a moment.

"Having a baby is serious, though. Isn't it?" Ryan finally said slowly.

"Yeah," Faith admitted. She gave Ryan a helpless sort of glance, and for some reason, the weightiness inherent to their conversation—their entire situation—temporarily lifted. Simultaneously Ryan grinned and Faith burst into hysterical laughter.

"I'm sorry," Faith said a moment later, wiping a few tears caused by her laughing jag off her cheek with a paper napkin. "This situation is so strange. I hope your sister doesn't think I'm an…*oddity.*"

"She'll think you're exactly what you are. She'll think you're wonderful," Ryan said simply. Her laughter faded when he touched her hand where it sat on the table, ever so briefly. Nerves all along the skin of her hand and forearm flickered to life.

After her heartbeat went back to normal following that caress, they managed to have a nice lunch together. Ryan's easy conversation about practical matters settled her unrest about his sudden presence in her life, and her confusion about how she was supposed to feel about it. After they'd eaten and cleaned up, Ryan resumed his furniture-moving project, and Faith hauled sacks filled with garbage out of the room. It fascinated her to watch him work, to observe how methodical and efficient he was in breaking down the bed into easily movable pieces, strapping the bureau drawers closed with duct tape, then maneuvering the large pieces of furniture through the door while he held them vertical on the metal truck.

In what seemed like no time, the furniture was neatly piled at the end of her driveway. Before she knew it, the Salvation Army truck had come to retrieve it, and a project she'd dreaded undertaking was done within a matter of hours.

"You're a miracle of efficiency," she told him as they both watched through the window as the two workers from the Salvation Army got into the truck and drove away. She turned and gazed at the nursery-to-be. Now that the room was empty, the possibilities of transforming it into a wonderful place for the baby filled her with excitement. She clapped her hands together eagerly and gave Ryan an irrepressible grin.

"Thank you so much."

"You're welcome," he said, his warm gaze running over her face.

"Do you want to know how I plan to decorate?" she asked, suddenly feeling like a kid with a secret she longed to share.

"Of course."

She swept across the room and gestured over the entire north wall. "I plan to paint a mural here—bright, eye-catching colors, and the cradle will go here, and a set of drawers here, and a baby changing table here," she explained as she moved around the room. "I'd like to hire someone to come in and do some built-in shelves on this wall—something that'll last, that can be used even when the baby is in high school. Now that you've cleaned out the room for me, I can order a new carpet. I haven't decided what color to do the walls in. It'll depend on whether or not I decide to know the sex during the next ultrasound."

She turned toward him and paused. "I mean, what *we* decide," she added weakly.

"Sounds like you have big plans," he said, inspecting the blank wall as if he saw something there she didn't. "I'll pay for half of the redecoration."

"Oh…I didn't mean…well, I suppose that'd be okay," she fumbled. He'd said it so unexpectedly, she hadn't had time to prepare. He was the baby's father. It was a perfectly reasonable offer.

"Can I build the shelves?"

"*Can* you do something like that?" Faith asked, eyes wide.

Ryan's nod was entirely confident. "My father taught me carpentry. We used to take on projects together as a hobby when I was a kid. I did the built-in bookshelves in my condominium in San Francisco. Here," he paused, digging in his jean pocket and extracting his cell phone. He tapped a few buttons and handed the device to her. "It doesn't have to look exactly like that. I can design it for whatever you want and need for the baby."

"Oh, it's amazing," Faith exclaimed, staring at a photo of beautifully crafted floor to ceiling maple shelves and cabinets. She glanced at Ryan with amazement. "I can't believe you built that. Jesse used to say you were the best pilot he'd ever met," she said quietly. "He said your reaction times were off the charts. And here you could have had a career as a carpenter, as well."

"Not likely," Ryan said, grinning and putting away his phone.

"Yeah, I guess you don't get the adrenaline rush with carpentry that you do with flying." For some reason a jolt of disappointment and irritation had gone through her when she saw his appealing, but undoubtedly cocky, smile. She was all too familiar with the rootless flyboy type. A man like Ryan would never be satisfied with a career like carpentry, or *anything* that kept him so grounded.

"My love of flying was never about the adrenaline rush. Or at least not primarily about that."

"Really?" Faith asked, her eyebrows quirked upward and a small, slightly incredulous smile on her face. She started to walk away, but blinked in surprise when Ryan caught her hand and pulled slightly until she swung to face him.

"Really," he said emphatically, an odd expression shadowing his visage. His gaze narrowed on her. "Why are you so convinced that I'm an adrenaline junkie, hell-raising pilot?"

"Come on, Ryan," she said with soft remonstrance. "I was a military wife. Do you think I don't know the personalities of the majority of Air Force pilots? I know it's a stereotype, but a pretty well-earned one, at least in my opinion…"

She trailed off, knowing she'd made a mistake when she saw the fire flash in his eyes. "So that's what I'm up against?" he asked, his voice quiet, but commanding. "Not just Jesse's bad behaviors, but your stereotype about all pilots being jacked-up jerks always looking for the next high over the horizon, be it with a hot, fast jet or a hot, fast woman. Is that it, Faith?"

She blushed at his graphic description, but bristled at it, as well. "I'm not going to apologize for my experience."

"Fine," he replied quickly, pulling her a little closer until the lapels of their shirts brushed together. This close, she could see the inky black color of his lashes and the gleam of the lamplight in his ebony eyes. "Just do me the favor of not judging me by it until you've had a chance to broaden your horizons."

"I suppose you think I need more of the experience that

I had with you on Christmas Eve?" she said sarcastically, and immediately regretted it. His nostrils flared at her challenge. His head lowered until their mouths were only inches apart. Against her will, Faith felt herself close the distance between them infinitesimally.

"That wasn't what I was talking about," he said quietly, his gaze roaming over her face and landing on her lips. "But honestly? Yeah, I think that's precisely the kind of experience you need. With *me*," he added succinctly, causing the burn in her cheeks to transfer to other parts of her body.

"I'm not about to make that kind of mistake anytime soon," she whispered shakily. She went still when he suddenly palmed her jaw and spoke so close to her mouth that she felt his warm breath fanning her lips.

"I'll be ready for you whenever you change your mind."

Faith blinked, disoriented, when he dropped his hand and walked away.

Ryan stalked to the kitchen, anger and arousal surging in equal measure through his veins. By the time he'd gathered all his tools, closed his toolbox and retrieved the rented metal truck, regret had joined the potent brew.

He should feel more compassionate toward Faith, given everything she'd been through with Jesse's faithless ways. He'd never been more infuriated at Jesse for what his friend had done, wounding such a lovely, generous woman.

What if Faith could never trust a man again? The possibility was too terrible to consider for long. Somehow he had to convince her that this strong, powerful attraction they shared for one another wasn't the sign of a lustful fling, but the stable basis for something real…something lasting.

He paused in the hallway next to the living room when he saw her approaching. His heart sank when he saw her expression.

"Ryan, I'm sorry—"

"No," he cut her off more abruptly than he'd intended and took a deep breath, briefly shutting his eyes. He opened them again, pinning her with his stare. "*I'm* sorry."

She gave him a shaky smile. He hated seeing the uncertainty in her green eyes. She waved at the metal truck. "Thank you again. I can't believe all you accomplished today."

"All *we* accomplished."

She nodded.

"I'll give you a call tomorrow morning and let you know about getting together with Mari? If you still want to, that is."

"I do want to," she said.

He gave her a small smile, appreciating her attempt to make things right between them again. All in all, he thought it was best that he get out of there before he said another stupid thing...or worse, touched her again. It was becoming increasingly hard to walk away after he felt her warm, soft skin beneath his fingertips, saw the way her lips parted as if in anticipation of his kiss—

He realized he was staring at her mouth again and charged toward the front door.

"I'll call you tomorrow, then."

"Okay," he heard her say in a small voice from behind him.

Fifteen minutes later he dropped the key to his hotel room on the night table and stalked toward the bathroom, where he turned on the shower.

A good dousing in cold water helped, but it couldn't extinguish the sound of Faith's voice ringing in his head like a sexy taunt.

He toweled off and shrugged on a pair of briefs and jeans, not bothering to button them all the way. He sat on the bed and grabbed the remote control. The baseball game on TV didn't distract him from hearing Faith's voice much better than the cold shower had.

I suppose you think I need more of the experience that I had with you on Christmas Eve?

Hell, *yes* that's what he thought. What sane male in existence wouldn't think about repeating such a phenomenal experience, almost to the exclusion of everything else?

Even though he'd ritualistically forced himself not to dwell on what had happened between them on Christmas Eve, his powers were running thin now that he'd seen Faith again. Now that he'd touched her.

Now that he'd witnessed firsthand the miraculous result of making love to her that night.

Christmas Eve.

He remembered Faith's radiant smile as they'd sat there together in the breakfast nook, sipping their Christmas punch. How could a woman possibly be so sweet and sexy as hell all at once?

"You're not a stranger," Faith said, beaming at him. "I feel like I know you as well as some people that I see every day of my life."

She faltered, as if suddenly second-guessing what she'd just said. Did she realize how uninhibited, how generous... how appealing *she'd sounded? She glanced away, her expression frozen. He saw her pulse thrumming delicately at her throat above the modest nightgown she wore with a white robe tied securely over it. As he watched, her heartbeat leaped.*

She peeked over at him cautiously through a fall of dark, glorious waves and curls. Her cheeks and lips were flushed a becoming pink. He wondered if it was wishful thinking on his part, but her green eyes looked glazed with desire.

She spilled punch on her robe when she stood too abruptly. Ryan sprang up almost as rapidly. She laughed awkwardly as she wiped her hand over the upper swell of a soft-looking, firm breast, trying to dry the red fluid.

"Clumsy. Uh, excuse me...I just need to..."

He followed her, drawn to her like a bee to honey. "Faith?" he called when she rushed over to the kitchen sink and turned on the water.

"Yes?" she asked, glancing around, her eyes huge in her face.

"You don't feel like a stranger to me, either."

The words had just popped out of his mouth. This entire interaction with Faith had taken on a charged tone. Something about it felt alarmingly imperative, as if he'd been planning it in some part of his brain he kept secret even from himself for a long time now...waiting for it for most of his life.

When he realized the bizarre direction of his thoughts, he blinked and stepped back. He was not typically a whimsical man.

He was never a whimsical man.

"I should go. It's late."

Her eyes widened. "Oh, don't rush off," she said regretfully as she wiped off her hands. "I don't know what's wrong with me. I'm not usually so jumpy—"

He shoved his hands in his jean pockets and gave a polite nod, looking away willfully when he noticed how pretty she was in her discomposure. "I'll just go get my coat."

Something had caught his eye as he'd tried to make a hasty exit. He paused, despite his better judgment, and then slowly walked to a bookcase in Faith's living room. He picked up one of the photos on her bookshelves.

"*That was taken at Bagram Airfield, I think,*" *Faith said from behind him, referring to the picture Ryan held.*

He set down the photograph of Jesse and him wearing flight suits and standing in front of the brand-new Raptor they'd just test piloted. As usual, Jesse looked unabashedly, boyishly happy, as if he couldn't think of a place he'd rather be in the world than in a blistering desert seven thousand miles from his wife.

"*Yeah,*" *Ryan said, turning to face her. The air seemed to hum with an electrical charge. Thus far on his unexpected visit, they hadn't broached the topic of Jesse or his death. Jesse and four other airmen had been on a search and rescue mission for a fellow pilot who had been forced to eject from his plane. Four of the search team had been killed in an accidental helicopter crash in the Kunar province in Afghanistan, including Jesse. Only the helicopter pilot had survived. Ryan's wing had been hit hard by the loss of five of their own.*

The pilot that had survived had, ironically, been Jesse's girlfriend, Melanie Shane.

Faith's smile looked a little sad. "Jesse always spoke very fondly of you. It was obvious how much he respected you."

"*He was a good friend,*" *he said, searching her face for some sign of what she thought of her dead husband.*

"*He'll have been gone for a year in January,*" *she said suddenly, studying the carpet.*

An awkward silence ensued.

"*I'm so sorry you lost such a—*"

"*I can't tell you how sorry I am for your—*"

Both of them stopped midsentence when they realized the other spoke a similar sentiment. Ryan winced slightly.

"*You shouldn't sympathize with me. Jesse was your husband. That's the cruelest loss of all.*"

Faith swallowed convulsively. He wished he could read her expression. "In many ways, the people you serve with are closer than family," she said quietly. "You spent time with Jesse, day in and day out. You depended on each other. I know how much he admired you. Of course you'd feel his loss deeply," she said, her gaze traveling over his face.

"Are you still struggling, Faith? With his loss?" Ryan asked, both curious and cautious about her answer.

She bit her lower lip and met his stare. "Jesse was gone for a lot of our marriage, Ryan," she said in a hushed voice. "It's not as if I didn't have to get used to being alone."

He nodded slowly, unable to unglue his gaze from her lovely face.

"You seem so sad. You took his death really hard, didn't you?" she asked. He was stunned that she seemed more concerned about his well-being than her own.

He felt a muscle flicker in his cheek.

"I do miss Jesse. But his death isn't why I'm feeling so regretful right now."

"Why, then?" she asked shakily, her clear green eyes intent on his face.

Had it been the tremor in her voice that made him do it? Maybe it'd been the mixture of uncertainty and desire shining in her eyes? Whatever it'd been, Ryan couldn't have done anything else in that moment but step forward and take Faith Holmes into his arms.

Chapter Six

*T*hey hugged for a long moment. Ryan felt as if he sensed her in every cell of his body, every square inch of his awareness. He wanted like hell to comfort her. He wanted to be utterly confident of her safety and happiness.

She shifted her head and buried her face in his chest, and Ryan forced himself to acknowledge the truth.

He wanted Faith more than anything. Period.

She tilted her head back when she felt the slight pressure of his forefinger beneath her chin. Was he really seeing so much unchecked longing in Faith's gaze at that moment? Or was it just what he was feeling reflected in her forest-green eyes?

"No matter how unwise and guilty I feel about it, I can't seem to stop myself from doing this, Faith."

He lowered his head so that their mouths were only inches apart. His gaze moved over her face, reading her re-action to his closeness. Her lips parted as if in anticipation.

He covered her mouth with his own.

The whimper that leaked out of her throat didn't sound distressed, but wondrous. Ryan could completely understand the sentiment. She tasted fantastic. His mouth moved over hers, molding, caressing, shaping her flesh to his... memorizing every sweet nuance of sensation. He sandwiched her lower lip between his, drawing it downward. His tongue slipped between her lips. His first taste was polite, a gentle dip beneath the surface. Then Faith touched him with the tip of her tongue, and her flavor penetrated his consciousness. Heat erupted in him. She glided her tongue against his and sucked lightly, teasing him to come farther...deeper.

He groaned and accepted her invitation wholeheartedly, sweeping his tongue into her mouth.

He cradled her chin at the side of her neck, holding her hostage to his kiss. His fingertips stroked her nape, amazed at her softness. It'd never happened to him before—that a woman's scent and taste could entirely obliterate logic. Apparently it wasn't just a myth, that passion had the ability to burn away rational thought.

She stepped closer and reached around his waist. He made a sound of satisfaction, highly gratified by the feeling of her feminine, firm curves pressing so tightly against him. He put a hand at the small of her back, sealing their bodies into a fit that made everything go black for a moment. Her knees seemed to sag. He broke their kiss and tightened his hold on her waist. He pushed back her dark, coiling hair and pressed his mouth to the side of her neck feverishly.

"Faith," he whispered roughly.

"I'm here," she said.

A poignant chord struck deep inside his spirit at her two simple words. So generous. So sweet. So inviting to this crazy, but somehow inevitable experience. She shifted her chin and nuzzled his jaw. Something sharp tore through him. He turned, his mouth finding hers. They fused in a kiss. This time he took her with a raw, elemental hunger that scorched away even the most stubborn lingering doubts and confusion about what was happening to him... what was happening to them.

She arched her back against his hands, offering the soft harbor of her body as a solace to his raging, burning need. The sensation of her breasts crushed against his ribs made him groan. She rubbed against him subtly. He moved in turn, stroking her even as his flesh hardened and thrilled to her sweetness.

He made a rough sound and broke their kiss.

"You're going to think I'm crazy, but when I was over there in that desert, I used to wish like hell you were mine and not Jesse's. How's that for a faithful friend?"

"Ryan," she whispered shakily. "I don't think you're crazy."

She went up on her toes and pressed her mouth to his. A shudder went through him. Suddenly, he was lifting her in his arms. His entire world shifted, until he didn't know left from right, up from down...

...right from wrong.

The only thing Ryan knew as he carried Faith into the living room and laid her on the couch was the recognition of her in the very marrow of his bones...the basic, powerful knowledge that she was his.

He swam in a sea of Faith's fragrance; soft, pale skin; eager, sweet lips and lush, supple curves. If he paused to think about what was happening, he'd stop, and he hated that idea.

Despised it.

He knelt next to the couch. He came down over her, his

knees still on the floor, his mouth immediately finding the juncture at her neck and shoulder.

"You smell so good," he muttered, inhaling her scent fully, feeling his blood pound in approval. She moaned softly. He relished the vibrations against his hungry lips. She arched her back. He paused, gritting his teeth at the sensation of full, firm breasts pressing against his chest. He was crazed to touch her, skin to skin. She ran her fingers through his hair, her touch causing prickles of pleasure to course down his neck and spine.

He bracketed her hips with his hands, taking her measure, finding her perfect. His fingers tugged lightly on the belt of her robe at the same time his mouth settled on warm, seeking lips. Her subtle perfume swamped his senses. He wanted to submerse himself in her and never come up for air. He probed the secrets of her mouth, relishing her unique flavor and uncommon responsiveness. She ran her hands beneath his shirt and molded his shoulder muscles into her palms.

The storm raging in his body gripped around flesh and bone, demanding release. He lifted his head a fraction of an inch, but couldn't entirely move away from the sweetest mouth he'd ever tasted.

"Tell me you want me to go away, Faith, because I can't seem to make myself do it," he muttered next to her damp lips.

"No. I can't do that," she said. Her fingers traced his neck, and then his collarbone. He tensed when she opened the first, then second button of his shirt and stroked his chest, her fingers avid. He clamped his eyes shut, feeling the inevitability of her touch...the impossibility of denying it.

She leaned forward and caught his mouth again, pluck-

ing at his lips, coaxing and tempting him until he thought
he would explode, then and there.

His hands moved on her hips, drawing up her robe and
nightgown. When his fingers skimmed the satiny skin of
her thighs, he grimaced, need clutching at him with talon-
sharp claws. He once again took control of their kiss, rav-
aging her tenderly. His hand moved, drawing down her
panties, finding her heat.

She was soft and warm and wet, and when he touched
her, her whimper pierced straight through him.

He never had a logical thought after that point. The
world became his hunger. His world became Faith.

He tried to remove his pants, but she held him fast in
her kiss, and goodness knows he was too wild for her taste
to protest. His need drove at him relentlessly, however. He
finally broke their kiss and pressed his mouth against the
upper curve of her breast. Her robe had fallen open. Only
a layer of thin cotton separated her skin from his caressing lips. She furrowed her fingers through his hair and
held him to her as he explored firm, feminine flesh. When
he reached the peak of a breast, he took it into his mouth,
laving the pebbled, turgid nipple through the fabric.

Her sharp cry was his siren call.

He moved over her, need making him blind to everything but sensation. He felt her wet heat on the tip of his
erection and muttered a curse that was a prayer.

"Oh...heavens," he heard her say as if from a great
distance. Desire pummeled him, gripping, squeezing...

He drove into her heat, feeling her deepest embrace in
every cell of his body.

"Are you all right?" he managed between a clenched
jaw. He pried open his eyelids. The vision of Faith laying
there while they were fused, her dark hair spread on the

cushion, her lovely face tight and glazed with desire, was scorched into his brain...quite possibly for an eternity.

She reached for him, her fervent kiss his answer.

The buzzing sound of his cell phone interrupted his heated memories. Ryan glanced at the number, scowling, and hit the receive button.

"Hey," Ryan greeted his sister gruffly.

"Did I wake you up?" Mari, his sister, asked.

"No, I was watching the Tigers game. I'm going to drive over to the airport here in a bit to meet with the owner of a Cessna I want to buy. What's up?"

"I just wanted to confirm lunch tomorrow. Did Faith say she'd come?"

Ryan and Mari had been close growing up, but the sudden, tragic loss of their parents when Mari was eighteen and Ryan was twenty had tightened their bond even more. He could hear the threads of anxiety and excitement in his sister's voice at the prospect of meeting Faith. When he'd told his sister last night about Faith and the pregnancy, she'd first expressed her worry about how he was handling things. After she'd listened to him describe Faith, however, excitement had started to filter into her voice.

"She'll be there. Are you sure you should make the trip?" Ryan asked, standing and turning off the television.

Mari laughed. In his mind's eye he could clearly see the droll roll of her whiskey-colored eyes. "I think I'm up to the hour drive from Chicago to Harbor Town. You'd better get used to the idea that a pregnant woman isn't disabled, Ryan."

"Between you and Faith constantly telling me, I'll likely learn the lesson soon enough," he mumbled dryly as he pulled a shirt out of the closet.

"Good. Faith sounds like she'll keep you in line. Can

you pick me up at Brigit's? I wouldn't ask, but I promised to meet with Deidre about the project she's started for veterans with post-traumatic stress syndrome at the center," Mari explained. She referred to The Family Center, the innovative community and treatment center for survivors of substance abuse that Mari had begun several years ago. Mari, the Reyes family, and all of the Kavanaugh children were intimately involved in the funding and workings of The Family Center, since all of them were direct survivors of substance abuse. Members of all three families had lost family members following a car wreck caused by Derry Kavanaugh when he'd been driving drunk seventeen years ago.

"Yeah, I wanted to double check with Deidre that she's all squared away with Scott to fly to Tahoe tomorrow, anyway," he said. "I'll pick you up at twelve-thirty," Ryan said before he bid her goodbye and hung up the phone.

He finished dressing, intent on going to the airport and finalizing the details for his purchase of the new plane for Eagle Air.

He only hoped Faith hadn't changed her mind about agreeing to come tomorrow.

Faith stood in her backyard the following morning watching Topsy poke her nose into every possible crevice she could. She soaked up the warm sunshine, glorying in the first bona fide springlike day of the year.

"Faith?"

She spun around at the sound of the deep voice calling from the front of the house. "Ryan, I'm back here!"

He came around the side of the house a moment later. She waited, appreciating the sight of him while he approached. He wore a pair of canvas pants along with a button-down blue-and-white twill shirt. Both items of clothing fitted him perfectly, highlighting long legs, narrow hips and the appealing slant of his torso from a lean waist to a powerful chest and shoulders.

He looked good enough to eat.

Recognizing her errant thought, she plastered a smile on her face as he opened the fence gate and approached her.

"You got here quicker than I'd expected. I thought I better let Topsy out before we left."

"There wasn't any traffic in town. I got here fast," he said, his dark eyes moving over her. She felt her cheeks warming beneath what appeared to be an appreciative male appraisal. "Isn't this weather amazing? The first real day of spring," she said breathlessly.

"You look like springtime," he murmured, his stare sweeping over her floral-colored skirt and lingering on the front of her lightweight peach-colored sweater.

"Thanks," she managed. Something about his low, gruff voice made her already warm cheeks burn. She'd purchased some springtime items for her wardrobe, well aware that her breasts were growing past the confines of her prepregnancy blouses. Even this new sweater seemed to highlight her growing curves, however. Ryan's appreciative glance didn't offend her like it would have if another man had perused her in such a manner.

In fact, his warm glance made her feel downright... desirable...

...aroused.

"Topsy!" she called, eager to derail her potentially dangerous train of thought. The puppy glanced around at her call and suddenly tore through the yard. She immediately went to Ryan, wiggling and hopping around his ankles. Ryan grinned and bent to pet the caramel-colored fluff ball, scratching Topsy behind the ears until she literally vibrated with pleasure.

"You've made a friend for life," Faith said, enjoying watching Ryan's long fingers stroke the puppy. No wonder Topsy appeared to be in a state of bliss. What was it about seeing a big, masculine man with something so tiny and adorable that appealed so much to a woman? A strange, powerful feeling tightened her chest.

What would it be like to see him hold their child?

"You think so?" Ryan asked, picking up Topsy and holding her in front of his face, examining the canine soberly. Faith burst out in laughter at the comical sound he made when Topsy lapped at his nose with a pink tongue.

"Why are you so quiet?" Ryan asked her several minutes later when they were on the road to Harbor Town.

"I'm worried about meeting your sister," Faith admitted, staring at the sun-gilded, blooming trees and meadows zooming past the car window.

"She'll love you. There's absolutely nothing to worry about."

"Easy for you to say," Faith said quietly. She glanced at Ryan when he reached across the console and put his hand on top of hers where it'd been resting on her thigh. His heat soaked down into her skin.

"It is easy for me to say, because I know Mari, and I know you. What specifically are you worried about?"

Faith bit at her lower lip, hesitant to reveal her insecurities. Ryan tightened his hold on her hand, as if in reassurance.

"I know it's ridiculous," she murmured, watching as they passed the city limit sign for Harbor Town. "I'm thirty years old, not a teenager, but I can't help but feel like she might think I'm...some kind of a..."

"What?" Ryan prodded when she faded off.

"Loose woman," Faith burst out. It sounded so ridiculous when she said it, she couldn't help but give Ryan a sheepish grin. He wore an incredulous expression that segued to amusement.

"*Loose woman?* This isn't the 1950s, Faith. Lots of women have babies who aren't married, or even in a serious relationship."

"I know. Maybe loose isn't the word. Maybe stupid is. Women in this day and age aren't supposed to get pregnant after a…a…" She struggled to finish her sentence, becoming increasingly uncomfortable when she couldn't. When Ryan released her hand, she looked at him in alarm. Had she offended him? She hadn't meant to minimize Christmas Eve, she just didn't know how to describe what had happened between them.

Still.

"Mari isn't going to judge you," he said as he stared out the front window and drove. "She's not a judgmental person, in the first place, and in the second place, there's nothing to judge. She's as aware as anyone that you can't always plan life. You just live it as best you can."

Faith inhaled slowly, studying his profile. He turned into a residential neighborhood featuring a tree-lined street and attractive older large homes. Of course he was right. How could she possibly feel the tiniest shame about the miracle of life growing inside her?

Ryan brought the car to a crawl.

"See that house there?" he asked, pointing to a lovely sprawling residence complete with a sweeping porch and swing that had been built in the Arts and Crafts style and lovingly restored. "That was our summer house."

"It's beautiful," Faith breathed. "Isn't there a beach down at the end of the street?" she asked, pointing to a wooded cul-de-sac. "What a wonderful neighborhood for kids this must have been."

"Yeah, the beach is on the other side of those trees. We lived on that beach during the summer. A bunch of the parents on the street conspired to serve dinner at the same time every night so that only one of them had to go down to round us all up for supper," Ryan said, smiling in memory.

"It's for sale," Faith said, pointing at the sign in the yard.

Ryan did a double take and frowned. "Mari and I just sold it to a couple a little over a year ago. They must have had a change of heart."

A moment later Ryan turned into the driveway of an appealing white-shingled Colonial Revival-style home. He put the car in Park, but instead of getting out, he turned toward her, his intent manner taking her off guard.

"If it bothers you that much, the idea of being single and having the baby—"

He paused, leaving Faith puzzled as to what he was about to say, his gaze fixed out the front windshield. Faith saw a beautiful woman with long dark hair coming down the front steps of the house toward them. She wore an attractive green dress that tied beneath her breasts and above the small roundness of her belly. Her leather lace-up sandals and matching shoulder bag gave her a hip, sophisticated appearance. As she approached the car, Ryan's sister smiled at Faith through the window. Faith stepped out of the car to greet her.

Within a minute of meeting Mari Kavanaugh, Faith fully recognized how baseless her fears were. Mari was one of the warmest, kindest people she'd ever met. The fact that she seemed as eager to know Faith as Faith was to know her helped matters greatly.

The three of them ate outdoors on the patio at a local restaurant, Jake's Place. The weather was ideal, the company excellent and the food good. Mari and Faith compared notes on their pregnancy while Ryan listened. Despite his impassive expression, Faith thought he paid close attention to what they said. It was obvious to Faith that Ryan deeply cared about his little sister. He leaned forward and took part in the conversation more animatedly when the topic turned to Mari's daughter, Riley. It warmed her heart to hear him speak with such fond pride of his niece.

"That's the last one I have on my cell phone," Ryan said as he showed Faith the final photo, this one of a grinning little girl sitting amongst a huge pile of torn Christmas wrapping, a red wrapping bow in her curly, dark hair.

"She liked the wrapping paper more than she did her presents," Mari told Faith with a twinkle in her eyes.

"She's absolutely adorable," Faith said sincerely, handing the phone back to Ryan. "Do you and your husband know if Riley is going to have a brother or sister?"

"A sister," Mari said, giving Ryan a knowing glance. "Another niece for Uncle Ryan to spoil. Speaking of which, what about *you*? Am I going to have a niece or nephew? My first time being an aunt!" Mari said with barely contained excitement.

Faith laughed. Mari's enthusiasm was contagious. The two women began talking excitedly, pausing to nod an acknowledgment when Ryan saw an old friend walk onto the patio and excused himself to go and greet him. Mari watched her brother walk away and glanced at Faith with a smile.

"He probably needs a break from all the estrogen we're exuding."

Faith chuckled, but shook her head a little sadly. She caught Mari's eye.

"He's got to be plowed under by all this, Mari. It was the last thing he expected."

Mari's grin faded. She reached across the table and patted Faith's hand. "The same must be true for you," she said feelingly.

"I'm okay," she assured. "You know how it is, being a mother. Sure, it took me by storm when I realized I was going to have a baby. But I've had months to come to terms with it, and the baby is here—" she touched her belly significantly "—growing inside me. It's different for Ryan."

"He'll get his footing. Ryan is nothing if not adaptable. He may be stunned, but he's also happy, Faith. Incredibly so," Mari added more quietly.

"Do you really think so?"

Mari nodded. "I could hear the wonder in his voice when he told me he was going to have a child. Family is very important to Ryan."

"I can imagine." Faith's expression tightened with compassion and she turned her hand, giving Mari's hand a squeeze. "You guys lost your family when you were so young. It's no wonder he values family ties the way he does. Did he…did Ryan tell you about his plans to move to Michigan?" Faith asked hesitantly.

Mari's golden brown eyes filled with concern. "I'm guessing you're not very pleased about that?"

"It's not that," Faith exclaimed. "His decision just took me by surprise, that's all." She sighed and leaned back in her chair. "To be honest, this whole thing with your brother has taken me off guard."

"I can only imagine. At least one little mystery has been cleared up for me," Mari said, a small smile tugging at her mouth.

"What's that?"

"Why Ryan was so fixed and determined to return to Michigan last Christmas Eve. I thought for sure he'd be less than thrilled at the idea of spending the holiday at Brigit's house, so I was shocked when he readily—even eagerly—agreed to come with us to Harbor Town. He obviously was looking forward to seeing you."

Faith's eyes widened in amazement at this news. Perhaps Mari noticed her unsettlement because she gave her a big smile.

"Like I said, time is what's needed. You two will figure things out. For my part, I'm thrilled to have met you."

"I'm so glad to have met you, as well," she returned sincerely. "I was really worried about it, earlier."

"Why?" Mari asked.

"I thought you might...you know...judge me for being pregnant when I'm not even dating your brother," she mumbled.

"Don't be silly. I'm the last person on earth to judge something like that. I hadn't seen Riley's father—Marc— for a decade when I accidentally got pregnant. We can't always plan life. We just have to—"

"Live it," Faith finished for her, repeating what Ryan had said in the car earlier.

Mari squeezed her hand before she let it go. "Babies are amazing things all on their own, but what's truly wonderful is the way they can pull people together," Mari said meaningfully before she glanced toward the far side of the patio. Faith followed the path of her gaze and saw Ryan walking toward them, his stare directly on her. Her heart began to pound erratically.

"That definitely sounds like the case with you and your husband," Faith said hesitantly. "It's different for Ryan and I. Our situation is...unusual."

"Babies also have a way of making the unusual more commonplace," Mari assured.

Faith smiled shakily. The baby was already bringing Ryan and her closer. It excited her to be near him, to feel his admiring glances and warm touches...to feel like an attractive, desirable woman again.

But what if they got *too* close?

Eventually, he'd fly away from her. He'd live a life separate from her as he traveled with his charter airline. He'd sleep in strange beds...possibly with strange women? The life of a pilot's wife was uncertain, lonely...unsecure. That was an experience she could not allow herself to repeat.

So why, Faith wondered anxiously as she watched Ryan come toward them, his gaze unwavering on her, did Ryan strike her as a veritable mountain of stability? Solid. Enduring.

When they dropped Mari off at Brigit Kavanaugh's later, Faith saw two women swaying on the front porch swing and recognized one of them.

"Would you mind very much if I went and said hello to Brigit?" Faith asked Ryan.

"No, of course not."

Before she got out of the car, she turned toward the backseat. "Did you by chance tell Brigit? About the baby?" she asked Mari.

Mari shook her head.

"Thank you. I'd rather not get into it right now, if that's all right with you?" she asked Ryan.

"Fine with me," Ryan stated. Something in his tone told Faith that he couldn't have agreed more with her decision. She recalled what Mari had said about how she'd expected Ryan to resist going to Brigit's house last Christmas Eve. It couldn't be easy for him, spending time in the house that was once owned by the man who had killed his parents in a case of involuntary manslaughter. How did he feel about his sister marrying Marc Kavanaugh, Derry Kavanaugh's oldest son?

Faith put her concerns on hold when Brigit came to the

top of the steps to greet her a moment later, a smile on her face and her arms outstretched. The pretty older woman gave her a warm hug.

"Imagine my surprise when Mari told me this morning she was having lunch with Faith Holmes!" Brigit exclaimed.

"I thought the same thing when Ryan mentioned you," Faith replied happily. She was glad to see Brigit looking so well. She was always attractive and well put together, but Faith had never seen her in such good spirits. She turned and saw the stunning young woman who had come to stand beside her mother, and wondered if Brigit's glow wasn't related to her. Brigit had mentioned once that Deidre and she had been estranged since the accident, but here they were, side by side, both of them smiling. The two women were an older and younger version of one another.

"You must be Deidre," Faith said, holding out her hand to Brigit's daughter. "Your mother has told me so much about you. I'm Faith."

"It's nice to meet you," Deidre said, glancing from Faith to Ryan with friendly curiosity.

They stayed and chatted for half an hour. When they finally stood to leave, Faith promised to keep in touch with Mari and they exchanged phone numbers.

"Let Nick know I'll be calling him next week. I have some important news to discus with him," Ryan told Deidre as they were leaving. Nick Malone was the CEO of DuBois Enterprises and Deidre's husband. The Malones had contracted Eagle Air for piloting services for their multibillion-dollar company, but Faith got the impression the couple and Ryan respected and liked each other.

Deidre's gaze flickered over Faith when Ryan took her hand as they stood on the stairs. "When do I get to hear this news?" she asked with a teasing grin.

"You know as well as I do that as soon as I tell Nick, you'll know, as well," Ryan grumbled dryly. "But I'll call you next week, as well."

"Good. You know I don't like to feel left out," Deidre joked, waving as they walked toward the car.

"That was nice," Faith murmured later as they drove back to Holland. "You were right about Mari. She's wonderful. It was nice to see Brigit, as well."

"Yeah. It was. Nice, I mean," Ryan said. She glanced at him in surprise, his tone had been so steadfast.

"I had the impression Brigit wasn't one of your favorite people."

"She didn't used to be," Ryan admitted, his gaze on the road. "The lawsuits that followed the accident years ago sort of put the Kavanaughs and us on opposite sides of the ring. It wasn't pretty."

"I can only imagine," Faith said, compassion filling her when she considered what people on all sides must have suffered following such a horrific accident. Ryan glanced at her quickly, a small smile on his face.

"But I have to admit…seeing how fond Brigit was of you, I have a new respect for her. She was doing what I wanted to do all along—making sure you were okay and safe and sound. I appreciate her in a whole new way for being here and looking out for you."

She opened her mouth to remind him she was very capable of looking out for herself, but halted. He'd sounded so warm and thoughtful just now, it was difficult to find fault in what he'd said. Was it really such a terrible thing that he worried about her, even though it was unwarranted? Didn't that mean he cared…even a little?

"Would you like to come in?" she asked him when he pulled into her driveway, damning her breathlessness.

"I would, if you don't mind," he said. "I brought my tape

measure. I was hoping to get some measurements for the bookcases so that I can start coming up with a sketch for you. We can bounce ideas off that."

"That'd be terrific," she said, watching as he reached in the backseat for a tape measure, ruler and a tablet of paper.

He immediately went into the nursery-to-be and began working. Faith let Topsy out into the backyard and fed the cats. She walked into the baby's room a half hour later. Ryan sat on the only chair in the room, the sketchpad open on his spread thighs. She peered over his shoulder at his sketch.

"It's just preliminary, but what would you think about something like this?" he asked, his pencil still moving over the paper. He moved aside the ruler to show her what he'd drawn. Fascinated, Faith sunk to her knees next to him, her forearms braced on the arms of his chair.

"Oh, that'd be amazing, Ryan," she enthused, admiring the multi-unit shelving and cabinet unit. "I can't believe you came up with that so quickly. I love it."

He waved his pencil over the two corner benches. "These can be used for both sitting and for toy storage, and these cabinets can hold anything from sports equipment to clothing to diapers. Then there's the book shelves, for displaying things and—"

"Books. Lots and lots of books."

Ryan glanced at her. Their heads were close enough that Faith could easily see the warm gleam in his eyes. She also could smell his clean, spicy scent. She breathed deeper, as if she wanted to absorb it.

"I'm glad you think books are so important," he said quietly.

"Of course I do."

She couldn't pull her gaze off his lips when they twitched in a smile. He leaned closer to her. She couldn't seem to stop herself from craning closer to him, until their mouths were only inches apart. He still watched her intently. She saw his nostrils flare, as if he was trying to capture her scent as she had his. Her heart stalled, and then began to race.

"I should have known that learning would be a top priority for a straight-A student."

"Don't forget gym class."

"I'm not forgetting anything," he said before his lips brushed against hers.

Chapter Seven

It was more of a gentle, skimming caress than a kiss, as if he was curious as to how her mouth felt and used his own to discover the information. Faith closed her eyes and just experienced him; firm, warm, fragrant flesh sliding and rubbing against her own sensitive, tingling lips. She pressed closer, eager for more of the sensation of him, molding her mouth against his, hungrier now...blindly seeking.

He put his hand on the back of her head and pierced her lips with his tongue. Excitement knifed through her, sharp and compelling. Her nipples prickled and tightened. A gnawing ache expanded at her core, a feeling she knew from experience that Ryan could build and mount in her flesh...and finally vanquish in a delicious rush of pure pleasure.

A loud, high-pitched wail penetrated her haze of arousal. Ryan closed their kiss and leaned back slightly, a mixture of alarm and puzzlement on his face.

"It's Topsy," she said in an apologetic tone. She snorted into soft laughter when the comically mournful howling continued. Faith pushed up on the arm of Ryan's chair and stood. "I'll just go and get her. I left her out in the yard."

"Her Highness doesn't like to be left waiting," Ryan said, grinning, although the embers of arousal remained in his eyes.

Thinking it was best to get some distance from him for a bit, considering how much she'd lost herself in that kiss, Faith busied herself in other rooms for the next several minutes. When she walked down the hallway to her bedroom a while later, Topsy panting after her on her heels, she noticed he was still in the baby's room, absorbed in his task. She entered her room and closed the door, leaving it open a crack. She quickly undressed and pulled on some jeans. Standing in her opened closet door, she searched for a blouse to wear, her hands skimming over several garments. Her fingers paused on the hanger for her evening dress that she planned to wear for the benefit Wednesday night for the Animal Advocates Alliance.

Impulsively she pulled out the dress and closed her closet door, peering into the mirror on the other side. It was a champagne-colored sleeveless silk number that she'd purchased last October, before she was pregnant. She held up the dress to the front of her body, her brow furrowed in worry. It was a tasteful dress, but more low-cut than Faith typically wore her necklines. She hadn't considered before—what if her slightly pregnancy-swollen breasts would be too obvious in the dress?

A knock sounded on her door. She started.

"Faith?"

"Yes?"

Ryan poked his head around the door. Faith's heart did

a flip-flop. She plastered the dress over the front of her. Ryan's gaze immediately dropped and widened.

"I'm sorry. I didn't mean to—" He paused and cleared his throat. "I was just coming to say goodbye."

"Oh, okay. Let me pull something on and I'll see you out," she said in a high-pitched voice.

His glance lowered again. "That's very pretty," he said, referring to the evening gown.

"Thanks. It's for the ball next Wednesday," she said, gathering herself a bit. It wasn't as if he could really *see* anything, with the dress held up over her mostly bare torso. This is what she told herself, anyway, when he stepped into the room. It struck her how large he appeared to be in her feminine retreat—how male. He came toward her and paused a few feet away, examining the dress.

"You'll look fantastic in that," he said.

She gave an awkward laugh. "I hope it fits. I was just wondering about that. I bought it when I wasn't pregnant. I'll probably be a total disaster."

He met her stare. "You won't be."

"How do you know?"

Instead of answering her, he calmly put his hand on the dress hanger. Faith released it hesitantly when he pulled. He tossed the gown over a nearby chair and put his hands on her shoulders. He turned her so that she faced the mirror and stood behind her.

Faith couldn't breathe.

"Look at you," Ryan said.

She inhaled with effort. He was following his own command, his eyes smoldering as they traveled over her image in the mirror. He placed his opened hand on her bare waist. Tendrils of pleasure curled through her belly when he moved it, sliding his palm over her hip and abdomen. His stare looked hot and worshipful as they both watched him touch her.

"I know Jesse pulled a number on you, but it's time you saw reality," he said quietly, his mouth near her right ear. She shivered when his fingers gently detailed her rib cage, his dark hand an erotic contrast to her pale skin. "You're a beautiful, sexy woman. Are you looking?" he asked, nudging her hair with his nose. His fingers coasted along the tender skin at her sides. She bit her lower lip to stifle a gasp.

"Yes," she managed.

"But are you *seeing?*" He stepped closer. She felt his groin brush against the top of her backside. "Flawless, soft skin," he murmured, stroking the inner part of her elbow. He palmed her hip. "Curves that fit my hand perfectly." His fingers traveled up the center of her rib cage, and then detoured to the left, tracing the skin beneath the cloth of her white bra. She couldn't take her gaze off the image of them in the mirror. Heat coursed through her. "Delicate and narrow in all the right places." He stepped closer as he caressed the sensitive skin, pressing his front more fully to her bottom. He brought his other hand around her and palmed both of her breasts, lifting slightly as if to test their weight.

A shaky sigh escaped her throat.

"Curvy and full in all the other ones," he added, his voice now low and husky. His fingertips flickered over her nipples, making them tighten against the clinging fabric of her bra. He made a low, rough sound of male appreciation. Much to her disappointment, however, he released her breasts. His hands gathered her hair and pulled it behind her shoulders.

"Hair a man wants to sink his fingers into," he continued, sliding his hands along her shoulders and collarbone.

He traced the line of her jaw, his stare on her intense. "And a face that haunts a man's dreams."

For a few seconds he remained still. They examined one another in the mirror while the air burned in Faith's lungs.

"At least this man's dreams," he added with a small, sheepish smile. He moved against her ever so slightly, leaving her in little doubt of his desire.

"Faith?"

"Yes?" she managed to whisper, even though her body was buzzing with sexual awareness and she was utterly entranced by Ryan's stare.

"Do you have a date to the ball on Wednesday?"

She started slightly. It hadn't been what she expected him to say.

"No," she blurted out before she had a chance to censor herself.

"I'd like to take you."

"Okay."

What else could she say, with such a gorgeous man pressed against her, hot and aroused? No sane woman could have resisted his smoky-eyed, wanting stare that seemed to promise untold sensual delights.

He leaned down and pressed his face to the side of her neck. A shudder of excitement went through her at the sensation of his warm lips moving against her skin.

Then he straightened and the hard pressure of his body was gone.

"Ryan?" she asked uncertainly when he stepped away.

"If I don't leave now, I'm not going to, Faith," he said, his voice sounding edgy. He glanced around, spearing her with his stare. His expression softened.

"I'll call you on Tuesday and we can make plans," he said. He briefly caressed her shoulder, turned and walked out of the room, leaving Faith standing there alone, a vibrating bundle of confusion and clamoring nerves.

On Wednesday at five-thirty Faith raced through her front door, laden down with dry cleaning, her briefcase and a large bag of dog chow. Topsy's loud yipping added another layer of chaos to her already overwhelmed state.

"I'm coming, I'm coming," she muttered in a regretful tone, dumping all the items she carried on the breakfast nook. Both Cleo and Smokey circled around her feet, meowing loudly for their supper. "I'm sorry for being late. My hair appointment had to be rescheduled because I had a patient emergency—an Irish setter managed to consume a jumbo package of toilet paper, including the plastic. Don't you ever think about pulling something like that, young lady," she lectured a squirming Topsy as she liberated her from her crate. The puppy shot like a torpedo through the back door when she opened it. She gave the cats their dinner in record time.

She only had a half an hour to get ready before Ryan would be here. Luckily, she'd gone to the salon in town to get her hair done, so the only thing that was required was a quick shower and makeup application.

At six o'clock, she stood in front of the bathroom mirror, inspecting the final result. Her skin looked smooth and glowing next to the champagne fabric of the dress. Her hairdresser had straightened her hair, and then used a curling iron to create loose curls that spilled down her shoulders and caressed her bare upper arms. The dress gathered beneath her breasts and then flowed in graceful folds to below her knees. Nervousness trickled through her when she saw the amount of cleavage revealed in the V-shape of the neckline. Was it entirely appropriate? She'd tried the dress on for Jane last night, however, and her friend had insisted it fit her perfectly.

"With curves like that, you ought to be flaunting it a little. It'll only help in getting a little extra cash from the male attendees during the silent auction you're running," Jane had said, her blue eyes twinkling. Faith had stood before a mirror at Jane's house while they both inspected her appearance. "And I doubt you'll hear that hunk of a man I met the other day in the office complaining."

After that it'd taken Jane about three seconds flat to get her to admit that Ryan Itani was, indeed, the father of her baby. When Jane had seen Faith's worried expression, she'd expressed confusion.

"Why are you upset that you're about to have that man's baby? He's gorgeous, and I saw the way he looked at you— like he wanted to eat you up in one bite. What's the problem?"

"Which one do you want me to start with?" Faith had asked drolly. She noticed Jane's mock stern expression in the mirror. "He's not in love with me or anything. That night—it was all a mistake...an impulse."

"Seems to me that your impulses are pretty good," Jane said dryly as she'd adjusted the bodice at Faith's back.

"He's not a one-woman man," Faith said, scowling at her reflection in the mirror. "Look at his job. Pilots live out of their suitcases. There's no...security in a man like that."

"Who are you talking about?" Jane asked, her gaze sharp in the mirror. "Ryan? Or Jesse?"

Faith sighed. Jane knew all about the heartache her former husband had caused her. "It doesn't matter. Ryan's not interested in me that way." Her cheeks grew pink when Jane gave her a give me a break glance. "I mean...

he's attracted to me. But he also told me he wants us to be friends."

Jane had just shrugged in a matter-of-fact manner. "Lust and friendship aren't a bad way to start, I'd say. Add a baby into the mix, and you've got the beginnings of a beautiful relationship."

A loud knock sounded on her front door, causing Faith to jump and jerking her out of her thoughts. She spun toward the vanity, the decadently soft folds of the skirt of the dress whisking around her hips and thighs. She tossed some money, a credit card, a comb and lipstick into her evening bag and hurried down the hallway, her heart starting to hammer out an erratic tempo in her ears.

Ryan had called yesterday, and they'd chatted for a few minutes. Other than that brief interaction, however, she hadn't had contact with him since last Sunday, when he'd touched her while they'd looked at one another in the mirror...when he'd *praised* her.

When he'd coaxed her into seeing herself in a whole new way.

"Hi," she greeted between pants a few seconds later, opening the outer door. Ryan caught it with his hand. Her frazzled brain fully took in his appearance for the first time. She froze, her eyes going wide.

"Oh, my goodness," she exclaimed. "You look great."

It was a bit of an understatement, she thought as her gaze ran over the considerable length of him.

It was a *lot* of an understatement.

He wore a classic black tux, white dress shirt with wing collar, points tucked behind a black bow tie. Faith always thought he looked completely natural wearing casual clothing and his leather flight jacket. She realized for the first time that he was so magnetically handsome, he could probably pull off wearing a paper bag.

Seeing him in an immaculate tuxedo was like a sock to the gut.

"You look amazing, yourself," Ryan said, his gaze going over her warmly.

"Where did you get that tuxedo?" she wondered incredulously. The elegant garment fit his large, lean body too well to have been anything but tailor made for him.

"I flew over to Chicago and had a rush job done on it. I needed to buy one anyway," Ryan said. "Since I've started working for Nick and Deidre, they've invited me to a few formal events. I needed a tux."

Faith realized she was standing there gaping at him while he stood on her front steps, holding the door.

"I'm sorry. Please come in. I just have to get my wrap." She flew to the kitchen, where she retrieved the pale, fluid evening wrap she'd had dry-cleaned. When she rejoined Ryan, her wrap draped over her arm, she saw that he carried a small plastic container.

"This is for you," he said, handing it to her.

Her eyes sprang wide. "A corsage?"

"No," he said. "It's just a single orchid. I thought it'd look great in your hair. If it doesn't, though, you can just put it in a vase."

"Oh, Ryan," she said, staring at the single, gorgeous bloom resting in the container. For some odd reason, her eyes smarted with tears. He'd recalled the color of her gown from last weekend, when he'd walked in and she'd been holding it up in the mirror. That such a masculine man remembered such a small detail and translated that knowledge into such a perfect gift struck a deep emotional chord in her. She looked at him.

"Thank you. I *will* wear it in my hair. You got the color

exactly. Give me just a second," she said, beaming at him before she hurried to the bathroom to find a pin to affix the orchid.

He couldn't have chosen better. The champagne-colored bloom looked lovely next to her dark hair. She removed the necklace she'd put on, allowing the flower to be her only accent besides a small pair of diamond studs in her ears.

His eyes seemed to glow when she joined him a second later.

"You're right. It is perfect," he said, smiling. He dipped his dark head and kissed her on the mouth, brief and electric.

Her breathing didn't return to normal until they were seated in the car and halfway to the Lake View restaurant.

"I hope you won't be too bored," Faith said worriedly when he pulled into the packed parking lot. "As the Alliance president I'll have to speak, and I'm responsible for the silent auction. The auction and cocktail party starts at six-thirty, and the dinner will follow. A couple of people from the board will be helping me do some last-minute things, so—"

"I'll be fine. You just do whatever you have to do," Ryan assured. She glanced over at his profile, sensing his calm confidence, and realized that of course he'd be fine. He was nothing if not self-sufficient.

She was aware of him all evening, despite the fact that she put considerable effort into socializing with all the guests during the combined cocktail hour and silent auction. He was at least a head taller than most of the attendees at the fundraiser, so it was easy to spot him above the crowd. He did, indeed, appear to be comfortable, meeting and chatting with strangers. Once she observed him talking to Sheila Maxwell, a local attorney. They made quite a striking pair standing next to each other, sipping their drinks, chatting and laughing. Jealousy made an unwanted appearance, swelling in her belly. It ducked its ugly head when she noticed that Ryan spoke just as long, and just as animatedly, to Mortimer Cohen, a wealthy octogenarian, as he had the statuesque Sheila.

She lost sight of him when the lights dimmed in the large dining room in order to show the brief film about the charitable work of the Animal Advocate Alliance.

"Those are your hands holding that dog. I'd recognize them anywhere," a deep voice said quietly in her right ear.

Faith turned around and saw Ryan's shadowed face just over her right shoulder. She smiled.

"You're amazing. I hadn't realized there was anything singular about my hands," she said, referring to the video that detailed the experience of one homeless dog from when it'd been taken in by the Alliance to when it had eventually been adopted by a family. Faith was shown in the video giving the canine a medical exam and providing its shots, although her face didn't appear on camera.

"I recognized your touch."

She blinked at having those sweet, intimate words murmured in her ear. She struggled to recover.

"Are you having an okay time?" she whispered.

"Yes. And I happen to know from mingling with your guests that you've got a ton of donations coming your way. I'm hoping the night will be a big success," he said quietly near her ear.

She craned her head around, trying to see him better in the shadowed room. "Thank you, Ryan."

She just made out his small smile and the gleam in his eyes before the video presentation ended and the lights came back up. Reluctantly Faith excused herself to call everyone to dinner and give her speech.

Afterward she sat down next to Ryan at the head table and gave a sigh of relief.

"It's finished. The hard part is over," she whispered, since another committee member now spoke at the podium.

"Congratulations for a job well done," he said quietly. She gratefully accepted the glass of ice water Ryan handed her. "I'd make it champagne, but under the circumstances..." He faded off, glancing down over her stomach.

"Water is just perfect," she said, sharing a smile with him.

After they'd finished their meal, a four-man band began to play music and couples moved onto the dance floor.

"What do you think? Are you too wiped out to dance?" Ryan asked, nodding toward the dance floor, which was situated directly in front of floor-to-ceiling windows and an outdoor terrace that overlooked the lake and the setting sun.

"I'd love to," Faith said.

She took his hand and they joined several other couples on the floor. He took her into his arms and they might have been the only people alive on the planet.

"Another gorgeous sunset," he murmured, even though his stare was on her face, not on the brilliant palette of streaking color in the western sky.

"Yes. It's nice. For the fundraiser, I mean," Faith breathed. "You're pretty light on your feet for a flyboy."

"You're not a bad dancer yourself, for a C-minus gym student," he replied, his mouth twitching in a grin. She laughed. He pulled her closer, sealing their fronts together, her breasts pressing against his ribs. His nostrils flared slightly as he looked down at her. She couldn't pull her gaze off him.

"Remember the other day, when you said that an adrenaline rush wasn't your main reason for becoming a pilot?"

she asked. He nodded. "What *was* the primary reason, then?"

He studied her face silently for a moment before he responded.

"It's kind of hard to put into words," he said eventually.

"Try me."

"Okay. The first time I ever flew in a plane, it was on a commercial airliner to Hawaii with my family. I was seven. I'll never forget it—the brute force of the plane lifting me, looking out the window and seeing an entire new world. It didn't hit me immediately that my mom and dad and sister weren't as blown away by the whole thing as I was. For me it was like a religious experience or something. I just *knew* I was meant to be up there."

Faith stared at him for a moment, touched by the force of his conviction.

"Do you miss it a lot? When you're…you know. On the ground?"

"Since I entered the academy, I was usually never on the ground long enough to go through withdrawal."

"I'd like to see you fly," she said. "I'd like to see you in your element."

"Name the day," he said quietly. She felt him studying her as she looked out at the radiant sunset as they slowly spun on the dance floor.

"Does it bother you?" he asked.

"What?" she asked, puzzled.

"That I love flying so much."

"Of course not. It's wonderful that you're so passionate about your job."

His gaze narrowed on her. "You're not being entirely honest. You associate a love of flying with an impermanent character."

She dropped her chin, looking sightlessly at his immaculate white shirt.

"Faith?"

"Yes?" she asked with false cheerfulness.

"Look at me," he said.

She slowly lifted her head and met his stare. It annoyed her that she found the topic so charged. What did it matter to her that Ryan had a passion for the freedom of the open skies?

"Maybe the reason I always got so homesick when I wasn't flying was that I never really had a permanent home after my parents died. I lived all over the globe in my years in the military. A plane became my refuge. That doesn't mean I can't eventually find a refuge somewhere else someday."

"On the ground?" She glanced out the floor-to-ceiling windows again, not wanting him to see the doubt in her yes.

"Yeah. On the ground. I don't think I'll ever stop loving to fly, but it's possible to feel at home in more than one place, isn't it?"

She put on a brave face and nodded. "Of course it is."

She was glad when the music came to an end. She had a feeling from Ryan's narrowed gaze that he didn't really believe her convicted tone. He tugged on her hand when she started to return to their seats at the table.

"Let's get your wrap and step onto the terrace for a moment," he said.

"Okay," Faith replied. Her heart started to do a drumroll on her breastbone as he led her out onto the empty terrace. The sun had sunk completely into Lake Michigan at this point, leaving a lingering residue of pink, purple and gold streaks in the western sky.

"What is it, Ryan?" Faith asked when they faced one another next to the rail of the terrace and she saw how somber his expression was. A chilly lake breeze swept past them. Faith shivered and pulled her wrap closer around her. Before she suspected what he planned, Ryan took her into his arms. She stiffened at first, but then found herself melting against him. She sighed, pressing her cheek to his lapel. The fortress of his embrace felt wonderful—solid, warm and secure.

"There's something important we need to talk about," he said. She became distracted when she felt him press his mouth to the top of her head, kissing her.

"What?" she asked, something in his serious tone making her wary.

"We need to talk about the baby—its security, both legally and financially."

Faith swallowed and lifted her head. She could just make out his stark features in the dim light from the restaurant.

"All right," she said. "What about it?"

He reached up and gently removed a windblown curl from her cheek. She shivered, but not from cold, when he tucked it behind her ear and his fingers grazed her skin.

"The thing of it is, Faith," he began, "given the circumstances, I think the right thing to do—the *only* thing to do—is for us to get married."

Chapter Eight

From her stunned expression of disbelief, Ryan realized it'd been the last thing she'd expected him to say. He felt himself sinking and forced himself to rally. He'd known this particular challenge wouldn't be easy.

"You can't be serious," she said.

"I'm dead serious. Think about it, Faith. If we marry, I'll have a legal responsibility for the child, no matter what."

Anxiety leaked into her expression. "You need it to be a *legal obligation* to be a father to the baby?"

"No. That's not what I mean. Of course I'll do my part no matter what. More—if you'll let me. But my point is, the legal contract of marriage makes things easier all around. The baby will automatically become my dependent. There won't be any hassles with the Air Force in regard to providing all the benefits that go along with the fact that I'm a veteran."

He saw her brows pinch together in dubious consideration at that. He pushed on. "Think about it, Faith. You have your own business. You know how expensive buying your own health care is. If we're married, you'll have coverage not only for the baby forever, but for yourself, as well. During the delivery."

She bit at her lower lip, looking bewildered.

"There's not only the legal and financial considerations," he continued. "I'd love to say that in this day and age, it doesn't matter to a child whether his parents have ever been married or not, but I think we'd both agree that just isn't the case." When he saw the doubt and anxiety lingering on her face, he threw out his trump card. He hadn't wanted to use it, but Faith wasn't going to give him any choice in this.

"We can get a divorce after the baby is born, if you like," he said. He forced himself not to grimace at the words.

He was desperate for Faith to accept him into her life. If he had to resort to partial measures in order to gain her compliance, he'd take what he could get. His only hope was that if she allowed him in partially, he could eventually coax her into accepting him completely. Faith clearly had doubts about his worthiness as a partner. Given her past with Jesse, he couldn't say he blamed her.

He just needed a chance. An opportunity to prove himself, once and for all.

He slid his hand into his jacket pocket. Her eyes went huge when he opened up the ring box. The lights from the interior of the restaurant glittered in the center diamond brilliant and glowed like a subdued fire in emeralds surrounding the band.

"I hope you like it," he said. "I chose the emeralds to match your eyes."

She looked bowled over.

"Are you really that shocked?" he asked. "I would have

thought you were at least partially expecting something like this. It's not like I haven't made it clear I have feelings for you."

He instantly regretted saying that. A panicked look entered her expression.

"Ryan, you're just saying that because of the circumstances. You're under no obligation to do this."

He shook his head and gave a small bark of laughter. "I don't feel obligated, Faith. I *want* to do this."

"For the baby, right?" she asked shakily.

"Right," he said grimly. It wasn't really a lie. He was partially doing this for the baby. The baby was his, after all.

The baby was *theirs*. As in, theirs *together*.

He just needed to prove to Faith that *she* was his, as well. And just as he'd suspected, he thought as he studied her anxious face, it wasn't going to be a simple challenge.

Faith stared at the most beautiful ring she'd ever seen and felt herself spinning. Her heart throbbed so loudly in her ears, she wondered if Ryan could hear it. He wanted her to marry again?

He wanted her to marry *him?*

She stared up at him helplessly, the lovely ring winking in the dim light as if to coax her.

"Ryan...I don't know what to say."

"Think about it, then. You can give me your answer when you're ready." Despite her doubts, a sharp pain of disappointment went through her when he closed the ring box and slipped it back into his pocket. He put his hands on her shoulders and pulled her closer, so that her lower belly was flush against his groin and her breasts pressed against his ribs. "But there's one thing I should make clear. I don't want there to be any doubt how much I want you. I kept my attraction for you buried while you were married to Jesse. I wasn't even aware of its magnitude until Christmas Eve. I'm not going to lie to myself about it anymore. And I'm not going to lie to you."

He bent and covered her mouth with his. He felt her small, surprised gasp, sensed the heat behind her parted lips. Altering the angle of the kiss, he sought with his tongue, relishing her sweetness. Just one taste and he found himself hardening for her, the lash of desire striking sharp, stinging nerve and flesh. He felt her mouth soften beneath him. Triumph soared through him when her tongue began to duel shyly with his. He pulled her closer in his arms, deepening the already ravenous kiss. His hands settled on her hips. He palmed her hungrily, loving how her curves fit his hands.

He pushed her even closer against his body, groaning quietly when he felt her softness cradle his arousal. He wanted her again, with the strength and heat of a thousand suns. He didn't think he could take much more of standing on the sidelines, ravenous and craving while Faith was just out of his reach.

He lifted his head, nipping at her lips.

"I want to make love to you again. I have every second…of every day…since that first time," he said quietly between gentle, hungry kisses on her mouth. "Tell me that you want that, too."

"I do," she said breathlessly, returning his feverish kisses avidly.

Arousal raged in him at her admission. "Then let's go. Would you like to come to my hotel room? Or would you prefer we go to your house?"

It took him a moment to realize she was no longer participating as eagerly in their kiss. He lifted his head and studied her face. The uncertainty he saw there sliced through his lust like a sharp blade. Perhaps she noticed his disappointment, because her tone sounded apologetic when she spoke.

"Ryan, if you want me to consider your proposal of marriage seriously, I don't think we should cloud the picture by sleeping together."

He pulled her closer next to his body, making sure she knew the profound effect she had on him. "It's kind of hard to be completely rational when I want you so much," he said. "Maybe we could think clearer if we just gave in to it?"

She gave him a suspicious look, and then laughed when she saw his small smile.

"You can't blame a guy for trying," he muttered. He released her with extreme reluctance. She gathered her wrap around her and looked up at him solemnly.

"I want to think this over," she explained. "It's hard to do that when you're...we're..."

"I understand." He sighed.

She bit her lip and stared out at the black lake. "I think I should probably go home. I have a lot to think about," she said.

He ran his hand along her shawl-covered arm.

"I'll be available. If you want to talk about the idea of marriage, just call me. But while you're thinking things over, I should return to San Francisco. There's a lot I need to do if I intend to move the charter airline business to Michigan."

"Do you still plan to do that? Even if we don't...marry?" she finished awkwardly.

He nodded. "I purchased the Cessna that was for sale at the airport, and I've arranged to rent space there for my planes and an office."

"Really? You've been busy," she said, sounding a little numb.

"I haven't changed my mind about wanting to be near my son or daughter. I don't think I could stand being that far away on a regular basis from my child." *Or from you,* he finished privately. If he said that out loud, she'd run scared. He'd already witnessed how skittish she could become at the idea of them in a romantic relationship. For now his best bet would be to give her the space she needed to feel confident in her decision. He touched her cheek with his fingertips, wishing he could erase the doubt and fear on her face.

"Take your time. I'll be here, whenever you need me," Ryan said.

"Thank you," she whispered, smiling up at him. Something twisted in his gut when he saw tears shining in her eyes.

Two weeks later Faith took off work a little early and stopped by the grocery store. Tonight was a special night. She wanted to make a nice dinner and there were still some last-minute details at the house that needed completing.

At around six that evening she finished making the bed in the guest bedroom, taking extra time to fluff the pillows. Her heart raced with nervous anticipation. She'd already showered and dressed in a manner that she hoped looked nice without seeming like she *tried* to look nice. The steaks she planned to make on the grill were marinating and the green bean, grape and pasta salad was ready to serve.

She ran her hand across the pillowcase, trying to picture Ryan's head resting there. It seemed surreal, but it was going to happen. Tonight. Ryan had already arrived in Holland. He would be at her house at any moment.

For a period of time—it would be *his* house, as well.

A week after the fundraiser ball, following a great deal of soul-searching, she'd called him in California and agreed to marry him. He'd taken another week to tidy up matters with his business and put his condo up for sale. In all that time Faith hadn't seen him. She missed him more than she cared to admit, his absence feeling like a raw ache in her belly, which she continually told herself was a figment of her imagination or quite possibly indigestion from her pregnant state.

She'd made clear her requirements for the marriage, of course. It would be in name only. Ryan could live at her house until the divorce was final—in the spare bedroom. They would remain married until the baby was born, giving their child at least the basics of legitimacy. Faith wouldn't have cared about such a thing; her baby would be loved to the ends of the earth, no matter what legal contract had been observed or not observed at the time of its birth. However she didn't want to deprive her baby of any of the benefits of a "normal" childhood.

Whatever "normal" meant.

She now had an inkling of what Ryan had meant about the social stigma associated with having a child out of wedlock, as much as she wished she hadn't gained knowledge of that particular prejudice. Her parents had been stunned and somewhat stiff when she'd informed them the day after the fundraiser that she was pregnant. When she'd called them back, and informed them that she planned to elope with Ryan—the father of her baby—they'd seemed somewhat mollified.

Faith knew her parents were utterly involved with each other, their friends and their social schedule. She wasn't offended that they'd seemed relieved when she said Ryan and she planned to elope in a small, private ceremony, and that they wouldn't be required to fly from their cozy condominium to Michigan. She routinely made excuses for her parents' lackluster interest in her life, and had long ago accepted the fact that Bob and Myra Blackwell were more interested in each other and their social network than they'd ever been in their only daughter. Faith described them as "deliriously happy in their golden years," for instance, while her friend Jane was known to dub them "self-involved excuses for parents."

In all honesty Faith wasn't much bothered by the idea that her parents couldn't be roused from their routine to attend her wedding. Given the facade of the marriage, she'd prefer not to have too many witnesses to the event.

She stood next to the bed and glanced around Ryan's new bedroom suite, anxious to make sure everything was neat and orderly. Her stomach seemed to leap into her chest cavity when she heard the brisk knock at her front door.

She opened her mouth to greet him when she opened the outer door, but nothing came out. He looked amazing to her. In the two weeks of his absence, his hair had grown a little bit. It now brushed his collar in the back and fell farther forward on his forehead. Along with a slight scruff on his lean jaw and the duffel bag flung casually over his shoulder, he appeared to be exactly what she'd subtly accused him of being in the past—a bad-boy, extremely sexy pilot with the promise of a new adventure gleaming in his eyes. Or maybe the reason her brain immediately leaped to "sex" had to do with the way his dark eyes trailed over her in a preylike perusal, as though he was calmly planning where he was going to take his first bite.

She cleared her throat and forced her ridiculous thoughts to scatter.

"Welcome back," she said breathlessly. "Or should I say, welcome home."

He grinned—a quick, brilliant flash of sex appeal.

"Thanks," he said, stepping into the foyer when she waved her hand and stepped back.

"Did everything go okay with your arrival in Holland?" Faith asked as she led him to his bedroom, her chin twisted over her shoulder. She was having trouble pulling her stare off his rugged male glory and nearly passed the doorway to his room.

"Yeah, all went well. Both planes are snug in their new homes at the airport, and I dropped Scott off at his new apartment," he said, referring to the other pilot for Eagle Air.

"So Scott is all settled?" Faith asked as they hovered outside the room.

"Yeah. He wants to thank you in person for all you've done in helping him. He liked the apartment a lot. I want to thank you, too, Faith, for looking at some places and sending him the apartment photos and the phone numbers for getting utilities connected and everything."

"Mari took care of some things, as well," she reminded him, flipping on the light and leading him into the room.

"I know. We're thankful to both of you. I'm glad Scott decided to make the move with me. He's too good of a pilot to lose. Besides, he's as much of a workhorse as I am," Ryan said distractedly, his gaze moving around the bedroom and finally landing on Faith.

"I can't believe you did all this," he said, sounding stunned.

"You...you like it, don't you?" Faith asked, referring to the newly refurbished bedroom.

"I can't believe you did all this," he repeated, looking almost grim. He plopped his large duffel bag on the bed and came toward her. "You shouldn't have, Faith," he admonished, looking all around the room again and then back at her. "I would have been happy sleeping on the couch. You didn't have to redecorate a whole room."

"It's just new bedding and curtains."

"And new lamps, and rugs...and was that painting there before?" he asked, referring to the framed Lake Michigan landscape.

"No," she admitted, feeling uncomfortable under his blazing stare.

He muttered something under his breath and stepped closer. Her breath stuck in her lungs when he took her into his arms, making the action seem as natural as climbing into the pilot's seat of an F-16.

"You shouldn't have spent all that time and money on me," he said quietly, his voice resonating above her fore-head. She looked up slowly. It overwhelmed her a little—a lot—to feel his rock-hard body next to hers, to see his bold-featured, much-missed visage so close. "I'll pay you back for everything you purchased."

"No, that's not necessary. I wanted to make it a nice place for you," she said, her voice just above a whisper, her eyes caught in his steady stare.

"I missed you while I was gone," he said.

"I...I missed you, too," she admitted shakily. She ducked her head when he lowered his. She was sorely tempted to lift it again, to accept his kiss—to glory in it. Because there was little doubt, given the glint in his eyes and the rigid expression of his features, kissing her had been *precisely* what Ryan was about to do. She couldn't allow their ar-rangement to derail from her planned course within three minutes of his arrival at the house.

"Why don't you get unpacked, and I'll go and get us some lemonade in the kitchen," Faith said, backing out of his arms. Her false cheeriness stood in stark contrast to Ryan's slanted brows and slightly irritated expression.

He entered the kitchen several minutes later. She glanced sideways at him as he bent to greet an ecstatic Topsy and ruffle the puppy's coat.

"Look at you. You've grown, haven't you, little girl?" he murmured, grinning.

It was an unusually warm spring day and he wore a short-sleeved white T-shirt and a pair of jeans. The shirt displayed his muscular arms ideally. Faith paused in the action of garnishing their drinks with lime slices.

"I didn't know you had a tattoo," she said, eyeing the only partially revealed depiction of what appeared to be a bird with outstretched wings etched on steely biceps just beneath a white sleeve.

He stood, a darkly amused look on his face. "You haven't given me the opportunity to show it to you yet."

She blushed and busied herself putting away the ice-cube container. It was true what he'd said—they'd been so wild with lust on Christmas Eve, they hadn't really had the opportunity for the niceties.

Like fully undressing, for instance.

What he'd said was also just a bit too *intimate,* given the comfortable, safe parameters she was trying to immediately establish in regard to their cohabitation.

"Ryan," she began with forced calmness, handing him his lemonade, "if we're going to make this work, we have to…respect each other's boundaries."

His dark brows lifted at her schoolmarm tone of voice. "I wasn't trying to be disrespectful. I was just stating the truth," he said, taking a sip of lemonade. She couldn't help but grin when he made a sound of appreciation, then swallowed the contents of the glass in three large swigs.

"Sorry," he said a moment later. "I was helping Scott move around some of his furniture, and it's hot out today. I was thirstier than I thought, and it tasted great."

"It's nice out in the shade on the back terrace. Do you want to sit out there?" Faith asked, holding up the pitcher to refill his glass. She was a little alarmed by his level of familiarity—not to mention the heat of his stare. She thought it would be advisable to take the opportunity to re-hash the "rules" of their arrangement before things slipped into foolish chaos.

He agreed about going to the terrace, and the three of them—Topsy, Ryan and Faith—retired to the back terrace.

"Everything's blooming," Ryan said as he sat down in a deck chair and surveyed the backyard. "Including you."

Faith paused in the action of settling in the chair next to him. Her glance dropped to her belly. It was definitely protruding a little next to the fabric of the cotton shorts she wore. She'd originally thought the embroidered peasant blouse she wore to be a modest, yet feminine choice for Ryan's arrival. Suddenly she wondered if instead of looking prim, she didn't more resemble the busty serving wench on the side of a beer bottle.

She froze, her lemonade glass trembling in her hand, when he leaned over on his hip and matter-of-factly placed his hand on her belly. After a second she inhaled sharply, stunned by the weight of his hand on her rising abdomen.

"Have you really been feeling okay?" Ryan asked, his voice sounding husky and nearer than she expected.

She nodded, keeping her gaze aimed straight ahead. He'd called every few days during his absence and always asked her about her health.

"I talked to Mari yesterday. She told me that you were showing—a little tiny bit, anyway," he said, shifting his hand upward. Prickles of pleasure went through her. Her breasts were growing so full that in her partially reclining position, his hand almost cradled them. "She said you two found a dress. For the wedding."

"We did," Faith said, trying to sound normal. She took a swig of her lemonade, feeling ridiculous doing something so mundane while Ryan touched her so intimately.

She knew she should tell him to stop touching her, but she couldn't help but feel it would draw attention to the significance of the contact…

…the *impact* it was having on her.

"I needed something new anyway. I've gone up a size, with the baby," she explained, hoping he didn't think she'd gone shopping like a breathless bride for her dream wedding dress. "Mari and I had a nice time, shopping together for it in downtown Holland. We went to lunch afterward." She risked a sideways glance. His gaze was glued to her face, but his hand lowered over her belly, as if he were tracing the slight convexness. He was just eager to feel his growing child, that's all. She tried like crazy to ignore the fireworks of sensation going off in her body as his hand reached the lower curve, his pinky resting at the top of her pelvis. A heavy, pleasant ache expanded at her core.

Focus, she told herself.

"Your sister is such a wonderful person. I can't wait to meet Marc," Faith said in a pressured fashion, desperate to turn her attention away from Ryan's stroking hand. "Are you close to Marc?" she asked in an odd, high-pitched voice as she blindly watched Topsy sink her sharp little teeth into a chew toy.

His deck chair squeaked next to her, and Faith realized he'd leaned closer. His hand moved yet again, the slight bump in her belly curving into his palm.

"We used to be best friends when we were kids," Ryan murmured, sounding distracted. Faith nervously took a sip of lemonade as his hand slid up her abdomen. This time he went farther, the ridge of his forefinger grazing her lower breasts. "Before the accident his father caused, that is," he added, moving his hand in a slight sawing motion, stimulating the sensitive skin of her ribs.

Faith stifled a choking sound. Her nipples drew tight against the clinging fabric of her bra.

"After the accident, Marc and I had a falling out," Ryan continued quietly. Faith struggled to recall the topic. His hand lowered again, this time detailing the side of her abdomen, making it very difficult for her to breathe. "A pretty severe falling out, actually. It came to blows during the lawsuit hearings, I remember."

"You two fought?" Faith asked, startled. She found herself examining his dark head and profile. He stared fixedly at his hand on her stomach. He nodded.

"Yeah. It almost came to blows again a few years ago when Mari got involved with him after all this time. They were teenage sweethearts, you know."

"No. I didn't."

"Then the accident happened. And the lawsuits," Ryan said so grimly that she temporarily forgot her discomfort—and arousal—at his possessive caress. Compassion for him filled her. She touched a crisp, short sideburn and he tilted his head, spearing her with his stare.

"It must have been so hard for you all—that accident, the losses…everything that came after it."

He said nothing, but his dark eyes spoke to her, nonetheless.

"Will it be difficult for you? To have Mari and Marc stand up for us when we get…married on Sunday?" she asked, fumbling and blushing at the mention of what they would be doing in three days time.

"No. It'll be fine," he said.

It suddenly struck her that they were touching each other very intimately and speaking in hushed tones. She'd called him out here to clarify the safe boundaries of their arrangement, and instead, Ryan's touch had turned her into a quivering, aroused bundle of nerves.

She dropped her hand and looked away. Slowly, Ryan removed his hand. She could almost feel his disappointment.

Or was it disapproval?

"So we're all set? For the wedding?" he said, the location of his voice informing her that he'd leaned back in his chair.

"Yes. Father Mike will meet all of us at the orchard," she said, trying to sound matter-of-fact, even though she was breathless and she could still feel the imprint of his hand on her abdomen. "It was a wonderful idea that you had, having the ceremony at the McKinley Farm and Orchard. The trees will be in full bloom. It'll be beautiful."

"Marc and Mari actually suggested it. They introduced me to it—and the Cherry Pie Café—last year. The McKinleys are nice people."

Faith smiled. She knew the orchard owners, Nathan and Clarisse McKinley, and had eaten several times at their delicious, lakeside restaurant on the grounds. It'd never occurred to her before how perfect the location would be for a spring wedding.

Not that this was a real wedding or anything, she quickly reminded herself.

Ryan checked his watch. He cursed quietly and sat up with a start.

"What's wrong?" Faith asked.

"I have to go. I have a flight. I'm taking a couple DuBois Enterprises executives from Chicago to New York."

"Oh," Faith said, taken aback. "I hadn't realized you'd start working so soon."

He grimaced slightly as he glanced at her and placed his long legs on either side of the lounge chair in preparation to stand. "You don't mind, do you? I'll be back by the time you wake up tomorrow. I was lucky to get a contract with DuBois. It's going to keep me busy. *Extremely* busy. I should be able to buy another plane soon, with as much work as Deidre and Nick are willing to send my way. I want to build a lucrative business, Faith. For the baby. For the future," he added, his dark eyes moving over her face.

"Of course," she said, feeling embarrassed, all thoughts of her warm welcome dinner for him fizzling to mist. Had she sounded whiny because he was leaving so soon after his arrival? She hadn't meant to. She admired him for working so hard to build up his company. "I'll go in with you and give you the key to the front door."

"Thanks." He touched her cheek and gently tucked a curl behind her ear. Faith tried to ignore the tendril of pleasure that coiled down her neck at his touch, just like she tried to ignore the fact that she was disappointed he was leaving.

After Ryan had left for the airport, she wondered why the house felt so empty. It made no sense whatsoever. She'd lived alone there for over a year, and never felt lonely. Now Ryan had blown through her front door and flown off after just an hour, and the house already felt empty in his absence.

It worried her, how easily she could get used to his presence; how much she could come to count on it.

It meant she'd be all that much more disappointed when he was gone. How much more proof did she need than tonight, that a man like Ryan wasn't meant to stay in one place for long?

No. That wasn't going to happen, she told herself firmly as she started down the hallway. She wasn't going to become dependent on his being there. Hadn't she been happy and satisfied for almost her entire adult life by calling her own shots?

So if she was so confident that she didn't need Ryan Itani one way or another, why did she pause outside his opened bedroom door? She hesitated, and then entered slowly. She stood at the mirrored chest of drawers and ran her fingers over a leather box, a bottle of his cologne and a handsome gold watch, dressier than the black casual one she'd seen on his wrist before he'd left.

He might be in his plane at this moment, preparing to fly away from Holland. But his things were here, hallmarks of his presence, reminders that even if it *was* temporary, for a period of time, this was Ryan's home.

She tried to ignore the feeling of satisfaction that tore through her at the thought, but it was just as hard to banish as her other feelings were when it came to Ryan.

She saved the dinner she'd made, in case Ryan wanted it tomorrow. By the time she made herself a grilled cheese sandwich and ate, it was getting late. She had a seven o'clock appointment at the office, so decided to retire early. She made sure some fresh towels were laid out for Ryan in his bathroom—he might want to shower when he got home early in the morning.

Now that she was pregnant, sleep came almost immediately the second her cheek hit the pillow. It took a little longer tonight, as thoughts and worries about Ryan moving in and their upcoming marriage whirled around her consciousness. Still, she was fast asleep by the time her bedside clock dial turned to ten o'clock.

She awoke with a start in the middle of the night. She just lay there, her heart racing, trying to figure out what had startled her. There hadn't been a noise, had there? It took her panicked brain several seconds to recall that it was probably Ryan returning home from his flight. She glanced at her clock. It read 4:35 a.m. She heard a tiny squeak from the hallway floor, as if someone was walking down it with caution.

It was *Ryan out there, wasn't it?* she thought anxiously.

She rose and scurried for her robe, donning it over the thigh-length nightshirt she wore. She gave a sigh of relief when she saw the light on in the kitchen in the distance and heard the sound of the refrigerator door open. Surely a burglar wouldn't make himself a late-night snack. Even knowing it was Ryan, however, anticipation coiled in her belly as she walked around the corner into the kitchen.

He stood next to the refrigerator, the door open.

"Hi," Faith said.

He peered around the door. The refrigerator swung closed. "I'm sorry," he said quietly. "I didn't mean to wake you. Was I too loud?"

Faith shook her head, staring. He was only wearing a pair of dark blue pajama bottoms. And by all things that were holy, she'd never seen a more beautiful man in her life.

She gaped at the vision before her of rippling, hard muscle covered by golden skin. She now could see that the tattoo on bulging, powerful-looking biceps was the Air Force logo that had been artfully depicted by the illustrator as transforming into a real eagle taking flight.

She swallowed with difficulty. Her throat had gone completely dry.

"Faith?" Ryan asked, looking a little worried.

"No, no. You weren't loud at all. I'm just used to living alone. I must have a sixth sense, about someone being in the house," she said, her gaze darting everywhere around the room, trying to avoid gawking at the awesome sight of his half-naked body. She cleared her throat and told herself to get a grip. "Would you like me to make you something to eat?"

"No. I was just going to make some toast or something, if that's okay. I haven't eaten since we left New York this morning."

Her expression collapsed in compassion. "You must be starved." She swept toward the refrigerator. He took a step back. "Just sit down over there in the breakfast nook, and I'll get something for you."

"Faith—"

"How about a cheese omelet and toast?" she asked, already grabbing the eggs. She paused, looking up at him when he put a hand on her forearm, halting her.

"I don't want you to cook for me. It's four-thirty in the morning. You should go back to bed."

She shrugged. "I'm up now. I have to be at the office at seven, anyway." His furrowed brow smoothed slightly when she gave him a smile of reassurance. "Will it help any if I eat with you?"

He shook his head and looked skyward, as though looking for patience in dealing with her. "Does it make any difference what I say?" he asked dryly.

She shook her head matter-of-factly. "Why don't you sit down in the breakfast nook? I'll bring you some juice."

"I don't want you to wait on me," he grumbled. He released her arm and reached into the refrigerator himself. "I'll pour the juice and make the toast."

"Deal. How was your flight?" she asked him a moment later as she whipped the eggs in a bowl and Ryan plugged in the toaster.

"Pretty uneventful. Just the way I like them." He gave her a backward glance. Her cheeks heated as she returned her attention to the eggs. He'd caught her staring at the way his back muscles rippled when he moved.

"Faith?"

"Yes?" she asked, looking around and hoping he didn't notice her pink cheeks.

He stepped toward her. His naked torso was like a miracle of taut ridges, valleys and dense, swelling muscle. His skin was beautiful—smooth and dark-honey colored. A smattering of dark hair grew on his chest, but not thickly. A thin, tempting trail of it led from his taut bellybutton and disappeared beneath the low-riding cotton pants.

She felt as if her lungs had failed her as he drew nearer.

"When I was looking in the refrigerator before you came in, I noticed—" He halted, looking a little uncomfortable. "Were you planning on making dinner? Last night?"

He definitely had to notice her blush now.

"Oh…yes. But it wasn't a big deal. I just thought I'd throw something on the grill, you know. Just a little welcome dinner…"

She faded off, feeling scored by his stare. She turned around and began beating the eggs again, pausing when she felt Ryan put his hands on her shoulders. He applied a slight pressure. Reluctantly she set the whisk in the bowl and turned to face him. He stood close enough that a bulging pectoral muscle was less than a foot away from her face. He pushed back her unbound hair from her cheek, smoothing it over her shoulder. Her neck tingled with pleasure. His fingertips brushed against the shell of her ear, and her shivering amplified.

"I'm sorry I ruined the evening," he said quietly.

"You didn't ruin anything," she insisted, looking up to reassure him. "You had a job. It wasn't a big deal."

His face looked somber as he studied her. He cradled her jaw with his hand. She felt so small in comparison to him. So feminine standing there next to his large, hard male body. She realized she was holding her breath.

"It *was* a big deal." She stared at him, mesmerized. His nostrils flared slightly and his face drew nearer. "I'll make it up to you, I promise."

"There's nothing to make up. It was nothing," she said, the words popping out of her with her expelled breath.

"I disagree," he murmured. His lips moved now just inches from her own. He stepped forward with his right foot, so that his inner thigh touched the outside of her hip. He leaned into her and she was wedged between Ryan and the counter. "It was sweet of you. *You're* incredibly sweet, Faith."

His hands tightened around her waist. He paused, his face just inches from her own. She met his stare, wide-eyed, and saw he was watching her like a hawk. Her lips parted.

He swooped down, seizing her mouth with his own.

Chapter Nine

His mouth moved over hers, a sensual drug that left her consciousness hazed by pleasure. He pressed closer, nudging her middle. Her eyes popped open, even though she kept avidly participating in the kiss. He wasn't wearing anything beneath the thin fabric of the pajama bottoms.

His obvious arousal made something squeeze tight deep inside her, made her recall all too well how he'd filled her on Christmas Eve, how he'd pulsed high and hard and alive deep inside her. Desire sluiced through her, so sharp she cried out softly into his hot, marauding mouth.

She touched his back with her hands, relishing the sensation of smooth skin gloving muscle and bone so tightly. Her fingertips moved eagerly, detailing the line of his spine. Her palms swept over the expanse of his back, pushing him closer.

He came up for air, making a hissing sound.

"I know you think we shouldn't give in to this, Faith,

but for the life of me, how can I forget what you felt like that night?" he whispered roughly next to her lips. "You were so small…" He plucked at her upturned lips. "So sweet. I can't sleep at night, remembering how good it felt," he muttered as he reined feverish kisses on her lips, her cheek, her ear. His hands moved at her waist, stroking her back, lowering to cup her hips possessively. He brought her closer, shifting his pelvis, rubbing their flesh together, stoking the fire.

Faith found herself sinking into heat.

"Please let me make love to you again," he said hoarsely, covering her ear with his mouth. The suction that came from his kiss caused prickles of excitement to reverberate down her spine. "I've thought about it since Christmas. How could something that feels this good be wrong?" His hand rose over her ribs, finding a breast. He covered her, nestling her flesh in his palm. She whimpered as he began to knead her gently. Her nipple grew hard against him. He gave a low growl of male approval. His body tensed and hardened next to hers.

She gasped in pleasure.

"You think so, too," he rasped.

"Yes," she whispered, her mouth seeking out his. "Yes," she breathed next to his lips before she pushed his head down to hers. They fastened together in another ravenous kiss. Sensual pleasure suffused every pore in her being. She said nothing when she felt him lift her off her feet. He strode out of the kitchen and through the living room, his stare scorching her. The bedroom was shadowed and dim, the only source of light the one in the distant kitchen and a glowing bedside clock.

He laid her on the bed and came down over her, immediately fusing their mouths again. His body covered hers, with plenty to spare. He felt so hard, so wonderful. Her mind went blank. Only pleasure existed…and Ryan.

His hands moved over her, conferring delight and heat wherever he touched. Faith was far from passive, however, touching him back just as heatedly, relishing the opportunity to feel what she'd barely allowed herself to look at earlier. His hands found their way to the belt of her robe, loosening it, and then moved to her thighs. He raised the fabric of her nightshirt to her waist, pausing to caress and enliven her tingling nerves with every stroke.

"So soft," he rasped, breaking their kiss. He lowered his head. She made a choking sound at the sensation of his mouth pressing between her rib cage. His lips nibbled at her tenderly, making her shiver. He tasted her, his tongue leaving damp spots on her pebbling skin. He pushed up her nightshirt. She gasped at the sensation of his mouth on her breast, moaning as he drew on her. Pleasure tore through her body. Her breasts had never felt so sensitive. He continued to use his mouth and tongue on one nipple, and used his fingertips to gently manipulate the other.

"Ryan," she said helplessly.

"I've never tasted anything as good you," he muttered thickly. He rose over her, his erection between her thighs. Faith's eyes sprang wide at the sensation. She twisted her head on the pillow. Her cheek brushed against the soft fabric of the pillowcase…

…the same pillowcase she'd just put on last evening. In Ryan's bedroom. The room where he was going to live while they shared a marriage of convenience for the benefit of their child.

She cried out in distress, moving her chin when Ryan bent again to ravish her mouth. He paused, his lips just inches from her averted jaw. She clamped her eyes shut when she felt a whole new type of tension enter his sleek muscles.

"We can't," she said shakily. "This isn't how this was supposed to go, Ryan."

"I thought things were going pretty damn great," he said grimly.

"Ryan…"

He cursed under his breath and rolled off her. She came up on her elbows, staring at his shadowed figure anxiously.

"I'm sorry," she said. "I shouldn't have agreed to this. This whole moving in together…the marriage idea. It was a mistake."

He lowered his arm. "No. You weren't at fault," he said, his voice hard. She heard him inhale slowly. When he resumed speaking, he sounded calmer. "It was my fault. I'm to blame. I agreed to respect your boundaries under this arrangement. I didn't."

"I was hardly complaining," she said miserably, moving to the side of the bed. He caught her hand and she paused.

"It won't happen again. Not unless you change your mind."

Her mouth fell open. Guilt surged through her. He was making it sound like he'd taken advantage of her, when goodness knows she'd been every bit as eager for him as he was her.

Not unless you change your mind.

She reluctantly pulled her hand from his and stood at the side of the bed.

The problem was, Faith couldn't trust herself. She couldn't tell Ryan that what she *wanted* was him.

What she *didn't* want was all the heartache she might receive if she opened herself up to him too far.

* * *

All was quiet in his bedroom when she crept out of the house on Friday morning. When she returned home that night, a heavy pregnancy-exhaustion weighting her muscles, she found a note in the kitchen from Ryan. It said he'd taken a flight to San Francisco, and that he'd just spend the night in his still-unsold condo before returning on Saturday.

Check the fridge, she read the last line few lines of his note. *A peace offering. I'm sorry about last night. I'm not sure how it is I'm always screwing things up when all I really want is to get it right with you.*

Tears burned her eyelids. She opened the refrigerator.

The first thing she saw was a luscious-looking dessert nestled in a paper cup with thick shavings of white chocolate nestled in frosting. She recognized it as her favorite guilty pleasure from the bakery downtown—a brownie with white chocolate chunks and Macadamia nuts. She pictured a smiling Georgiana at the bakery telling Ryan about Faith's preferred dessert.

Beneath the confection was a plastic-covered plate. She grabbed it and the brownie and set them on the counter. When she peeled back the plastic on the plate, she saw that he'd grilled the steak she'd prepared for his thwarted welcome dinner. He'd placed a helping of her green bean, grape and pasta salad next to it.

She stared blankly at the meal he'd made for a full minute, her throat feeling tight. She'd treated him unfairly last night. Her guilt mounted over the fact that he kept apologizing for a sin she'd participated in every bit as enthusiastically as he had. There was a singular, powerful attraction between them. Ryan was just a man; one who was undoubtedly unused to having his sexual advances denied.

Faith knew firsthand how difficult it was to deny him.

How fair was it for her to agree to this arrangement between them, knowing full well that she was making him uncomfortable?

Miserable?

What if, even now, he was finding the gratification she'd denied him last night in the arms of another woman?

"Don't be stupid," she snapped at herself out loud. She picked up the plate and cupcake and set them on the breakfast nook table.

She'd drive herself absolutely mad by having thoughts like that every time Ryan took off in a plane.

She arose the next morning to a pristine, sunny spring day. As she was preparing some breakfast, she heard her cell phone ringing. She answered it when she saw it was Mari calling.

"Good morning," she greeted, setting her steaming bowl of oatmeal on the table.

"Good morning!" Mari returned cheerfully. "How are you feeling?"

"Wonderful," Faith said honestly. "I'm always energized in the mornings."

"And wiped out by two o'clock, right?" Mari said knowingly. "The fatigue is supposed to go away for a lot of women during the second trimester and come back for the last, but I know for me, I'm affected the whole time."

"Unfortunately, I think we might have that in common," Faith said dryly, touching her abdomen. "I'm not complaining, though. Luckily, I can go into my office if it gets too bad and close my eyes for fifteen minutes."

"Those catnaps make a world of difference. I just wanted to tell you that Marc and I are spending the night with Brigit tonight in Harbor Town. I can drive over this afternoon if there are any last-minute details you'd like me to see to for the wedding. Ryan called last night, and said he would be in San Francisco until later today. He thought you might need some help."

Warmth rushed through her at the mention of Ryan's concern for her. "Oh, no. I'm fine. There really isn't much to plan, it's going to be such a simple ceremony. Ryan has gotten the license, and you helped me with the dress and Ryan's ring. Clarisse is going to make the four of us a nice lunch on the terrace after the ceremony. I hear the weather is supposed to be wonderful. Everything is all taken care of."

"So you don't have any errands you need run today?"

"No, I'm actually seeing some patients at the office this morning, I got so backed up this week. But I really appreciate you asking, Mari," she said sincerely.

"Well, call me if you change your mind. Oh…I spoke with Deidre on the phone earlier. She wants me to tell you congratulations. Ryan told her and Nick about you and the baby and his plans to headquarter Eagle Air out of Michigan. Nick thinks it's a good thing, as so many DuBois employees have to regularly go coast-to-coast, and Ryan will be more centrally located."

"Tell Deidre thank you. And as for Eagle Air, I'm happy to hear it's going to work for everybody."

They reaffirmed the time they would meet at the orchard tomorrow and said goodbye.

As Mari had predicted, Faith was exhausted by the time she returned home at a little past three that afternoon. She fed the cats and let Topsy into the yard. After she let the puppy back inside, she kicked off her pumps and flopped down on the couch in the living room. The sun shone through the large picture window next to the couch, warming her. After a minute Topsy came up to the couch, whining plaintively.

"Hi you," Faith murmured, leaning down to scoop up the fluffy puppy in her arms. She curled on her left side, Topsy snuggling between her body and the back of the couch. She closed her eyes and drifted into a contented sleep.

Ryan pulled into the driveway, his eyes feeling gritty with fatigue. He hadn't slept well last night, tossing and turning, recalling in vivid detail what had occurred with Faith the night before, wishing it hadn't happened…

…wanting like hell for it to happen again.

He had to rise early to fly a DuBois executive from San Francisco to Houston. He'd been forced to wait two hours before being cleared for takeoff in Houston, chomping at the bit the whole time for his return to Michigan.

To Faith.

The interior of the house was bright and warm when he entered. "Faith?" he called, his voice trailing off at the utter silence of the house. He walked out of the foyer and immediately saw her curled up on the couch. He approached her cautiously, a smile tugging at his mouth when he noticed Topsy tucked next to her body, both of them taking the even, shallow breaths of sleep.

He sat down at the end of the couch, careful that his movements wouldn't wake her. He sank into the cushion with a restrained sigh, his tired muscles relaxing at last. Faith hadn't changed since she'd returned home from the office. He'd noticed that she tended to only wear the tailored, knee-length skirts for work. Her bare legs looked smooth, pale and shapely next to the taupe fabric of the couch. The bottoms of her feet looked feminine and pink and…extremely touchable.

He'd promised not to touch her, though, he recalled with a stab of grim disappointment. Instead he grabbed the decorative pillow wedged behind his back and the couch and wrapped his arms around it. It was nowhere near as warm as Faith, or as soft, or as shapely.

But it'd have to do.

Faith felt Topsy's warm body moving and shifted, stretching her legs. Her feet were chilly. She sunk almost immediately back into sleep.

When she finally pried open her eyelids a while later, the light outside the window had dimmed. It was early evening. Her intended catnap had turned into a two-hour deep sleep. She felt so warm and cozy, she was tempted to get up and go back to her bed.

She lifted her head off the pillow and started. She blinked, bringing her sleepy eyes into focus, assuring herself she saw what she *thought* she was seeing. Ryan came into clearer view. He sat at the end of the couch, his long, jean-covered legs sprawled before him. Topsy had abandoned her only to relocate next to him. The puppy snuggled against his hip, her nose pressed next to his thigh. Faith's feet were in his lap, his hand draped over her toes in a relaxed grip. Her eyes widened when she saw—and felt—just how intimately her feet were pressed against the fly of his jeans.

She started to extricate her feet from the compromising position, but paused when Ryan's head moved on the back of the couch. She froze. She vaguely recalled stretching her feet earlier and finding a warm crevice in which to snuggle them.

To her rising horror, she saw Ryan open his eyes.

For a few tense seconds they just stared at each other, unmoving. His heat seemed to amplify beneath her, resonating into her feet. His hand tightened as if convulsively over her toes, then loosened.

Faith jerked her feet out of his lap.

"I'm sorry," he muttered, his voice sounding sleep-roughened and sexy. He blinked, as if clearing his vision. "I drifted off when I got home. Didn't sleep well last night."

"Neither did I," Faith said, smoothing her skirt over her thighs. She swung her feet to the floor and sat up, avoiding his gaze. "How long...I mean...when did you get home?" she asked awkwardly, running her fingers through her hair.

"About an hour ago, I think."

Topsy made a sound between a grunt and a whine. Faith turned. Topsy was blinking sleepily. Ryan was watching her face with a narrow-eyed stare.

"I didn't..." He glanced down toward his lap, clearly uncomfortable. "It was... Your feet were just *there* when I woke up."

"I know," she said, standing, suddenly wishing she were anywhere but there. "I know you didn't do it. I think I did. Sleeping...feet cold," she mumbled stupidly before she grabbed her pumps and rushed out of the living room to the safety of her bedroom.

She felt so discombobulated by the experience, so vulnerable, that she closed her bedroom door and drew a hot bath. She took her time bathing, trying to piece together her discordant feelings about Ryan...her attraction to him, her uncontrollable desire...her fear of getting hurt.

An hour later she stood at the mirror in her bathroom, brushing her hair. A soft knock came at her door. She glanced around, her eyes going wide and her heartbeat escalating. She stood there for several seconds, undecided about whether or not she should answer. If she remained quiet, Ryan might assume she was sleeping and go away.

She grabbed her robe and hurriedly shoved her arms into the sleeves, then opened the door. He stood in the dim hallway, still dressed as he had been when they'd awakened on the couch. He looked at her from below a lowered brow.

"I got you a salad from the deli. It's in the fridge," he said quietly.

"Oh, thank you. But I'm not very hungry."

"You should eat."

"Maybe later," she said, her voice barely above a whisper.

He nodded, his gaze flickering over her. "I think I'll go for a jog and try to get to bed early. Big day tomorrow."

She attempted a smile and nodded. Awkwardness flooded her. They were getting married tomorrow, and here they stood, talking to each other like acquaintances through a crack in the door.

"We're still leaving at eleven tomorrow, right?" he asked.

"Yes."

Did he exhale, as if relieved? Had he been thinking she'd changed her mind about tomorrow?

"Well, good night, then," he said.

"Good night. Ryan?" she called impulsively when he turned to walk away. He paused, looking back at her.

"Thank you for making dinner for me last night. And the brownie was delicious."

He smiled. "You made the dinner. I just cooked it."

"Well, thank you anyway," she said emphatically.

He nodded once, his expression tight, his gaze searching. He turned. Faith opened her mouth to halt him again, but uncertainty tightened her throat, silencing her.

The next day dawned even more brilliant than its predecessor. Faith peered out her bedroom window as soon as she arose. The leaves of the oak tree in the side yard had completely unfurled, looking brilliantly green against the backdrop of a cloudless, periwinkle-blue sky. A soft, mild breeze wafted through the window screen.

When she opened her bedroom door, she paused on the threshold. She could hear the muted sound of Ryan moving around in the kitchen. A ridiculous thought occurred to her that she should go back in her room and close the door.

It's unlucky for the groom to see the bride before the wedding.

Where in the world had *that* come from? Faith wondered in amused puzzlement. It wasn't as if they were a real bride and groom, after all.

She peered into the kitchen cautiously, breathing a sigh of relief when she saw that Ryan wore a gray cotton T-shirt along with his pajama bottoms.

"Good morning," she said, feeling shy for some stupid reason.

He looked around, holding a pan lid in his hand.

"Good morning. I made oatmeal. Hungry?"

"I'm starving," she admitted, entering the kitchen and opening the refrigerator. She pulled out a carton of orange juice and poured it into two glasses.

"You never ate your salad last night," he said. "No wonder you're starved. Were you nauseated? Because of the baby?"

"No. I think that's mostly passed, thank goodness." She returned the carton to the refrigerator and pulled out some English muffins. "I think I might have just been a little… keyed up."

"Nervous, you mean?"

She paused in the action of forking apart a muffin. Ryan leaned next to the counter. It didn't matter that he'd covered his museum-worthy torso with a T-shirt. He still looked roll-out-of-bed delicious.

"Yes," she admitted, dropping her gaze. "Aren't you?

A little?" She looked at his face again when he didn't immediately answer.

"I thought you were going to tell me last night that you
didn't want to go through with it," he said starkly.

"Oh…well, I was sort of having doubts last night. It's
kind of an unusual situation, isn't it?" she asked, turning
to put the muffins in the toaster.

"It's for the best. We have the baby to think about."

"I know."

A strained silence ensued.

"Do you feel any different this morning?" he asked.

She looked out the window on to the brilliant spring
day. She gave him a small, sheepish smile.

"This morning I'm feeling like…it's an awfully pretty
day for a wedding."

His face remained sober for a stretched moment.

Then he smiled the sort of smile a woman remembers
for a long, long time.

At ten forty-five that morning, Faith was cursing herself for not asking Mari or Jane or *anyone* to help her get
ready. Yes, she knew very well that this was a marriage
of convenience, so why in the world had she let Mari talk
her into buying the highly romantic silk, strapless, vintage-
inspired gown? She started to work up a sweat as she tried
to zip it herself, and had to force herself to pause and take
some calming breaths.

Her face looked anxious in the reflection of the bathroom mirror. Her heart pounded in her ears. She hadn't
been anywhere near this nervous for her wedding to Jesse.

If you don't want to do it, don't, a voice in her head
said firmly.

It was as if reminding herself that she had a choice
helped to stabilize her faltering resolution. She was doing

this for one reason—a *good* reason. The baby. It had nothing to do with how she felt about Ryan, or how he felt about her…or even how he *didn't* feel about her.

Surely she wasn't so selfish as to deny her child the most secure future she could possibly grant it?

She twisted the dress sufficiently to zip it and slid it back into place. She examined herself in the mirror. Maybe Mari's advice had been perfect, after all. The vintage ivory color worked well with her skin tone. She wore her hair down and curled loosely. It spilled around her bare shoulders. She had a wrap, but thanks to the ideal spring day with temperatures in the mid-seventies, she wouldn't need it. The intricate ruched detail around the bodice did a nice job of disguising her expanding breasts. The thing she loved most about the dress, however, was the flowing, light skirt. It made her feel airy and feminine and…

…very much like a bride.

She felt every bit as jittery as a bride on her wedding day when she left her bedroom a moment later and walked into the living room. Ryan was waiting for her, his hands folded behind his back and staring out the front picture window on to the bright spring day.

He turned. She froze.

He wore his Air Force dress uniform, and he looked… amazing. The dark blue coat and trousers were perfectly tailored to his tall form. A matching bow tie, silver trimmed shoulder boards and sleeve braid added to his immaculate, elegant, yet utterly masculine appearance.

She smiled.

"I had no idea you were going to wear your uniform."

"I hope it's okay."

"You look…fantastic."

"You look like something out of a dream."

Faith blinked. He'd sounded so quiet, so matter-of-fact, it took her a moment to absorb his compliment. She blushed.

"Thank you."

"Just a second," he said, walking toward the kitchen. When he returned, he held a gorgeous bouquet of white roses, pale orchids and sprays of apple and cherry blossoms. "Every bride is supposed to have flowers."

She accepted the bouquet. "Oh, thank you," she said feelingly. "It's gorgeous. When did you ever have time to get it?"

"I picked it up this morning while you were in the shower. After I got my haircut," he said.

"It's almost military short again."

"We're not allowed to wear a dress uniform without a regulation haircut. Even as veterans," he said, returning her smile. "Well? Are you ready to go?"

Something new had joined her anxiety when she'd seen Ryan standing there in his dress uniform, so handsome, tall and proud. A fullness unlike anything she'd ever experienced in her life filled her chest cavity, making her feel breathless with anticipation, excited and thrilled to be alive.

"Are you ready?" he asked quietly.

Faith nodded, unable to pull her gaze off him. He touched the back of her waist and guided her out the door.

Chapter Ten

Faith gasped in pleasure when Ryan turned down the entrance drive to the McKinley Orchards. The lane was lined with brilliantly pink redbud trees in full blossom.

"Oh, look. I've never seen anything so pretty in my life," she said a few minutes later when Ryan opened the car door for her and she alighted. The garden and landscape blazed so bright with spring color, it was almost blinding to the eyes. Brilliant tulips lined the path to the café, but beyond their tame, orderly border, Clarisse and Nathan had let nature do the gardening. Amaryllis, begonia, bluebell and grape hyacinth waved in the gentle breeze. In the distance stood the groves of blooming fruit trees—fuchsia peach blossoms, snow-white apple and pear, lavender plum and pink cherry. The smooth blue sky and the ruffled, sparkling lake provided a soothing backdrop to the vibrant palette of color.

She glanced at Ryan and they shared a smile.

Several people were walking to greet them along the stone-paved path that led to the café. Mari looked like part of the landscape in a magenta-colored dress with her hair spilling around her shoulders. The tall, arrestingly handsome man with the golden-brown hair and tawny skin who walked by her side must be Marc Kavanaugh. She recognized the sunburned, white-haired, thin man with a camera strapped around his neck as Nathan McKinley, the orchard owner. The man who brought up the rear of the party must be Father Mike.

"Could you possibly have picked a more perfect day for this?" Mari enthused as she reached them, hugging Faith first and her brother second. She beamed at both of them as she stepped back. "Oh, my. You two *are* a picture."

"Lucky I'm ready to take one, then," Nathan said, holding up his camera as Ryan shook hands with and greeted him, Marc and Father Mike. He introduced Faith to Marc and Father Mike.

"It's very nice to meet you. I've known Ryan and Mari since they were as tall as my knee," Father Mike said, taking Faith's hand. "As you can see, a lot has changed since then," the priest joked, tilting his thumb at Ryan. The top of Father Mike's head currently was even with one of Ryan's silver shoulder boards.

"Father Mike married us, too," Marc said, taking Faith's hand.

Faith smiled tremulously. She'd worried before about the idea of having a priest marry them versus a justice of the peace. She understood from Mari that they had been brought up as Maronite Christians by their parents, who were very orthodox in their practice, even if Mari and Ryan had not remained strict adherents as adults. Having a priest marry them seemed so much more...*binding* than a justice of the peace, although Ryan had assured her that when it came to the law, which is why they were marrying, it made no difference whatsoever.

She'd *previously* had those doubts.

As she stood there at Ryan's side with all those kind, smiling people, the spring day surrounding them like a blessing, she was glad they'd get married by an old family friend…a man of God.

"Well, should we proceed?" Father Mike asked, waving toward the blossoming groves, a twinkle in his eye.

"Absolutely," Ryan said, his eyes on Faith, his gaze warmer than the sunshine. He held out his arm for her, and she took it.

Later she wished she could remember more details of the brief ceremony. It was as if the whole experience passed in a blaze of sensation: golden sunshine, brilliant blooms, the sweet scent wafting off the trees, the sound of the waves breaking on the beach in the distance…the warm, steady look in Ryan's eyes as they repeated their vows. She recalled the cool sensation of the white gold on her skin as Ryan slipped the ring on her finger, the sound of Father Mike's voice saying, *I now pronounce you husband and wife.* She remembered the radiant expression on Mari's face as she looked on, tears spilling down her cheek.

But she'd never forget the first time Ryan kissed her as her husband.

His mouth felt warm and cherishing as it moved over hers. When they parted, a thrill of anticipation went through her when she saw the possessive gleam in his eyes.

Clarisse served them lunch on the terrace, where they sat in shade and looked out on to a sunny, sparkling Lake Michigan. Ryan hardly saw the view, however, as busy as he was touching Faith's bare shoulder and staring. She looked more radiant than he'd ever seen her.

He managed to tear his gaze off her for a split second and saw Marc looking at his wife, his head close to hers.

"Do you remember the last time we sat at this table? You were pregnant then, too," he murmured.

"Of course I remember," she said softly, exchanging a meaningful glance with her husband. "This place is charmed. That's why I suggested it for you two." She transferred her gaze to Ryan and Faith. Faith looked up at him shyly. He leaned down to kiss her mouth.

"So you two plan to just return home after this?" Mari asked later, after they'd eaten the delicious cake Clarisse had prepared for them from scratch.

Ryan cupped Faith's shoulder in the palm of his hand and squeezed lightly. Was that a blush spreading on her cheeks as she toyed with her cake fork?

"That's right," Ryan said. "I was wondering if I can have a word with you before we leave, Marc?"

Everyone at the table stilled, but Marc looked the most stunned of all at Ryan's request.

"Sure," Marc said. He took his napkin from his lap and pointed toward the picturesque stone path that ran between the lake bluff and the orchard. "Do you want to take a walk?"

Ryan nodded, gave Faith a smile and one last squeeze of her petal-soft shoulder, and stood. Mari looked puzzled and a little worried about Ryan's request to talk to Marc in private. He felt guilty about that and tried to give her a reassuring smile. His sister had put up with his unresolved issues with Marc Kavanaugh for too long, now.

He and Marc walked for a ways in silence, finally pausing when they reached a low, circular stone wall that served as a lookout to the lake. They stood gazing out at the rippling, sun-dappled water.

"I've been reading in the papers that the polls have you far ahead of your opponent for the senate race," Ryan began. "It looks like we're going to have a U.S. Senator in the family."

Marc made a doubtful noise. "Anything can change between now and November."

"It won't," Ryan said, sitting on the stone wall. "Remember when we were in high school, and I used to say you'd probably be president some day?"

Marc gave a wry smile. "And you were going to be my Air Force One pilot."

"I still will be, if the need should ever arise," Ryan said, grinning swiftly.

"It won't. I would never put Mari through that mess. This campaign has been hard enough on the family. I'll go back to being a prosecutor after I serve my term," Marc said.

Marc spoke amiably enough, but Ryan noticed his slightly puzzled expression. He couldn't understand why Ryan had called him out here for this little discussion.

"I have something that I want to…confess, I guess," Ryan said after a pause.

"Okay," Marc said slowly, his brows bunching together in consternation.

He exhaled and looked out at the dancing water. "When Mari first told me she was pregnant with Riley, when I took her back to San Francisco with me, there were a few times that I encouraged her not to tell you she was going to have your baby."

Only the waves crashing on the beach broke the stony silence that followed.

"She never agreed, of course. I know now that I was wrong to tell her that," Ryan said. "I'm sorry."

"And you realize that because of your experience with Faith?" Marc asked. "You wouldn't want to be cut out of the picture any more than I would have, would you?"

"No," Ryan said, meeting his onetime friend's stare. Anger sparked in Marc's blue eyes. "And in answer to your question about Faith, *yes*. That was part of why I wanted to bring up the topic to you today. But there's more."

"Go on," Marc said after a tense moment.

"The accident happened a long, long time ago. In a different lifetime. I won't lie that I've been angry and resentful about losing my parents. I took out a lot of my anger on you, but I know you didn't deserve it. It hasn't been fair, to you, or to Mari or to Riley." He looked at Marc. "We used to be friends once. Good friends."

"The best," Marc said grimly.

He watched a wave break on a rock, sending up a tall spray.

"You've made Mari so happy. More happy than she's ever been in her life. I've considered Riley as my family, but not you," Ryan stated baldly. He looked at Marc. "I want that to change. I want you to be a real uncle to my child, just like I am to Riley. I want us to be brothers. *If* you can see your way to forgive all my misplaced anger over the years, that is."

"Of course I forgive you. If you can forgive me in the same way," Marc said.

He stood and held out his hand. Marc shook it.

"What's family for, if not to forgive our worst faults?" Ryan asked with a small smile.

"Exactly," Marc agreed. He slapped Ryan's upper arm. "Now, let's get you back to your bride."

* * *

"Ryan? Why did you want to talk to Marc earlier? You guys looked so serious when you left. And when you got back, you both seemed...relieved."

Ryan opened the front door for her. The house felt a little stuffy, so Faith flipped the air-conditioning on low. She turned to face Ryan.

"I was saying something to him that I should have said a long time ago," Ryan said, removing his coat. "I guess you could say that the specialness of the day sort of... popped it out of me."

The specialness of the day.

His words reverberated in her brain. That, along with some other phrases that had kept reoccurring with alarming frequency as she'd sat by Ryan's side during the lunch, exquisitely aware of his touch on her shoulder and arm. Phrases like, *I, Faith, take you, Ryan, to be my wedded husband.*

Or Father Mike saying, *an institution ordained by God, which is not to be entered into lightly or unadvisedly.*

Faith took a step toward him.

"It was a special day, Ryan. I want to thank you. It... it couldn't have been any lovelier if we'd planned it for a year."

He draped his coat on the back of a chair and stepped toward her, his eyes intense. "Did you really think so?"

"Yes," she whispered.

"You felt it, too?"

She swallowed. She knew precisely what he meant. No matter how much she wanted to cling on to the comfort of a marriage of convenience, something *larger* than she'd expected had happened out in the orchard today. Call it the divinely inspired weather, or the fact that Ryan was the most handsome, dashing man she'd ever laid eyes on, or her own foolish heart, but the day would forever be treasured in her memory.

"Yes," she said softly. "I felt it."

He stepped closer to her. She looked up at him solemnly. He touched her cheek.

"The day isn't over yet. Let's make it last, Faith."

She swallowed through a constricted throat. She knew exactly what he meant, of course. There was no other way to interpret the hot, possessive gleam in his eyes.

"I'm not sure that'd be a good idea. It's not what we planned."

He opened his hand along the side of her neck. His other hand caressed her shoulder, reminding her of how aware—how excited—she'd been while he stroked her during their wedding lunch. He lowered his head.

"To hell with the plan. Life isn't meant to be planned. It's meant to be…"

"Lived," she finished for him shakily. She looked into his eyes. He didn't move. She knew he wouldn't, either. He was waiting for her.

She placed her hand on the back of his head and pushed him down to her. She fit her mouth to his, sliding and caressing, nibbling at him…memorizing the feel of him. When she slicked the tip of her tongue between his closed lips, she felt his body leap in arousal next to hers. He groaned, his hands sliding to her waist.

His kiss was like chained desire set free. Faith gave herself to it—to him—completely. Doubt and fear were for another day, not this sunny, glorious, blessed one.

Not her wedding day.

Ryan took her hand and led her down the hallway. He hesitated in front of his bedroom.

"Should we…here?" he asked, waving at the door.

Faith nodded. Her mouth suddenly felt too dry to speak. "Yes," she managed. "It's all new."

He gave her a small smile of understanding and started to lead her into the bedroom. He looked back when Faith didn't follow.

"I'm going to go and change," she said breathlessly. Heat scalded her cheeks. "I'll be right back."

He just nodded. It was so odd to consider Ryan off balance, so she couldn't be sure, but she had the strangest impression he was speechless.

She hurried to her bedroom and closed the door. She pulled an ivory-colored silk negligee from her drawer. The exquisite nightgown had been ordered from an online catalogue. Faith hadn't allowed herself to dwell for long on why she'd bought it. She told herself that it'd been an impulse buy. Didn't she deserve to spoil herself with luxurious, sexy things once in a while?

She certainly hadn't allowed herself to consider the meaning of the fact that she'd made the order the day after she'd called Ryan and agreed to marry him.

Changing quickly, she then brushed her hair until it shone. She could see her pulse throbbing at her throat when she inspected her reflection.

Moments later she tapped lightly at Ryan's partially opened door.

"Come in," he said.

He turned from where he'd been standing at his open closet, a leather belt in his hand. He froze when he saw her. Never taking his eyes off her, he draped the belt on a hook and spun to face her. He wore only the dark blue trousers from his uniform.

"You look beautiful," he said, his voice low.

"So do you," she said sincerely, giving him a shaky smile.

He came toward her. Suddenly she was in his arms, surrounded by his solid male strength and breathing in the subtle, spicy scent of his aftershave. That full, wonderful feeling she'd been experiencing on and off all day swelled tight in her chest cavity.

"Are you sure you want to do this, Faith?" he murmured, his gaze scoring her.

"Yes. Today, I'm sure," she whispered.

His nostrils flared slightly. He bent to kiss her and their mouths fused. Just like during their wedding, a brilliant palette of sensation suffused her consciousness. His mouth was so demanding, and yet so gentle, warm and firm. His smooth skin and dense muscles flowed like a sensual blessing through her seeking fingers. He parted her lips with his tongue, and she felt herself melting into him. She delved her fingertips into the thick, crisp hair on his head and pushed him down closer to her. He bent his knees and put his hands on her hips, pressing their bodies almost as close as a man and woman could get.

Almost.

She gave a soft cry when he lifted her and carried her over to the bed.

"I've waited for this for what feels like forever," he said after he'd laid her on the bed. He stood over her, his expression almost grim with desire as he looked down at her.

"Let's not wait anymore," she said, reaching for him.

He came down over her, pressing her into the mattress. She loved his solid weight, adored the way he kissed her with feverish possession. She felt burned by him, scorched by his intensity. She made a sound of protest when he broke their kiss and rolled onto his side, his front facing her. He placed his hand below her ribs. It looked dark and masculine next to the pale, soft fabric. Her breath stuck in her lungs when he ran his hand over the fullness of her breasts. He brushed the thin straps off her shoulders and lowered the fabric.

For a few seconds he said nothing as he stared at her bare breasts. His heated gaze caused an ache of longing at her core.

"So beautiful. So feminine." He touched the side of a breast. "So soft." His gaze rose to meet hers. She stilled when she saw the deep emotion in his dark eyes. "Our child is going to nurse here, one day."

"Yes," she mouthed.

"Faith…" he whispered heatedly. She watched, enthralled, as his dark head dipped. She trembled as she watched him kiss a pink nipple, then slip it between his lips. Her entire body seemed to sizzle in sympathy with the flesh in his warm mouth when he drew on her so sweetly.

A sharp cry broke free of her lips.

His large hand closed gently over her other breast, his fingertips gently manipulating the beading center. He shaped her to his palm and lifted his head, holding her breast in his hand and slipping the other nipple into his mouth.

She whimpered in rising need and raked her fingers through his thick hair. Desire pinched at her almost painfully, but he seemed so intent on his task, she couldn't bear to make him stop. She stared sightlessly at the ceiling while he teased and manipulated and worshipped her sensitive flesh, mounting her desire unbearably.

"Ryan," she finally pleaded softly.

He lifted his head from her flushed, aching breasts. His eyelids looked heavy with arousal.

"I'm sorry," he whispered, his hand moving along her sides, stroking her sensitive skin even as he lowered the fabric down over her waist, and then her hips. Soon, she was lying before him, naked. His gaze burned her. His hands followed, worshiping and stimulating all at once. He traced the shape of her hip and thigh with his palm, and then lowered his head to her stomach. She moaned at the sensation of his open mouth on her bellybutton, the ache at the center of her becoming unbearable. She clamped her thighs shut to alleviate the pressure.

"Shhhh," he soothed, rising over her, his hip next to hers, one elbow bracing him. He touched between her thighs, his fingertips gentle and knowing. He kissed her mouth softly when she cried out.

"Open your thighs, Faith," he whispered hoarsely next to her lips.

She hadn't realized she'd been closing them so tightly, as if she was unconsciously protecting herself from the rush of sensation and feeling that would come if she exposed herself. She looked at Ryan through heavy eyelids, his face so rigid with desire, and knew she'd been foolish to try to keep herself separate from him…safe from him.

Only a coward would keep themselves safe from the one they loved.

She parted her thighs. A slight convulsion went through his tight facial muscles.

"Oh, Faith," he muttered thickly. "You're so sweet."

"Ryan," she whispered, trembling. His hand moved, tenderly exploring the folds of her sex, granting pleasure wherever he touched.

He kissed her, and she tasted the salt of the sheen of sweat from his upper lip. Or was that from her tears? His fingers stroked her and the pleasurable friction mounted. Her hand moved frantically along his shoulders and neck, clutching spasmodically as the pressure swelled.

"All those flowers out there today, and here's the loveliest one by far," she heard him say as if from a great distance. She cried out sharply as pleasure broke over her.

Ryan kissed her deliberately while she shook, making sure she could breathe, but seeming to relish the sensation of parted lips and her small cries falling past his own. His warm hand remained between her thighs, coaxing every last shudder of pleasure from her flesh.

Faith blinked a moment later, coming back to herself. Her eyes widened when she saw that Ryan had removed his pants. He lay next to her naked, his thigh draped over her leg. She felt his firm, warm arousal pressed against her hip.

She moved without conscious thought, touching him. He shut his eyes and made a low, restrained sound in his throat. He felt so heavy in her sliding palm, the skin softer to the touch than she would have expected…like warm silk stretched tight over steel.

"Faith," he mumbled, his voice gravely with arousal. She met his gaze and continued to caress him. "Will it… will it hurt the baby?"

"No," she whispered. "Absolutely not. The baby is very well protected, and I'm a low-risk pregnancy."

He stretched toward the bedside table. She watched, wide-eyed as he rolled on a condom, and then he was coming over her, his arms taking his upper-body weight, his hips between her opened thighs.

A cry of amazement leaked out of her lips when he entered her slowly. He paused.

Every muscle in his body looked like it was flexed tight and hard. It was a wondrous sight.

"I don't want to hurt you," he grated out.

She touched his narrow hips. "You're not hurting anything. It feels wonderful," she whispered. She urged him with her hands, welcoming him.

His groan sounded like it was ripped out of him. Faith cried out shakily, for suddenly she was filled with Ryan again, and he throbbed high and deep inside her. How could she have forgotten how exquisite the sensation was?

How right.

He began to move, and pleasure rippled through her in shocking waves. She watched his face, and knew he experienced the same bliss, that their desire fused them, made them one. He stroked her faster, and her entire world began to quake. Sweat gleamed on his rigid muscles as he took them both higher, and she joined in the dance, moving in the rhythm he set with perfect synchrony.

She gritted her teeth together and cried out in longing when she felt his desire swell hard and deeper inside her. He paused and bent his elbows, bringing his mouth to hers. As he kissed her again, both of them hovered on the edge of ecstasy.

"You're mine, Faith. Can't you feel it?"

She cried out sharply, his incendiary words igniting her release. She felt him move, sensed him straining, eager to leap into the fire with her.

Sharing that sweet, inevitable explosion of desire with Ryan hurled Faith into a whole new territory of existence.

Chapter Eleven

"Faith? Are you asleep?" Ryan asked her.

She smiled. She loved the sound of his deep voice roughed by both sleep and desire. They both lay on their side, Ryan spooning her. He moved his hand slowly and lazily across her bare belly, ribs and breasts. The sunlight filtering through the window had taken on the warm, golden cast of sunset.

"No," she said quietly.

"Do you love this house? I mean…was it your dream to always come back here as an adult?"

"No," she snorted. She glanced around when he remained silent. Had he been super-serious? "I mean I *like* this house and everything, but I didn't buy it because of *that*. The circumstances just all collided. That's how I ended up here. I'd started my practice, and it was going really well. My parents were planning to retire to Florida, and then Jesse died. So—" she shrugged "—I bought their house."

"Right," he said. "So it's not like it's your dream house or anything?"

"Hardly," she murmured.

"Is there space in the garage for me to set up a workshop? I want to get started on the baby's shelving unit."

She twisted her head farther on the pillow to see him better. He gently pushed her hair out of her face.

"My father had a workshop in the basement. Do you think that would work?"

His hand paused in the action of smoothing her hair. "Of course it would. I didn't know you had a basement."

"You didn't know *we* did," she corrected, smiling and snuggling back in the pillow.

His chuckle was low and gruff and delicious. He swept his hand over her shoulder and chest. "Is your father's workshop far enough away from the living area? I don't want to bother you with too much sound or a sawdust smell."

"There's good ventilation in it, and it's technically in a room beneath the garage. I should have thought to tell you about it before. I think it'd be perfect," she said, distracted because now he was caressing the upper swells of her breasts and it felt very good. She inhaled sharply when his fingertips detailed a nipple.

"Your breasts are extremely sensitive," he murmured, his mouth near her ear. She shivered at the sensation of his warm breath.

"From the pregnancy, I suppose."

She felt him harden next to her and hid a smile. They'd made love, and touched, and talked and repeated the cycle several times now, but Ryan didn't appear to be tiring of the routine.

"Not just from the pregnancy," he said. He slid his other arm beneath her and touched the other breast. Faith moaned softly, desire swelling in her yet again as he finessed both nipples at once. "I remember how sensitive they were on Christmas Eve." He shaped the flesh of one breast into his palm, molding and squeezing gently, while he continued to pluck at a nipple. She cried out shakily and instinctively curled her body into his, sealing their skin, feeling his arousal next to her backside. "How lovely they were," he continued to rasp in her ear. "If you had any idea how often I've thought about your breasts since then, you'd probably run for the hills."

She snorted with laughter, and then moaned as he took both of her breasts into his hands. "There aren't any hills around here."

He removed one hand and she heard the bedside drawer open.

"You'd run for a sand dune then," he assured gruffly a moment later.

He slid inside her at the same time his hand wedged between her thighs, stimulating her. Faith gasped in undiluted pleasure. He grunted gutturally as pulled her to him and flexed toward her at once, and their flesh fused.

He kissed her ear. "You're the sweetest thing in existence, bar none."

Morning sunlight peaked around the curtains as Ryan stuck his nose into the fragrant juncture of Faith's neck and shoulder. He nuzzled her. She stirred and murmured.

"Wake up," he said. "You may have plans to keep me in this bed as a slave to your every whim, but even slaves need food. Come on. Let's take a shower and I'll take you to brunch in town."

"I can make us something here," Faith mumbled sleepily.

"Uh-uh," he said, playfully slapping the sweet swell of her hip to rouse her. "You're not cooking. It's your honeymoon, remember?"

She looked over at him, her heavy eyelids widening slightly.

"Okay. It's not much of a honeymoon," he agreed. "But I'll make it up to you, someday."

Her smile made something curl tight in his gut. "It's been a wonderful honeymoon. I have no complaints whatsoever."

He rubbed her hip, considering. She looked downright edible, lying there with her dark hair in disarray on the pillow, the tops of her breasts peeking over the edge of the sheet, that sexy, thoroughly feminine smile shaping her lips.

"Okay, you talked me into it. Who needs food," he growled, kissing her shoulder and neck hungrily. She broke into giggles and twisted away from him.

"No, no, you're right. We should eat. We never did last night."

He watched her getting up, disappointment swamping him when she picked up her nightgown from the floor and held it over her. Was he *nuts* for suggesting they get out of bed?

"Where are you going?" he asked, thoroughly bemused when Faith started to leave the room.

"To shower," she said, turning so that he could see the lovely profile of her back and rear end.

"The shower is right there," he said, scowling as he pointed to the bathroom adjoined to the bedroom.

"I have my own."

He rose from the bed like there was a fire. Her green eyes widened as he approached her.

"We'll shower together," he said, brushing her soft hair behind her shoulder.

He saw her nostrils flare slightly as she glanced down over him. He paused, his fingers in her hair, when he saw a flicker of uncertainty cross her features. He sighed and lowered his hand.

"I haven't seen that particular expression in over twenty-four hours now," he said quietly.

"What expression?" she asked.

"The doubtful one."

He saw her throat convulse as she swallowed.

"It's…it's not that, Ryan. I just need a little privacy, that's all. I'm…I'm not used to showering with anyone," she said awkwardly.

He sighed, hating to see her discomfort.

"I understand," he said. He kissed her quickly and urged her toward the door with a hand on her shoulder. "Hurry up getting ready, though. I want to show off my new wife."

She gave him a furtive glance over her shoulder and witnessed him admiring her backside. She threw him a repressive glance, hiding a smile.

He chuckled as she scurried out of the room, trying to ignore the disappointment he experienced at her going. Patience was what was required.

Winning Faith's trust would be a process, not a decisive battle.

They'd been blessed with a day that was every bit as glorious as their wedding day. They sat outside on the patio at Boatwerks on the edge of Lake Macatawa. Ryan attacked his Boatwerks biscuits with gusto. Faith watched him for a moment, grinning.

"You really are making me feel guilty now for keeping you in bed," she said.

He wiggled his eyebrows salaciously and forked up more fresh biscuit, sausage and poached egg. "A hard-working man has a big appetite."

Hard-*loving* man, she thought to herself. He grinned as if he'd read her thought and she laughed. She'd never seen him so playful, so carefree. It was a little addictive. Ryan was typically so hard, so...*strong*. She couldn't think of how else to describe him. He was rarely impassive with her, of course, but generally he exuded a steely, deliberate sort of male strength. He was the kind of man other men trusted immediately. If it weren't for the fact that he also possessed a potent sex appeal without even trying, Faith would have found him just as easy to trust.

She blinked when she recognized her thought. Was she really going to hold it against him because he was so good-looking and appealing to the opposite sex? That seemed blatantly unfair—

"Are you going to eat?" Ryan asked, looking puzzled. Faith realized she'd paused with her fork hovering over her vegetable and cheese omelet.

"Oh, yes," she said, banishing her worries to the periphery of her consciousness.

After they'd eaten and paid the bill, they walked out onto the dock, breathing the fresh air off the lake and holding hands.

"I like that place," Ryan said, referring to Boatwerks. "Reminds me of the places I used to eat with my family when I was a kid."

They came to a stop at the end of the dock. "It must have been wonderful for you and Mari to spend the whole summer in Harbor Town."

"Yeah. Those summers went on for an eternity," Ryan murmured, looking lost in memory as he stared out at the lake. He gave her a sideways glance. "Or it seemed like they would at the time."

"That's one of the many wonderful things about children," Faith said. "A moment can stretch into eternity. I remember thinking that, growing up here in Holland," she said, nodding toward the lake, which was really a swollen, drowned river that stretched like a finger inland from the massive great lake.

Ryan nodded thoughtfully. "You were right. This part of Michigan really is ideal for raising a child." He squeezed her hand and she looked up at him. His short bangs flickered on his forehead in the soft breeze. He hadn't shaved this morning; his jaw was sexily shadowed by a scruff. His gaze on her was warm as he turned toward her, their middles brushing together.

"Thanks for bringing it back for me, how special it is here. After the accident all my great memories must have…receded into the background. They're still there. They didn't really disappear," he said, his gaze on the horizon as if he was seeing something Faith couldn't. He suddenly lowered his head to hers. A devilish smile tilted his lips. "When summer gets here, I'm going to take you to all my favorite beaches."

"No you won't," she scolded, grinning. "I'll be starting to show soon. There's no way in hell I'm putting on a swimsuit."

"You have a beautiful body," he said, pulling her closer in his arms. "Pregnant or not, you're gorgeous."

She narrowed her eyes on him in mock suspicion. "I read about men like you."

"What am I like?" he wondered, his gaze narrowed in a predatory fashion on her lips.

"The type that gets turned on by pregnant women."

His male laughter echoed across the bay. She chuckled,

liking the sound. He bent, nuzzling her curving lips with his nose. "I don't get turned on by pregnant *women*." Their lips brushed together and his smile faded. "I get turned on by *you,* pregnant or not."

He proved the truth of his words with a deep, devouring kiss. He pressed with his hand at the small of her back and she arched into him. He leaned down over her, slaking his thirst. The warm sun shone down and the lake rippled around them, but Faith only knew the taste, scent and sensation of Ryan.

This is what it was to fall in love. *Really* fall in love, Faith thought dizzily when Ryan sealed their kiss. For an instant as she'd been under the spell of his kiss, the moment had stretched into an eternity.

But you're not a child anymore, an annoying voice cracked in her head. *You're an adult who should know that the magic* always *ends.*

Always.

Ryan's hand tightened on hers. Her heart throbbed when he smiled. She silently told the offending voice to shut up, but it was very persistent.

"You have to be back at work tomorrow, don't you?" Ryan asked when they passed her office on the ride home.

She nodded regretfully. "I originally took today off with the intent of picking out paint for the nursery and choosing new carpet to have installed, and I haven't accomplished a thing yet."

He took her hand. "It was worth it, wasn't it?"

"Of course it was."

"I'll give you a real honeymoon sometime soon. You name the place and I'll fly you there."

A sharp pain went through her at his words. "That's not necessary, Ryan."

"Why not?"

She gave him a beseeching glance and spoke before she could stop herself. "Because it wasn't a *real* wedding."

She immediately regretted it when she saw his jaw stiffen.

"I'm sorry," she said, wincing. What was wrong with her? She let go of his hand and stifled a curse. She didn't know why she'd felt the need to say it. Did it have something to do with the fact that she'd recognized fully just how vulnerable she'd made herself as she'd stood out on that dock with Ryan?

"Why should you be?" he asked, the hard sound of his voice making her wince again. "I know that's how you feel. It isn't like you haven't made it clear."

"You were the one who proposed the whole thing as a marriage of convenience for the baby, Ryan," she exclaimed.

He glanced at her, quick and sharp. She exhaled in disbelief. She felt burned by his stare.

"I know I said that then," he said as he drove, staring straight ahead. "But I meant what I said yesterday."

An hour later Faith was in the process of letting Topsy through the back door when Ryan walked into the kitchen. She glanced at him nervously. They hadn't really spoken since that uncomfortable conversation in the car. She'd been beating herself up repeatedly while he'd been down in the basement, apparently exploring the workshop area.

Despite her concern he seemed fairly relaxed as he paused by the counter holding the notebook in his hand that she recognized as being the one where he'd started sketches for the nursery bookshelves.

"I'm going out to the airport, and then to run some errands. I have to go to the sawmill to give some measurements for pieces for the shelving unit. I'm leaving for an overnight in San Francisco early tomorrow morning, so I want to get started on it while I can."

"Oh, okay," Faith said, feeling off balance by his friendly, relaxed manner, not to mention the news that he was leaving town again tomorrow. He'd told her that he was looking for another pilot now that he had two planes, along with an administrative assistant to help him with arranging flights and keeping the books. Until those employees were hired, however, she knew he and Scott would be extremely busy.

But despite all of that didn't he want to talk about what had happened in the car? Despite her outburst she wasn't at all sure she wanted to go back to respecting each other's space. She'd admitted to herself she'd fallen in love with Ryan, after all. Another part of her was sure she'd made a mistake yesterday by giving in to her desire for him, for falling prey to the magic of the day.

Her ambivalence seemed to be having the effect of freezing her up completely.

As far as Ryan went there could be little doubt he was swayed by the fact that they were going to have a child. She understood at this point, both from Mari and from Ryan himself, just how crucial family was to him. Their physical attraction for each other combined with his euphoria over becoming a father was confusing him into thinking he should spend the rest of his life with her.

"Are you okay?"

Faith blinked at the sound of his voice.

"Yes. Of course."

His dark eyes toured her face quickly before he spoke. "I'll probably stop by the hardware store on the way home for some supplies. Do you want me to pick up some paint and carpet samples for you?"

"That'd be terrific," she said gratefully.

He nodded once and turned to leave.

"Ryan."

"Yeah?" he asked calmly, looking over his shoulder.

She hesitated. She wanted to apologize for her outburst in the car, but she wasn't entirely certain she'd been wrong in what she'd said. Bewilderment swelled in her chest. She grabbed desperately for a certainty.

"I…I wanted to let you know that I have an appointment at the obstetrician's this Thursday. I don't think very much exciting is going to happen, but…well, you can come. If you have time. And…want to," she added lamely.

"Thursday at what time?"

"Two o'clock?"

"I'll make sure Scott is available on Thursday then," he said.

Faith stood there, watching helplessly as he walked away.

Ryan was gone for most of the day on Monday. When he finally did return home that night, he carried some wood and supplies with him. He greeted her pleasantly enough, explaining that the lumberyard would deliver the majority of the supplies for the bookcase later in the week. What he carried was just enough to get things started in a small way. He immediately disappeared into the basement, leaving Faith to stew in her confusion.

The next morning when she woke up in her room, Faith knew he was gone by the flat, empty feel to the house. She dragged herself out of bed with a heavy heart. Her work helped to ground her for the next two days. On Tuesday night, however, she succumbed to a wave of gloom, recalling the golden glory of the wedding in the tranquil, color-soaked orchard, the look in Ryan's eyes when he'd repeated his vows, the full, incendiary moment when he'd uttered those words...

You're mine, Faith. Can't you feel it?

Then she remembered all too clearly what she'd said in the car in a fit of fear.

Because it wasn't a real *wedding.*

A pain went through her at the memory, causing her to clutch at her chest. She walked out onto the back terrace and took deep breaths of the mild spring air, staring at the thousands of stars in the sky, and feeling her loneliness like an ache deep in her spirit.

The next afternoon at closing time, she was talking to Jane about a lab order and glanced up to see Brigit Kavanaugh walking into her office.

"Brigit! How wonderful to see you," Faith exclaimed. She came around the reception desk into the waiting area and greeted her friend with a hug.

"I haven't had a chance to offer my congratulations on your wedding," Brigit said, smiling. She handed Faith a flat, thin package wrapped in silver paper. "This is for you."

"Oh, thank you! You shouldn't have, Brigit."

"It's not much. Derry and I had one from an aunt of mine, and I always treasured it."

Faith gave her a warm smile. "Come back to my office and we'll chat."

"Go ahead and open it," Brigit encouraged a moment later after they'd both sat in chairs in her sunny office. "Ryan won't mind. He's a man, and this is something that goes in the china cabinet. I'm quite sure Derry never had a clue what was in ours."

Faith laughed and unwrapped the gift. Inside the box was a lovely sterling silver filigreed platter with a simple inscription bearing their names and the date of their wedding. Seeing Brigit's thoughtful gift made tears well in her eyes for some reason. Much to her embarrassment, they spilled down her cheeks unchecked.

"Oh, I'm sorry. It's…just beautiful," Faith managed shakily as she hastily dried her cheeks with the back of her hand.

Brigit reached for some tissues on her desk and passed them to her, looking mildly concerned. "Is everything all right, Faith?"

"Oh, yes," Faith assured. She glanced into Brigit's face, however, and another shudder of emotion went through her. More tears spilled down her cheeks. She'd never had a nurturing, overly involved mother figure in her life, and something about Brigit's kind, concerned expression at that moment undid her. She sobbed, holding the tissue to her face as if to hide from her misery when she felt Brigit's touch on her shoulder. "It's just…well…I'm pregnant, Brigit," she wailed, as if that explained everything.

Which, perhaps, it did.

Brigit just made soothing sounds while she had her cry. After a minute she took several more tissues and mopped up her face, feeling contrite.

"I'm really sorry," she mumbled. "I feel like I cry at the drop of a hat these days. The platter is absolutely beautiful."

Brigit waved her elegant hand, making it clear her gift was hardly crucial.

"How far along are you?" Brigit asked.

"Fifteen weeks," Faith hiccupped.

"And Ryan…"

"Is the father, yes. He came to my house last Christmas Eve—after he spent the holiday with you and your family, actually," Faith explained wetly. "He said he wanted to see if I was all right. He and Jesse were…good friends, you know," she said brokenly. She inhaled to calm herself, but more tears spilled down her cheeks. "That's when it happened. The baby I mean. Well...everything."

She swallowed painfully and gave Brigit an apologetic glance, saw that the older woman's face was tight with understanding. She stroked Faith's shoulder as another wave of emotion shuddered through her.

"And so you two decided to marry because of the baby?" Brigit asked.

Faith nodded, ignoring the new tears that spilled down her cheeks this time. They just seemed to keep coming.

"It's supposed to be in name only," she said miserably. Brigit patted her when her face clenched up and she sobbed again quietly.

"Shhhh, try to calm down now, honey," Brigit murmured comfortingly. She stood and made her way to a small refrigerator Faith kept in her office. She opened the bottle of water she found there and handed it to Faith. Faith thankfully took several sips of the cool water, feeling herself calm.

"From what you've said so far, I'm gathering that you care about Ryan," Brigit said, sitting down across from her again.

Faith just nodded.

"And how does he feel about you?"

"He thinks he cares about me, but it's all wrapped up in his need to sort of...protect me or something ever since Jesse died. We're attracted to each other. Obviously," Faith said, glancing down at her stomach and then back up at Brigit. When she saw a look of amusement pass over Brigit's face, she couldn't help but grin tiredly. "Oh, Brigit," she said, shaking her head. "How is anybody supposed to know *what* they feel in a strange situation like this one?"

"Are you talking about you, or Ryan?"

"Both, I suppose. Ryan is being incredibly sweet about the baby. He's very excited. Mari told me he's always wanted to have a child."

Brigit nodded. "I can see that. The Itanis were a very close-knit family, and Ryan has always been loyal to the bone. I had reason to resent his familial loyalty after the accident and during the lawsuit, but that was years and years ago. I understand his need now to protect Mari—his only family—and provide her with whatever compensation was available to her for the loss of their parents. Not that money can replace a loved one, but…well…" She faded off for a moment, looking thoughtful. "Ryan was practically a kid himself then, but he took on the full responsibility of a man, making all the decisions and fulfilling all the obligations that came along with the death of both of his parents."

Faith sniffed. "I guess I'm not the only one he gets protective over."

Brigit smiled and patted her hand. "He cares deeply about his sister. For a while she was his only living family. If Ryan is concerned for you, it means he cares."

Faith's lower lip trembled. She wanted to believe what Brigit said was true, but…

"But he's gone so much, Brigit. He's a pilot…like Jesse."

Brigit's blue eyes sharpened on her. "Oh, I see."

Faith blushed. Brigit Kavanaugh could be quite formidable, at times. When Brigit said she saw, she *saw* with that incising gaze of hers.

"You're afraid that Ryan is going to turn out to be the rootless, womanizing type."

Faith said nothing, but her cheeks turned warmer.

Brigit sighed after a moment. "There are no guarantees when it comes to marriage, Faith. But if it helps you any to hear it, I've known Ryan since he was about six years old. He and Marc were best friends. In the summer months he was practically one of my own children, he was around the house so much. By the time he was thirteen, practically every girl in Harbor Town had a crush on him, including my Deidre," she added wryly.

Faith smiled uneasily.

"Lots of men as good-looking, as athletic and smart as a boy like Ryan would have let it go to their head. But he wasn't like that. He had girlfriends, all right, but to my knowledge, he was always loyal to them. And trust me, I would have heard about it if he wasn't, with two teenage daughters in the house who somehow always knew what everyone else in Harbor Town was doing."

Faith laughed.

"There. That's better," Brigit said, her gaze warm on Faith.

"Thank you, Brigit," she said, squeezing the other woman's hand.

"It's my pleasure. I wish I could say something more to assure you. In the end I think the only thing you can do, though, is take it one day at a time. Try to trust in Ryan unless you see some clear reason you shouldn't. I know it's hard, when you've known heartache and betrayal. Trust me. I *know.* Derry and I made our mistakes in the early part of our marriage, and there were times I wondered if I'd ever be able to trust him again. But in the end, you either choose to have faith or not. I know it's like tying a blindfold around your eyes and walking along a ledge. It's terrifying, but it gets easier over time. And that's just…"

"Life," Faith whispered, giving Brigit a grateful smile. She stared out the window on to the sunny day, feeling the shadows of her doubts recede into the corners of her mind.

Chapter Twelve

Faith left her bedroom hastily that night when she heard the front door open at around seven. Ryan paused at the entryway of the living room when he saw her.

"Hi," she said, smiling.

"Hi."

For a second or two they just stood there, gazing at each other. He looked wonderful to her, wearing a pair of dark jeans and a blue-and-white button-down shirt, his overnight bag slung over his shoulder. The mail had come late today. He clutched the envelopes in one hand. As usual his good looks and utterly masculine aura left her a little breathless. Would it feel like this every time he returned home after an absence?

"Did you have a good trip?"

"Yeah," he said, taking a step into the room. "I met with Nick Malone while I was out there. He told me that I can take Eagle Air as far as I want. DuBois Enterprises can give me enough work to keep nine or ten planes moving alone, and that doesn't even include the new business contacts I've made. I'm thinking of keeping some hangar space in the Bay Area, as well, and keeping some planes there for a more convenient turnaround."

She beamed at him. "Ryan, that's wonderful. Nick really believes in your work ethic."

He shrugged and swung his overnight bag off his shoulder. "He's ex-Air Force, too," he said, as if that explained all Nick's faith in him.

"I think it's more than just that," Faith said, smiling knowingly. She noticed him turn his head toward the kitchen and wondered if he'd caught the aroma of the chicken she had baking. "Are you hungry?"

"I'm starving."

"Good. I made baked chicken and homemade potato salad."

"Sounds great," he said, but she saw puzzlement flicker across his features. Obviously he was confused about her running from hot to cold to hot. She inhaled slowly for courage and stepped toward him.

"Ryan, I want to apologize for what I said in the car the other day. It was wrong of me. I shouldn't have been so disrespectful about the good feelings we were having, being together. I was…scared."

She saw his throat convulse as he looked at her. "I know. I understand."

She sighed and gave a small laugh. "I'm glad one of us does, then. My point is, I realized while you were gone that we just have to take this one day at a time. I'll try not to give in to my insecurities, but that's all I can really promise for now."

"One day at a time is good enough for me."

She gave him a tremulous smile. "Thank you, Ryan."

She straightened and took a deep breath. "Now…dinner is almost ready. Do you want to take a shower before we eat?"

"If there's time."

"There's time," she told him with a smile before she walked to the kitchen.

Faith set the table in the dining room, complete with lit candelabra. "Wow, I've never eaten in here before," Ryan said when he entered, looking appealing in jeans and a fresh shirt, his dark hair still slightly wet.

"Too bad it's not a very fancy meal," Faith said, setting their filled plates on the table.

"Fancy or not, it's fantastic," Ryan said a few minutes later as he ate, appearing to completely appreciate her efforts.

They talked comfortably enough during dinner about some immediate plans for Eagle Air, including the fact that Ryan was interviewing two potential candidates for the administrative assistant position in addition to a pilot the following morning.

"I'll still be available for the doctor's appointment, though," he said after they'd finished eating, but they remained sitting at the table, sipping their water and iced tea. "Have you been feeling all right?"

"Yes. Very good, actually. I haven't been tired at all at the office for the past few days."

"Good. I'm glad," he said, reaching up to touch her hand where it rested on her placemat. It seemed like a completely natural gesture, given their comfort with one another during dinner. But as he continued to stroke her hand warmly, and prickles of pleasurable sensation shot through her arm, Faith became aware of a shift in the atmosphere. She glanced at him hesitantly and saw that his eyes were on her, dark and intense.

"Earlier you said one day at a time," he said quietly.

"And I'll do whatever I can to make this work for you, Faith. But I have to be honest—now that I've made love to you again, I'm not sure I can go back to abstinence. It just doesn't seem…natural to be here in this house with you and not touch you."

Her cheeks warmed. She looked at her plate. "I understand. For some things, it's impossible to go backward. I hadn't really expected that we could, either."

He squeezed her hand softly. She met his stare.

"And you're okay with that?"

"Yes. I don't want to run anymore from what's happening between us," she said in a hushed tone.

He nodded slowly, still stroking her wrist with his thumb.

"I appreciate you saying that. I know this isn't easy for you."

"Making love with you is the easiest, nicest thing in the world, Ryan. It's not that part that's hard."

His expression went flat. His caressing thumb stilled. She sensed his incredulity at her words.

"You honestly didn't think I wasn't loving *that* part, did you, Ryan?"

He blinked, as if awakening from a trance. "To be honest, I wasn't quite sure what to think after Monday morning."

"I know. I'm sorry."

"I didn't mean for you to apologize again."

"I know," she whispered.

He inhaled slowly. "Why don't you go and relax while I clean up the dishes?"

"That's not necessary, I can—"

He surprised her by leaning across the corner of the table and kissing her, quick and potent.

"You cooked. I'll clean up."

"Okay," she said when she'd recovered her voice. "Maybe I'll just go...take a shower." Despite what she'd said, she remained seated, and so did he. Faith grasped for her courage and finally found it. "You can sleep in my room tonight. If you want."

He raised his eyebrows in a subtle, wry gesture that said loud and clear that he most certainly *wanted.* Faith chuckled softly, and he smiled.

Faith was in bed when he tapped on the door later. She wore a dark green nightgown that left her shoulders and a good portion of her chest bare. Her skin gleamed in the golden light of the lamp. Her dark hair was piled on her head, but some of the rebellious tendrils had escaped down her back and coiled at her shoulders. She was wearing glasses and reading a publication called the *American Journal of Veterinary Research.* He paused next to the door, his body going on instant alert at the tempting sight she made.

He closed the door and approached the bed, smiling.

"Looks like fascinating reading," he said.

"Oh, it is," she said so confidently that his smile widened. She had to be the most adorable woman he'd ever seen. Her green eyes flickered down over his bare torso, making his nerves tickle in awareness, and landed on the envelope he carried.

"What's that?" she asked.

He sat on the edge of the bed. She scooted over, giving him room. He hesitated for a second. Maybe this wasn't such a good idea. She might think he had mercenary reasons for his actions, but in truth, he'd done what he'd done out of concern for Faith and their child.

He handed her the envelope. She opened it, a curious expression on her face, and withdrew the papers inside.

"I had these medical tests done just before the wedding.

I know with the baby, you've probably had lots of blood tests done to make sure you were healthy. I thought it was only fair for me to do the same. I wasn't promiscuous when I was single, by any stretch of the imagination, but I wasn't abstinent, either. I've always practiced safe sex, Faith," he said in a quieter tone.

She glanced up at him, a startled expression on her face.

"Except for Christmas Eve," he said sheepishly. "I thought maybe given our first night together, you might have very good reason to doubt my assurances in that regard." He nodded toward the envelope. "I got a completely clean bill of health."

"Ryan, you didn't have to do this," she said, her voice shaking a little.

"Yes, I did," he said firmly. He took the papers and set them on the bedside table. The journal she'd been reading slid off her blanket-covered thighs onto the floor, but neither of them paid any notice. He took her hand.

"I'm not going to be with another woman, Faith. Not for as long as we're together."

Tears swelled in her eyes. "I'm not going to be with anyone else, either," she said in a choked voice.

He leaned forward and caught her soft gasp with his mouth. Her arms flew around his neck, and she pulled him closer. He came down on the bed, partially sprawled on her, kissing her like she was his very breath. Her scent filled his nose—flowers and some singular scent that came from her skin. He came up for air from their kiss and buried his nose in the fragrant juncture of her neck and shoulder.

"I can't believe I was only gone for two days. It feels like weeks since I touched you," he said between feverish kisses. A shudder went through him at the sensation of fingernails scraping his scalp.

"I missed you, too," she said breathlessly.

His mouth coasted down her throat, nibbling hungrily at her skin. She moaned and grabbed at his waist when he gently took a love bite from her shoulder. He'd never known a flame of desire to leap so high and powerful so quickly as it did with Faith. It was like he existed constantly on a low simmer for her, and a touch, a kiss, could send that fire to the boiling point instantly.

He ran his mouth over her chest, breathing her scent, testing her skin with his lips and tongue. Her hands moved restlessly over the bare skin of his back, making him shiver uncontrollably. He felt need swell in him, hard and hot, as he moved his lips over the lace of her nightgown and the upper swells of her breasts. He tugged on the straps of her gown, suddenly impatient to taste her…drown in her sweetness.

She cried out sharply when he slipped a nipple between his lips and drew on her, so he softened, laving his tongue over the stiffening tip, soothing and exciting her at once. His hunger mounted soon enough, however, breaking through his feeble restraints when it came to Faith. He gently gathered her breast in his hand, molding her softly to his palm, while he applied a steady suction with his mouth. She tasted like woman and sex and something so sweet, so precious, he couldn't find the word if he tried.

He pushed her gown down lower. The skin over her ribs tasted just as good, and so did the exquisitely soft stretch along her sensitive sides. He heard her whimpers of excitement through the sound of his heart pounding in his ears as he licked and kissed and nibbled at the skin there. An almost unbearable ache of longing went through him when he kissed her abdomen. Was it his imagination, or had it swelled slightly even since the last time he'd kissed her there? It felt so warm, taut and smooth beneath his cherishing lips.

Her fingernails raking his scalp—this time more forcefully—added a welcome spice to his excitement as he kissed the tender strip of skin below the slight swell of her belly and ran his hands along her silky thighs. He lifted his head and worked her gown down over her legs. He sensed the tension rise in her muscles when he lowered her panties. For a few strained seconds he just looked down at her, stunned by her beauty. He glanced up at her face and saw the glaze of desire in her eyes.

A ripple of excitement went through her when he kissed her just above her pelvis. He lowered his head, closed his eyes and tasted her for the first time. He moaned softly, and was lost.

He was gentle with her, focusing exclusively on the soft, nectar-sweet folds of her outer sex and the precious kernel of nerve-packed flesh nestled between them. The essence of Faith filled him, her flavor, her scent, the sexy sounds of her soft whimpers and increasingly desperate moans.

She called his name wildly when she bucked in release. He came at her bidding, waiting until she'd quieted beneath his kiss.

When he slid into her, his mouth fused to hers, it was like a sharp blade of distilled pleasure knifing through his flesh. He'd only ever been inside a woman naked once before. Faith had been his first.

As he began to move, and ecstasy became his entire world, Ryan sent up a silent prayer that she would be his last.

Ryan and Faith stood when Dr. Feingold, her obstetrician, greeted them both in the waiting area of the clinic.

"Are you the baby's father?" the friendly doctor, who was in her late forties, asked Ryan unabashedly.

"Yes."

"Would you like him to come back for your visit?" Dr. Feingold asked Faith.

"Yes, that'd be wonderful," Faith said, giving Ryan a warm smile. He seemed a little embarrassed, walking back with her and Dr. Feingold to the exam room, but all in all, she thought he handled the appointment with calm aplomb. It was a singularly female environment, of course, decorated in soft colors with tasteful paintings on the wall, many of them alluding to the theme of mother and child, or families. They passed several women in varying stages of pregnancy in the hallway.

After Dr. Feingold had completed her brief exam, she asked Ryan if he had any questions for her. Much to Faith's surprise, he did. He asked first about how frequently Faith would need to come for prenatal care from now until the pregnancy was over. Then he asked about the pros and cons of ultrasounds.

"We'll do an ultrasound for the fetal anatomy survey in…" Dr. Feingold flipped through Faith's chart. "Four weeks, just to make sure all is well with the fetus. Faith is very healthy. She's a low-risk pregnancy. If all goes well, there won't be any need for another ultrasound after that."

"Will we be able to identify the sex then, if we choose to?" Ryan asked.

"Absolutely," Dr. Feingold said.

"One last question. Should Faith be painting the nursery? I can do the regular painting, but she's been planning to do a wall mural."

Faith blinked in surprise. Why hadn't she thought to ask about that?

"We generally recommend that someone else do the painting, Faith," Dr. Feingold said kindly. "It's probably too low of a toxicity to matter, but might as well play it safe, right? Luckily enough, you seem to have an interested party here," she said, smiling at Ryan, "or you can just wait to do the project after the baby is born."

Faith glanced at Ryan a little shyly on the way home from the appointment.

"What?" he asked, noticing her covert stare.

"Nothing. It's just…have you been reading up on pregnancy and prenatal care? I just thought…because of those questions you asked during the appointment…"

"Sure I have," he said matter-of-factly. He stopped at a stoplight. "It's my first baby, too, Faith."

"I'm so glad you asked that question about the paint. Thank you."

She grinned. She couldn't help it. It was so…nice to think of him caring enough to research the pregnancy on his own, amazing to think of him looking out for her. He smiled along with her, and suddenly all her concerns about the wisdom of her relationship with Ryan were millions of miles away.

Ryan was crazy busy for the next two weeks. He hired an administrative assistant and got her set up in the small office space he was renting at the airport. He also hired a new pilot, an ex-Navy, ex-commercial airline pilot who was in her fifties and looking for full-time work now that her two children were off at college. The new hire, whose name was Sylvia Aaron, gave Ryan a tip about a medium-turbo prop plane for sale in Detroit. Ryan was interested in adding a larger plane to his fleet, something that could fly up to ten passengers at a time to conferences or larger meetings. He did an overnight trip to Detroit, and came home the following day triumphant at his latest purchase.

"Congratulations!" Faith enthused when he'd given her his good news. She gave him a huge hug and a kiss, the latter of which ended up lasting for the better part of several minutes. When they finally broke apart, she smiled as he rained hungry kisses on her cheek and neck.

"I missed you," he said.

"I missed you, too," she replied, distracted by the movements of his mouth on her throat. "But, Ryan...before you get carried away—"

He gave her a slightly harassed look when she pried herself out of his arms. She grinned at his surly expression. He reminded her a little of how Topsy might look if she gave her a dish filled with food, only to whip it away at the last second.

"I have a surprise for you. I had a feeling you were going to get the plane. I made you a special dinner."

She beamed a moment later when she saw his expression of pleasant surprise when she showed him what she'd made him.

"Shish taouk," she said excitedly, referring to the white meat chicken skewers that she'd grilled. The dish smelled delicious, the meat having been marinated in olive oil, lemon, parsley and sumac. She'd arranged it on the platter just as Mari had described, on a bed of saffron rice with a tahini sauce. "I got the recipe from Mari. She told me it was your favorite when you were a boy. I know it won't be anywhere near as good as your mother's or Mari's, but—"

"It'll be fantastic," he interrupted. He took the platter from her hands, set it on the counter and proceeded to kiss her even more fervently than he had upon his return home. When they finally broke apart, he said, "It's an awesome surprise. Thank you."

"You're welcome," she said, flushed with happiness.

He nipped quickly at her lips before he released her. "And guess what? I have a surprise for you, too. I'll show it to you tomorrow, after work. I'm a little worried you won't like it, but...well, we'll see I guess."

No matter how much she prodded him, he wouldn't give her a hint as to the nature of his surprise. After dinner, they made love. Faith was drifting contentedly into sleep, surrounded by Ryan's arms, when his cell phone started to ring on the bedside table.

She sat up drowsily when he moved, turning over on her side to face him. It was a little late for someone to be calling. Through heavy eyelids, she watched him answer.

"Hello?"

His brow furrowed as he listened.

"Oh...hi," he said after a moment. He gave Faith a flickering glance and sat up straighter in bed. She sensed his tension. Her nerves prickled into alertness when she distantly heard a female's voice resounding from the receiver. Whoever it was, she sounded upset.

"I don't know. I don't think that'd be a very good idea," Ryan said cautiously. This time, Faith was sure of it. His glance at her was furtive. Wary.

It suddenly felt as if lead had replaced her insides when he suddenly stood and walked out of the room, closing the door behind him, the phone still pressed to his ear.

Faith just lay there, trying to sort out why the phone call had upset her so much. She realized it was because she'd been in this position before. She'd been with Jesse a few times—maybe more times than she cared to remember—when he'd gotten a phone call and suddenly walked out of the room. It wasn't until that moment, that very moment, that Faith realized those awkward phone calls had probably been from other women.

His lovers.

The realization had just never hit her until now. She'd found out about Jesse's infidelities while he'd still been overseas. He'd died soon afterward. She'd never had any reason to put two and two together and resolve puzzling little moments like that from her previous marriage.

Feeling cold and heavy, Faith turned over and curled up beneath the covers. When Ryan came back to bed later, she pretended to be sleeping.

By the next afternoon her glacial insides had thawed out quite a bit. Her busy day at her office had gone a long way to bringing her around to her senses. That phone call last night might have been anything—an old school friend, an old girlfriend, even his new female employee, for all she knew. By the time Ryan walked through her office front door to pick her up, she'd recalled what Brigit had told her.

Try to trust in Ryan unless you see some clear reason why you shouldn't.

He certainly had done nothing offensive, she reminded herself. She became so disgusted with her paranoia that she vowed to herself not to even ask him about the strange phone call.

When he came to her office to pick her up at around five-thirty that evening, he seemed preoccupied.

"Are you all right?" she asked him when they got in the car and he pulled out of the parking lot. "You seem sort of…worried or something."

"No, no I'm fine. Well, maybe a little concerned. But it'll be okay," he seemed to say to himself as much as to her. "If you don't like it, it's no big deal. You're not under any obligation to—"

"Ryan, what in the world are you talking about?" she interrupted, starting to get worried now herself.

"You'll see," he said, giving her a smile of reassurance and grabbing her hand.

"Are we going to visit Brigit?" she asked a while later

when he drove into Harbor Town and turned right onto Sycamore Avenue. "Is Mari in town or something?"

"No. It's not that."

"Well, what th…" She paused when he slowed down the car, staring out the window in bewilderment when he pulled into the drive of the house she recognized as being the large, handsome one that had once been the Itani summer home. A woman wearing a beige-colored suit walked down the front steps as if to greet them. Faith gaped, aghast, when she saw that the for sale sign that had conspicuously been displayed when they'd passed weeks ago was missing.

"Ryan," she began numbly. "You didn't…we're not…"

"I put down a small fee to hold this house until you saw it," he said quietly. "I'd like to buy it, Faith. For us."

Chapter Thirteen

"What? *Why?*" Faith asked, utterly floored.

He took her hand. "It's a beautiful house. I don't know when it'll come up for sale again, if ever." Ryan scanned her expression, looking anxious.

Faith's dazed shock was fractured slightly when she saw movement near Ryan's window. He glanced around.

"That's Mrs. Reynolds, the real estate agent. Why don't you just take a look at the house? You don't have to say yes. It's not like I put down a full down payment or anything, I just asked her to put it on hold for us until the weekend."

Faith managed to shake her head and mutter a passable greeting to a smiling Mrs. Reynolds. Her numbness fractured slightly when she entered the beautiful home and saw the gleaming hardwood floors, the spacious rooms, the luxurious kitchen, the wonderful detailing and craftsmanship that had gone into the building of the house. She'd regained the power of speech by the time they entered the dining room with the lovely built-in china cabinet and elegant chandelier.

"This was your family's *summer* home?" she asked Ryan in weak disbelief. She knew that Ryan's father was a top executive for a car company in Detroit, but she'd never really thought before about how affluent Ryan's life must have been growing up.

"Yeah, but I don't remember ever eating in this dining room once. We always ate on the back terrace or in the kitchen during the summertime," he said, smiling in memory. She pictured it, Mari and Ryan—both of them suntanned and full of the buoyancy of youth—sitting on the shaded back terrace with the lovely climbing hydrangea in full bloom, regaling their parents with stories of their day's adventures. Suddenly the image altered and she saw Ryan and she sitting at the same patio table, listening patiently to their dark-haired child's excited retelling of their day.

They were touring one of the large, well-proportioned bedroom suites, which was filled with golden evening sunlight when Ryan suddenly asked Mrs. Reynolds if they could have some privacy. The real estate agent gave them a knowing glance, assured them she'd be out on the front porch, and told them to take their time.

"I hope I didn't upset you," Ryan said quietly, studying her from across the large room.

"You didn't upset me! But I can't figure out what you were thinking," she exclaimed, a large measure of her incredulity sweeping over her again now that they were alone.

"You don't like the house?" he asked.

"Are you kidding? It's amazing. It's perfect. I've never even considered living in a house like this. I grew up in this area. I know what a house like this so close to the beach must cost."

"I can afford it."

She stared at him, mute.

"Mari and I both received large trusts from our parents' estate. I spent my entire adult life in the service. The military provided me with almost everything I needed. I didn't have to spend as much as most people, so I was able to save a lot of money. Invest."

Her mouth had gone dry. "But, Ryan, that's your money."

"It's ours," he said firmly, stepping toward her. His face looked gilded and solemn in the luminescent, golden light. "We're married, Faith."

Unexpectedly the topic of their future had come up again. She hadn't prepared for it. She didn't know what to say.

Ryan touched her shoulder. She looked up at him helplessly.

"I know when I first brought up the topic of marriage, I said we could divorce after the baby is born. I'll still do whatever you want in that regard, Faith. But you must know by now that isn't what *I* want. I'd like us to remain as a family." He touched her cheek. "I'd like that more than anything. But no matter what you decide about the house, I'm still considering buying it as an investment property." He glanced around the sunny room. "It hurt to give up this house before. I'd like to keep it in the family."

Utterly caught in his solemn-eyed stare, she jumped slightly when his cell phone began to ring. He muttered under his breath and reached into his pocket to get it. He scowled when he saw the number, tapped a button and stuffed the phone back in his pocket.

"Aren't you going to answer it?" Faith asked bemusedly.

"No," he said. He reached for her hand. "Did I happen to mention this was my bedroom, growing up?"

"It was?" Faith asked, glancing around for a fresh take on the room.

"Yeah. Come on. Let me show you the master bedroom. I have some ideas for renovation in there that'd make it incredible…"

"What are you thinking?" Ryan asked her later on the drive back to Holland.

Faith bit at her bottom lip anxiously. The idea of moving into that gorgeous home with Ryan, of raising their child there, was like being told an amazing dream could come true. But in order for them to step so firmly into the future, didn't they need to confirm their feelings for one another? Was it really enough for Ryan to choose a future based solely on his love for family and his child?

Wasn't love and partnership important, as well?

She realized that Ryan was patiently awaiting her answer.

"I think it was incredibly generous of you to make this offer, Ryan. The house is fantastic. And you're right…a house like that doesn't go up on the market frequently in Harbor Town. I can understand why you'd want to own it again. They tend to be kept in families for generations."

"I'm glad you liked it."

"I loved it," she said, looking at him as he drove. "Do you think I could have a little time to think over the idea of us moving there together, though?"

"Of course."

"Thank you," Faith said, her heart filled with the strangest, most potent combination of dread and hope at once.

The next afternoon she retired to her office after her last patient and sank into her office chair. She was surprised she'd gotten any work done, she'd been so preoccupied with making the decision about the house. Of course the house was only at the surface of the core of the dilemma. Ryan hadn't probably meant to do it, but by showing her that home last night, he'd brought the entire issue of their arranged marriage to a head.

In order to make such a game-altering decision, she knew she had no choice but to put all her cards on the table and hope that Ryan did the same.

She was going to have to bite the bullet and tell Ryan that she'd fallen in love with him. How else was it possible for him to make an informed choice about his future? How else was it conceivable for her? She was going to have to march home and tell him the truth.

When she saw his reaction to the fact that she loved him, body and soul, she'd have her answer as to how to proceed.

Ryan was down in the workshop assembling one of the many units of the bookshelf when he heard knocking at the front door. Had Faith forgotten her key? He glanced around hastily for his shirt, but didn't see where he'd tossed it when he'd whipped it off earlier. The air-conditioning didn't work very well here in the basement, and he'd been working up a sweat.

"Coming," he shouted as he lunged up the stairs, two at a time. "Did you forget your—"

He paused in midsentence as he flung open the front door when he saw Jesse's old girlfriend, Melanie Shane, standing on the front stoop.

"I told you I didn't think it was a good idea for you to come here," Ryan said coolly a minute after he'd let Melanie inside. They stood in the living room, exchanging tense words.

A tear leaked down Melanie's face. She'd always been a good-looking woman, but her appearance had altered since

Ryan had last seen her while they were both still stationed in Afghanistan. After Jesse had died, she'd started to lose weight. She'd lost even more since Ryan had left the service. Weight loss agreed with Melanie, making her voluptuous curves more streamlined and her blue eyes larger and even more haunted in appearance than they'd been when Ryan had last seen her.

"I had to come," she said, her usually cigarette-roughed, tough-girl voice trembling with emotion. "You're the only person I could talk to, Ryan. You were Jesse's good friend. The only one who knew how close Jesse and I were. I mean…I know you didn't entirely approve of Jesse's and my relationship, but you're the only one who could understand what his death meant to me. I've left the Air Force," she said starkly after a pause.

"You did?"

She nodded and sniffed. Ryan sighed and walked across the room to get her some tissues.

"Look, Melanie, I've got nothing against you, but—"

"Don't give me that line, Ryan." Her jaw tilted up defiantly. "I know you always looked down on my and Jesse's relationship. I suppose you thought even less of me because of that night we celebrated Shaunessy's birthday."

Ryan didn't reply. He just stuck out the box of Kleenex tissues for Melanie. If she wanted to rehash the night she'd gotten drunk at Mike Shaunessy's party and come on to Ryan because Jesse had been flirting heavily with a nurse from the hospital, she was going to have to do it with someone else. It wasn't as if he hated Melanie. He actually felt sorry for her, and he had a good idea of why she was here…

…why she was feeling so miserable in regard to Jesse's death.

But there was nothing he could do for her. He couldn't

offer Melanie the peace—or the solace—for which she longed.

"Like I've been telling you when you've called the past couple times, there's nothing for us to discuss, Melanie. I want you to go. This is Faith's home. You know that. You shouldn't be here. It's disrespectful."

Melanie's eyes flashed with anger at that. Her gaze landed on a photo on the corner table of Faith holding a tiny version of Topsy up to her cheek.

"So that's the paragon of virtue herself," Melanie said scathingly. She glanced around the house as if seeing it for the first time. Her gaze landed on Ryan. She gave him a thoroughly amused feminine appraisal, her eyes lowering over his naked torso. "I can't believe you married Jesse's widow. Isn't that a little…*sick?*"

"Get out," Ryan said quietly.

He'd been hoping to get rid of Melanie politely, but that clearly wasn't going to happen. Melanie could be all right at times, but she also could get herself worked up into a real state. Jesse had used to joke that he didn't know whether to dread or adore Melanie's temper tantrums, because they were hell to endure, but heaven to make up from.

"So you really envied Jesse his sappy, sweet little animal-loving wife. Funny," Melanie said, stepping closer to him, her voice going husky, "I would have pegged you above all men for needing a strong, hot-blooded female."

Ryan halted her attempt to press against him by grabbing her elbows.

"Cut it out, Melanie. What are you trying to prove by acting so stupid?" he asked, his patience running thin. "It's not going to get you anywhere here with me. No more than it ever did," he seethed.

As if his angry words had popped a cap off a geyser,

she sobbed, her entire body heaving with uncontrollable emotion.

"Oh, God, Ryan, I know you know the truth. I know you know the real reason I'm here. I can't stand it anymore. You're the only one who knew how badly Jesse and I had been fighting before we got that emergency call about Langley's plane going down in the Kunar. You're the only one who knows the truth. *I* killed Jesse and the others."

Ryan ground his teeth together as she shook with misery. Here it was. Melanie had been piloting the chopper that had gone down on the rescue mission. He exhaled, wishing like hell Melanie had chosen another time and another place to have her little mental breakdown.

Still…she was a soldier in arms and more importantly, another pilot. What she was experiencing right now was every pilot's worst nightmare. He couldn't help but feel compassion for her.

"You didn't kill Jesse or anyone. It was an accident, pure and simple. You were down low, on the lookout for Langley, and the chopper hit a power line. You know as well as I do other choppers have run into similar problems with those low lines. They're a menace."

"But if Jesse and I hadn't been arguing before, maybe I would have been less distracted and more alert. Maybe—"

"It wasn't your fault," Ryan repeated, tightening his hold on her upper arms. She was near hysteria. Her guilt must have been building up in her for a while now. "I know a pilot feels total responsibility for their passengers and mission, but that's not the same as saying that you killed someone. It was an *accident*. Those wires are uncharted and damn near invisible outside of twenty feet. There was nothing you could have done," he said, shaking her slightly, trying to break through her misery.

"I loved him," Melanie said in a strained, vibrating

voice. "I know you don't believe I'm capable of it, but I am. I miss him so much." She collapsed against him. Ryan gripped her tighter, trying to keep her from falling.

"Melanie," Ryan pleaded.

"I have never, ever loved like this. It hurts so much," she said against his chest, her hands grasping at his shoulders desperately.

Ryan opened his mouth, wildly searching for something to say that would bring both comfort and closure to this awkward situation. He glanced over Melanie's head and froze.

Faith stood at the entryway to the living room, holding a sack of groceries, her green eyes huge, wearing an expression he'd seen before on shell-shocked soldiers.

Faith was so stunned she didn't at first know how to interpret what she was seeing. Ryan held a tall, willowy blonde against him. The image of the woman's red-tipped fingernails clutching at the dense muscle of his naked shoulders was scored on her consciousness, as was Ryan's returned tight hold on her upper arms.

"I have never, ever loved like this. It hurts so much," she heard the woman moan as if through a barrier of thick cotton. Her fingers clutched tighter at Ryan.

"Faith."

She looked up into his face. It looked rigid with tension. The woman whipped her head around. Her face was wet with tears.

"I...this is Melanie," Ryan said in gruff tone. "Melanie Shane."

"Hello," Faith said hollowly. She hardly knew what she was saying. She hardly knew what she was doing as she set down the grocery bag on a nearby table. A strange noise had started up in her ears, like a fierce wind blowing.

"Excuse me."

"Faith," Ryan's voice came from just behind her a few seconds later as she walked toward her car. "That wasn't... it wasn't what it might have looked like. Let me explain."

"So that's Melanie?" Faith asked as she opened her car door. Ryan caught it. They stood in the driveway, separated by the door.

"Yes. She shouldn't have come here. I'm sorry. I've been telling her not to, but she's upset. She wanted to talk to me about—"

"You weren't being entirely honest when you said *some* men would find her attractive. She's very pretty. You shouldn't leave her standing in there alone, Ryan," she said flatly before she got in the car.

"Dammit, Faith—" He lifted his hands to try and reach for her and she swung the door closed. Hard. He whipped his hands out of the opening just before the door would have banged forcefully into his fingers. Faith started up the car and put it into Reverse. He thumped his hand on the window as it began to move away from him. "Faith, come back here. You're jumping to the wrong conclusion," he boomed.

But Faith could hardly hear him. Her heart was beating like she'd just narrowly escaped the monster trap of a lifetime.

She blinked fifteen minutes later when she saw the sign welcoming her to Harbor Town's city limits. She'd driven blindly, unaware of any goal or destination.

Or had her numb brain perhaps chosen this route purposefully, to remind her of all she'd been about to put on the line...all she'd been about to sacrifice by exposing her soul and taking a chance on the future with Ryan?

She pulled into the parking lot of White Sands Beach. She'd chosen the location randomly, seeing its entrance from Travertine Road. It had suddenly struck her that she should pull over. She felt ill. She shouldn't be driving. It wasn't safe.

She just sat there behind the wheel of the car for the better part of an hour, staring at the sparkling lake in the distance, waiting for her brain to stop vibrating in shock.

What the hell had just happened?

She closed her eyes and tried to piece together the events of the past several hours. Her brain didn't seem to be working properly, and she felt as if she might throw up.

She'd decided to pick up the ingredients for a nice dinner for Ryan. She wanted to lay everything on the line… tell him the truth. She was in love with him. If he didn't balk at her admission, if he, too, thought they had a future together as a true husband and wife, she'd be able to read it in his face. She knew somehow that she'd see his hesitancy once she admitted she loved him.

If there was one thing she knew about Ryan, it was that he worried about her. He'd feel responsible if he asked her to continue the marriage for the sake of the baby and him having the family he'd always wanted, knowing all along that he risked hurting her because she'd truly fallen for him.

She'd made that risky choice, and returned home with her heart on her sleeve, so to speak. And then…

The image of the woman's red fingernails clutching at Ryan's naked shoulders flashed into her mind's eye like a visual slap to the face. Suddenly she knew for a fact that had been Melanie who had been calling Ryan for the past several days. A pain went through her and faded to a dull, cramp-like ache. She clutched at her abdomen, applying a slight pressure, trying to soothe it.

So *that* had been Melanie Shane. Jesse's lover.

She'd certainly seemed close to Ryan, as well.

Ryan had insisted she'd misunderstood what she'd seen, but what she'd seen had been pretty damn inflammatory.

Since Melanie had contacted her by email, breaking the news about her affair with Jesse, Faith had imagined the other woman countless times. She knew it'd been stupid, but she defied any wife who discovered that her husband had been cheating not to wonder about the other woman.

Imagining Jesse with Melanie Shane had been nothing...absolutely *nothing* to seeing Ryan holding her.

The vision of the lake blurred before her eyes. Faith opened the car door and vomited. Another cramp went through her. She bent over in the car seat, gasping for air.

For the first time real fear pierced her chaotic emotional state.

Chapter Fourteen

Ryan plowed through the doors leading to the Acute Care Unit at Harbor Town Memorial, barely moving in time to stop from plowing into a maid's cart and knocking over all her supplies.

"Sorry," he said, not pausing to stop in his rapid forward motion. "Is the Acute Care Unit down that way?" he asked the startled maid, pointing toward the hallway to the left. The woman nodded, her eyes wide.

Ryan plunged down the hallway, ignoring the nurses' station.

"Sir. Can I help you?" one of the nurses called after him, standing. "Sir, you're going to have to come back here!"

"It's all right," Ryan heard a woman say. "Ryan!"

He paused, panting. He didn't want to stop until he located Faith, but whoever this was knew his name. Maybe she knew which room was Faith's—

God, let her be all right, he thought as he whipped around.

"Dr. Feingold," he said, recognizing Faith's obstetrician as she came toward him. "What happened? Where is she? Is she okay?"

"Yes," Dr. Feingold said firmly, staring straight at him as she approached, as if she wanted to make sure she had his complete attention. "She's absolutely fine. And so is the baby."

Ryan exhaled raggedly. He'd been in a panic ever since he'd received the phone call from an intake nurse at the Emergency Room at Harbor Town Hospital.

I'm afraid your wife came into the E.R. earlier. She'd been experiencing some pretty severe cramping and spotting. We've contacted Dr. Feingold, your wife's obstetrician. She's on staff here at Harbor Town Memorial. The doctor has arrived and has ordered a series of tests. She'd like to admit Faith. That's all we know right now, sir, the nurse had added when Ryan had demanded to know if Faith would be all right.

He'd driven to Harbor Town in record time, the entire time his brain ablaze with wild concern and regrets. What if something terrible happened to Faith and he'd never told her he loved her? If there was one thing he'd thought he'd had on his side, it was time. Surely Faith would learn to trust him, the more time they spent together. Surely she'd gain faith that the only thing he wanted to do was to see her happy...to know she was loved.

Her shattered expression as she'd stood there looking at Melanie Shane in his arms earlier rose up to haunt him. That was the reason she'd grown ill. He hadn't intended to hurt her in any way, but he had, nevertheless.

"I want to see her," Ryan demanded. "Where is she, Dr. Feingold?"

"She's resting. She's in Room 212. But why don't you sit down over here for a second with me. You look very shaken up. I'll explain about the test results."

Renewed terror tore through him. "You said she'd be all right."

"And she *will* be," Dr. Feingold assured, urging him to sit down next to her on a bench. Ryan sat stiffly.

"What happened?" Ryan asked.

"She was having some breakthrough bleeding and some cramping. She was right to come into the Emergency Room. We did all the routine tests, though, and everything is fine, both with Faith and the fetus."

"Why was she bleeding then?"

"It's not uncommon. Lots of women have spotting while they're pregnant. It was more the cramping I was concerned about, but as it turns out, Faith had vomited. Her cramps were more associated with an upset stomach than the baby."

Ryan nodded numbly. "She was upset," he mumbled, his gaze turning down the hallway. "I have to see her, Dr. Feingold."

"All right. Just try to keep her calm. I'm going to keep her overnight, just for observation. She can go home in the morning."

Ryan nodded, barely hearing the doctor, his entire focus on seeing Faith.

Faith stared out the hospital room window. Light was fading. It would soon be night. It was funny, how a scare like the one she'd just been through made you reconsider so much, really made you appreciate the things you daily overlooked and took for granted, like the beauty of a new day or the simple touch or smile of a loved one. A visit to

the hospital really made you think about what was important, and what wasn't.

She turned eagerly at the sound of the knock at her door.

"Ryan," she called, smiling. Tears burned in her eyelids. He looked so tall and straight and wonderful...and
worried, she realized regretfully as he entered the room.

"I'm so glad to see you," she said, a rush of love going
through her at the sight of him. "The baby is going to be
okay. Did anyone tell you?"

She couldn't quite read his expression as he came next
to the bed.

"Ryan? Did you hear me?" she asked. "The baby is
going to be fine."

His dark eyes looked desperate...a little wild.

"I only wanted to know you were all right," he said.

For a few seconds they just stared at each other. What
he'd said had pierced straight to her heart. Why had she
been so certain he was only interested in her out of pity
because of Jesse's infidelities or because she carried his
child? How else could she possibly interpret the worry and
love pouring out of his eyes at this very minute?

"Oh, Ryan, I'm so sorry about running off like that
without letting you explain. It's just...Jesse...and Melanie...and seeing you holding her," she choked out tearfully.

"She's been trying to get in contact with me because
she's carrying around a guilt complex about the crash. She
feels responsible."

Faith froze. "Was she?"

"No. It's not uncommon for a pilot to feel that way after
an accident. I'm not best friends with Melanie or anything, but I do feel bad for her. It's hard for a pilot not to
feel compassion for another one in that situation. It's all of
our worst nightmare. Anyway, Melanie misses Jesse and
was breaking down when you walked in. I've been telling

her it was inappropriate for her to come to your house, but she's been so persistent—"

"I figured it was probably something like that, once I had the chance to really think about it. Being in the hospital like this, feeling terrified that something was wrong with the baby...well, it really gives you a chance to reflect on things," she said, sobbing softly.

"Don't get upset, honey. Please," Ryan implored.

"No, no, it's okay. I'm all right. I'm just sorry for judging you like that."

"It's okay," he said, his heart plastered all over his usually impassive, top-gun facade. He set his hip on the bed and hugged her tightly.

"Oh, Ryan, I love you," she said in a pressured fashion against his shirt.

"I love you, too, Faith," he said, running his hand over her hair, soothing her. "I think I've been in love with you since Christmas Eve. At first I doubted what I was feeling. Later, after I returned to Michigan, I started to trust in it. But I could tell you weren't going to buy it after all you'd been through with Jesse...with me...with us falling for each other so hard and so fast."

She sniffed and rubbed her cheek against his shirt. "I should have trusted you, Ryan. I should have trusted this," she said, hugging him closer to her.

He cupped her head in his hand, urging her to lean her head back. She did so, never finding the sight of his face so compelling as she did at that moment, with his love exposed.

"I told myself all we needed was time," he said. "I knew I could gain your trust...your love if I just had the time to prove myself to you. After today I realized that I might never have any of those things."

"No," she whispered fervently, hating the haunted look

that shadowed his rugged features. She pressed her lips to his warmly. "You have all those things—time, trust and love. My love, most of all."

Epilogue

Ethan Kassim Itani's first day at the new house on Sycamore Avenue was the family's first day, as well. It felt like living a miracle to Faith to walk into their beautiful new home carrying her beautiful new son.

"I'll take him, so you can look around better," Ryan said quietly when they reached the landing at the top of the stairs of the house.

"Oh, *Ryan*," Faith whispered as she looked at the newly polished floors and painted walls. The house on Sycamore Avenue had been beautiful when they'd viewed it four and a half months ago, but what Ryan had done to it in the meantime made it downright stunning.

"I can't believe it, you painted the hallway and put in the wall sconces," she breathed, glancing around in wonder. "You've been working too hard, doing this and everything with the business, too," she admonished as she turned to hand him the bundle in her arms. She looked down into

Ethan's tiny face as Ryan took him. The baby wrinkled his nose and made a pursing movement with his mouth before he resumed sleeping again. Faith glanced up into Ryan's face and they shared a smile.

"The most gorgeous baby in the world, the most beautiful house and the most wonderful husband," Faith whispered. "How is it possible for one woman to feel so much happiness at once?"

"Does that mean you can't take any more?"

She grinned and narrowed her gaze on him. "What do you mean?" she asked suspiciously. "Did you finish the nursery?"

His grin widened. He led her down the hallway. She gasped when she walked into the room. Faith had insisted on putting up the stenciling for the wall mural, even though she wouldn't be able to actually paint it until after the baby was born, so that part remained unfinished. Ryan had completed every other possible conceivable detail of the nursery, however. The walls were painted in a rich cobalt-blue, the white furniture they'd chosen contrasting with it handsomely. She walked over to the finished, dark walnut shelving unit that Ryan had fashioned, admiring the gleaming wood and all the useful cabinets and shelves.

Tears smarted in her eyes when she turned to face her husband and son.

"It's perfect. It's absolutely perfect," she said.

"Come here," he said, his gaze on her warm. She hugged him around his waist, careful not to wake Ethan. She smiled at her beautiful boys.

"Should we see how Ethan likes his new cradle?" she asked. Ryan nodded and she watched, spellbound, as he laid the baby inside and gently covered him.

He turned and took Faith into his arms.

"To think," she whispered. "You used to sleep in this

room at night and dream about the next day's summer-time adventure."

A smile tilted Ryan's mouth. Warmth and love suffused every pore of her being when Ryan leaned down and fastened his mouth to hers.

"And one day," he said quietly next to her upturned lips a moment later, "Ethan will scheme up his own dreams, and a whole new generation of adventures will take place in Harbor Town."

* * * * *

FROM BEST FRIEND TO DADDY

JULES BENNETT

Marrying my best friend was the best decision of my life. Love you, Michael.

Chapter One

"It's just one glass."

Kate McCoy stared at the champagne flute the best man held. He'd flirted with her all night during the wedding rehearsal dinner—and by her estimate in smelling his overwhelming breath, he'd had more than enough for both of them. Thankfully he was just Noah's cousin and visiting from out of town. As in, he'd be leaving after the nuptials tomorrow afternoon.

One of Kate's three best friends, Lucy, was marrying her very own cowboy, and Kate couldn't be happier. She could, however, do without Noah's cousin all up in her face.

"She doesn't drink."

That low, growly tone belonged to Gray Gallagher, her only male best friend and the man who always came to her rescue whether she needed him to or not. She could've handled herself, but she wasn't about to turn away backup since Bryan with a Y wasn't taking her subtle hints.

Kate glanced over her shoulder and smiled, but Gray's eyes weren't on her. That dark, narrowed gaze was focused downward at the best man. Which wasn't difficult. Gray easily had five inches and an exorbitant amount of muscle tone on Best Man Bryan.

"Oh, well." Bryan awkwardly held two flutes in his hand, tossing one back with a shrug. "Perhaps I could get you a soda or some water."

"We were just leaving," Gray growled.

He slid his arm around her waist and escorted her from the dining area of the country club. Apparently they were indeed leaving because he kept heading toward the exit.

"I need to at least get my purse before you manhandle me out the door," she said, swiping her clutch off the table closest to the door, where she'd been chatting with some guests. "And for your information, I was going to have a glass."

Gray stopped short in the hallway and turned to her. "You wanted to have a drink with that lame guy? You've never drank in your life."

Kate shrugged. "It's my thirtieth birthday."

"I'm aware of that." Eyes as dark as midnight narrowed. "You're not drinking with him."

Should she clue Gray in on her reasoning for wanting to have her first drink on her birthday and at her friend's wedding?

True, Kate hadn't so much as tried a drop of alcohol since her parents had been tragically killed in an accident. Her father had been thirty-five, her mother only thirty-two.

Now that Kate had hit the big 3-0, she'd started reevaluating everything about her carefully detailed life.

"C'mon." Gray slid his hand around her arm and escorted her out the door into the humid Tennessee heat. "If you're going to have a drink, it's not going to be with someone who can't handle champagne at a damn formal dinner."

Kate couldn't help but laugh. "That wasn't nice."

"Wasn't meant to be. I don't like how he looked at you."

What was up with this grouchy attitude tonight? Well, not just tonight. Gray seemed to be out of sorts for months now and with each passing day, he seemed to be getting worse and worse.

Gray headed toward his truck. He'd picked her up earlier and presented her with a box of chocolate-covered strawberries for her birthday. He knew those were her weakness and it was a tradition he'd started years ago when he'd first come back from the army only days before her birthday. Gray had told her he'd actually ordered her something this year, but it hadn't arrived yet.

"I'm picking you up for the wedding tomorrow, too."

Kate McCoy calculated everything, from matching her underwear to her outfit to the precise inches of curling ribbon she needed when wrapping packages. She had every detail in her life down to perfection and even owned a company that specialized in organizing the lives of others—everything from closets to finances. The Savvy Scheduler was still fairly new, but it was growing thanks to her social media accounts that drove interested viewers to her blog and ultimately resulted in many new clients.

Kate had anal-retentive down to a science. So she didn't like when her plans got changed.

"I'm driving myself in the morning."

Gray knew she calculated everything in her life well in advance. Hell, her planner had a planner. Everything in her personal life and business was not only on paper but also in e-format.

He was perfectly aware of how meticulous she was with every detail. They'd met in grade school on the playground when she made fun of his new haircut. Considering he'd hated it as well, they had a good laugh and bonded when other children would've fought over the mocking. They knew each other better than most married couples, which was why she couldn't pinpoint why he'd been surlier than usual tonight.

From scowling when he'd picked her up and muttered something about her dress, to the rude way he'd just escorted her out without saying goodbye to their friends, Gray's manners were seriously lacking.

"Plans change," he said with a shrug as he released his hold and walked ahead. "Relax."

Relax? The man had been uptight all night, glaring at any male guest who talked to her, but she was supposed to relax? What was up with him?

The wind picked up, threatening to blow her short skirt higher than was within her comfort zone and expose said matching panties. Kate fisted the bottom of her flare dress in one hand as she marched across the parking lot after Gray—which wasn't easy, considering she'd gone with three-inch stilettos for the special occasion.

Stubborn man. He always wanted to bicker, and tonight was apparently no exception. But his unexplained behavior was starting to wear on her nerves.

Honestly, though, she didn't have time to analyze Gray's snarly attitude. It was late and she was tired and sweaty from this damn heat. Coupled with the unforgiving humidity wave hitting Stonerock, she was becoming rather grouchy herself. What happened to spring?

"I *planned* on getting to the church early to make sure everything was ready for when Lucy got there in the morning." Why was she yelling at his retreating back? "Would you stop and listen to me?"

Gray didn't stop until he got to the passenger door

of his black truck. When he turned to face her, he released an exasperated sigh. He hadn't shaved for a few days, had that whole messy head of dark hair going on, and his tattoos peeked from beneath each sleeve that he'd cuffed up over his forearms. If she went for the dark, mysterious type, Gray would fit the bill perfectly. Well, also if he weren't her best friend.

Kate could easily see why women flocked to Gallagher's to flirt and throw themselves at the third-generation bar owner. He was a sexy man, had the whole "I don't give a damn" attitude, but she knew something those women didn't. Gray was loyal to a fault and didn't do flings. He may have looked like the quintessential bad boy, but he was all heart and a true Southern gentleman.

"Noah asked if I would bring you," he told her. "He said Lucy was worried about parking for the guests and he was trying to make things as simple as possible by having the wedding party carpool. I'll pick you up whatever time you want. Is this seriously something we have to argue about?"

One dark brow quirked and she thought for a scant second that maybe this was something they didn't have to argue about. Not that she was ready to concede the upper hand. First the angry attitude, now a lame argument?

"I'll pick you up," she stated, swiping away a hair that had landed right on her lip gloss. "I want my own vehicle there."

"Fine. Hop in." He motioned toward the truck. "I have to swing by the bar and get champagne out of the back stock since more was consumed tonight than originally planned. I'll give you a drink of whatever you want. But your first one will be with me."

"It's late, Gray. You don't have to do that. My list isn't going anywhere."

"List?" He shook his head, muttering something under his breath she couldn't quite make out. "Get in the truck. I should've known you'd have a damn list about taking a sip of alcohol."

Kate blew out a sigh. "I'm not sure, though. Maybe I should just mark it off and move on to the next item."

Gray reached out and tucked a strand behind her ear. "First of all, one drink of champagne or wine is a far cry from the ten empty vodka bottles found in the car of the person who hit your parents. Second, I'd never let you get in over your head. Third, what the hell is this list you keep referring to?"

The breeze kicked up, thankfully sending some relief over her bare shoulders, but making it impossible to let go of her dress. She'd left her hair down, which was a huge mistake. With that thick mass sticking to her neck and back, she'd give anything for a rubber band about now.

"It's silly."

"I live for silly."

Even without the dry humor, she knew Gray was as far removed from silly as any human being.

"Since I was turning thirty, I decided to make a list of things I want to do. Kind of a way to give myself a life makeover." She shrugged, because saying this out loud sounded even more ridiculous. "Trying a drink is on there."

"What else made the list?"

His eyes raked over her. Sometimes he did that. Like she was fragile. Just because life had knocked her down at times didn't mean she couldn't handle herself.

"Nothing for you to worry about."

She started to edge around him and reach for her handle when he stepped in her path. "Tell me."

Her eyes met his and she could tell by the hard stare that he wasn't backing down.

"I don't know what's up with you lately. You've been a bit of a Neanderthal." Might as well point out the proverbial elephant in the room. "You're pushy and hovering and...well, demanding. Just because some guy flirts with me doesn't mean I'm going to repeat old mistakes. And if I want a drink, I can do that for myself, too. I know you want to protect me, but you can't always do that, Gray. I'm a big girl and—"

In a quick move he spun her around and had her caged between the truck door and his hard chest. Mercy, he was ripped...and strong.

"Wh-what are you—"

"Putting that mouth to better use."

The words had barely processed before he covered

her lips with his. There was nothing gentle, nothing sweet or calm about Gray. He was a storm, sweeping her up before she even knew what hit her.

Wait. She shouldn't be kissing her best friend. Should she?

He touched her nowhere else and she still clutched her dress in one hand. On a low growl, he shifted and changed the angle of the kiss before diving back in for more. The way he towered over her, covering her body from lips to hips, made her feel protected and ravaged all at the same time.

Heat flooded through her in a way that had nothing to do with the weather.

Just as fiercely as he started, Gray pulled back. Cursing under his breath, he raked a hand through his already messy hair. Clearly he was waging some war with himself. Well, he could just get in line, because she had no idea what to do about what had just happened.

"Gray—"

"Get in the truck, Kate."

His raspy voice slid over her, making her shiver despite the heat.

What the hell did that mean? What did any of the past few minutes mean? Kate couldn't wrap her mind around his actions, his words. One minute she was trying to get to the bottom of his behavior and the next…well, she was being kissed by her best friend, and not just any kiss. No, he'd all but devoured her, almost as if he were trying to ruin her for another man.

Gray reached around her for the door handle, giving her no choice but to move. She settled inside and stared ahead, completely dazed. With his taste still on her lips and countless questions swirling through her mind, Kate didn't dare say another word out loud as she buckled her seat belt.

What on earth had triggered such an intense response? And then to just leave like that? She'd already told him that they couldn't be more than friends, but damn it, that kiss sparked something inside her she'd never experienced before.

Why did he have to go and do that to her? Why did he have to make her question her stance on their relationship and leave her aching for more?

More wasn't an option.

Chapter Two

The ride from the country club to Gallagher's had been too damn quiet. Tension had settled between them like an unwanted third party. Never before had things been this tense between them. They bantered, they bickered…that's just who they were.

But now, thanks to his inability to control himself, the dynamics had shifted completely.

Gray wasn't even going to question what had gotten into him. He knew full well that years of pent-up frustration from being relegated to the friend category, seeing her flirt and dance with other men at his bar and then being engaged and heartbroken, and finally that damn dress and heels tonight had all caused him to snap. There was only so much a man could take…especially from a woman like Kate.

And then the list. He wanted to know what the hell was on it and why she thought she needed to revamp herself. Not a thing was wrong with her. Who was she proving herself to?

Losing his cool and kissing her may not have been his finest moment, but every man had a breaking point and Kate McCoy had been his for far too long.

Damn, she'd tasted good and she'd felt even better all pressed against him. He wasn't sorry he'd kissed her, wasn't regretting in the slightest that he'd finally taken what he'd wanted. She'd leaned into him and obviously had wanted it just as much.

No, what angered him was the shocked look on her face and the fact he'd just pulled them both across a line they could never come back from. He was her friend, her self-appointed protector. She didn't have many constants in her life and she counted on him, damn it. She *trusted* him.

Now Kate stood at the bar, her eyes never meeting his. No doubt she was replaying that kiss just as he'd been over the past ten minutes.

Gray didn't say anything as he went to the back and pulled out a bottle of champagne that none of his customers would ever be interested in, but it was perfect for Kate. Once he got her home and came back, though, he was going to need something much stronger. Thankfully he could just crawl upstairs to his apartment after throwing one back.

Gray returned to the bar to find Kate exactly how he'd left her. He reached for a glass and carried that and the bottle around to the front side of the bar.

"I assume you still want that drink."

Finally, her blue eyes darted to his. "If anything in my life warranted a drink, this night would be it."

He poured her a small amount and slid the glass over to her. Kate stared at the peach-toned liquid for only a moment before picking it up and smelling the contents.

All of that long, dark hair curtained her face as she leaned down. With those creamy shoulders exposed, he was having a difficult time not reaching out to touch her.

Had he severed that right? Had he ruined everything innocent about their friendship when he'd put his lips on hers?

Damn it. He didn't like the idea of another man coming into her life. It had damn near killed him when she'd gotten engaged while he'd been in the army. Then, when the jerk had broken her heart, it had taken all of Gray's willpower not to pummel the guy.

Tonight he'd nearly lost it when Noah's best man had gotten flirty. Gray saw how Bryan looked at her, like she was going to be easy to take home. That wasn't his Kate. She didn't go home with random strangers.

Kate slammed her empty glass on the bar. "More."

He added a bit more to her glass and was a little

surprised when she tipped it back and swallowed it in one drink. Then belched like a champ.

"Wow. That's bubbly."

Gray couldn't help but smile. "It is. Had enough?"

"I can still taste your lips, so probably not."

His gut tightened as arousal spiraled through him. "Don't say things like that."

She lifted a slender shoulder. "Why not? It's the truth."

Gray took her glass away and set it aside with the bottle. The last thing she needed was to start buzzing, get all talkative and then regret spilling her secrets come morning. Though part of him—the part that had kissed her—would love to keep pouring and get her true feelings to come out into the open.

The low lighting behind the bottles lining the mirror along the bar wall sent a warm glow throughout the space. The main dining section and dance floor were still dark and Gray had never been more aware of a woman or his desire.

Over the years he'd purposely never allowed himself to be in a compromising situation with Kate, yet here he was only moments after plastering her against the side of his truck and claiming her lips.

"You can't be attracted to me," she murmured. "You *can't*, Gray."

If her words had any heat to them, if he thought for a second she didn't feel anything toward him, he'd ignore his need. But the only emotion he heard in her tone was fear and she'd kissed him right back earlier, so...

"You know I'm attracted to you." He closed the space between them. "I've never made it a secret."

"I'm the only woman who comes in your bar and hasn't thrown herself at you. I'm a conquest."

Anger settled heavily inside him. "Never call yourself that."

"Then what's the reasoning?" she tossed back. "Why me? After all these years, you're telling me... what? I need you to talk to me instead of being so damn irritated. Why now?"

"Maybe I'm tired of seeing other guys flirt with you. Maybe I'm sick of you dating losers since your breakup because you know your heart won't get involved."

She'd been burned and her defense mechanism to set her standards low was slowly driving him out of his ever-loving mind. Couldn't she see that she deserved more? She should actually be expecting more.

"Why did you kiss me back?" he asked, shifting the direction back to her.

Gray adjusted his body to cage her in against the bar with one hand on either side of her hips. He didn't want her to dodge him or look away or find an excuse not to hash this out right here, right now.

Maybe it was the late hour, maybe it was the near-darkness surrounding them. Or perhaps it was just time that his war with himself came to an end one way or another.

Kate's eyes widened, then darted to his mouth. That innocent act had arousal pumping through him. His frustrating friend could stir up quite the gamut of emotions. One of the reasons he had always been so fascinated by her. Nobody could get to him the way she could. And nobody could match him in conversation the way Kate could.

She flattened her palms on his chest. "Gray, I can't lose you as a friend."

"I never said I was going anywhere." He leaned in just a bit closer, close enough to see those navy flecks in her bright blue eyes. Close enough for her to realize he wasn't messing around anymore. "Tell me you don't want me kissing you again."

Because as much as he worried he was pushing her, he kept returning to the fact that she'd kissed him back.

Kate's mouth opened, then closed. That was all the green light he needed.

Gray didn't waste time gripping her hips and capturing her mouth. Those fingertips against his chest curled in, biting into his skin through the fabric. She let out a soft moan as her body melted against his. He wanted to hoist her up onto this bar and see exactly what she wore beneath this damn dress that had driven him crazy all night. He wanted those legs wrapped around him, her body arched against his.

Kate tore her mouth away. "We can't... Why does this feel so good? It can't go anywhere."

Like hell it couldn't. She was just as turned on as

he was if the way she'd rubbed herself against him proved anything.

Gray slid his hands over the curve of her hips, to the dip in her waist, and back down. "Tell me to stop and I will."

He leaned in, trailing his lips over her collarbone, breathing in that jasmine scent that belonged only on her.

"Tell me, Kate," he whispered, smiling when she trembled beneath his touch. "I have to hear the words."

He was torturing himself. If she told him to stop right now he would. But damn it, being pulled away after having a sample would be hell.

Slowly her hands slid up around his neck, and her fingers threaded through his hair. "Gray," she murmured.

Music to his ears. He'd always wondered how his name would sound sliding through her lips on a whispered sigh. Now he knew…and he wanted more.

Gray hovered with his mouth right over hers, his hands circling her waist. "You want me."

She nodded.

"Say it."

"I want you," she murmured. "But I need you as a friend. Please. Tell me we won't lose that."

He didn't want to lose anything. He wanted to build on what they had. They couldn't ignore this pull between them, so taking this risk to see where things went was the only option.

When he said nothing, she eased back as much as she could with the bar at her back. "Gray, this night is all we can have. We'll still be friends come morning."

One night? Did she think she'd be done with him that soon?

"And nobody can know," she added. "I don't want Lucy or Tara to know."

Her girl posse. He understood the need for privacy, but at the same time, he didn't want to be her dirty little secret and he sure as hell wanted more than one night.

He was a guy. Wasn't he supposed to be thrilled at the idea of a one-night stand with no strings? He should've had her dress off by now.

But this was Kate and she was special. Always had been.

"I wondered."

Her words stopped every single thought. "What?"

Bright blue eyes came up to his. "About this. I wondered before."

"Kate," he growled.

"I mean it, Gray. Just this night and it stays here, between us."

There was so much he wanted to say, so much he wanted to fight for because Kate was worth fighting for. He'd worry about the semantics tomorrow. He'd come too far and had a willing woman in his arms right now. There was only one thing to do.

Gray lifted her up onto the bar and kissed her.

Chapter Three

Kate didn't want to think about why this could potentially be a disastrous idea. How could she form a coherent thought when her best friend had his mouth and hands all over her? She'd never felt this good in her life and her clothes were still on.

Was it the champagne? Surely not. She'd only had two small glasses.

No, it couldn't be the alcohol. Gray was more potent than any drink he could give her. Why was she just discovering this fact?

Kate's head spun as she continued to clutch his shirt. She didn't want to analyze this moment or her emotions. She only wanted to feel.

Part of her wanted to rip off his clothes, but she'd

never been that brazen a woman. The few lovers she'd had were all calm, tame…and she'd never tingled like this for any of them.

She'd never ached with desire for her best friend, either, but here they were. A new wave of emotions swept her up, giving her no choice but to go along for the ride and enjoy every glorious moment.

Gray's firm hands rested on her knees as he spread them wide and stepped into the open space. He continued kissing her as his fingertips slid beneath her short skirt. Every single nerve ending inside her sizzled. When was the last time she'd sizzled?

Oh, right. Never. How did he know exactly what to do and how was she just realizing that her bestie had skills?

Kate tipped her head back as Gray's lips traveled over her chin and down the column of her throat. She circled his waist with her legs, toeing off her heels. The double thumps of her shoes hitting the hardwood floor sliced through the moment. Gray eased back and pinned her with his dark gaze. She'd never seen that look on his face before—pure hunger, passion, desire. All directed toward her.

Kate looked in his eyes and the need that stared back had her figuring maybe this wasn't a bad idea at all. No one had ever looked at her with such a need before. Something churned within her, not just arousal, but some emotion she wasn't ready to identify that coupled right along beside it, making her feel more alive and needed than ever.

Keeping his eyes locked on hers, Gray flipped her skirt up and jerked her by the waist toward the edge of the bar. Kate was completely captivated by the man before her. This passionate, sexual side of Gray had her reaching for the buckle on his belt, more than ready to hurry this process along. He quickly shoved her hands aside and reached for his wallet.

The second he procured a foil packet everything clicked in her mind. This was real. All of this was actually happening. She was about to have sex with her best friend…and she'd never been more thrilled, more excited in her life.

Shouldn't she be freaking out? Where had all of this come from? Clearly the desire had built up over time.

But she didn't. Kate waited, anticipation coiling through her. She'd address those questions later. Right now, she had a need, an ache, and judging by Gray's urgency, he did, too.

He tossed the packet next to her hip on the bar and unfastened his pants. Then, in a move that both shocked and aroused her, he reached beneath her dress, gripped the strip of satin that lay against her hip, and gave a jerk until the rip resounded through the quiet bar. So much for that pair of panties. They were a worthy sacrifice to the cause.

Kate didn't even get to enjoy the view before Gray sheathed himself and stepped toward her. With his hands firmly circling her waist, he nudged her forward once again, until he slowly joined their bodies.

Oh…my…

On a groan, Kate took a moment to allow her body time to adjust, but Gray clearly was in a hurry. He framed her face with his strong hands, tipped her head and covered her mouth as his hips jerked forward once again.

There was not much she could do but lock her ankles behind his back and match the perfect rhythm he set with their bodies.

"Kate," he muttered against her mouth.

She didn't want words. She had no clue what he was about to say, but she didn't want anything breaking into this moment. Words couldn't even begin to cover the tumultuous emotions flowing between them and she just wanted to feel. For right now, she wanted this man and nothing else.

Fisting his hair in her hands, Kate slammed his mouth back down onto hers. His hips pumped harder and in the next second, Kate's entire body trembled. She arched against Gray, pulling from the kiss. Her head dropped back, eyes shut as the euphoria spiraled through her.

She felt him lifting her before he settled her onto the bar. He whispered something just as his fingertips dug into her waist and he rose to tower above her. For a moment she marveled at his strength, but he started shifting again, moving faster and giving her no choice but to clutch his muscular arms.

Gray's body stilled as he rested his forearms on either side of her head, aligning their torsos. His mouth came down onto her shoulder. The sudden nip of his teeth against her flesh stunned her, arousing her even as she came down from her high. He kissed her there and trailed his lips across her heated skin.

Kate held onto Gray's shoulders even when their bodies completely stopped trembling. She had no idea what to say at this point. They lay on top of his bar half-dressed and had never so much as kissed more than in a friendly manner before, yet they'd just had explosive sex.

That was one hell of a birthday present.

Okay, maybe those shouldn't be the first words out of her mouth. But really, what was the protocol for a situation like this? She prided herself on always being prepared, but nothing could prepare her for what just took place. On a bar top, no less.

Gray came up onto his hands and looked down at her. Fear curled low in her belly. Was he waiting on her to say something and cut through the tension? Did they joke about this or did they fix their clothes like nothing happened?

Considering she analyzed everything from every angle, they would have to talk about this at some point. Maybe not right now when her emotions were too raw and she was still reeling from the fact that Gray had pursued her and torn off her underwear. Just the memory had chills popping up over her skin.

Exactly how long had he wanted her like this? There had been quite a bit of pent-up sexual need inside her bestie. Not that she was complaining. Definitely not complaining. Just…confused, and there were so many questions whirling inside her head, she had no clue where to start.

The muscle in Gray's jaw clenched and the way he continued to study her had Kate fidgeting. The top of her dress had slid down, so she adjusted to cover herself. She lifted onto her elbows and glanced around, anything but having to look right into those dark eyes to see…

She didn't know what she'd see, but she knew awkward tension had already started settling in.

Gray eased down off the bar and took a step back. Kate started to climb down, but he reached up, lifted her carefully into his arms, and placed her on the floor. The cool wood beneath her feet had her shivering, as did the sweet gesture of how he'd just handled her.

Of course, she could be shivering because her underwear was in shreds on the floor and her best friend was walking away. So much for him being sweet.

Apparently he wasn't one for chatter after sex, either. The silence only left her alone with thoughts she wasn't quite ready to tackle.

Kate's pale pink heels lay on their sides and she padded over to retrieve them. She clutched them against her chest like they could ward off the unknown, because she truly had no clue what was going to happen next.

Hell, it wasn't only the next few minutes she was

concerned with. What about long-term? Did this change everything between them? She hadn't been lying when she said she couldn't lose him. Gray was her everything. Absolutely everything.

The only constant in her life other than Tara and Lucy, but Gray was different. He was…well, he was special.

Right now, though, Kate could use some space to think and here on his turf, where her tattered panties lay mocking her, was not the place to clear her head and regroup.

Of all the times not to have her car. Damn it. This was why she always planned things, always had a plan B. But neither plan A nor B had been to leave the rehearsal dinner and have a quickie on the bar top at Gallagher's.

She was at the mercy of Gray whenever he came back and chose to take her home. Maybe then they'd talk and she'd get a feel for what was going on in that head of his.

Kate was stunned at the way her body still tingled. Gray had awakened something inside her, something she hadn't even known existed. But she'd made him promise just one night and that's exactly what she was going to hold on to.

She couldn't afford to lose him as a friend simply because she'd just experienced the best sex of her life. Gray was the one constant male in her life. He had been in that role since they were in junior high, and he'd come to rescue her from some bullying jerk who was new at the school. Not that she'd needed rescuing, but she'd appreciated it at the time, and he'd been her self-appointed white knight since.

So who was going to save her from him? Because now that she'd had him, Kate knew he'd ruined her for other men.

Gray Gallagher had infiltrated her, body and soul, and she'd better just live with the tantalizing memories, because they were definitely one and done.

She couldn't emotionally afford to have it any other way.

Gray took a minute longer than necessary in his private bathroom attached to the back office. The second he'd come back to reality and looked down into Kate's eyes, he'd seen her withdrawing. He'd instantly wanted her to reconsider that one-night rule. But he hadn't even gotten her completely undressed. He'd ripped her panties off, and they'd had a quickie on his bar.

Yeah, real smooth. Perfect way to show her she was special and he wanted to do it all over again. He'd be lucky if she didn't haul off and smack him when he walked back in there. Hadn't he always told her she deserved better? That she deserved to be treated like she was the most valuable woman in a man's life?

Gray slammed his hand against the wall and cursed himself for being such a jerk to the one woman he cared most about. Now he was going to have to go out and face her, make some excuse as to his behavior, and then drive her home in what he was sure would be uncomfortable silence.

What a fantastic way to end an already crappy day. He'd already been in a bitch of a mood when he'd seen that best man flirting with her. He shouldn't be jealous, but damn it, he couldn't help how he felt.

He'd faced death when he'd lost his mother at the tender age of five. He'd faced the enemy when he'd been overseas in the army. He faced his father, who was disappointed because Gray hadn't settled down and started a family. But Gray was not looking forward to facing his best friend, because if he saw even the slightest hint of regret or disappointment in her eyes, he would absolutely be destroyed.

Knowing he couldn't stay hidden forever, he made sure his clothes were adjusted before he headed out. The second he rounded the corner from the back hallway, he stilled.

Kate stood frozen just where he'd left her. She clutched her shoes, worried her bottom lip with her teeth, and stared at the spot where he'd taken her like some horny teen with no experience.

But it was the pale pink bite mark on her shoulder that had him cringing and cursing himself all over again.

Damn it. What the hell was wrong with him? His Kate was a lady. She was classy. She was so far above him and he'd treated her like a one-night stand.

Oh, wait. That's exactly what this was, per her

last-minute request. It wasn't like he gave her ample time to get used to the idea of the two of them together.

Still, Kate deserved better and he damn well was going to show her. Screw the one-night rule. If anyone should be proving to her exactly how she should be treated, it was him.

"I'll take you home."

Kate jumped and turned to face him, her eyes wide. His voice came out gruffer than he'd intended.

With a simple nod, she headed toward the back door. Gray didn't move from his position and ultimately blocked the opening to the hallway. He waited until she stopped right before him. He shouldn't touch her, shouldn't push this topic, but damn if he couldn't help himself. There had to be something he could do to redeem his actions.

Reaching out, he traced one fingertip over the faint mark on her shoulder.

"We good?"

Wow. He'd had several minutes to think of something tender, kind, and apologetic to say, and that's the best he could come up with?

Yes, he saw confusion looking back at him, but there was more. Kate wasn't upset, not at all. She had questions, of that he was sure, but she wasn't angry. Thankfully he hadn't botched this night up too much.

Kate attempted a smile. "We're good," she murmured as her eyes darted away.

She may not be angry, but she was no doubt wondering what they should do next. Kate planned everything and this whole experience had definitely not been planned.

Enter the awkward tension he swore wouldn't be there. He promised her they wouldn't change. He promised they'd be friends just like before.

Yet she couldn't even look him in the eyes.

"Kate."

Her focus darted back to him, but he didn't see regret. Kate's pretty blue eyes were full of desire... Damn if that didn't just confuse the hell out of him. She might be wanting to ask him about what just happened, but she also wasn't sorry.

Gray didn't know what else to say at this moment. The dynamics had changed, the intimacy too fresh. Maybe once they had some time apart and saw each other at the wedding tomorrow they'd laugh and joke and go back to the Gray and Kate they'd been hours ago.

Or maybe they'd find the nearest closet and rip each other's clothes off. Things could go either way at this point.

Gray moved out of her way so she could pass. Her hair hung down her back in dark waves, her dress was slightly askew, and she still clutched her shoes. He'd turned a moment of intimacy with his best friend into forcing her to do a walk of shame from his bar.

He was no better than the prick who'd cheated on her and broke her heart. But Gray would make this up to her. He had to.

Kate adjusted her one-shoulder bridesmaid's dress for the fifth time in as many minutes. Thankfully Lucy hadn't chosen strapless dresses. Kate needed this chiffon strap to cover Gray's mark. She didn't know what she would've done had he chosen the other shoulder.

Part of her loved the mark. She'd be lying if she said otherwise. She'd never had a man lose such control, and the fact he hadn't even been able to get them out of their clothes was thrilling. Sex should be thrilling, or so she'd heard before, and she'd always wondered if that was a myth. Now she knew.

Analyzing this over and over wasn't going to change the future. Gray wasn't going to happen again. On that they'd agreed, so now she had to figure out how to not compare any other man to her best friend. But at least the standards were set and she wasn't going to settle for someone who didn't at least give her a little spark.

Kate had definitely had a happy birthday. At least she had until he'd come from the bathroom and couldn't get her out of the bar fast enough. Did he regret what they'd done? Or worse. Was she a disappointment?

"Hey, you okay?" Tara whispered.

"Fine."

Kate smiled for the camera and hoped they were nearly done with all the photos. What did it matter if Gray found her lacking in the skill department? They weren't doing anything again anyway.

He'd barely said a word when she'd picked him up this morning and she hadn't seen him at the wedding. But the church had been packed, so that wasn't a surprise. She'd see him at the reception for sure. He was in charge of all the drinks and had brought a few of his employees to serve as waiters.

She felt a bit odd not sharing her epic, mind-blowing, toe-curling experience with Lucy and Tara. If this had been any other man she'd had wild sex with late at night in a closed bar, she would've texted them immediately after, but this was Gray. He was different and what they shared was…well, it was something she still couldn't describe.

"I think we got them," the photographer announced. "We'll do more at the reception."

Kate resisted the urge to groan. This was Lucy and Noah's day. She shouldn't be so grouchy, but smiling and posing and pretending to be in a good mood was not working for her. All she could think of was Gray: what they'd done, what she had missed from him that led up to that moment, how he'd react seeing her again.

Kate lifted the long skirt of her dress and stepped off the stage. A hand slid over her elbow.

"Wait a second," Tara said.

Turning her attention to her friend, Kate dropped her dress and clutched the bouquet. "What's up?"

"That's what I want to know."

Tara's questioning gaze held Kate in place. "I'm just going to hop on the shuttle to take me to the reception so I can get some food. I'm starving."

Rolling her eyes, Tara stepped closer. "You've been acting weird all day. What happened from last night to this morning?"

What happened? Oh, just a quickie on the bar top at Gallagher's, third stool from the left. Well, Gray had shoved the stool out of the way when he'd climbed up to her, but still. She'd never be able to look at that space again without bursting into internal flames. Her panties would probably melt right off.

"I just had a late night." Kate opted to go with some form of the truth. "Gray and I left the rehearsal and headed back to the bar so he could pull more champagne and wine from the back stock. I just didn't get much sleep before we had to be up and ready."

Tara's bright blue eyes studied Kate a moment longer than she was comfortable with. Gathering her skirt in her hand once again, Kate forced a smile.

"C'mon," she said, nodding toward the front of the church. "Let's go get on the shuttle so they can take us over to the food and dancing. I'm ready to get rid of these heels."

Tara nodded. "Will you get some pictures of me dancing with Marley?"

Marley, Tara's five-year-old daughter. She shared custody with her ex, Sam Bailey. Sam had brought Marley to the wedding since this was his weekend to have her. Tara had been surprised that Sam had taken Marley to get her hair done and her nails painted.

Kate knew Sam had some issues several months ago, but she saw the man was trying. Okay, using the word "issues" was really sugarcoating things. But addiction was such a delicate topic and Kate still wasn't sure how to approach it with Tara.

But Kate saw Sam fighting to get his family back. The man had gone to rehab, he'd gotten a new job, he'd gone to counseling. There was a determination in him now that Kate hadn't seen before. Tara wasn't ready to see it and Kate worried irreparable damage had been done and their marriage was over for good.

None of that was Kate's business and she had her own issues to worry about right now. Like seeing Gray at the reception. She didn't like the silence that had settled between them this morning. That wasn't like them. They were always bantering or arguing or joking about something. It was their thing. They lived to annoy the hell out of each other and for some strange reason, it worked for them.

Damn it. She knew sleeping with him would change things, but she'd been unable to prevent herself from giving in. One second they were friends, and the next he'd kissed her against his truck and made her want things she never realized she was missing.

Well, she had to just suck it up and get over this awkward hurdle. She wanted her friend back and she wasn't going to let great sex stand in their way.

Chapter Four

Gray checked on the status of the bottles, confident they'd be just fine with the extras he'd brought. He asked around with his staff to see if they were doing okay or if anyone needed a break. None of them took him up on his offer.

He had such amazing, loyal employees at his bar who would work any venue when he asked. Honestly, they could run the whole place themselves and probably didn't even need him around.

Damn it. He was out of things to do other than watch Bryan try to hit on Kate again. Didn't the guy take the not-so-subtle hint from the rehearsal dinner?

Gray had been jealous last night, but seeing him make a play again tonight had him feeling all sorts of rage. Which was absurd. Kate was a grown woman and they were just friends. They'd slept together and now he was letting that incident cloud his judgment.

Actually, he didn't care. Kate was better than Bryan and Gray didn't like the way the guy kept looking at her.

Gray walked around the perimeter of the country club dining area and glared at Bryan as he stepped in behind Kate on the dance floor. What the hell was wrong with that guy?

Kate turned and glanced at Bryan, then shook her head and held up her hands as if to ward him off. Bryan smiled and reached out to touch her bare shoulder. Seeing that man's hand against Kate's creamy skin had Gray making his way across the floor.

The jerk stepped into her when a slow song started and the tension on Kate's face made Gray's anger skyrocket. He was sure his face showed his every emotion but right now he didn't give a damn who saw him or what others thought. He was putting a stop to this now.

"Go have another drink, Bryan. This dance is mine."

Gray instantly wrapped an arm around Kate's waist and took her hand in his. From the corner of his eye, Gray saw Bryan still standing there. Spinning Kate in a circle, Gray stepped on Bryan's foot and was rewarded with a grunt.

"Still there?" Gray asked over his shoulder.

The guy finally disappeared through the crowd of dancers.

Kate's eyes were wide, but Gray would rather she be uncomfortable with him than with some idiot who didn't know what a treasure Kate was.

"He's harmless."

Gray narrowed his gaze. "And I'm not?"

She merely tipped her chin in defiance. "I could've handled it myself."

Gray offered her a smile. "You always say that."

"Because I can."

"I'm aware." He spun her around again, keeping his firm hold on her. His Kate was extra prickly today. "But we haven't danced yet and I had a few minutes to spare."

Her eyes continued to hold his. "And what were you doing those few minutes you were glaring this way?"

Damn if she wasn't adorable when she was fired up. "Some people take a smoke break. I don't smoke, so I take a glare break."

Kate stared for another moment before she finally shook her head and let out a soft laugh. "You're incorrigible. You know that, right?"

A bit of tension eased from his chest at her sweet laugh. "It's only because I care and Bryan is not the guy for you. Not even as a dance partner. Hell, he's not even your drink provider."

Kate arched a brow. "So now you're screening my guys?"

Screening them? Hell, if that was a possibility he damn well would be first in line to sign up for that job. If he hadn't been overseas during her ill-fated engagement, perhaps he could've prevented her heartache. But Gray hadn't even met the ex because he'd come and gone while Gray had been serving. So, yeah, perhaps he was looking out for her. Isn't that what friends did?

"Maybe dancing with a guy like Bryan made my list."

Here she went with that damn list again. He'd like to see exactly what was on that thing.

"Tell me more about this infamous list."

He spun her around again, slowly leading the way toward the edge of the dance floor, where there weren't as many people. He found he didn't want to share Kate right now. He wanted to keep her talking, keep her dancing. Though dancing wasn't his thing, it was an excuse to get her in his arms.

He glanced around as he led her. He recognized many people from town. The St. John brothers and their wives were all dancing. Several other couples who frequented his bar were also dancing and having a good time.

Gray actually hadn't seen the bride and groom for a while, though. Perhaps they'd already slipped out once the bouquet and the garter had been tossed. Most likely they'd been in a hurry to get to their honeymoon.

"I'm keeping my list to myself for now," she replied.

Gray stared down into her blue eyes. She hadn't brought up last night and he wasn't about to, either. They hadn't wanted things to change between them, but the tension had become palpable and he wasn't sure how to erase it.

Eventually they would have to discuss what happened. Might as well be now, while he had her undivided attention. Maybe having everyone around would help ease the tension. If they were alone again and trying to talk, Gray wasn't so sure he could prevent himself from touching her again. Touching her now was safe, smart.

"About last night—"

Kate's eyes widened a fraction. "I need to find Tara," she said, breaking from his hold. "We'll talk later."

And then she was gone, leaving him all alone with a slew of couples dancing around him. Gray fisted his hands at his sides. He hadn't expected Kate to run. He hadn't expected their night to scare her away. She'd always been comfortable with him.

But then he'd turned into the guy who had sex with his best friend on top of a bar.

Raking a hand through his hair, Gray left the dance floor and went back to what he could control. The alcohol and the servers. Right now, Kate was utterly out of his control. Perhaps they needed space. Maybe she needed a breather after what had happened.

One thing was certain, though. He'd had her only one time and he knew without a doubt he wanted more.

Kate sank onto the chaise in the seating area of the women's restroom. She slid out of her heels and resisted the urge to moan. Between all the food she ate and dancing and the lack of sleep, she was ready for bed.

It was that whole lack of sleep—or the reason behind it—that had her escaping to the restroom to hide for a bit. She'd known Gray would bring up their situation, but their friend's wedding was sure as hell not the place she wanted to hash things out.

She couldn't think when he was holding her, because now that they'd been intimate, any type of touch triggered her memories…not that the images of last night had ever faded to the background. Would they ever?

Besides, Kate had no clue what she wanted to say anyway. Did she say thank you? Did she compliment him? Or did she broach the fact that she'd had her first taste of alcohol and it wasn't that bad? What exactly did she lead in with after such an epic, mind-boggling night?

The bathroom door opened, but Kate kept her eyes in her lap, not wanting to face any guests.

"Who are we hiding from?"

So much for not facing anyone.

Kate glanced up to see Tara and Lucy holding the skirts of their gowns and coming in from the madness and noise outside. Once the door shut, her friends waited for her answer in silence.

"Tara—"

"Is it Bryan?" Lucy asked, rolling her eyes. "I swear, he and Noah are close, but I had no idea how annoying that man could be when presented with a single woman. Guess he thinks he has a chance with you."

Kate blew out a sigh. If her only problem involved a man who was a complete goober and found her attractive, she'd be golden and certainly wouldn't be hiding in the bathroom.

No, her issues came in the form of a six-foot-four-inch bar owner who could make her tingle just from the slightest brush of his fingertips.

"This isn't about Bryan. I'm just taking a breather," she told them, which was the absolute truth.

Lucy gathered the full skirt of her wedding dress and flopped next to Kate on the chaise. Tara crossed and sat in the floral armchair.

"I told you something was up," Tara stated, looking at Lucy.

"This is her wedding day." Kate glared at her friend. "You told her you thought something was up with me when she should be focusing on how quickly she and Noah can get out of here and head to their honeymoon?"

Tara's eyes widened as she shrugged. "We're friends. She can go have sex with Noah whenever. I need to know what's going on with you and Gray."

"Are you two arguing again?" Lucy asked. "I swear, you're like an old married couple, just without the sex."

Kate nearly choked on the gasp that lodged in her throat. Fortunately, she recovered before giving herself away. She was nowhere near ready to spill her secret. Her friends would be completely shocked if they learned she'd had sex with Gray. Kate was still reeling from the fact herself.

"What? No, we're not arguing." They couldn't argue when she was running away and dodging the issue. "Why would you think that?"

"Because you two were dancing, then you rushed out in the middle of the song."

Kate stared at Tara. "I didn't see you on the dance floor."

"I wasn't there. I was getting Marley another plate of fruit and dip when you scurried by," Tara explained. She pinned her with those bright eyes. "I'd assumed you were running from Bryan, but I saw Gray's face as he watched you."

Oh, no. *Damn it.* Kate didn't want to ask what emotions Tara had seen on his face, what feelings he'd been unable to mask. She honestly had no clue what he was feeling because he'd been so good at keeping that to himself since last night.

Of course, if she'd waited to hear what he had to say, maybe she'd be better in tune with what was happening in his mind.

"He stepped in and saved me from Bryan. You know how Gray is," Kate explained, smoothing down her chiffon-overlay skirt. She had to convince them there was nothing more than what was on the surface. "We just danced a few minutes until Bryan was gone. That's all."

Silence filled the room, which was good because the door opened again and an elderly lady came in. Kate didn't know her, but she'd seen her on the groom's side during the ceremony. Considering Noah wasn't from here, it would make sense that there were guests Kate didn't know.

"Would you go back out to your husband?" Kate hissed. "I'm just taking a break from those killer heels. Nothing is wrong."

Lucy took Kate's hand and squeezed. "Promise?"

"Of course." Kate nodded. "Go on."

Lucy finally got up and left. Once the other guest left as well, Kate was alone with Tara and her questioning gaze.

"What?" Kate demanded. "Can't a girl just take a break?"

"Lucy can and I can, but not you." Tara crossed her legs and leaned back in the seat. "You are always on the go, always planning the next thing, and I've never seen you relax. So what's really going on? And don't lie. I'm done with lies."

Kate swallowed a lump of guilt. Tara had been dealt too much lately, but there were just some things Kate wasn't about to share. That was not a reflection of their friendship. She'd tell her and Lucy… someday.

"Not now, okay?"

Tara's curiosity quickly turned to concern. "Promise me you'll come to us if you need anything. I know what it's like to be lost in your own thoughts and worry what to do next."

True story. Tara and Sam were going through hell all while trying to keep their daughter out of the fires.

"Same goes." Kate reached over and took her friend's hand. "Sam looked like he was doing really well."

Tara nodded. "He is. He left me a note on my windshield this morning."

How could anyone not find Sam and his handwritten notes simply heart-melting? He'd done that when they'd been married and since their split, he continued to leave her notes. Tara always mentioned them and Kate wondered what it would be like to have a man who cared that much.

The man was a hopeless romantic who'd just made some bad choices. Kate didn't blame Tara for being cautious, though. Some obstacles were just too great to overcome.

"We should get back out there." Kate came to her feet and stared down at her heels. "If I ever get married, we're all going barefoot."

Tara laughed as she stood up. "Deal."

Kate had pushed marriage thoughts out of her head long ago when her engagement ended. The whole ordeal had left her a bit jaded, but seeing Noah and Lucy come together after they'd both experienced such devastation in their lives gave Kate hope. She wanted to marry one day, to have a husband who loved her, start a family and live in the picturesque mountains of Tennessee.

One day, she vowed. But first she was going to have to figure out how to get back on that friendship ground with Gray. Every time she thought of him now, she only remembered him tearing off her underwear and climbing up on that bar to get to her.

And her body heated all over again. She had a feeling the line they'd crossed had been erased. There was nowhere for them to go that was familiar and comfortable because they were both in unknown territory.

Chapter Five

Gray slid another tray of glasses beneath the bar. For the past five days he'd gone about his business and mundane, day-to-day activities. This wasn't the first time, and wouldn't be the last, that he couldn't shake the void inside him. Something was missing, had been for quite some time, but he'd never been able to quite place it.

His father always said it was a wife and children, but Gray didn't believe that. He wasn't looking to settle down and worry about feeding a relationship. His parents had been completely in love up until his mother's death when Gray had been five. He'd seen how the loss had affected his father, seen how the man had mourned for decades. Gray didn't want to subject himself to that type of pain.

Besides, he'd never found anyone who would make him even think about marriage.

He'd been hand-delivered this bar when he'd come home from the army, just like his father before him. Gray's grandfather, Ewan Gallagher, had opened the doors when he'd retired from the army after World War II. Right after that, he'd married the love of his life and started a family. Same with Gray's father, Reece.

They'd both had a plan and been the happiest men Gray had ever known. Not that Gray wasn't happy. He knew how fortunate he was to have served his country and come home to a business with deep familial roots and heritage. Some men never came home, and some guys who did weren't even close to the men they'd been before they were deployed.

But beyond all of that, something inside him felt empty. The void that accompanied him every single day had settled in deep and he had no clue how to rid himself of it.

Gray pushed those thoughts aside and headed to the back office. He needed to get his payroll done before they opened this afternoon.

He sank into his worn leather office chair and blew out a sigh. He couldn't even lie to himself. It wasn't just the monotonous life he led that had him in a pissy mood. He hadn't seen Kate once since she'd deserted him on the dance floor.

They'd texted a few times, but only about safe topics.

Safe. That word summed up Kate. She did things by the book. Hell, the book she carried with her was like her lifeline to the world. She always had a plan, excelled at making her life organized and perfect.

Gray was anything but organized and perfect. He ran a bar. Things got messy and out of control at times. He'd obliterated her perfect little world when he'd taken their relationship to an entirely unsafe level.

Still, he was going to let her hide for only so long. "Hello?"

Gray stilled at the unfamiliar voice coming from the front of the bar. He came to his feet and rounded his desk. He always left the doors unlocked while he was here working. Stonerock was a small town where everybody knew everybody. Crime was low and people usually respected his bar's hours.

Sometimes his buddy Sam would stop in during the day to talk or just to unwind. After all that man had been through, Gray wasn't about to lock him out. Sam needed support now more than ever and if he was here, at least Gray could keep an eye on him and be part of that support team.

"Anyone here?"

Definitely not Sam. Gray had no idea who'd decided to waltz right into his bar in the middle of the morning.

He stepped from the back hall and came to stand

behind the bar. The man who stood in the middle of Gray's restaurant clearly had the wrong address. Nobody came in here wearing a three-piece suit and carrying a briefcase. Who the hell even owned a suit like that? Nobody in Stonerock, that was for damn sure.

Gray flattened his palms on the bar top. "Can I help you?"

The stranger offered a toothy smile and crossed the space to the bar…third stool from the left. Now his favorite place in the entire building.

"You the owner?"

Gray nodded. People came in looking for donations for schools, ball teams, charity events…but Gray couldn't pinpoint exactly what this guy was nosing around about.

"My name is Preston Anderson. I'm from Knoxville."

Preston Anderson sounded exactly like the type of man who'd own a suit as confining and stiff as this one. Gray eyed the man's extended hand and ultimately gave it a quick shake.

"I have enough staff," Gray replied. "But the bank might be hiring."

The guy laughed and propped his briefcase on a bar stool. "I'm here to see you. I assume you're Gray Gallagher."

"You would assume correctly."

He pulled a business card from his pocket and

placed it on the bar. Gray didn't even give it a glance, let alone touch it.

"My partner and I are looking to buy a number of properties here in Stonerock and doing some minor revamping of the town."

Gray crossed his arms over his chest. "Is that so?"

"We'd like to make it a mini-Nashville, if you will. The area is perfect for day tourists to pop over to get away from the city, but still have a city feel."

Pulling in a breath, Gray eyed the business card, then glanced back to Preston. "And you want to buy my bar."

Preston nodded. "We'll make it more than worth your while."

He took a pen from inside his jacket pocket, flipped the card over, and wrote a number. Using his fingertip, he slid the card across the bar. Again, Gray didn't pick it up, but he did eye the number and it took every ounce of his resolve to not react. There was a hell of a lot of numbers after that dollar sign.

"You really want this bar," Gray replied.

Preston nodded. "We're eager to dive into this venture. We'd like to have firm answers within a month and finalize the sales within thirty days after that. All cash. Our goal is to have all of our properties up and running before fall for when the tourists come to the mountains for getaways."

Gray had never thought of selling this place before, and now he had a month to make a decision.

His initial reaction was hell no. This was his family's legacy, what his grandfather had dreamed of.

But reality kicked in, too. That void he'd been feeling? He still didn't know what was causing it, but all of those zeroes would go a long way in helping him find what was missing...or at least pass the time until he could figure out what the hell he wanted to be when he grew up.

Gray never had a set goal in mind. He'd done what was expected and never questioned it. But more and more lately he wondered if this was really where he was supposed to be. And if it was, then why did he still feel like something was lacking?

Preston went on to explain they'd still keep the establishment a bar, but it would be modernized for the crowds they were hoping to bring in. Gray had no idea what to say, so he merely nodded and listened.

The figure on the untouched card between them spoke more than anything Preston could've said.

"So, think about it," Preston stated, picking up his briefcase. "My number is on the card if you have any questions. This isn't an opportunity that will present itself again, Mr. Gallagher."

"I imagine not," Gray muttered.

Preston let himself out the front door, leaving Gray to process everything that had happened over the past ten minutes. He reached for the card, turning it from front to back.

What the hell did he do with this proposal? True, he'd never actually wanted the bar, but it was his.

And while he may have wanted to pursue other things in his life, there were some loyalties that came with keeping up tradition. Gray would never purposely go against his family.

Family was absolutely everything to him. His father never remarried, so Gray and his dad had been a team. Then Gray's grandfather had passed only a few years ago, leaving Gray and his father once again reeling from loss.

Now that they were all each other had, this business deal wasn't going to be something easy to say yes or no to. This was definitely a decision he needed to discuss with his father. But Gray wanted to weigh his options and have some idea of what he wanted before that discussion took place.

Gray already knew where his father would stand on this from a sentimental standpoint, but his father also didn't know that Gray hadn't been happy for a while now.

Ultimately, the final decision would belong to Gray.

There was one other person he wanted to talk to. One other person who'd been his voice of reason since junior high, when she talked him out of beating the hell out of some new jock who had mouthed off one too many times.

Sliding Preston's card into the pocket of his jeans, Gray went back to working on the payroll. Kate had one more day to come to him…and then he was going to her.

* * *

Kate's color-coded binder lay open to the red section. The red section was reserved for her most important clients. Not that all of them weren't important, but some needed more attention than others.

Mrs. Clements was by far her best client. That woman wanted help with everything from organizing her daughter's bridal shower to setting up her new home office. Kate also had a standing seasonal job with the middle-aged lady when it was time to change out her closets for the weather.

Kate stared at the time on her phone. It was nearly two in the morning, but she wasn't the slightest bit tired. This plan for Mrs. Clements wasn't due for nineteen days, but Kate wanted it to be perfect before she presented it to her.

Pulling her green fine-tip marker from the matching green pouch, Kate started jotting down possible strategies. The definite plans were always in blue and those were already completed and in the folder.

Kate tapped on her phone to fire up her music playlist before she started compiling a list of possible caterers.

The knock on her door had Kate jumping in her seat. She jerked around and waited. Who would be knocking on her door in the middle of the night? Probably some crazy teenagers out pulling pranks. But the knock sounded again, more determined than just a random tap.

She contemplated ignoring the unwanted guest,

but figured murderers didn't go around knocking on doors. Plus, this was Stonerock. She knew the entire police force. She could have anyone over here in a flash if something was wrong.

Kate paused her music and carried her phone to the door in case she needed to call upon one of those said officers. Of course Noah was still on his honeymoon with Lucy, so he wasn't an option.

As she padded through the hall, Kate tipped her head slightly to glance out the sidelight. Her heart kicked up. Gray. She knew it was only a matter of time, but she certainly didn't expect him in the middle of the night.

This man…always keeping her guessing and on her toes.

Blowing out a breath, Kate set her phone on the accent table by the door. She flicked the dead bolt and turned the knob.

Without waiting for her to invite him in, Gray pulled open the screen door and stepped inside.

"Won't you come in," she muttered.

"Considering I rarely knock anyway, I figured you wouldn't mind."

She closed the door, locking it before she turned to face him. "And what on earth do you possibly need at this time of the night?"

"You weren't asleep. I saw your lights on."

No, she wasn't asleep, and he'd just come from the bar. His black T-shirt with the bar logo on his left pec stretched tightly across his broad shoulders.

She could never look at those shoulders the same way again, not after clutching them the other night as he'd given her the most intensely satisfying experience of her life.

Suddenly the foyer in her townhome seemed too small. She couldn't be this close to Gray, not with those memories replaying through her head. The memories that made her question everything and want more than she should.

Clearing her throat, Kate turned and headed to the back of the house, where she'd turned a spare bedroom into her home office.

Gray fell in step behind her. She went back to her cushy chair at her corner desk and spun around to see Gray fold his frame onto the delicate yellow sofa she'd found at a yard sale a couple of years ago.

"Why am I not surprised you're working?" he asked, nodding toward the organized piles on her desk.

"I couldn't sleep."

"There's a surefire remedy for that."

Kate stared at him for a moment before she rolled her eyes. "Did you seriously come here thinking we'd have sex again?"

Gray quirked one dark brow. He stretched his long, denim-clad legs out in front of him and crossed his ankles. He placed one tattooed arm on the armrest. Gray was clearly comfortable with this topic based on the way he looked at her, taking in her thin tank and ratty old shorts.

His gaze was anything but friendly. Well, it was friendly in the sense that he looked like he wanted to strip her out of her clothes again.

Wait. He'd never gotten her out of her clothes the first time. Perhaps that's why he was staring so intently. But he'd seen her in a bathing suit and he'd most definitely seen her lower half.

Boobs. Men always wanted boobs. It was a ridiculous thing she would never understand. Still, he continued to stare across the office as if he knew exactly what she looked like in her birthday suit.

Had he always been this intense? This potent?

Kate shivered and tucked one leg beneath her. "Why did you really stop by?"

"I missed you."

The way those words settled between them had Kate's breath catching in her throat. He said them so simply, as if the question were silly and it should be obvious why he was here.

They hadn't gone this long without seeing each other since he'd served in the army. She appreciated how he put himself out there and used complete and utter honesty.

Another reason why he was her everything. Gray never sugarcoated anything and had always been up front with her. Considering her ex had been so deceitful, having Gray in her life was refreshing and made her realize there were good men out there. This good man, however, just couldn't be for her.

"I missed you, too," she replied, because she

wanted to be just as honest right back. "I've been busy with the Savvy Scheduler, the blogs and the scheduling for upcoming giveaways, and then getting ready for the next Helping Hands meeting. With Lucy gone—"

"You're hiding from me."

She really was getting ready for the next meeting. Kate, Tara and Lucy all led a weekly support group that helped to uplift those hurting from loss. They'd all experienced it themselves on some level, so it was a labor of love.

But perhaps she was using her work and the group to hide from Gray. Still, she'd always made time for him before and he'd never pushed her away. Not once.

Fine. So maybe she wasn't being totally honest with him, but how could she be when she was trying to fumble around with her own emotions and figure it all out herself?

Kate glanced down to her lap and stared at her pale pink polish. "I don't know what to do now."

Silence settled in the room. She had no clue what he was thinking, no clue how to get them back on the comfortable ground they'd been walking on for years. How could one moment undo years of friendship? How did sex muddle so much?

When the awkward tension became unbearable, Kate turned slightly and started straightening her desk. There had never been awkwardness between them and she desperately needed to rid this moment of it. She needed her Gray back—her best friend back.

She glanced at the outline for her next week and mentally tried to prepare herself and focus. At least this was something she could control, because she sure as hell couldn't control her feelings—not now that he was in her house and staring at her as if he wanted an encore bar performance.

No. No more sex—at least not with him. She shouldn't pay attention to her body when it started getting all revved up again at just the sight of Gray. She shouldn't keep remembering how he'd felt as he'd joined their bodies. And she sure as hell shouldn't keep wondering if there was any man who could measure up to him.

"We do what we've always done, Kate."

She shivered as his soft words pierced the silence and washed over her. Leave it to him to find a simple resolution to their tension. Maybe he didn't have the juxtaposition of feelings running through him like she did. Maybe he slept just fine at night and hadn't given her or their encounter another thought.

Kate slid the green marker back into the pouch, set Mrs. Clements's folder in her desk organizer labeled Things to Do, and worked the corners of the rest of the folders until they were perfectly lined up. Now what? There was nothing else to straighten or fiddle with.

"Look at me."

Oh, that low, sultry tone. Now that they'd been intimate, she could appreciate it so much more.

Kate gritted her teeth and spun around in her chair. That piercing stare had her gripping the edge of her chair. Anticipation curled low in her belly at what he would say or do next. She'd never been on the edge of her seat with him before.

Honestly, sex changed everything. Hadn't she warned herself about that in the few moments between the kiss and the torn underwear? But her hormones had taken over and Gray had been all too convincing…and she was human.

"We're still Gray and Kate," he reminded her, pinning her with that dark gaze. "We annoy each other for fun. We watch old movies and argue over the classics. I still worry you're going to choose another loser, so I'm extra cautious and overprotective. Yes, we had sex, but we're still us."

He made things sound so simple and easy, as if sex hadn't changed a thing. But it had changed everything. She found herself looking at him differently, seeing him in a completely different light. Because for a short time he'd been not only her best friend, but also her lover.

"That's why you came?" she asked.

"You didn't think I'd let you hide forever, did you?"

Kate smiled. "I would've been at Ladies' Night this week."

That side grin flashed over his face. "You missed last week, so I wasn't sure."

Kate picked at one of the threads on the edge of her shorts. "I just needed some space."

"Had enough?"

She chewed the inside of her cheek. "Maybe."

Gray came to his feet and crossed to her. He took her hands and pulled her up against him. Kate tipped her head back to look him directly in the eyes. A punch of lust hit her faster than she'd expected. She'd hoped that need, that ache, had vanished or had been all in her mind. But no. Gray had crossed the line and had settled deep into a place inside her. And she had no clue how to categorize him.

"You're done hiding or running, or whatever the hell else you were doing." He flashed her that devilish grin. "I need you, Kate. We've been together too long to let anything come between our friendship. Can we just get back there again?"

Something akin to relief slid through her at how easily he was putting them both back on stable ground. At the same time, though, she hated that they were going back to being just friends.

How could she just ignore how she felt now that he was this close? How could she forget how he'd kissed her? How he'd looked at her, touched her?

She couldn't forget. Gray had imbedded himself so far into her soul, she truly wasn't sure she could go back. She wasn't even entirely sure she wanted to.

"We are friends," she agreed. "You have to admit this is a bit awkward."

Gray laughed. "So stop making it awkward."

He pulled her into a hug just like he'd done for years. Only this time she couldn't prevent herself from pulling in a deep breath of that masculine scent, remembering how she'd been completely enveloped by that familiar aroma and the man. His potency had been all-consuming when he'd ripped off her panties and taken her on that bar top. Would she ever get that image, that *feeling* from her mind?

"You in a hurry to get home?" she asked into his chest.

"Not really."

Kate tipped her head back and smiled. "How about a movie?"

Gray kissed her forehead. "Perfect."

Chapter Six

"Tell me about this list."

Kate stopped tapping her toes on the side of his thigh. He sat on one end of the sofa and she had relaxed on the other, stretching those legs out, propping her dainty feet against his denim-clad thigh, and driving him out of his ever-loving mind.

Gray had known facing her would be difficult. Of course they'd seen each other at the wedding, but this was the first time they'd been alone and forced to really discuss what had happened at the bar. The tension still hovered between them, but he was going to push through because as much as he wanted her physically, he refused to lose her altogether.

Other than the obvious fact she'd been dodging

him, he knew she was panicking about where they were now. He knew she'd be trying to analyze things from every which angle and she wouldn't be able to. He'd wanted her for a while, longer than he probably wanted to admit even to himself, so there was no way she could decipher what the hell truly happened when he couldn't explain it himself.

For years, he'd been able to control himself out of respect for her and their friendship. Then, over the past several months, little by little, seeing her at the bar dancing with other guys, then at the rehearsal with Bryan, it had all just become too much and he'd snapped. Every man had a breaking point and she'd definitely hit his.

"It's nothing," she finally replied.

He curled his hand around her bare toes. "Tell me about the infamous list or I'll crack your toes."

Kate's legs jerked from his lap as she laughed. "Watch the movie and leave me alone."

"We've seen this at least a hundred times," he told her as he shifted on the couch to face her. He grabbed the remote from the back of the couch and muted the TV before tossing the device between them on the cushion. "Talk to me, Kate. You can't hide it forever. I'm going to get the truth out of you, you know."

She let out a sigh and shook her head. "Fine."

When she started to get up, Gray reached out and gripped her arm. "You don't have to go get some color-coded spreadsheet that no doubt you've laminated. Just tell me. I want to hear your words, not read some damn paper."

Kate smiled as she settled onto the couch. She swung her legs back up and he instantly started rubbing her feet. Maybe if she was relaxed she'd talk, and if she was talking about this mystery list, then perhaps he would focus on that and not the fact that he wanted his best friend now more than ever.

There was still the matter of discussing the business proposition with her, but right now there were much more important things to work out. It was just another area of his life he was confused as hell about. Once he talked to Kate and his father, he'd have a clearer picture of the future...he hoped.

"Tell me why you made a list," he started, needing to reel himself in from his wayward thoughts.

Kate adjusted the throw pillow between her head and the arm of the couch. Tipping her head sideways, she stared down at him. "My thirtieth birthday just passed."

"Yes, I'm aware of that." His thumb slid up over the arch of her foot. "So, what? You think you're old now that you're thirty? I'm thirty-one. We're barely getting started."

She smiled, which is exactly the response he wanted. He loved seeing that smile, loved knowing he could get such a quick, heartfelt reaction from her.

Lacing her hands over her abdomen, Kate blew out a deep sigh. "I don't think we're old. My mom was only thirty-two when she died, which was way too young. I just… I don't know. I guess I've been thinking too much over the past year. My mom probably thought she had her whole life ahead of her with raising me. Maybe she even wanted more kids. I have no clue. All I know is I don't want to lose out on anything because I was too busy working or assumed I had more time."

Gray's hands stilled. Her words hit hard. She was absolutely right. What if he kept up his day-to-day life, wondering what else was out there, what he was missing out on? Life was fleeting and nothing was guaranteed.

Should he take that business deal? Should he accept the money and sell Gallagher's, finally moving on to fill that void? The possibilities for him would be endless and the money would allow him to fully explore his options.

But at what cost? Disappointment from his father and the unknown of what he'd do next or if he would even stay in Stonerock. The risk from either decision weighed heavily on him.

"You okay?" Kate asked, pulling him away from his thoughts.

"Fine." He switched to her other foot and circled back to her needs. He wasn't quite ready to express his own just yet. "Tell me what you've put on the list."

"You'll think I'm silly."

"We've already established I live for silly."

Kate rolled her eyes and laughed—music to his ears. "Well, I'd like to go camping."

Gray couldn't help but laugh. "Camping? What in the world brought that up?"

"I don't know. It's just something I haven't done." She stretched her legs and rotated her ankles before dropping them back to his lap. "I live in the mountains, for crying out loud, and I've never been camping."

"So you made a bucket list?"

She nodded. "I titled it My Life List."

"Of course you gave it a title. What else is on there?" he asked, resting his hands on her legs.

"I'd like to get a dog and name her Sprout. A kennel dog or a stray. I can't handle the thought of all those abandoned animals while people are paying for novelty pets. It's heartbreaking. So I'll start with one dog. Who knows how many I'll end up with."

Someone as passionate and caring as Kate would want to help the less fortunate. Just another aspect he'd always admired about her. She was always looking at how to spread her light, even when she didn't always shine it on herself.

Kate kept her eyes on his as she discussed the items from her list. "I want to go to the beach since I've never seen the ocean. I'd love to throw a *Great Gatsby*–themed party and dress up and have fun all night. I think I'd like to go on a road trip. Of course I'd have to have it mapped out, but I want to just take off in the car and visit some national landmarks.

Once I get closer to checking that one off the list, I'll make a spreadsheet."

As he listened to her, Gray realized her goals were all so obtainable and there was no reason she couldn't do those things.

"I wanted to try alcohol, so that box is already ticked off," she added.

"In bright blue marker, I'm sure."

She reached up to swat his shoulder. "No, smarty-pants. Yellow is clearly the only choice."

Gray couldn't help but laugh. Kate took her feet from his lap and crisscrossed them in front of her on the cushion.

"So what else do you have?" he asked.

"I want to do something utterly spontaneous."

Gray stared at her, waiting for her to smile or give some hint that she was kidding. But she merely stared at him, completely serious.

"Darlin', you do realize you're missing the whole point of being spontaneous if you put it on a list and schedule it."

She toyed with the frayed ends of her shorts. Gray couldn't help but watch her movements, torment-ing himself further as he stared at the white threads lying against her tanned skin. He wanted to run his hands up those shapely legs. He wanted to strip her and have her right here on this couch.

Being together in the middle of the night with nothing around to interrupt them was probably not the smartest idea, but he couldn't bring himself to leave. He was dead-tired now, but she was talking. They were getting back to a place of comfort and familiarity. And she wasn't trying to make excuses for the mistake they'd made.

Only having sex hadn't been a mistake. It had been perfect and he was hell-bent on making sure it happened again. But above all, he didn't want her to worry about the future of their relationship. He'd never let anything—including his all-consuming desire for her—jeopardize that, because he needed her just as much.

While he respected her stipulation that their one night of passion stay just that, he wasn't going to let her ignore the attraction. If the opportunity arose again, if she gave the slightest hint she wanted more, he'd be all over it...and her.

"Well, I don't know what the spontaneous moment will be," she explained. "So it's not completely ridiculous that I listed it. I just want to try to be more... I don't know. Like you. You're so laid-back and carefree. I don't even know what that would feel like. But it's a short-term goal."

He wasn't going to state the obvious of the spontaneity on the bar. She'd probably already labeled that under something else.

"If you say so," he chuckled. "Anything else on the list?"

"Well..."

She was driving him crazy. "What? You want to

jump out of a plane? See the Mayan ruins? Take an Alaskan cruise? Just spit it out."

"Jump out of a plane?" She jerked back. "First of all, I wouldn't pick something so predictable, and second of all, hell no."

Gray laughed and curled his hands over her toes. "Tell me or I start cracking."

"I want to trace my heritage."

Intrigued at her statement, he relaxed his hands and stared over at her. "Seriously?"

Kate nodded and tipped her head to the side, resting on the back of the couch. "With my parents gone, I just want to know where I came from, you know? I don't have any other family and I was just a teen when they passed. It's not something I ever thought of asking them about."

Gray had never thought of that before. His grandfather had died only two years ago, but his father was alive and well and more than willing to pass down the family stories that could trace all the way back to their roots in Ireland. Kate didn't have anything like that.

While Gray had lost his mother at a young age and always had that hole in his heart, he couldn't imagine how Kate felt, essentially alone other than having friends. But that wasn't the same as family. Nothing could ever replace parents.

She'd lived with her grandmother for a while, but ultimately she passed, too. Thankfully Kate was older when that happened.

"I want to know where I got the combination of black hair and blue eyes," she went on with a slight smile. "It's a little silly, I know, but I guess I just feel like I need those answers. Maybe I have family out there and a long-distance relative I can connect with."

Gray hated that lost tone. She'd never mentioned feeling alone before. She'd never talked like she was hurting. At least, she hadn't said as much to him. Of course, she suffered from her parents' absence. That was something she'd never get over. But he really had no idea she'd been longing to find out where she came from. Kate should have every opportunity to trace her family roots. He'd make damn sure of it.

As she went through her list, he realized that he wanted to be the one to experience those things with her. They were best friends. Yes, she had Tara and Lucy, but Lucy was newly married and Tara was still struggling with Sam and their own sordid mess.

Gray wasn't going to let Kate feel alone any longer. Hell, he'd already helped her knock trying alcohol off her list. The rest would be a joy to share with her.

"We'll do this together," he told her.

Bright blue eyes snapped up, focusing on him. "Don't be ridiculous. I wasn't hinting that I needed a partner. I wasn't going to tell anyone about this list. It's just something I'm doing for me."

"I don't plan on telling anyone," he replied. "Keep

all the secrets about it you want, but I'm not going to let you do this alone."

Kate stared at him another minute before swinging her feet to the floor. She grabbed the remote and turned the television off, then put it back on the table.

"I really should get to bed." She stretched her arms above her head, giving him a glimpse of pale skin between her tank and her shorts. "I think I'm finally tired."

Yeah, well, he wasn't. Well, he was tired in the sense that he needed sleep, but he didn't want to leave. He could sit here all night and talk with her like they had when they were younger, with fewer responsibilities. Besides, she couldn't brush him off that easily. She was running scared again. He'd offered to help and she flipped out, jumping off the couch to get away from his touch. How could she choose this over intimacy?

If they just went with the sexual pull, the undeniable attraction, it would have to be less stressful than what was brewing between them now. How could she not see that? Was she simply too afraid to face the truth?

An idea formed in his head, but he kept the piece of brilliance locked away as he came to his feet. He knew she was tired, so he'd go. But he was done letting her hide behind her fear of the unknown and what was happening here.

"You look like you're ready to drop."

Gray took in her sleepy eyes, her relaxed clothing,

and there was nothing more he wanted to do than to pick her up and carry her to bed…and stay the rest of the night. Maybe he would one day. Maybe she'd realize that the one time wasn't enough and she wanted more.

He had every intention of respecting her wishes to stay in the friend zone—but that didn't mean he wouldn't keep showing her how perfect they were together. There was nothing wrong with exploring what they'd started. Besides, he knew Kate better than she knew herself at times. She had analyzed that night from every different angle and their intimacy was never far from the front of her mind. He'd bet his bar on it.

Said bar might not be his for much longer, though. But she wasn't in the right mind-set to discuss the potential sale now, and honestly, neither was he. Tomorrow, he vowed. There was too much at stake no matter which way he decided to go. Both choices were life-altering and would change not only his entire world, but that of his father and the town.

Gallagher's had been the pride of three generations now. His grandfather had wanted to set down roots, to have something that brought people together, because he'd seen so much ugliness tearing them apart. Ewan Gallagher had started a tradition, one that the people in this tiny town had come to appreciate and rely upon.

Gray didn't want that niggle of doubt and guilt to sway his decision. He wanted to look at this from a business and personal standpoint, but it was so difficult when the two were so inherently connected.

He dropped an innocent kiss on Kate's forehead and let himself out the front door. Gray waited until he heard her click the lock back into place before he headed to his car.

He knew he needed to grab sleep, but as soon as he got up, he was putting a few plans into motion. Kate was about to check off more items on her bucket list and he was personally going to see that she accomplished exactly what she set out to do.

Morning runs sucked. They sucked even more when little sleep was a factor and really all she'd wanted was to run to the bakery and buy a donut the size of her face. And by run, she meant drive.

Kate took a hearty chug from her water bottle as she pulled her key from the tiny pouch on her running shorts. She'd ended up falling asleep on the couch after Gray left, then stumbled to her room at about six and climbed into bed. When she'd woken up for good at nine, Kate realized she'd slept later than usual, so she'd hopped out of bed and quickly headed out the door to get in her miles.

She hated running. But that was the only way she could enjoy her donuts and still fit in her clothes. Besides, the exercise was a great stress reliever...so were pastries, but whatever.

As Kate opened her front door, she heard a vehicle pulling into her drive. Kate glanced over her shoulder, her heart skipping a beat at the sight of Gray's large black truck. The thing was as menacing as the man himself. He might look like the quintessential bad boy, but he'd listened to her drone on and on about her bucket list all while rubbing her feet.

Damn it. Why did he have to be her best friend? He was the perfect catch for any woman…just not her. She couldn't—no, she *wouldn't*—risk losing him as a friend. If she'd jumped at her initial reaction after the great sex and ignored common sense altogether, she might have made a play for him. But he was the only stable man in her life. He'd filled that role for far too long for her to just throw it aside and take the risk for something more.

Even if she went for more, what would it be? Gray wasn't the type to settle down. In fact, she knew his father mentioned Gray's bachelor status quite often and Gray brushed the notion aside. He seemed just fine keeping busy with his bar. The man rarely dated and even when he did, he kept it all so private. He was definitely not someone looking for happily-ever-after.

Kate took another drink as she waited on the porch for Gray to come up her flower-lined walk.

"Didn't you just leave here?" she joked.

He glanced up, flashing that megawatt smile he didn't always hand out freely. Mercy, the man was too sexy for his own good, and now that she'd had a sample of that sexiness, she was positive no other man would ever measure up.

How did one encounter have such an epic impact? Kate had to push aside what happened. It couldn't have been that great…could it? Surely she was just conjuring up more vivid details than actually happened.

Or maybe not. Gray did in fact tear her panties off and climb up the bar to get to her.

"I feel like I did," he replied as he mounted the steps. "You're sweating."

Kate rolled her eyes. "That happens when I go for a run."

"Well, you have ten minutes to get a bag together." He hooked his thumbs through his belt loops. "And if you want to shower, you better squeeze it in that time frame."

Kate jerked back. "Excuse me? Pack a bag?"

A mischievous smile spread across his face. "We're going camping."

"What?" Shocked, she turned and let herself in her house, trying to wrap her mind around his announcement. "I can't just go camping right now. I have things to do."

Her planner lay on the table just inside the door. She fingered through the colored tabs until she landed on the red. Flipping it over, she quickly glanced at her mounting list—color-coded with her favorite fine-point markers, of course.

"You can see there's no time," she stated as Gray followed her in. She used the tip of her finger to tap on the upcoming days. "I have to finish outlining a bridal shower and start on a new client's vacation schedule. Then I have to try to come up with some way to fit in my neighbor, who swears her closets are full but won't get rid of anything. Same story with her kitchen, so at this point I'm afraid her entire house needs an overhaul. I also have eight online clients I'm working with who found me just last week through my social media sites and referrals."

"And do you plan on doing all of that today?" he asked, crossing his arms and leaning against the wall beside her.

"Well, no, but—"

"You're down to eight minutes, Kate. If you hurry, I can even swing by and get a box of donuts on our way out of town so we can have breakfast in the morning."

"That's a low blow," she stated, narrowing her eyes.

"You need a break."

She slapped her planner shut and faced him. "I can't go camping last minute. I'd need sufficient time to strategize and make a detailed list of all the things I need to take. Hell, I need to research *what* to take. I've never been, so I have no clue."

That smile assaulted her once again. Damn cocky man.

"You're in luck," he replied. "I have been multiple times so I have everything you need, minus your clothes and the donuts I'll stop and get on the road.

Look at it this way—you can check off two things on your list. Camping and spontaneity."

Kate shook her head and sighed. "I can't mark off being spontaneous when it was your idea."

And she still hadn't marked it in regards to the bar sex. That needed a whole other label of its own. How could something so life-altering be checked off so simply? No, that encounter deserved more respect than just a quick X by the words spontaneous quickie.

Gray pushed off the wall and started for the steps. "You'll want a pair of jeans for when we go hiking, plus shorts, maybe a swimsuit, comfortable shoes that can get wet. It gets cooler at night so grab a sweatshirt or something with sleeves."

Kate watched as he just headed up to her bedroom like she hadn't just laid out several reasons she couldn't go. Did the man ever take no for an answer?

Her mind flashed back to the bar as her body trembled with the onslaught of memories.

So no. No, he didn't.

And here she was, contemplating going camping? Being alone with him all night and not invoking how she felt when he'd touched her, kissed her. This was not smart. Not smart at all.

Kate headed for the steps, rushing up to her bedroom.

"You're not getting out of this," he told her before she could open her mouth.

He opened her closet and jerked a sweatshirt off

the top shelf. Two more shirts fell to the floor as a result and Kate cringed.

"You're messing up my system here, Gallagher." She crossed over and instantly started sorting the mess back into neat piles. "You cannot just start packing my bag."

He shot her a wink. "Does that mean you're cuddling up to me for warmth and skinny dipping? Hey, I'm game, but you might be more comfortable with clothes."

Kate blew out a breath and leaned back against her open closet door. "You're not going to let this go, are you?"

"Nope." He took a step closer to her, his eyes all serious now. Gone was the playful smile. "Listen, if I didn't push you into this, I'm not sure you'd actually do it. Making a list is one thing, but following through is another."

"I would do it," She felt the need to defend herself because, damn it, she would do it…at some point. "I don't know when, but I would."

He tossed the sweatshirt behind him onto her four-poster bed, then took her by her shoulders. "My truck is packed. I literally have everything we need: a large tent, food, supplies, blankets. I got Jacob to cover at the bar for me tonight. We'll be back late tomorrow evening."

Kate stared into those dark eyes and knew if anyone could help her check items off her list, it was this man. He'd clearly gone to great lengths to set this up for her and she'd be a terrible friend, not to mention flat-out rude, to turn him down.

He'd literally thought of everything and he stood before her, having rearranged his entire life for two days just to make her happy.

Kate's heart flipped in her chest. Gray always did amazing things for her, but since the sex, his actions had taken on a deeper, more intimate meaning.

"Fine," she conceded. "But step away from my neatly organized closet and let me pack. I don't trust you over there and I promise I won't be long. You swear we're stopping for donuts?"

"I promise." Gray leaned forward and wrinkled his nose. "I'll give you an extra five minutes to shower. You smell."

Laughing, Kate smacked his arm. "Get out of my room. I'll be down in twenty minutes."

Once he was gone, Kate closed her bedroom door and started stripping on her way to the shower. She dropped her clothes into the color-coded piles in her laundry sorter just inside her bathroom.

Gray Gallagher was slowly making her reconsider that whole one-night rule. For a half second she thought about packing some pretty underwear, but then snorted.

Seriously? Even if she was after an encore performance, they were camping. She'd never been, but she had a feeling lace and satin didn't pair well with bug spray and campfire smoke.

Kate stepped under the hot shower and mentally started packing. No matter how this trip went down, she had a feeling lasting memories would be made.

Chapter Seven

"I did it," Kate exclaimed, jumping up and down.

Gray glanced over to the tent she'd put together. He'd set everything out and given her instructions, and damn if she hadn't erected their tent like a pro. He knew she wouldn't give up, but she'd definitely gotten it done much quicker than he thought she would. He was proud of her.

This was by far his favorite campground, but the spot he usually chose had already been taken and he'd had to choose another. He found one closest to a hiking trail near his favorite areas in the forest. He couldn't wait to share all of these experiences with Kate.

"Looks good." Gray came to his feet and wiped

his hands on his pants. "The fire is ready if you want to roast some hot dogs for lunch."

"I don't recall the last time I had a roasted hot dog."

Gray rolled over another large log and stood it up on its end as a makeshift stool. He'd found several near the designated fire area, but set up only the two.

"We had one at the bonfire last fall," he said. "Remember the fundraiser for Drake?"

Drake St. John had been a firefighter who had encountered several issues with the then mayor. Drake had decided to run for office himself and ultimately won. Drake and his brothers were pillars in the community and Gray had happily voted for him.

"Oh, yeah." Kate picked up one of the roasting sticks and held it out for him to put the hot dog on. "So I guess that was the last time I had one."

"Then you're long overdue," he replied, getting his own roasting stick ready.

The crackling fire kept his focus on cooking his lunch....and away from the swell of her breasts peeking from the top of her fitted tank. He had no business going there. This was about Kate. He wanted this to be an easy trip, something where she could relax and just be herself, take a break from work and all those damn schedules. He was here to make sure she was taken care of, first and foremost.

Silence settled easily between them, but so much swirled through Gray's mind. Kate, their turning point, the bar, the possibilities…the unknowns came at him from every single angle.

He still hadn't spoken to his father about the proposal. There were pros and cons that Gray could easily see now, but there was no clear answer.

"I jotted down some things for us to do," Kate said after a minute. "I looked on my phone for area suggestions while you were driving and made a list—"

"I saw you. You just had to bring your planner, didn't you?"

Kate gasped and stared at him as if he'd just asked if the sky was purple. "Of course I had to bring it. How else would I know what to do? I can't keep all these places and a timeline of when to visit them straight without writing them down."

Shaking his head, Gray rotated the stick. "You can relax for a day, damn it. I've got the trip planned and details covered. We'll be fine. Chill."

"I'm relaxed," she argued. "Look at me. Cooking a hot dog over a fire, sitting on a tree stump, completely relaxed."

"Where's the planner?"

She pursed her lips and shrugged.

"It's beside you, isn't it?"

Kate blinked. "I don't know what you're talking about."

Gray pulled his charred hot dog from the fire and tested it with his fingers. Black and crispy on the outside, just the way he liked it.

"What would you do if you didn't have that colorful binder?"

"I'd be lost. This is my personal one. But I need both personal and business or I'd never be able to function."

He threw her a sideways glance. "You've got to be kidding."

Kate came to her feet and pulled her hot dog from the fire. "Why is that so strange? I have too much to remember so I just keep it all nice and neat in my planner."

"But that's just your personal one," he stated. "You still have one for work."

Gray pulled the pack of buns out and set them on the old picnic table before grabbing bottles of water from the cooler.

"This is supposed to be a nice, calm overnight trip," he reminded her. "We don't need an itinerary."

She took a seat on one of the benches and grabbed a bun. "I need a plan or I'm going to miss out on things. So, like I was saying—"

"You've got me." Gray threw a leg over the bench and took a seat. "I have plans for us so put your planner in my truck and forget about it until we start to head home."

Kate's eyes widened. "You're joking."

He stared across the table. "Do I look like I'm joking?"

"I don't like camping already," she muttered around a bite.

Gray couldn't help but smile. He was going to get her to relax if it was the last thing he did.

"After we eat there's a little place I want to show you."

"What do I need to wear?"

"You're fine the way you are."

She'd come down the stairs at her house freshly showered. Her hair had been pulled up on top of her head in some wet bun thing she sometimes wore. She'd thrown on a tank that fit her curvy body perfectly, and her shorts showed off those legs she kept toned and shapely by her constant running. Though she'd looked perfectly fine before she'd taken up that hobby. She'd started running after her jerk fiancé left. Gray never did figure out if she was using the exercise as a natural form of therapy or if she thought something was wrong with her body.

Kate was pretty damn perfect no matter her look or her shape…at least in his eyes.

They finished their lunch and cleaned up, making sure to burn what they could before putting the food back in a sealed cooler to keep the hungry animals away.

"We've got things to do that do not involve spreadsheets or strict schedules," he informed her. "I'll wait while you put your planner and cell in my truck."

Kate hesitated, but he quirked his brow and crossed his arms. Groaning, she picked up her things and put them in the cab of his truck before coming back beside him.

"Happy now?"

Gray nodded and turned to head toward the marked trail. He wasn't sure if this camping idea was the greatest or dumbest move he'd ever made. On one hand, at least he was getting her out of her scheduled shell and she was checking things off her list.

On the other, though, they would be sharing a tent. Which wouldn't be a big deal if they hadn't already slept together. He'd warned her not to make things awkward between them, so he needed to take his own advice.

Still, anticipation had settled in deep because he had no idea how the night would play out once they were alone lying mere inches from each other.

"How far are we going?" she asked from behind him.

"About a mile."

She came up beside him. "I could've skipped my run this morning."

"You could skip it every morning and be just fine," he growled.

He hadn't meant to sound grouchy, but she worried about her body when her body was perfect. Why did women obsess about such things? Confidence was more of a turn-on to him than anything. Kate had to know how amazing she looked. Damn that ex of hers for ever making her doubt it.

They walked on a bit more in silence before they came to the top of a hill. He reached for her arm to stop her. With careful movements, he shifted her to stand and turn exactly to the spot he'd been dying for her to see.

"Oh my word," she gasped. "That's gorgeous."

Gray looked down into the valley at the natural waterfall spilling over the rocks. "This is one of my favorite places."

She glanced over her shoulder. "How often do you come here?"

"Not enough. Maybe once a year."

"And you've never brought me?"

Gray shrugged. "I tend to come alone to recharge, plus I never knew you had an interest in camping."

Kate turned her attention back to the breathtaking view. "I didn't know I had an interest, either, but I'm starting to love it. There's not a worry in the world up here. How could anyone even think of their day-to-day lives when this is so…magical?"

Something turned deep inside him. He couldn't put his finger on it, but as he stood behind her, seeing her take in this sight for the first time, Gray knew he'd be bringing her back.

This one night out here with her wouldn't be enough. Just like the one night of sex wouldn't be enough. Kate was a huge part of his life. He couldn't just ignore this continual pull between them.

Gray had always loved being outside, there was a sense of freedom he didn't have when he was be-hind the bar or doing office work. Knowing that Kate might share this…well, he was starting to wonder just how right they were together in areas he'd never fathomed.

"Can we climb down there and get a closer look?" she asked.

"We can, but you'll want to change."

She turned back to face him. "Why?"

"There's a natural spring you can swim in."

Her face lit up and she smacked his chest. "Then what are we waiting for? Let's get to it."

She circled around him and started heading back down the narrow, wooded trail. Gray watched her go and raked a hand down his face. First camping alone and now getting her in a bathing suit. Yeah, this whole adventurous weekend was a brilliant idea... for a masochist.

Kate smoothed her wet hair back from her face as she climbed back up the shoreline toward the grassy area with a large fallen tree serving as a makeshift bench. She grabbed her towel from the tree and patted her face.

Pulling in a deep breath and starting to dry her legs, she threw a smile at Gray, who had yet to put his shirt back on.

How long was he going to stand there? They'd splashed in the water, floated on their backs, then chatted a bit while just wading. Thankfully the conversation had stayed light, mostly about the beauty of the area and its peacefulness. There was something so calming and perfect about it. Kate was convinced no problems existed here.

Gray had gotten out of the water several minutes ago but still wasn't making any moves to get dressed. And that was pretty much the only reason she'd gotten out. They needed to get back to camp so he could put some damn clothes on and stop driving her out of her mind. Those water droplets glistening all over his well-defined shoulders, pecs and abs. The dark ink curving over his shoulder. There wasn't a thing about her best friend that she didn't find attractive.

Yes. He was definitely driving her out of her mind.

Unfortunately, Kate had a feeling he wasn't even trying.

She pushed aside her lustful thoughts. Okay, she didn't push them aside so much as kept them to herself as she turned her attention toward the brooding man. Something was up with him, but it could just be the sexual tension that continued to thicken between them with each passing day.

"That was amazing," she stated, blowing out a breath and glancing toward the crisp blue sky before looking back at Gray. He said nothing, didn't even so much as crack a smile. "But I guess we can't stay here forever."

Kate tightened the knot on her towel and when she lifted her eyes back up, those dark, mesmerizing eyes were directed right at her. She couldn't quite decipher the look, but whatever it was had her clutching the knot she'd just tied.

"What's wrong?" she asked.

Gray wrapped his towel around his neck, gripping the ends in one hand. "I've had something on my mind I want to discuss with you."

Instantly, Kate stilled. The only major thing between them was the new state of their relationship that they hadn't fully fleshed out. They'd brushed it aside in an attempt to get back on safer ground.

Was he about to open the memory bank and dig deeper? Fine. She needed to just remain calm and do this. They had to hash it out at some point, and better before they fell into bed together than later, so to speak.

Gray sank down onto the large old tree stretched across the ground. Without waiting to see what he was about to say or do, she took a seat beside him.

"What's up?"

Gray rested his forearms on his knees and leaned forward, staring out at the waterfall. The way stress settled over his face, Kate worried something else was wrong. If he wanted to discuss the other night, he'd be more confident. Right now, Gray appeared to be…torn.

Kate honestly had no idea what he was going to say, but the silence certainly wasn't helping her nerves. *Was* there something else wrong? Had he actually brought her out here to tell her he was sick or dying?

"Gray, come on," she said, smacking his leg. "You know my anxiety and overactive imagination can't handle this."

"I had a visitor at the bar yesterday morning."

Okay, so he wasn't dying. That was good. So what had him so upset and speechless?

Kate shifted to block the sun from her eyes. She waited for him to go on, but at this rate it would be nightfall before he finished the story. Whoever this visitor was had Gray struggling for words. Either that or he was battling something major and trying to figure out how to tell her.

"He offered me an insane amount of money to buy the bar."

His words settled heavily between them, rendering her speechless as well. Sell the bar? Is that something he actually wanted to do? She'd never heard him mention wanting away from something that she'd always thought held so much meaning. What would his dad say? Had he even talked to his dad?

There were so many questions crammed into one space and she wanted all of the answers now.

"Are you selling?" she finally asked when it was clear he wasn't going to add more to his verbal bomb.

Gray lifted one bare shoulder and glanced over. "I have no idea. I never wanted the bar, it was just assumed I'd take it over. When I came home from the army, it was there, so I stepped into role of owner."

"What would you do without it?"

He raked a hand over his wet hair and blew out

a sigh. "I have no idea, but I've always wondered. I mean, with the amount I was offered, I could do anything."

"You haven't talked to your dad."

Gray shook his head, though she hadn't actually been asking.

"Is that why you brought me camping?" she asked. "So you could get my opinion?"

Gray reached for her hand. "No. I mean, I knew I wanted to talk to you, but the second you mentioned that list and started naming things off, I knew I was going to bring you here as soon as I could get everything lined up. It just happened to be rather quickly."

Kate couldn't help but smile as she glanced down to their joined hands. "Have you made a list of reasons to stay and reasons to go?"

His lips twitched into a grin of their own as he shook his head. "No, ma'am. I leave the list-making to you."

Her mind started rolling on all the good things about owning a family business. There was just so much, but only Gray knew what he loved most about the place.

On the downside, once you owned a business, you were married to it. Randomly he would take a day, like this, but the man was loyal and that bar was his wife, baby. Plus, he carried on the small-town tradition his grandfather had started.

Family heritage meant everything to someone like Gray. Money could only go so far. She was surprised he even considered selling the bar, which meant he must really be looking for something else in his life.

Kate's heart ached for him, for this decision. If she were in his place she wouldn't even have to think about it. She had no family and would kill to carry on this kind of legacy.

"Your silence is making me nervous."

Kate smiled and patted his leg. "You should be nervous. The pros and cons are already lining up inside my head."

Gray led her back to camp and she was somewhat grateful for the distraction. Though she didn't think anything could fully take her mind off the ripped torso covered with tats that he still hadn't covered. She'd be lying if she didn't admit her nerves had settled in at the thought of spending the night in that tent with him.

But first, she'd help him figure out what to do about this business proposition. Surely that would crush any desires…wouldn't it?

Yes, if they just continued to focus on the bar and his proposal, then any desires they shared would be pushed aside and they could reconfigure their friendship.

Kate would keep telling herself that until it became the truth.

Chapter Eight

The fire crackled, the stars were vibrant in the sky, and beside him, Kate continued to jot down notes. She'd mutter something, then mark out what she'd just written. Every now and then she'd ask him a question and scribble something else down.

Her system was driving him insane. She fidgeted, pulling her hair up into a knot, then taking it down and raking her fingers through it. Then she'd start the process all over again. Watching her was killing him, mostly because her mind was working overtime, but just seeing her in her element was too damn sexy.

Kate let out a groan. "I need my colored markers so I can see the overall picture clearer."

Gray had had enough. He reached over, jerked the planner from her lap and tossed it into the fire.

"Gray!" Kate leaped to her feet and stared down as the pages curled, turned black, and drifted up in ashes. "That was my personal planner. You can't just—"

"Too late. I just did."

Okay, maybe he should feel bad, but she needed to relax because until she did, he couldn't. She'd brought the damn thing camping when this whole night should be about taking a break from reality.

Now she sat here working on his life like he was one of her damn clients. No more.

"Not only does that have my whole life in it, I had the lists for you about the bar."

Kate spun around and propped her hands on her hips as she stared down at him. He picked up the long stick he'd had beside him and poked around at the fire, shoving the last bit of the planner further into the flames for good measure. It was better than seeing that snug little tank pulling across her chest or the creamy patch of skin between the hem of her shirt and the top of her pants.

"You're a jerk."

She stomped off into the darkness, heading toward his truck. Gray bit the inside of his cheek to keep from laughing. She most likely had a backup planner at home and he knew she kept duplicate electronic files. He felt only a little guilty. She'd be fine. Knowing Kate, she had everything logged into her memory bank anyway. Someone who was so focused on details and schedules and color coding the hell out of every minute of life would definitely know her schedule by heart.

The slam of his truck door had Gray glancing in that direction. Seconds later, Kate came stomping back with her cell in hand. She flopped back onto the fat stump she'd been using as her seat. The glow of her phone added a bit more light to their campfire area.

"You can't be serious," he grumbled.

Without looking up, she started typing like a mad woman. "Oh, when it comes to schedules, I'm dead serious. And even though you just ruined my life by burning my planner, I'm still going to help you work this out."

Gray tossed the stick back to the ground. "I'm not making a decision tonight, so relax."

"You keep telling me to relax, but if I don't worry about it and try to come to a conclusion, who will?"

Gray stood and took a step toward her. She jerked her phone behind her back and tipped her chin up in defiance.

"You're not throwing this in the fire," she said, and he thought he saw a ghost of a smile on her lips.

"No," he laughed. "But I'm not worrying and neither are you. I'm tired and it's late so I thought we could get our sleeping bags rolled out and get some rest. I want to get up early and hike to the top of the peak so you can see the sunrise."

"Sounds beautiful."

"Words can't describe it." Gray held out his hand to help her up. "So you may want to get some sleep or you'll be grouchy when I wake you."

"I'm grouchy now," she muttered, placing her hand in his. "You owe me a new planner, but I get to pick it out. I don't trust you anymore."

He helped her up, but didn't let go of her hand. "Now, where's the fun in that? You may love the one I choose."

"Please," she said, and snorted. "You have terrible taste. I've seen that painting over your sofa."

"Hey, *Dogs Playing Poker* is a classic. I paid good money for that."

"From a flea market, maybe," she muttered. Kate shook her head and blew out a sigh. "We better just go to bed and stop arguing."

Gray wasn't sure why he hadn't let her go, or why he continued to watch as the orange glow from the flames tinted her cheeks. Now her hair was down from the knot she'd been wearing. It had air-dried from the swim earlier…a swim that he took way too long to recover from. She'd only worn a simple black one-piece, but he knew exactly what she had hidden beneath that suit. She may as well have been naked. The V in the front and the low scoop in the back had been so damn arousing, he'd had to recite all fifty states in alphabetical order to get himself under control.

Gray kept hold of her hand, pulling it up to his

chest. Her eyes remained locked on his. Sounds from crickets filled the night, the crackling of the fire randomly broke into the moment.

"Gray," she whispered.

"Kate."

Her eyes closed as she pulled in a deep breath. "You're making this difficult."

"None of this has to be difficult," he countered. No reason to pretend he didn't know what she spoke of. They both had the same exact thing on their minds.

"No, it shouldn't be," she agreed, lifting her lids to look at him again. "But when I'm around you, I just remember the bar and how that felt. And then I wonder if my memory is just making the whole scenario better than it actually was."

Good. He'd been banking on her replaying that night, but he hadn't expected such an honest compliment. He sure as hell remembered, too, and not just when he was with her.

Even when he was alone or working, especially working, he recalled how stunning she'd been all spread out across the gleaming mahogany bar top. She was like a fantasy come to life.

There wasn't a doubt in his mind that she wanted him, too. He could see the way her gaze kept dropping to his mouth, the fact she hadn't let go of his hand, the way she'd avoided him for days after their intimacy. She was afraid of her feelings, of taking what she wanted.

"I don't expect anything once we go in that tent," he explained. The last thing he wanted was for her to think that was why he actually brought her here.

"I didn't think that." She licked her lips and curled her fingers more tightly around his hand. "You understand why I made the one-night rule. Right?"

She might need him to know, but that didn't mean he wanted to. All Gray cared about was how they felt, and ignoring such intense emotions was only going to complicate things further down the line. The resulting tension would eat away at their friendship and drive a wedge between them much more than taking a risk would.

"I can't lose you, Gray," she went on, staring up at him like he was everything in her life. "It would destroy me."

Kate had looked at him that way before, when her parents died and when he'd come home from the army. He didn't want to be some type of hero to anybody.

No, that wasn't right. He did want to be her hero, but not someone she thought needed to be on a pedestal. He wanted to be her equal, to prove to her that they were good together.

Fortunately, he didn't need to prove such things. She already knew just how good they were…and that's what scared the hell out of her.

"You're the only constant man in my life." She squeezed his hand. "Do you even know how important that is to me? Tara and Lucy are great, but they're not you."

Gray swallowed the lump in his throat. He didn't get emotional. Ever. But something about her raw honesty, her vulnerability got to him.

"You really think I'd let something happen to our friendship?" he asked, staring into her expressive eyes.

"Neither of us would mean for anything to happen to it," she countered. "But are you willing to take that chance?"

"I'd never risk hurting you," he stated. Gray palmed one side of her face, stroking his thumb beneath her eye. "You think I don't understand where you're coming from? You have to notice you're the only constant woman in my life basically since we met."

A smile played over her mouth. "You date."

"I do, but serious relationships aren't my thing. I'm too busy with work to feed a relationship or worry about a woman." He took a half-step closer until they were toe to toe. "I need this friendship just as much as you do, but I'm not going to ignore these feelings forever, Kate."

Her eyes widened. "You promised—"

"—that I wouldn't let you lose this friendship and that I wasn't pressuring you for anything tonight. But you can't run from your feelings forever. I won't let you deny your own feelings, either."

Unable to resist, Gray dropped a quick kiss on

her lips, not lingering nearly as long as he would've liked. After releasing her and taking a step back, he finally turned and headed to the tent.

This was going to be one long, uncomfortable night.

Kate rolled over in her sleeping bag for what seemed like the eighteenth time in as many minutes. Facing Gray now, she narrowed her gaze to adjust to the darkness and make out his silhouette.

How dare he throw down that gauntlet and then lie there and get a good night's sleep? How did the man turn his emotions off and on so easily?

She wanted to know the secret because this jumbled up mess inside her head, inside her heart, was causing some serious anxiety issues. As if she didn't have enough to handle where this man was concerned.

Kate couldn't make out his face in the dark. But she knew it by heart just as well as she knew her own. The faint lines around his eyes and between his brows gave him that distinguished look she found sexier than she should. His dark lashes always made the perfect frame for those dark as night eyes. She'd bet they were fanned out over his cheeks right now as he slept peacefully.

When he'd come home from the army, he'd been harder than when he'd left. Whatever he'd seen overseas had done something to him, something she never could put her finger on. But then he'd jumped right in and taken over the family business.

Some men came home a shell of who they'd once been. While Gray might be harder and more closed off to some, he was alive and thriving in their little town. He might not like the word *hero*, but he was hers. Honestly, he always had been.

Just another reason she couldn't keep exploring these new sexual feelings. The friendship was so, so much more important.

When Gray had implemented Ladies' Night at Gallagher's, the women around town had flocked there, all trying to catch the attention of the town's most eligible bachelor. Ladies from surrounding towns also came in to see the sexy new vet turned bartender.

Kate had always been aware of Gray's ridiculously good looks. She wasn't blind or stupid. She'd just never thought about acting on her attraction. She could be attracted to someone and still be friends... right?

Well, she'd been doing just fine at managing both until he propositioned her on the bar top. The sex couldn't have been as good as she remembered. It simply couldn't. And yet it was all of those overexaggerated flashes in her mind that had her all jumbled and aching now when she had no right to be.

"Are you going to stare at me all night?"

Kate jerked at Gray's mumbled words. He hadn't even cracked an eyelid open, so how did he know she was staring? Her heart beat faster at the abrupt break in the peaceful silence.

"I can't sleep," she answered honestly. No need to tell him her insomnia was due to him. Gray wasn't stupid.

"I can tell from all the flopping around you've been doing."

Now he did open his eyes. Even though she couldn't make out the color in the dark tent, she knew they were fixed on her.

"Sorry I kept you awake," she whispered, though why she was whispering was lost on her. Maybe because everything was so peaceful around them and she needed to hold on to that just a bit longer. Lately, so much in her life didn't seem calm. Well, maybe not so much. Mostly just Gray and their friendship, which trickled down to everything else because she couldn't stop thinking of him, of what had happened, and how to move on.

Gray shifted in his sleeping bag. When his knee bumped hers, a jolt shot through her. Being hyper-aware of him in the middle of the night with these sexual urges spiraling through her was not good. Not good at all.

But there wasn't one thing she could do to stop how she felt. Why did these feelings have to be awakened inside her? How long had she had them and not even realized it?

Yes, she'd wondered if they could ever be more than friends. She'd thought of sex with him. He was hot. She was a woman. It was the natural order of things. But she'd always pushed those thoughts aside and focused on their friendship.

That wasn't the case right now.

"Your movement didn't keep me awake," he countered.

Kate curled her fingers around the top of her sleeping bag and tried to resist the urge to reach out. So close. He was so close she would only have to lift her hand slightly to brush the side of his face. She knew from firsthand experience exactly how that bristle would feel against her skin.

Kate swallowed. She shouldn't be fantasizing about that stubbled jaw beneath her palm. She shouldn't wonder if they both could fit into one sleeping bag. And she sure as hell shouldn't be thinking how quickly they could get their clothes off.

"What's keeping you awake?" he asked.

Kate snorted. "You're joking, right?"

"Do I sound like I'm joking?"

No. He sounded sexy with that low, growly voice she'd never fully appreciated until now.

"You've got me so confused and worked up," she confessed. "Why couldn't we just keep things the way they were?"

"Because attraction doesn't follow your rules."

Kate closed her eyes and chewed on her lip. What could she say to that? He was right, but that didn't mean she wouldn't keep trying to compartmentalize her emotions. They had to stay in the friend box.

They had to. Everyone in her life had a special area inside her heart, but Gray kept stepping out of his designated spot and causing all sorts of confusion.

"You're not the only one losing sleep over this, Kate."

Oh, mercy. Those were words she wished he hadn't thrown out there to settle between them. Not now, when they were being held hostage by the circumstances surrounding them. The dark night, the enclosed tent, the sexually charged energy that seemed to be pulling them closer together.

Her heart beating a fast, steady rhythm, she reached out. When her fingers found his jawline, she slid her hand up the side of his face. That prickle of his coarse hair beneath her palm had her entire body heating up.

"What if…"

She couldn't finish. This was insane. This entire idea was absolutely insane and not smart. But she ached…for this man.

His warm, strong hand covered hers as he whispered, "What if what?"

"One more time," she murmured. "We do this just once more."

"Are you going to regret it this time?"

Kate eased her body closer. "I didn't regret it last time."

He released her hand and jerked on the zipper of his bag before sliding hers down as well. In another swift move, he was on her, taking her hands and holding them on either side of her head.

"Tell me now if you want me to stop."

Kate arched against him, pulling against his hold. "Now, Gray."

Chapter Nine

The green light couldn't be brighter. And one time? Sure, he'd heard that before. Whatever. He'd take this time and show her again exactly how perfect their special bond was.

Gray eased up just enough to slide his hands beneath the long-sleeved T-shirt she had on. He hadn't been able to appreciate her before at the bar, and it was so damn dark he could barely see, but he was going to get her naked and not fumble around ripping underwear like some inexperienced, out-of-control teen.

With some careful maneuvering and assistance from Kate, Gray had her clothes off in record time.

His hands settled on her bare hips as she reached up to frame his face.

"You're still wearing clothes."

Gray gripped her wrist, kissed her palm and put her hand on his shirt. "Then take them off."

Her hands trembled as she brought them to the hem of his tee. She jerked the material up and over his head. When she grabbed the waistband of his shorts, he sucked in a breath. Those delicate fingers on his body might be more than he could handle. To say he was hanging on by a thread would be a vast understatement.

Since she'd paraded around in that swimsuit, he'd been fighting the ache to take her hard and fast. Gray covered her hands with his and took over. Within seconds, he was just as bare as her.

Kate eased her knees apart, making room for him. Her fingertips grazed up his arms and over his shoulders. "I wish I could see you better."

Gray reached over, taking the lantern-style light he'd brought. He flicked the switch on and left it against the edge of the tent. When he turned his attention back to Kate, his breath got caught in his throat. A vise-like grip formed around his chest.

She lay beneath him, all of that dark hair spread around her, her eyes bright and beautiful and solely focused on him.

"You're stunning."

He hadn't meant to say the words out loud. He'd wanted to keep this simple—or as simple as they could be, considering their circumstances. But now that they were out, he wasn't sorry. Maybe Kate needed to hear this more often. Maybe she needed to realize just how special and amazing she was.

A smile spread across her face. "I'm already naked," she joked. "You don't need to flatter me."

If she wanted to keep things light, that was fine. Having Kate here with him, like this, was more than he thought would happen.

But he didn't want more words coming between them. All he wanted was to feel this woman, to take his time with her, and show her how much she was treasured. Above all else, he never wanted her to feel like she was just a one-night stand. Even if they agreed to stay friends, he needed her to know she was worth more than quick actions and meaning-less words.

Gray covered her body. Then he covered her mouth. Her delicate arms and legs wrapped all around him.

"I need to get protection," he muttered against her lips.

Her hold tightened. "I'm on birth control and I trust you."

The whispered declaration had him battling over what he should do. There was nothing more he wanted than to have no barrier between them and he trusted her, too. He'd never gone without because there wasn't a woman he trusted that much.

But he knew his Kate and he wasn't about to move

from this spot, not when she was holding on so tight and looking at him like she couldn't take another second without his touch.

Gray settled himself between her thighs, bracing his forearms on either side of her face. He smoothed her hair back, wanting to see every emotion that flashed across her face when he joined their bodies.

And he wasn't disappointed.

The second they became one, her lids fluttered down, her breath came out on a soft sigh, and she arched against him.

Kate's fingertips threaded through his hair as she urged him down, opening for another kiss. How could he ever agree to just one time with her? Hell, he already knew that twice wouldn't be enough.

She muttered something against his lips, but he couldn't make out what. Her hands traveled down to his shoulders, then his back as she tossed her head to the side. Raven hair covered a portion of her face as she cried out, her legs tightening around him.

Gray shoved her hair out of the way, basking in the play of emotions. He'd never seen a more beautiful, expressive woman than Kate. His Kate. No matter what happened, friends or more, she'd always be his.

In no time he was pumping his hips, capturing her mouth beneath his. Kate's nails bit into his back and that was all he needed to send him over the edge. Nothing had ever felt like this…well, nothing except their encounter at his bar.

Gray held on to her, nipping at her lips as he trembled. After several moments, and once his body stilled, he gathered her close and pulled the open sleeping bag over them. He didn't care about their clothes, didn't care that there was a little chill in the mountain air. He leaned over with his free hand and clicked the light off.

"That was the last time," she muttered against his chest. "I mean it."

Gray smiled into the dark. He'd never agreed to that bargain to begin with.

"These new pamphlets turned out so nice."

Kate glanced to Tara, who was waving around the stack of brand-new promotional material for their grief center. Judging by the look on her face, she'd been talking for a while, but Kate had zoned out.

"What? Oh, yes. They're pretty. Lucy did a great job with the design and the colors."

They'd just had new pamphlets done a few months ago, but with the popularity of their weekly meetings, Lucy had taken it upon herself to design the new ones, adding some testimonials from the regulars and having nicer pages printed online.

"You're distracted," Tara stated, dropping the stack to the table at the entryway of the community center. "Does this have anything to do with the camping trip?"

Kate shook her head. "No. Gray and I just went away for a day. It was pretty cool. I can't believe

I live in this gorgeous state and have never taken advantage of the mountains. I'm definitely going camping again."

The waterfall had been amazing, but the sunrise only hours after making love had been something special. She wasn't sure where Gray's thoughts were, but for her, something had changed. She needed a breather and she needed to do some serious reevaluating of where she stood on her feelings for her best friend.

What had she been thinking, telling him not to use protection? Not that she didn't believe him that he was safe, but that bold move was, well…bold. They'd taken their intimacy to another level when she knew full well they couldn't do that ever, ever again.

But when she'd been lying beneath him, cradled by his strength and seeing how he looked at her, she simply hadn't wanted him to move away for anything. She'd wanted him and only him.

Besides, they were fine. She was on the pill and neither of them had ever gone without protection before.

"What's up with the two of you lately?" Tara asked.

Before Kate could answer, she was saved by the adorable five-year-old running around the tables and singing something Kate didn't recognize.

"Marley Jo Bailey," Tara scolded. "You cannot run in here. I brought your bag in and put it back in the kitchen. You have crayons, a coloring book and your new baby doll to play with."

Marley stopped at her mother's abrupt tone, or maybe it was the use of her full name. Either way, the little cutie started skipping toward the back of the building, where the kitchen was located.

"Sorry about that," Tara said, turning her focus back to Kate.

She wasn't sorry one bit. Marley's running got Kate out of answering the question that had been weighing on her, because honestly, Kate had no idea what was going on with Gray.

"Is Sam working?"

Tara nodded. "He's always good to keep her on meeting nights, but he got a new job and he's worried about asking off."

Kate smiled. "Sounds like he's getting things back in order."

"He left me another note."

"He wants forgiveness," Kate stated. "It's obvious he loves you."

Her friend nodded and glanced back toward the kitchen area. "I know he does. That's never been the issue."

Kate couldn't imagine what her friend struggled with. Between losing her husband to addiction only to have him fight and claw his way back, and having a sweet, innocent child in the mix…there was so much to take in and Tara was handling things like a champ.

"So, back to Gray."

Kate resisted moaning. There was no way she was going to offer up everything that had happened between them. She and Gray were still friends and that's what they'd stay, because the other night was it. No more taking her clothes off for her best friend.

"He's just going through some personal things right now and needed to escape and get some advice."

There. That wasn't a total lie. She'd offered him advice, hadn't she? She'd told him to take his clothes off.

"And you gave him advice?" Tara asked, her raised brows almost mocking.

"Well, I was trying to until he tossed my planner into the fire."

Something she was still pissed about, but seemed to have forgotten about the second he'd touched her and made her toes curl all over again. Damn that man for making her want things she couldn't have—and for destroying her beloved planner.

And in answer to her question from days ago, yes. Yes, the sex was just as fabulous as she'd remembered. Maybe more so since they'd both gotten out of their clothes this time. Gray had been rather thorough and her body continued to tingle at just the mere thought of how gloriously his hands had roamed over her as if memorizing every aspect.

"The fire?" Tara gasped, throwing a hand to her chest. "Tell me he didn't burn the cherished planner."

"Very funny." Kate playfully smacked Tara's shoulder. "He said I needed to relax."

Tara laughed. No, she doubled over laughing, which had Marley running from the kitchen with some blond baby doll tucked beneath her arm.

"What's so funny?" Marley asked, her wide eyes bouncing between her mother and Kate.

"Oh, just something Kate said, honey." Tara swiped beneath her eyes and attempted to control her laughter. "So he told you to relax, which I'm sure you immediately did. And then he watched your planner turn to ash?"

Kate crossed her arms. "Pretty much."

"And he's still breathing?"

"Barely," Kate replied. "He owes me a new planner and don't think I'm not going to pick out the most expensive, thickest one I can find. It will have quotes on every page and a gold-embossed font, and I may just have him spring for the twenty-four-month one instead of the twelve."

Uninterested in the grown-ups' conversation, Marley started skipping around the room with her baby in the air.

"Oh, hitting him in his wallet." Tara feigned a shudder. "That will teach him never to mess with your schedules."

Kate dropped her arms to her sides and rolled her shoulders. "I don't know why the closest people in my life mock my work," she joked. "I mean, I make a killer living off organizing lives. I could help with yours if you'd let me."

Tara held up her hands. "I already let you into my closet. I'm still afraid to mess up those white shirts hanging next to the gray for fear you've set some alarm in there and you'll know if I get them out of order."

Kate laughed as she went to the food table on the back wall. "I'm not that bad," she called over her shoulder. "Besides, your closet was a disaster."

After Sam had left, Tara had needed something to occupy her time, and she'd had Kate and Lucy come over for a girls' night. One thing turned into another and the next thing Kate knew, she was knee-deep in a three-day project to revamp her friend's closet.

"I'm still upset you tossed my favorite sweatshirt," Tara griped, coming to lean against the wall by the table.

Kate rolled her eyes as she straightened up the plastic cups next to the lemonade and sweet tea. "That sweatshirt needed a proper burial and I just helped things along."

"It was a classic."

"No, it was from the junior high volleyball camp we went to and it was hideous."

"Still fit," Tara muttered.

Kate patted her friend's arm. "And that's why I threw it away and secretly hate you. You have never gained an ounce of fat other than when you were pregnant."

Tara quirked a brow. "High metabolism and good gene pool?"

"Still, I can hate you." Kate stepped back and glanced around. "I think we're good to go."

The meeting was due to start in fifteen minutes, which meant people should be rolling in anytime. They always had their regulars, accounting for about eight people. Randomly others would filter in. Some stayed only a few sessions. Some they never saw again.

Ironically, this uplifting support group was how Lucy and Noah met. They would've eventually met at work since he was an officer and Lucy had been a dispatcher. But, as fate would have it, Noah had slipped into the back of the meeting one day and Lucy had made a beeline for him when he tried to sneak out. Noah had lost his wife before coming to Stonerock and Lucy had lost her husband in the war a few years ago. If nothing else came from Helping Hands, at least Lucy and Noah had found true love and a second chance at happiness.

Kate wished that Tara and Sam could do the same, but things weren't looking good. Marley skipped back into the room and ran up to her mom. Tara picked her daughter up and squeezed her tight.

Something flipped in Kate's chest. She wanted a family, a husband to share her life with. But she'd been too busy with her career, a failed engagement and the launch of Helping Hands to make it happen.

An image of Gray flashed through her mind.

No. That was not the direction she needed to take her thoughts. Gray wasn't the marrying type. His father had pressured him over the past few years to settle down, but obviously that wasn't something Gray wanted.

And she needed to remember that he was her everything. She couldn't allow herself to hope for more with him. No, when she married and settled down it wouldn't be with a hunky bar owner with a naughty side and a sleeve of tattoos.

Chapter Ten

Gray finished pulling the wood chairs off the table-tops. He still needed to complete the invoice for next week's beer order and return a call to a new vendor before they opened in two hours.

Owning a bar wasn't just mixing drinks and writing paychecks. There was so much more that went into it, but he'd done it so long—hell, he'd grown up here—he pretty much did everything on autopilot.

Is that how he wanted to spend the rest of his life? Doing the same thing day in and day out? How could a thirty-one-year-old man not have a clue what he wanted to do with his life?

The tempting business proposal from the random

stranger still weighed heavily on him and kept him awake at night.

Granted, the looming deadline wasn't the only thing keeping him awake. A raven-haired vixen posing as his best friend had him questioning everything he'd ever thought to be a truth.

Gray set the last chair on the floor and turned to head toward his office. The old black-and-white picture hanging behind the bar stopped him. He'd seen that picture countless times, passed it constantly, but the image of his grandfather standing in his army uniform outside the bar on the day he bought it seemed to hit home this time.

The back door opened and slammed shut. Only a handful of people used the back door. A sliver of hope hit him as he stared at the doorway to the hall, thinking he'd see Kate step through.

But when his father rounded the corner, Gray smiled, hating how disappointment over not seeing Kate had been his first reaction.

She'd retreated again after their trip. Her pattern shouldn't surprise him, but it did. Whatever she was afraid of, he could battle it. Seriously. Did she not think all of this was freaking him out a little, as well? But there was no way in hell he was just going to ignore this pull toward her. He knew without a doubt that she was being pulled just as fiercely.

"Want a beer?" Gray asked as he circled the bar.

Reece Gallagher went to the opposite side of the

bar and took a seat on one of the stools. "You know what I like."

Gray smiled as he reached for a frosted mug and flipped the tap of his father's favorite brew. He tipped the mug enough to keep the head of the beer just right. Another thing he simply did without thinking.

He'd been meaning to call his dad, but now that he was here, there was no better time to discuss the future of Gallagher's.

Gray set the beer in front of his dad, the frothy top spilling over. He pulled a rag from below the counter and swiped up the moisture.

"Had a visitor the other day," he told his dad.

"Oh, yeah?" Reece took a hearty drink of his beer before setting the mug back on the bar. "Something tells me there's more to the story."

"He offered me more money than I'd know what to do with if I sell him this bar."

His father's dark eyes instantly met his. "Sell Gallagher's? I hope you told him where he could stick his money. Who the hell was this guy?"

Gray swallowed, resting his palms on the smooth bar top. "Businessman from Knoxville. He left me his card and told me I had a month to think about it."

His dad's silver brows drew in as he shifted on his stool and seemed as if he was about ready to come over the bar. "What's there to think about, son?"

Gray figured his father would have this reaction. The bar had been in their family for years and selling had never been an option. Hell, Gray had never thought about selling the place until he'd been presented with the option.

He had to be honest with his dad. There was no reason to gloss this over and pretend everything was fine and he wasn't contemplating the change.

"Maybe I'm not meant to run this bar."

Silence settled between them as the words hung in the air. Gray didn't back down. If his father and the military taught him one thing, it was to never back down from what you believed in.

"You're actually considering this."

Gray nodded even though his father hadn't actually asked. "Something is missing in my life," he said.

His father's response was another pull of his beer. Gray figured he should just lay it all out there. His dad might not like the direction of Gray's thoughts, but he did appreciate and expect honesty.

"I'm thankful for this, all of it. I know you and Grandpa worked hard." He pulled in a deep breath. "I'm just not sure this is what I was meant to do in life."

Reece Gallagher tapped the side of his mug. Whatever was rolling around in his mind, Gray knew his father was formulating a plan to convince him to stay.

"How much were you offered?" his dad finally asked.

Gray threw out the number which resulted in a long, slow whistle from his father.

"That's a hell of a number," he agreed. "And you think this money will ultimately buy you what you want in life? Which is what, exactly?"

Gray shrugged. "I have no clue. There's a void, though. I haven't been able to put my finger on it."

"A wife? Kids?" his dad suggested. "Settling down is a logical step."

Gray pushed off the bar. He was going to need a beer of his own if this was the path the conversation was going to head down.

"I'm not looking for a wife, let alone children."

He pulled a bottle from the cooler behind the bar. Quickly he popped the top and tossed it into the trash.

"I know that's what worked for you and Grandpa," he went on, resting his bottle on the bar. "But I'm not you or him. I'm my own person, and is it so bad that I'm not sure what I want?"

"No," his father agreed. "But I also don't want you making decisions based on money alone, and I certainly don't want you letting all of this go only to find that what you were looking for was here all along."

What the hell did that mean? Stonerock was a great town, but it wasn't necessarily where he wanted to spend his future.

"The decision is ultimately up to you," he dad went on. "You have to understand that I'm not giving you my blessing if you choose to sell. What does he want to do with the bar, anyway?"

Gray took a drink of his beer, then leaned onto his

elbows. "He and his business partner want to make Stonerock like a mini-Nashville. I guess they're looking to buy more businesses in the area and revamp them to draw more tourists."

Reece wrinkled his nose. "That's absurd. Stonerock is just fine the way it is."

Gray finished his beer and tossed his bottle. Then he grabbed his dad's empty mug and set it in the sink below the bar.

"I won't contact him without talking to you first," Gray assured his dad. "I don't want you to think that your opinion doesn't matter or that I'm only looking at dollar signs."

His dad came to his feet and tapped his fingertips on the bar. "I know money can sound good, especially that much, but family is everything, Gray. At the end of the day you only have a few friends and your family that you can count on. Money is just paper."

Why did his dad have to make him feel guilty? Why did he have to add more doubts in his head when he was so close to making a decision?

Reece headed for the back hallway.

"Wait a second," Gray called out. "What did you stop by for to begin with?"

Tossing a glance over his shoulder, his father shook his head. "It's not important."

His footsteps echoed down the hall until they disappeared behind the closing door. Gray stared out at the empty bar, knowing that in just over an hour it would be bustling. That was definitely the main perk to this place. He'd never had to worry about patrons or making money. Gallagher's was the only bar in town and it was a nice place to hang. He was proud of that accomplishment, of the tradition he carried on here.

Emotions filled his throat and squeezed his chest. No matter the decision he made, he'd always wonder if he'd made the right one. If he left, he'd look back and wonder if his father thought him a disappointment. If he stayed, he'd always be looking for something to fill the void. Could he achieve what his heart desired?

Gray wasn't going to be making any decisions tonight. Between the bar and Kate, he wasn't sure how the hell he was supposed to maintain his sanity.

"I have to go," Kate said around a yawn. "I have to meet a client early in the morning to discuss reorganizing her basement for a play-work area."

Lucy put a hand on Kate's arm. "Don't go. I haven't even gotten to the part about the hammock."

Tara busted out laughing and Kate groaned. "Seriously, Lucy. Keep the honeymoon stories to yourself. You came back just as pale as when you left so I know what you were doing."

Lucy shrugged. "But the hammock story is hilarious. Can you even imagine how difficult—"

Kate held up her hands. "I'm getting the visual."

Lucy had been back from her honeymoon only a

day, but they'd been in need of some long overdue girl time. The wedding planning and showers and anticipation had filled their schedules over the past several months.

Tara had invited them over to her house and opened a bottle of wine, and they'd proceeded to just decompress and gossip. Sweet Marley had gone to bed an hour ago, leaving the women to some much-needed adult conversation that wasn't centered around dresses, registries and invitations.

Kate didn't partake in the wine, though. The last time she drank, the *only* time she'd drunk, had changed her entire life, and she was still reeling from the results. Maybe this would just her new normal and she'd have to get used to these unfamiliar emotions that seemed to have taken up residence in her heart.

"Will you hang a bit longer if I promise to hold off on describing the hammock incident?" Lucy asked as she refilled her own wineglass.

Kate shook her head. "I've seriously got so much to do."

"Did you tell Lucy about the planner and the campfire?"

Kate shot a glare at Tara, who sat across on the opposite sofa. The smirk on her friend's face was not funny. Not funny at all.

"A fire and your planner?" Lucy gasped. "I have to hear this. I swear, tell me this and I won't bring up the hammock again."

Kate realized she wasn't going anywhere anytime soon. She sank back into her corner of the couch and replayed her camping story—minus the sex and lustful glances—to her best friends.

"Wait." Lucy held up her hands. "You went camping? That's almost as shocking as the fact Gray burned your planner."

"He forced my hand on the camping thing," she stated. "Well, he didn't force me. Camping was on my life list and he just showed up unannounced—"

"Hold up," Lucy said, incredulous. "What's this life list? Good grief. A girl gets married, has awkward sex in a hammock and misses so much that has happened. Start at the beginning."

"No hammock talk," Kate reminded her.

Lucy shrugged. "Minor slip."

Tara refilled her glass, then propped her bare feet on the couch. "Yes. The beginning of this camping adventure, please."

Kate rolled her eyes. "You already know everything."

"Still makes for a good bedtime story." Tara shrugged. "Besides, I think something is brewing between you and Gray."

"Nothing is brewing. You know we drive each other insane on a good day."

Kate was quick to Δdefend herself, but she and Gray were friends. No, really. No more sex. Just the one time...times two.

"I made a list," Kate started. "I guess you could

call it a bucket list. With turning thirty, I started getting a little anxiety about inching closer to the age my mom was when she died. I figured I better start doing some of the things I really want to try. You just never know how much time you have left."

"Camping made your list?" Lucy asked. "I'm intrigued by what else you've put on there."

Kate slipped off her sandals and pulled her feet back under her. She didn't want to get into the full details of her wishes because…well, she felt that was something she and Gray shared. As strange as that sounded, she'd originally wanted to keep it all to herself, but since he knew, Kate wanted to keep things just between them.

The secrets between her and Gray were mounting up.

"I tried to think of things I'd never done, so, yeah. Camping ranked high," Kate explained. "Once we got settled in and took a hike, I could tell something was bothering Gray. He finally opened up and dropped a bomb on me that someone wants to buy his bar."

"What?" Lucy and Tara both asked.

Kate met her friends' wide eyes and dropped jaws with a nod. "He said some guy came in and offered him an insane amount of money to purchase Gallagher's. Said something about buying properties around the town to update them and make them more city-like."

"Our town doesn't need updating," Lucy stated.

"The reason people live here is because they like the small-town atmosphere. If they wanted a city feel, they'd move there. I wonder if Drake is aware of this. Surely these guys had the decency to talk to our mayor."

Kate shrugged. "Just telling you what I know."

Tara set her wineglass on the coffee table and shifted to face Kate. "Is Gray seriously considering giving up the bar?"

"He hasn't turned the offer down."

Which honestly surprised her. He'd explained the whole thing about feeling something missing in his life, but at the same time, this was his family's legacy. A piece of history that had just been handed to him. Did he even realize how lucky he was? She'd give anything to have a piece of her parents handed down to her, some way to still hold on to them.

Which was why tracing her family genealogy had made her list.

"Wow." Lucy took another sip of her wine. "When will he decide what he's doing?"

"The guy gave him a deadline. Next week sometime." Kate stretched her legs out and felt around for her shoes. She really did need to get going. Not just because of the work thing. She didn't want to get back into the camping conversation and Tara's speculation that something was up. "He's going to talk to his dad and feel him out, though I imagine that won't go very well."

No doubt he'd let her know exactly how that talk

went. Then he'd probably call her out on dodging him since they'd returned from their trip. She hadn't been dodging him, exactly. She'd been working and she assumed he had, as well.

Besides, she just needed a break after those two days together. The man consumed her every thought lately and when they were together he was...well, even more irresistible and in her face.

What did all of this mean? How could she let her Gray go from being her best friend to lover, then try to put him back in the best friend zone? It shouldn't be that difficult to keep him locked away in that particular section of her heart. Isn't that what she did for a living? Put everything in a neat and tidy order?

So why the hell couldn't she do that with her personal life?

Kate finally said her goodbyes to her best girlfriends and agreed to meet them at Ladies' Night on Wednesday. She hadn't been for a while and was overdue—something Gray had noticed and called her out on. And, well, she could use a night of dancing and just having a good time.

That would prove to Gray that she wasn't dodging him...right?

Kate headed home, her mind working through all she needed to get done over the next couple of days. She was still in need of a good personal planner. She had looked at a few, but hadn't made a commitment yet. Whatever she chose, Gray would feel it in his wallet. That would teach him not to mess with her things anymore.

As she pulled into her drive, she noticed a sporty black car parked on the street directly in front of her house. Her eyes darted to the porch, where a man in a suit sat on one of her white rockers.

Kate barely took her eyes off him as she put the car in Park and killed the engine. Of all people to make an unexpected visit, her cheating, lying ex was the last man she ever expected to see again.

Chapter Eleven

Gripping her purse, Kate headed up her stone walk-way. "What are you doing here, Chris?"

Always clean-cut and polished, Chris Percell came to his feet and shoved his hands in his pockets.

Who wore a suit at this time of night? And in this humidity? Not that his wardrobe was a concern of hers. No, the main issues here were that he stood on her porch without an invitation and she hadn't heard a word from him in years. Granted, once he'd left, she hadn't wanted to hear a word from the cheating bastard.

Kate didn't mount the steps. He had about three seconds to state his business and then she was going in her house and locking the door. She hadn't been lying when she told her friends she was tired and still had some work to do, so this unexpected visitor was not putting her in the best of moods.

"You look good, Kate."

Chris started down the steps toward her. Now she did dodge him and go on up to her porch. When she turned, he stood on the bottom step, smiling up at her.

"It's been a long time," he stated.

"Not long enough. What do you want?"

With a shrug, he crossed his arms and shifted his stance. "I was hoping we could talk."

"Most people just text." She'd deleted him from her phone long ago, but still. Showing up unannounced was flat-out rude. Not that he had many morals or even common decency.

"I wasn't sure if you'd respond."

"I wouldn't," she told him.

He propped one foot on the next step and smoothed a hand over his perfectly parted hair. "After all these years, you're still angry?"

She didn't know whether to laugh at his stupidity or throw her purse at him and pray she hit him in the head hard enough to knock some damn sense into him.

No purse should be treated that way, so she adjusted the strap on her shoulder and held it tight.

"Angry?" she asked with a slight laugh. "I'd have to feel something to actually be angry with you."

"Kate." Chris lowered his tone as if to appeal to

her good side. She no longer had one where he was concerned. "Could I come in for a bit just to talk?"

"No. And actually, it's a bit creepy that you're on my porch waiting on me to get home."

"I haven't been here long," he assured her. "Maybe I should come back tomorrow. Can I take you for coffee?"

Kate stared down at the clean-cut man who probably still got bimonthly manicures. She couldn't help but wonder what in the hell she'd ever seen in him to begin with. Coffee with a man wearing a suit? She'd prefer champagne served up by a sexy tattooed-up bar owner.

Oh, no.

No, no, no.

Now was not the time to discover that her feelings were sliding into more than just friendship with Gray. Chris continued to stare at her, waiting for her answer, but she was having a minor mental breakdown.

"I'm busy tomorrow," she finally replied. "Good night, Chris."

Without waiting for him to respond, Kate pulled her key from her purse and quickly let herself into the house. She flicked the dead bolt back into place and smacked the porch lights off.

What on earth had flashed through her mind when Chris mentioned taking her for coffee? She loved coffee and Stonerock had the best little coffee house on the edge of town. Not that she would even entertain the thought of having coffee with that slime bag.

But Gray?

Everything in her thought process lately circled back to that man. Her planner, her bucket list, her drinks, her most satisfying sexual experiences.

Kate groaned as she made her way toward her bedroom. What she needed to do was spend more time with Tara and Lucy. So much one-on-one with Gray had obviously clouded her judgment and left her confused and mixing amazing sex with feelings that shouldn't be developing.

But Tara was busy with her own life and Lucy was still in that newlywed bliss phase. Ladies' Night would definitely be her best bet to get back to where she needed to be mentally. Letting lose, being carefree, and not worrying about anything would surely cleanse her mind of all lustful thoughts of her best friend.

Sex really did cloud the mind. And great sex… well, maybe she just needed sleep. If she weren't so exhausted, perhaps Gray wouldn't have filled her mind the second Chris started talking about taking her out.

Gray hadn't even taken her out. They weren't in any way dating. They were going on about their way like always—just adding in a few toe-curling orgasms along the way.

Kate pushed aside all thoughts of Chris showing up, Gray and his ability to make her want more than she should and the fact he may be selling his bar and leaving. She couldn't get wrapped up in lives and circumstances she had no control over. As much as she thrived on micromanaging, realistically, she had to let go.

After pulling on her favorite sleep shirt, Kate slid beneath her sheets and adjusted her pillows against the upholstered headboard. She unplugged her iPad from the nightstand and pulled up her schedule for the following day. Yes, her schedule was in both paper and e-format.

After glancing over her schedule, she went to her personal blog. So many blogs failed, but Kate prided herself on being a marketing genius. She honed in on her niche market, taking full advantage of social media platforms that drove her clients to her site, thus turning them into paying customers.

Not many people could do their dream job and work from home. Kate knew how blessed and lucky she was to have such a fabulous life.

Though seeing Lucy so happy with love and Tara with sweet Marley made Kate wonder if she was missing out.

Tara clicked on the tab to bring up her bucket list. At the bottom she added the word "family" in bold font. Ultimately that would be her main goal once she'd achieved the others. She wasn't going to rush it, she wanted to wait on the right man to come along. She was definitely ready to take that step toward a broader future.

Stifling a yawn, Kate placed her device back on her nightstand and clicked the light off. As she fluffed her pillows and rolled over, she hoped she would fall asleep right away and not dream of the sexy bar owner who had occupied her thoughts every night.

But she found herself smiling. She couldn't help herself. There was no greater man in her life, and even though things were a little unbalanced right now, she fully intended on keeping him at an arm's length. For real this time.

"Thanks, darlin', but I'm busy tonight."

Ladies' Night always brought in the flirtatious women with short skirts and plunging necklines. Being single didn't hurt business, either, but he'd never picked up a woman in his bar. That wasn't good business and certainly not a reputation he wanted hovering over his establishment.

Gray extracted himself from the clutches of the blonde at the table in the corner. That's what he got for coming out from behind his post. His staff had been busy so he'd taken the table their drinks.

Back behind the safety of the bar, Gray tapped on the computer and started filling more drink orders. Jacob ran the finger foods from the kitchen. The menu remained small and simple but enough to keep people thirsty, because the drinks were by far the moneymaker.

The DJ switched the song to one that seriously

made Gray's teeth itch. "It's Raining Men" blared through the hidden surround sound speakers. Considering the crowd and the cheers and squeals, Gray was definitely in the minority here.

One night. He could live through terrible music for one night a week. Wednesday nights brought in the most revenue. Women from all walks of life came out in droves. Some were celebrating bachelorette parties. Some were stay-at-home moms who needed a break. Sometimes a group of employees got together to decompress after work. Whatever their situation was, Gray—and his bottom line—was thrilled he'd decided to add this night when he'd taken over.

As he placed three margaritas on the bar for one of his staff to take to table eleven, he glanced at the front door when it opened.

Finally.

Gray didn't even care that his heart skipped a little at the sight of Kate. He was done ignoring the way he felt when she was near. He just…damn it, he wanted her to stop avoiding him. He needed her stability, the security she brought to their friendship.

He hadn't spoken with her since he'd talked to his dad. Just the thought of that conversation had him questioning what to do. Clearly his father would be heartbroken over losing Gallagher's, but Gray just kept thinking back to how free he would be if he was able to explore his own interests.

His eyes drifted back to Kate. She'd settled in a booth with Tara and Lucy. When her gaze landed on him, she might as well have touched him with her bare hands. Immediate heat spread through him, and the second she flashed that radiant smile, Gray nearly toppled the glass he'd been holding.

After returning her smile, he returned his focus to the orders. No woman had ever made him falter on the job before. Then again, no woman was Kate McCoy.

As he worked on filling orders, he randomly glanced her way. He knew exactly which drinks were going to that table. Those three were so predictable. Tara always wanted a cosmo, Lucy stuck with a light beer and Kate went with soda.

It wasn't long before another song blared through the speakers that had Gray cringing, but the dance floor instantly filled with women. Kate and her friends were right in the midst of the action.

That little dress she wore had his gut tightening. The loose hem slid all over her thighs as she wiggled that sweet body on the dance floor. She'd piled her hair up on top of her head, but the longer she danced, the more stray strands fell around her face, her neck.

Get a grip.

"Hey, baby. You ever take time for a dance?"

Gray flashed a smile to the redhead leaning over the bar at just the right angle to give him a complete visual of her cleavage and bra of choice.

"Who would make all these drinks if I went dancing?" he yelled over the music.

She reached across the bar and ran her fingertip down his chest. "I think if you got on that dance floor, we'd all forget about our drinks. At least for a little while."

Someone slammed a glass next to him, jerking Gray's attention from the flirtatious patron.

He turned just in time to see Kate walking away, her empty glass on the bar.

"Looks like you made someone's drink wrong," the redhead stated, lowering her lids. "You can make me anything you want."

Gray stepped back, causing her hand to fall from his chest. "Where are you and your friends sitting?" he asked. "I'll send over a pitcher of margaritas."

Her smile widened as she gestured to their table. Apparently the idea of free booze was more appealing than him...which was perfectly fine. Right now, he was more intrigued with the way Kate had acted. She'd slammed that glass pretty close to his arm on purpose and then walked away without a word.

Jealous?

Gray couldn't help but smile as he got the pitcher ready. If Kate was jealous, then maybe she was ready to see where this new level of friendship would take them. Perhaps she'd missed him in the days they'd been apart and she'd thought more about their time in the mountains.

Maybe she'd finally realized how good they were together and that it was silly to put restrictions on their intimacy. He spotted her back out on the dance floor talking to Lucy. Lucy nodded in response to whatever she said and Kate walked away.

Gray picked up empty glasses and wiped off the bar where a few ladies had just sat, all the while keeping his gaze on Kate. She went back to the booth and grabbed her purse.

Well, hell. She was pissed and leaving? All because some woman flirted with him?

If she was that upset, then she was definitely jealous. Gray had every intention of playing right into that little nugget of information.

Gray lost track of Kate, but he never saw the front door open, which meant she had to be inside somewhere. He glanced at his watch and realized they still had another two business hours to go. He couldn't get to Kate for a while, but she better be ready for him, because he wasn't backing down from this fight. He was damn well going to call her out on her jealousy and forbid her to make any excuses for why they shouldn't be together.

Gray couldn't wait to get her alone again.

Chapter Twelve

This was the most ridiculous thing she'd ever done in her entire life. But hey, at least she could mark spontaneity off her life list.

Kate stared at the clock on Gray's nightstand. The bar had closed thirty minutes ago. She knew he had cleanup down to a science and he should be wrapping things up any minute.

She thought coming up here to cool off would help. Seeing that trampy redhead raking her false nail down Gray's chest had set something off inside Kate she didn't want to label…because it smacked her right in the face with jealousy.

Why was she jealous? Kate knew full well that women found Gray sexy and did nearly anything to get his attention. But things were different now. Yes, they were just friends, but everything had changed.

What would he say when he came up here and found her in his bed? Would he tell her they'd agreed to call it quits after the camping? Would he climb in bed and give her another night to remember?

Kate came to her feet and grabbed the dress she'd flung at the bottom of the bed. This was a mistake. She looked like an utter fool. No, a desperate fool, and she needed to get the hell out of here before Gray came in.

The front door to his apartment clicked shut, followed by the dead bolt. Too late to run.

She clutched the dress to her chest, feeling even more ridiculous now. Why had she put that damn "be more spontaneous" idea on her list? And why had she let that busty tramp bring out the green-eyed monster?

Heavy footsteps sounded down the hall seconds before Gray filled the doorway. His dark eyes widened as they raked over her. There was no way she could move. Just that simple, visual lick he gave her had her rooted in place.

His eyes snapped back up to hers. "Put the dress down."

Kate dropped it at her feet before thinking twice. That low command gave her little choice but to obey. Warmth spread through her. There was no denying exactly why she'd come up here, just as there was no denying that heated look in his eyes.

"You came up here a while ago." He leaned one broad shoulder against the door frame and continued to rake his eyes across her body. "What have you been doing?"

"Second-guessing myself," she murmured.

Gray's lips twitched. "Is that so? I don't recall sneaking into a man's bedroom on your life list."

"I was trying to check off spontaneity."

"Is that so?"

Kate crossed her arms over her chest. "I'm feeling a little silly standing here like this. Are you just going to stay over there and stare at me?"

"Maybe I'm looking at you because you deserve to be valued."

Oh, no. He couldn't say things like that to her. Statements so bold only pushed them deeper into this …whatever the technical term was. *Friends* seemed too tame of a label considering she stood in his bedroom wearing only her underwear.

"Chris showed up at my house."

Why did she blurt that out? She prided herself on planning everything, even her words. But somehow hearing him mention her being valued made her think of the jerk who thought the opposite.

Gray stood straight up and took a step toward her. "What the hell did he want?"

Kate laughed. "To talk. He invited me to coffee."

The muscle in his jaw clenched. "Did you go?" he all but growled.

"No. I demanded he leave and I haven't heard from him since."

Gray's eyes narrowed. "He's trying to get you back."

"After all this time and after what he did? He's a fool."

"Tell me if he comes back."

Kate stared up into those dark eyes. "You're jealous."

Gray slid his palms up her bare arms, over her shoulders, and hooked his thumbs in her bra straps. "Like you were jealous downstairs?"

Tipping her chin up, she met his mocking stare. "I was not jealous."

Gray's fingertips left the straps and slid over the swell of her breasts. Tingles raced through her body.

"You cracked the glass you slammed down." One finger slid between her breasts and back up. "Seemed like you were upset about something."

"Consider the glass payment for the panties you ripped off me."

If possible, his eyes darkened at the mention of her underwear. In one swift move, he flicked the front closure of her bra and had it off. When he gripped the edge of her panties and met her eyes, she smiled.

"You going for two?" she asked, quirking a brow.

He gave a yank, and the sound of ripping material answered her question. Suddenly she stood before him completely naked and in the bright light of his bedroom while he was completely clothed.

"This is hardly fair," she informed him.

"You snuck up to my apartment and came to my bed," he reminded her. "You're playing by my rules now, Kate."

How did the man continually get sexier? Seriously. Looks were one thing, but the way he treated her, spoke to her...how would she feel when this came to an end?

"I wasn't going to do this again," she muttered, mostly to herself.

"And I wasn't going to let you run, either." He banded an arm around her waist and jerked her body against his. "Why is there a time limit on what we're doing? We both like it. Neither one of us is dating anyone. It makes sense."

Kate closed her eyes. "Because we could lose ourselves and forget who we really are."

He leaned down and nipped her lips. "Maybe we're only just discovering who we really are."

Those words barely registered before he lifted her off her feet and carried her to his bed. He eased her down onto the plain gray sheets that were still rumpled from when he'd gotten out of them. She'd never been in his bedroom. They'd been friends forever, but crossing this threshold was taking things to a whole new territory.

Gray eased back, leaving her lying spread out. She watched as he reached behind his neck and jerked the black tee up and over his head. After he tossed it into the corner, he started unfastening his jeans, all while keeping those heavy-lidded eyes on her.

"You look good here, Kate."

She closed her eyes. Maybe if she didn't look at him when he said such meaningful words, they wouldn't penetrate her soul. But he kept saying little things. No, not little, not in the terms of the impact they had.

Instead of responding, because she truly had no words, she lifted her knees to make room for him. Once he'd gotten protection from his nightstand, she reached out, taking him in her arms. His weight pressed her further into the bed. She wasn't sure how she looked here, but she knew she liked it. Being wrapped up in Gray and knowing they shared something no one else knew about…there was a thrill to what they were doing.

A thrill she wasn't sure she ever wanted to see end.

But was he on the same page? If she threw out that she was having stronger feelings, what would he say? Would he tell her they were done with sex? Would he tell her they could be friends and have sex only as long as they were both single? Because suddenly, she wondered if there could be more.

"Hey."

Kate focused on the man who flanked her head with his forearms and smoothed her hair away from her face.

"Stay with me," he murmured.

Curling her fingers around his bare shoulders, Kate smiled. "I wouldn't be anywhere else."

Gray joined their bodies and Kate locked her ankles behind his back. She wanted to stay just like this, to forget the outside world, to ignore any warning that went off in her head about what could go wrong. Because right now, everything in her world was absolutely perfect.

Gray's lips slid over her skin, along her jawline, down her neck, along her chest. Kate arched into him, needing more and silently begging him to give it to her. Gray murmured something into her ear and she couldn't make it out. He'd done that before and she wondered what he was saying, but that was something she'd ask later. She'd rather enjoy the euphoria and sweet bliss of being in his arms…in his bed.

In a move that shocked her, Gray held on to her and flipped them until he was on his back and she straddled him. The way he looked up at her…

A girl could get used to a man looking at her like she was the only good thing in his world.

Gray gripped her hips and Kate's body instantly responded to his strength. His fingers bit into her as she flattened her palms on his chest and let the moment completely consume her.

Before Kate's body ceased trembling, Gray's stilled beneath her. His lips thinned. His head tipped back. His eyes shut. But his grip on her never lightened. She remained where she was, watching the play of emotions across his face.

Slowly he relaxed beneath her. As he slid his hands up over the dip in her waist and urged her down, Kate smiled. She fell against his chest and closed her eyes.

"What now?" she asked, unable to stop herself.

His chest vibrated with the soft rumble of laughter. "We don't need to plan the next move. Relax."

When she started to set up, he flattened his hand on her back. "You can stay just like this a few more minutes."

She could, but she had questions. So many questions and only he could answer them. Well, they could figure them out together, but what was going to happen when she told him she might want more? He'd never even acted like he wanted a relationship. They had sex. They had never even been on a real date.

Kate couldn't take it anymore. She sat up and shifted off him. With her back to Gray, she sat on the edge of the bed and leaned down to pick up her discarded dress.

"We really need to talk."

Silence filled the air, as she'd expected it would once she uttered those five words that would put any man's hackles up.

Kate threw a glance over her shoulder. Gray lay there naked as you please, with his arms folded behind his head. His eyes held hers, but he still said nothing even when she raised a brow, silently begging him to speak.

"Why are you making this difficult?" she asked.

She came to her feet and threw her dress on, sans all undergarments. When she spun around toward the bed and crossed her arms over her chest, Gray merely smiled. Still naked, still fully in charge of this situation, because he just watched her. The man could be utterly infuriating.

"What are we doing?" she muttered, shaking her head. "Seriously? Are we going to keep doing this? Is there more?"

Her heart beat so fast, she wondered if he could see the pulse in her neck. Again without a word, Gray came to his feet and strutted from the room.

She threw her arms out. "Well, that went well," she whispered to the empty room.

Moments later, he came back in, still not the least bit concerned with his state of undress. He carried two wine stems between his fingers and in the other hand he had a champagne bottle.

"This is another bottle of what you had the other night." He set everything on the nightstand and poured her a glass. "You need another drink if we're going to get into this discussion."

"Drinking isn't the answer," she retorted.

He picked up the glass and handed it to her. "I never said it was. But I brought this bottle up earlier and got sidetracked when I found you naked in my room."

She took the glass but didn't take a sip yet. "Why

did you bring it to begin with? I didn't take you for a champagne drinker."

"I'm not, but I knew you were up here so I brought it for you."

Kate jerked. "How did you know I came up here? I was discreet."

Gray laughed as he filled his own glass and then downed it in one gulp. He set the glass back on the nightstand and turned toward her.

"I'm a pretty smart guy, Kate." He pointed toward her glass. "You're going to want to start on that."

She took a small drink, relishing the bubbles that burst in her mouth. Champagne really wasn't bad at all.

"You were jealous," he started, holding up his hand when she opened her mouth to argue. "You were, so be quiet for a minute."

Kate took another drink and sank onto the edge of the bed. "Could you at least put something on? It's hard to concentrate with all that hanging out."

Gray laughed and turned toward his dresser, where a stack of clean laundry lay neatly folded. He grabbed a pair of black boxer briefs and tugged them on.

"Better?"

Actually, no. The briefs hugged his narrow hips, drawing her attention to that perfect V of muscles leading south. Mercy, how had she missed all of his flawless features in the past?

She took another drink.

"So you were jealous," he went on.

"Move to something else," she growled.

Gray laughed, propping his hands on those hips she tried so hard to stop staring at. "Fine. Then I saw you grab your purse and disappear, only the front door didn't open and I couldn't get a clear view of the back hall. Nobody goes that way, but I had a feeling my Kate had done just that."

She narrowed her eyes. "Jacob told you."

"He didn't have to say anything."

Kate polished off her champagne and set her empty glass next to his. When she glanced back up at him, she shivered at the look in his eyes.

"You didn't like that woman flirting with me. That was a good piece of information to have."

Kate hated that she'd let her emotions get the better of her. "Fine. I was jealous."

Gray knelt down in front of her and clasped her hands in his. "I didn't think you'd admit it."

"Why hide it? We may just be having sex, but that doesn't mean I want to see some woman pawing you."

Kate stared down at their joined hands and willed herself to be strong and just say what she wanted to say. But before she could tell him her thoughts, he placed one hand beneath her chin and tipped her face to meet his.

Gray leaned forward and nipped at her lips before murmuring, "Marry me."

Chapter Thirteen

Why wasn't she saying anything?

Gray waited.

"Kate?"

She blinked. "Marry you? But we've never discussed anything like that."

When she came to her feet, her abrupt movement had him standing as well. Then she began to pace his room. She couldn't go far in the small space, but since he had only a bed and dresser, she didn't have much to maneuver around.

"Marry you," she repeated beneath her breath as she turned on her heel to walk in the other direction.

"Why not?" he asked. "We get along, we're good

together in bed, and we just understand each other. That's more than most married couples have."

She stopped and stared at him as if he had grown another nose on the side of his head. "Why on earth do you want to marry me?"

"I talked to Dad about selling the bar." Now it was his turn to pace because the thought of everything closing in on him made him twitchy. "He's most definitely not on board and he seems to think I just need to settle down. Perhaps this way, I could sell it and you and I could use that money to start over somewhere. Or hell, build a house here. Whatever. We'd have freedom and that's all that matters."

He'd come to stand directly in front of her, but she continued to stare. No, glare would best describe what she was doing now. There was something he couldn't quite pinpoint in her eyes. Gone was the desire he'd seen moments ago.

"So, what, I'm just a means to pacify your dad so you can collect a check?" she asked. With a shake of her head, she let out a humorless laugh. "I was already going to marry one jerk who obviously didn't get me. It's quite clear you never understood me either if you think I'll marry you."

Anger simmered within him, but he didn't want to lash out.

"What the hell is wrong with marrying me?" he asked.

"I want to know your first thought when I asked why you wanted to marry me. Don't think about what I want to hear. Just tell me the first thing that comes into your head."

This was a trap. Somewhere in that statement she'd set a trap for him and he was about to fall headfirst into it.

"I think it makes sense," he answered honestly. "What's there to think about?"

She stared at him a bit longer and that's when he saw it. Hurt. That emotion he couldn't pin down before had been pain and it stared back at him plain as day. He'd seen that look before from patrons who wanted to drink their worries away. He'd seen it too often. But he was completely baffled by why the hell she stared at him with such anguish.

"What did I say?"

She chewed on her bottom lip for a moment before skirting around him and picking up her underwear and bra. He watched as she dressed fully and then sat on the edge of his bed to pull her sandals on.

"Where are you going?"

Without looking up, she adjusted her shoe and came to her feet. "Home. I've had enough of…whatever this is. We never should've slept together."

He crossed the room and took her shoulders, forcing her to face him. "What the hell are you talking about? Is this because I asked you to marry me?"

Her eyes swam with unshed tears and he wished like hell he knew why she was this upset.

"Do you love me, Gray?"

"What?" Her question stunned him. "Of course

I love you. I've loved you since the seventh grade. What kind of a question is that?"

She blinked, causing a tear to spill down her cheek. He swiped the pad of his thumb over her creamy skin. His heart ached at seeing her hurt, but hell if he knew how to fix this.

"It's a legitimate question, considering you proposed," she said, her voice soft, sad. "This isn't working for me anymore."

Kate shrugged from his arms and stepped back. She tilted her chin and squared her shoulders as if going into warrior mode before his eyes.

"You want freedom?" she asked. "Then go. Take that fat check, sell the bar and just go."

"What the hell are you so angry about?" he asked...well, more like yelled, because damn it, he could not figure her out.

"I never thought you'd use me or consider me plan B for your life." She swatted at another tear that streaked down her cheek. "You're only asking me to marry you to pacify your father. That man would do anything for you and he's all you have left. Do you know how lucky you are? Do you understand that if I had a parent in my life, I'd do anything to make them proud of me?"

Now he was pissed. Gray fisted his hands at his sides and towered over her as he took a step forward. "You think my father isn't proud of me? Of what I've done here? You know I'm sorry about your parents, but damn it, Kate, you can't always throw that in my face."

She recoiled as if he'd hit her. Gray muttered a string of curses beneath his breath as he raked a hand through his hair.

"That's not what I meant," he said.

She held up her hands. "You said exactly what you meant. We don't see eye to eye on things anymore. Just another reason why I need to go and this…all of it has to stop."

His heart clenched. "What do you mean, 'all of it'?"

"I knew we couldn't keep our friendship and sex separate," she cried. Tears streamed down her cheeks and she didn't even bother swiping them away. "Then you throw out an engagement like it's a simple fix to your problems. Did you ever think that maybe I'd want to marry someone who actually loves me? That I don't just want to settle?"

"I said I loved you," he practically shouted. "What more do you want?"

The brief smile that flashed amid the tears nearly gutted him. Pain radiated from her and if he knew what he'd done to crush her, he'd fix it.

"You don't mean it," she whispered. "Not in the way I need you to."

A rumble of thunder and a quick flash of lightning interrupted the tense moment. Within seconds, rain pelted the windows. Kate stared at him another second before she turned away and headed toward the door. Gray had a sinking feeling that if she walked out that door, she might never come back...not even as his friend.

"Don't go, Kate. Not like this."

She stilled, but didn't face him.

"We can work this out."

"I think we've said enough," she replied.

He took a step toward her, but didn't reach for her like he desperately wanted to. "At least let me drive you home. You're upset and it's starting to storm."

Those bright blue eyes shining with tears peered over her shoulder. "I'd rather take my chances with the storm outside than the one surrounding us."

And then she was gone.

Gray stared at the spot where she'd just stood, then he glanced to the empty glasses, the rumpled sheets.

What the hell had just happened here?

Well, there was the proposal that had taken them both by surprise. But in his defense, the moment the words were out of his mouth, he hadn't regretted them.

He did love her. They'd been friends forever, so what kind of question was that? And what did she mean by saying he didn't love her the way she needed him to? He'd always been there for her, hadn't he?

Gray turned from the bedroom. He couldn't stay in there, not when the sheets smelled like her, not when just the sight of that bed had him recalling how perfect she'd looked lying there.

He stalked down the hall and into the living room. The storm grew closer as the thunder and lightning hit simultaneously. The electricity flickered once, twice, then went out.

Perfect. Pitch black to match his mood.

Gray went to the window and looked down into the parking lot beside the bar. Kate's car still sat there.

Without thinking, he fumbled his way through the dark to throw on a pair of jeans, not bothering with shoes. He raced down the back steps and out the rear entrance.

Instantly he was soaked, but he didn't care. If Kate was still here, she was sitting in her car, upset. He knew that as well as he knew his name.

He tapped on the driver's window. Kate started the car and slid the window down a sliver.

"Get out of the storm," she yelled.

"I will when I know you're all right."

The damn street lights were out so he couldn't see her face, but he saw enough shimmer in her eyes to know she wasn't fine, not at all.

"You're soaked. Go inside, Gray. We're done."

He jerked open her door, propping one arm up on the car, and leaned down to get right in her face. "We're not done, Kate. You can't brush me aside."

The lights from her dash lit up her face. She stared at him for a moment before shaking her head.

"I'm going home. I need some space."

He knew what that was code for. She wanted

to push him away and try to figure everything out herself. Hell no. Yes, he'd upset her, but he wasn't backing down. This was bigger than selling the bar, pleasing his father or some lame marriage proposal.

Kate had legitimately been hurt by their conversation. She'd opened herself and came to his room. He could only imagine the courage that had taken.

"You can have your space," he told her, swiping the rain from his eyes. "But know that you can't keep me away. I'm not going anywhere, Kate."

He didn't give her a chance to reply. Gray gripped the back of her head and covered her mouth with his. Quick, fierce, impossible to forget, that's the kiss he delivered before he stepped back and closed her car door.

The window slid up as she put the car in Drive and pulled out of the lot. He stood in the midst of the storm, watching her taillights disappear into the dark night.

The thunder continued to rumble and a bolt of lightning streaked across the sky. Gray rubbed his chest as he headed back inside. He'd always ached for her when she'd gotten upset. But this was different.

Somehow with that surprise proposal, he'd severed something they shared. He'd tainted their friendship and put a dark cloud over their lives. All he'd wanted to do was make his father happy and somehow that had blown up in his face.

Gray knew sleep wasn't coming anytime soon,

so he started plotting. If the damn electricity would come back on, he could put his plan into motion and maybe salvage some semblance of this friendship.

Chapter Fourteen

Kate clicked Send on her blog and sat back to admire the new layout she'd implemented on her site. Thanks to sleepless nights, she'd had plenty of time to work on cleaning up her pages a bit. She now had everything organized and easier to maneuver.

But she was in no mood to celebrate. For the past two mornings she'd been sick as a dog. She'd also missed her period and there was a home pregnancy test in her bathroom that mocked her every time she went in. There was no need to take it. She knew.

The birth control she'd switched from pill to patch had come during their camping trip, there was no questioning how this happened.

She hadn't heard from Gray in two weeks. The

deadline had passed for him to make a decision on the bar, but he hadn't told her anything. He hadn't texted, hadn't called. He'd warned her he'd give her space and he'd kept his word.

Damn it, why did she have to miss him so much? What was he going to say when she told him about the baby? Most likely he'd take that Neanderthal attitude and try to convince her to marry him.

Kate glanced at the clock. She really needed to get some lunch. The crackers and ginger ale this morning had worn off. Well, they hadn't stayed down, so they'd worn off immediately.

She scrolled through her newly uploaded blog discussing why organization made for a better attitude. People in general were calmer if the world around them was in order so they didn't feel as if they were living in chaos. She'd even added a new buy button to the site, along with a note stating that all first-time clients would receive a 10 percent discount.

Her newsletter was set to go out this evening, so the timing of this post was perfect. Of course, she'd planned it that way.

Kate pushed her chair back and came to her feet. A slight wave of dizziness overcame her. Gripping the edge of her desk, she closed her eyes and waited for it to pass.

What would Lucy and Tara say? They didn't even know she and Gray had been intimate. They would be hurt that she hadn't confided in them, but she just hadn't been ready and then she thought things were going to go back to normal and now…well, this was her new normal.

Kate's cell buzzed and vibrated on her desk top. She sank back into her chair and stared at the screen, not recognizing the number. New clients contacted her all the time, so ignoring the call wasn't an option.

"Hello?"

"Ms. McCoy?"

She didn't recognize the male voice on the other end. "Yes."

"My name is Steven Sanders. I'm with a group out of Nashville called Lost and Found Family."

Intrigued, Kate eased back in her seat and kept her eyes shut. The room had stopped spinning, but she wasn't taking any chances right now.

"What can I do for you, Mr. Sanders?"

"Actually, it's what I can do for you," he countered. "I was given your contact information by Gray Gallagher. He wanted me to talk with you about tracing your family and finding your heritage. Is this a good time to talk?"

So many things swirled around in her mind. Gray had called someone to help her find her family? But he hadn't talked to her or even texted. Why hadn't he told her about this? Why was he being so nice when she'd turned him down and left in the midst of a storm?

"Sure," she replied. "Um…sorry. This is all just a bit of a surprise."

The man chuckled on the other end of the line.

"Gray was adamant I call you as soon as I could, but I was trying to get another case wrapped up before contacting you. He made me vow to give your case special attention."

Something warmed inside her, something that brought tears to her eyes. She leaned forward, resting her elbows on her desk.

"Well, I appreciate that," she replied. "But I understand I'm probably not your only client. What information do you need from me?"

Steven went on to explain the information Gray had already delivered to him. He asked her about her mother's maiden name, her skin color, eye color, hair color. He went through her father's description. Then he asked for birthdays, where they were born and any grandparents' names she might know.

"This gives me a bit to go on to get started," Steven said after about a half hour of gathering information. "Should I call or email you when I have more questions?"

"I'm fine with either," she replied. "I can't thank you enough. I never knew really who to call to get started on this. You can bill me through email and I'll—"

"Oh, no, ma'am. Mr. Gallagher already took care of the bill, and any further charges will be sent to him."

Kate wasn't going to get into an argument with this guy. He had no clue about the whirlwind of emotions that continued to swirl around her and Gray. The poor guy was just doing his job.

"Thanks so much for taking on this case," she replied. "I look forward to hearing from you."

"I'll be in touch."

She disconnected the call and stood back up, thankfully no longer dizzy. As she made her way toward the kitchen, she went over in her mind what she wanted to say to Gray. He'd already helped her by tracking down someone who could research her ancestry. He didn't need to pay for it, too. And he'd done all of this after they'd stopped speaking.

The idea that he'd started working on a portion of her life list had tears burning her eyes. No matter what had transpired between them, he was still determined to be there for her.

Kate made a quick peanut butter sandwich and grabbed a bottle of water and a banana before heading back to her office. There was no dodging Gray anymore. She needed to thank him for hiring the genealogy investigator, plus tell him about the baby.

If she thought their dynamics had been changed before with just sex, this would certainly alter everything they'd ever known. She had to be positive before going to him and she had to know exactly what to say.

Kate would definitely take the test to be sure, but he deserved to know. This was definitely something they needed to work on together.

Looked like she wasn't going to be putting him in

that friend category anymore. She wasn't ready to put him in the husband category, either. He'd honestly hurt her when he'd said why he wanted to marry her.

How could he be so blind? How could he not see that she wanted someone who genuinely loved her? Like *in love* with her?

She'd been on the verge of telling him she was falling for him when he blurted out the proposal, destroying any hope she might have had that their bond could go deeper than friendship. And now she was carrying his child. If this wasn't the most warped situation ever, she didn't know what was.

Ladies' Night was tonight and in their group texts, Lucy and Tara had already been vocal about wanting to go. Kate figured now would be as good a time as any to go out, try to have fun and not freak out about her entire life getting turned upside down.

Because as scared, nervous and anxious as she was about this child—along with a gamut of other emotions—the truth of the matter was…she was happy. She had no family, but she was creating her very own. No, this was definitely not planned and, surprisingly, she was okay.

This wasn't a schedule or a job. This was a child. Her child.

Would Gray still want to take the money from the sale of the bar? She couldn't stand the thought of him leaving, but he needed to be aware of just how much their lives were about to change.

Tonight. She'd go tonight and thank him for the

genealogy specialist. Then, once the bar closed, she'd take him upstairs and tell him about the baby.

First, though, she had a test to take.

As Wednesday nights went, the bar was crazier than usual. He'd begged one of his waitresses to come in on her night off. He never begged. He'd even offered her an extra paid day off if she just came in for a few hours to help bartend. Jacob was in the kitchen filling in for the cook, who'd come down with some cold or whatever.

It was just a crazy, messed up day.

And Kate had strolled in with her friends and hadn't come up to the bar once to speak to him. In the two weeks he'd given her space, he'd damn near lost his mind.

More orders flooded the system and Gray didn't slow down or stop. If Kate was here, then she was here to talk. She'd missed Ladies' Night last week and, like a fool, he'd watched the door. But he'd been so busy over the past fourteen days trying to get this place ready to sell that he'd let himself get wrapped up in the business.

He still hadn't made up his mind, but he had texted the guy and bought more time. Gray was inching closer to realizing he might never get a chance like this again. If he ever wanted to get out and see what he'd been missing in his life, now was the time.

What seemed like an eternity later, the crowd started winding down. Gray had caught glimpses of Kate, Lucy and Tara dancing, but now he only saw Kate in the corner booth alone and looking at something on her phone.

He left the bar to his employee and promised to be away only two minutes. Now that things weren't so insane, he wanted to talk to Kate.

As he crossed the bar, weaving through the tables and the stragglers who were still hanging out, Kate looked up and caught his gaze. Her eyes widened and with her tense shoulders and tight smile, Gray knew something was up.

Without asking, he slid into the booth across from her. "Didn't expect you to show up tonight."

She laid her phone in front of her and shrugged. "I needed to get out of the house. Plus, I needed to thank you for having Steven Sanders call me."

Gray eased back in the seat. "So he's on it. Good. I was giving him two more days to contact you before I called him again."

"He has other clients, you know."

Gray didn't care. What he cared about was helping Kate with her list and finding some sort of family for her to call her own.

"I hope he can find what you need," Gray replied.

Silence settled between them as she glanced down at her hands. She'd laced her fingers together and the way her knuckles were turning white made him wonder what was really on her mind.

"You're upset that I contacted him?" he guessed.

"No, no. I'm surprised and thankful," she corrected him.

"What's wrong?" he asked, leaning forward. "Lucy and Tara took off a while ago but you're still here."

Her eyes darted to the dancing women on the dance floor.

"Kate."

She turned her focus to him, but that didn't last long. Her gaze dropped once again to her clasped hands. "We need to talk. Can I wait until you're closed?"

Gray glanced to his watch. "We've got another hour. Do you want to go upstairs? You look like you could fall over."

And she did. She'd gone sans makeup, which wasn't unusual, but he could see the dark circles under her eyes, and she was a bit paler than normal.

"You feeling all right?" he asked.

She attempted a smile, but it was lame and forced. "Fine. I think I will go upstairs if you don't care. I can't leave without talking to you alone."

When she slid out of the booth, Gray came to his feet as well. She reached for the table with one hand and her head with the other as she teetered.

"Kate." He grasped her arms, holding tight. "I didn't make a drink for you. What have you had?"

She waved a hand away as she straightened. "I'm just tired and stood up too fast. I've only had water."

"Do you need something to eat?"

Shaking her head, she tried for a smile once again. "Really, I'm okay. I'll meet you upstairs when you're done."

He watched her head behind the bar and into the back hallway. Never in all his years as owner had he wanted to close up early and tell everyone to get the hell out.

Something was wrong with Kate. After all the running she'd done, something had pulled her back to him and he knew it wasn't the fact he'd called a genealogy specialist.

The next hour seemed to drag as he busted his butt to get the place ready to shut down for the night. He could sweep the floors and do a thorough wipe down in the morning. Once all the alcohol was taken care of, the kitchen was shut down properly and the employees were gone, Gray locked up and headed upstairs.

When he opened the door and stepped into the living room, he froze. There on his sofa was Kate all curled up in one corner. She'd removed her shoes and her little bare feet were tucked at her side.

She didn't look too comfortable at the angle her head had fallen against the back of the couch. Had she not been sleeping at home? Had she thought about his proposal and was here to…what? Take him up on it?

Gray turned the knob and slowly shut the door, careful not to click it into place. He crossed the room and took a seat directly in front of her on the old metal trunk he used as a coffee table. He watched her for a minute, torn between waking her and letting her get the sleep she seemed to desperately need.

After several minutes of feeling like a creeper, Gray reached out and tapped her leg. She didn't move. He flattened his hand around her thigh and gave a gentle squeeze.

"Kate," he said in a soft tone.

She started to stir. Her lids fluttered, then lifted. She blinked a few times as if focusing. Then she shot up on the sofa.

"Oh my gosh." Her hands immediately went to her hair, pushing wayward strands back from her face. "I didn't mean to fall asleep."

He held out his hands. "Relax. It's no big deal."

She swung her legs around and placed them on the area rug. The side of her knee brushed his as she propped her elbows on her thighs and rubbed her face.

"What's wrong, Kate?" He couldn't stand it any longer. "I gave you the space you asked for, but you show up here looking like a small gust of wind could blow you over. Are you sick? Don't lie to me."

Damn it, fear gripped him and he didn't like this feeling. Not one bit.

"I'm not sick." She dropped her hands in her lap and met his gaze dead-on. "I'm pregnant."

Chapter Fifteen

Kate stared at him, worried when the silence stretched longer than was comfortable.

She hadn't meant to just blurt that out, but honestly, was there a lead-in to such a bomb? Gray sat so close, their knees bumped. And for the second time in their years of friendship, she couldn't make out the expression on his face.

His eyes never wavered from her, but he reached out and gripped her hands in his. "Pregnant? Are you sure?"

Before she could answer, he shook his head. "That was stupid. You wouldn't tell me unless you were sure."

"I've suspected for a few days, but just took the test today."

Now his eyes did drop to her stomach. "I don't even know what to say. Are you… I mean, you feel okay?"

"I'm nauseous, tired, look like hell. Other than that, I'm fine."

Gray shifted his focus from her flat abdomen to her eyes. "You've never looked like hell in your life."

"You didn't see me hugging the commode this morning," she muttered.

His thumb raked over the back of her hand. "Did you come here to tell me you'd marry me?"

She'd been so afraid he'd say that. That he would just assume a baby would be a reason to marry. If the marriage wasn't going to be forever, how was joining lives the right thing to do?

"I'm not marrying you, Gray."

His dark brows drew in as he continued to stare at her. "Why not? This is all the more reason to get married. We're going to be parents. I can sell the bar, get the money, and we can go wherever you want. Hell, we'll travel and then decide where to settle down. Name it."

Kate shook her head and removed her hands from his. She leaned back on the couch and curled her feet back up beside her where they'd been.

"That's not the answer," she countered. "I don't want to keep doing this with you. We have time to figure out what the best plan will be for our baby."

"So if I sell the bar and leave, you'll what? Stay here? I want to be part of our child's life."

She knew he would. She expected him to be. Gray would be a wonderful father. He'd be a fabulous husband, just not in the way he was proposing. Literally.

"I'd never keep you away from the baby," she told him. "I'm hurt you would even suggest such a thing. If you leave, that's on you. I'll be right here in Stonerock."

He stared at her another minute and then finally pushed to his feet. "Stay here tonight," he said, looking down at her. "Just stay here so we can figure this out."

Kate smiled, but shook her head. "Sex isn't going to solve anything."

"Maybe I just want you here," he retorted. "Maybe I've missed you and now, knowing that you're carrying my child, I want to take care of you."

The tenderness in his voice warmed her. She knew he'd want to take over and make sure everything was perfect for her. He'd want to make her as comfortable as possible.

Unfortunately, through all of that, he just couldn't love her the way she wanted to be loved. The way she loved him.

Tears pricked her eyes. She dropped her head and brought her hands up to shield her face. Damn hormones.

"Kate." The cushion on the sofa sank next to her. One strong arm wrapped around her and she felt herself being pulled against his side. "Don't cry. Please. I'll figure something out."

Couldn't he see? This had nothing to do with the bar and if he kept it or sold it. If he loved her, truly loved her like a man loved a woman, she'd go anywhere with him. But she couldn't just uproot her life for a man who was settling and only trying to do the right thing.

"Stay," he whispered into her ear as he stroked her hair. "Sleeping. Nothing more."

She tipped her head back to peer up at him.

"Please."

She knew he only wanted to keep an eye on her, plus it was late and she was exhausted. Kate nodded. "I'll stay."

Gray left Kate sleeping and eased out of the bed. He glanced back down to where she lay wearing one of his shirts, her raven hair in a tangled mess around her, dark circles beneath her eyes. She'd been so exhausted when she'd come to the bar last night.

And she'd dropped the biggest bomb of his life.

A baby. He was having a baby with his best friend and she refused to marry him.

Gray had to convince her to. Before she'd changed his entire life with one sentence, he'd nearly talked himself into selling Gallagher's. Now that he knew he was going to be a father, well, he was sure he wanted to sell. He could use that money and make a nice life for his family...just as soon as he convinced

Kate to marry him. Didn't she see that this was the most logical step?

He hadn't planned on getting married, but with his dad always hinting that he should, with the new chapter of selling the bar, and with Kate pregnant... hell, he had to move forward with his plan and make her see this was the best option for their future.

Quietly he eased the door shut and went to the kitchen to make breakfast. He had no clue what was on her agenda today, but hopefully after a good night's sleep, they could talk and try to work things out. Well, he'd try to get her to see reason.

Gray checked his fridge and realized he hadn't been to the store in... Honestly, he couldn't remember the last time he went to the store.

He headed down to the bar and raided that kitchen, then ran back upstairs. Now he could actually start cooking something. Kate still slept, so he tried to be quiet. His apartment wasn't that big, but it worked for him.

That is, this space had always worked until now. He couldn't exactly expect Kate to raise a baby here. She valued family and the importance of home. Kate and the baby deserved a house with a yard, somewhere they could put a swing set. Something the total opposite of a bachelor pad above a bar.

Gray fried some potatoes he'd snagged from downstairs and pulled out the ham steaks from his freezer. Kate was more of a pancake girl, but she'd have to adapt today. He would see to it that she was cared for, whether she liked it or not.

He'd just dished up the plates when he heard running down the hall and then the bathroom door slamming shut.

Muttering a curse, he left the breakfast and went to the closed door. Yeah, she was definitely sick. He rubbed his hands down his face and stared up at the ceiling. How the hell could he make her feel better? He couldn't exactly fix this or take it from her.

He stood on the other side of the door and waited until the toilet flushed. He heard water running and, moments later, she opened the door. Gray hated how pale she was, how her hand shook as she shoved her hair away from her face.

"Sorry about that," she murmured, leaning against the door frame. "It hits quick."

He reached out and framed her face in his hands. "Never apologize to me. I made breakfast, but I'm thinking maybe you're not in the mood."

Her eyes shut as she wrinkled her nose. "Do you just have some juice?"

"Downstairs I do. I'll be right back."

In record time he had the juice and was racing back upstairs. As soon as he stepped into the apartment, he heard Kate talking.

"No, Chris. This isn't a good time."

Gray set the bottle on the small dining table and headed down the hall toward her voice. Chris, the bastard ex.

"I never agreed to meet up with you, so if you thought I did, then you're mistaken."

When Gray hit the doorway of his bedroom, he saw Kate sitting on the edge of his bed, her back to him. She had her head down and was rubbing it.

Anger bubbled within him. Who the hell was this guy who suddenly came back into her life? Why did he think she would want anything at all to do with him after the way he'd treated her?

"I don't care how long you're in town," she replied. "I'm busy."

She tapped the screen and tossed her cell on the bed.

"Has he been bothering you?" Gray asked, stepping into the room.

Kate turned to glance over her shoulder. "Just a few calls and texts. He only showed up at my house the one time."

If this jerk planned on staying in town, Gray intended to track him down. It was time for Chris to find out for good that he'd lost his chance at anything with Kate.

"I have your juice in the kitchen," he told her. "How are you feeling?"

She let out a slight laugh. "Confused. Scared. Powerless."

It probably wasn't the best time to tell her he felt the same way. Kate needed him to be strong, needed him to be there like he always had been. Even more so now.

Gray crossed the room and came to stand in front of her. "Don't answer me now, but think about marriage, Kate. There are so many reasons this is a good idea."

She stood, easing around him. "Not now, Gray. Just…not now."

"I'm just asking you to think about it."

He followed her down the hall to the kitchen. Grabbing a glass from the cabinet, he set it on the counter and poured her juice.

"I'm not asking for an answer today," he told her as she drank. "But you can't dismiss the idea completely."

She licked her lips and leveled her gaze. "Are you selling the bar?"

Gray swallowed, knowing he was going to have to say it out loud at some point. "Yes."

Kate pulled in a slow breath and nodded. Then she finished the last of the juice and handed him back the glass.

"Then go do what you need to do," she told him. "You wanted to figure out what your life was missing, and I sure as hell don't want to be the reason you stay. I won't be someone's burden and I won't let this baby feel that way, either."

Gray slammed the glass on the counter and took her by her shoulders. "You're not listening to me, damn it. You're not a burden, Kate. This baby isn't a burden. But selling the bar makes more sense now than ever. What? You want to live up here and raise a child?"

"We're not getting married or living together, so it's a moot point," she threw back at him. "I don't like this, Gray. We're always arguing and I just want my friend back."

Her voice cracked on that last word and he hauled her against his chest. He wanted his friend back, too, but they'd obliterated the friendship line and now they were adding a baby to the mix.

"We can't go back," he told her. "But I won't let you go through this alone. I'm here."

She eased back, piercing him with those blue eyes full of questions, but she asked only one.

"For how long?"

Chapter Sixteen

Well, there was no more dodging the inevitable.

Kate had asked the girls over since she knew Sam had Marley. This was definitely not a conversation for little ears.

She'd ordered pizza, made cookies, had wine and water on hand—everything was all set for the big reveal. Just then, her front door opened and Tara and Lucy came in, chattering.

Kate heard Lucy saying something about her stepdaughter, but couldn't make out exactly what it was. When she'd married Noah, she'd gotten an instant family and was filling the role of mom beautifully. Tara excelled at motherhood, despite the roller coaster she'd had to endure these past several months with Sam and his addiction.

Looked like Kate couldn't have asked for two better women to call on for support. She only hoped they weren't too angry with her for keeping the situation with Gray a secret.

Kate stepped from the kitchen into the living room. "Hey, guys."

"I smell pizza," Tara stated. "Please, tell me you got extra bacon on at least part of it."

Kate rolled her eyes. "Have I ever let you down? I even bought your favorite wine, though wine and pizza always sounded like a bad combo to me."

Lucy set her purse on the accent chair and dropped her keys inside. "Wine goes with everything and so does pizza, so it only makes sense to pair them together."

Kate attempted a smile, but her nerves were spiraling out of control. She could do this. There was nothing to be afraid of and her friends would be there for her. Isn't that what they did? They banded together during the best and worst of times.

"Oh, no." Tara took a slow step forward. "I thought we were just having a random girls' night. What's wrong, Kate?"

"You guys might want to sit down with a glass of wine first."

Lucy crossed her arms over her chest and shook her head. "Not until you tell us what's wrong."

"Nothing is wrong, exactly," she replied. "Gray and I—"

"Finally." Tara threw her hands in the air. "I knew something was going on with the two of you. What is it, though? You seem, I don't know...nervous."

"Are you and Gray together?" Lucy whispered as if this was some sacred secret.

"You could say that."

Kate looked from one friend to the other. They'd barely made it inside the front door, and from the determined look on their faces, they weren't moving any further until she confessed.

"I'm pregnant."

Tara's eyes widened. Lucy's mouth dropped. Neither said a word, but their shock spoke volumes.

"We were just fooling around," Kate went on. "I mean, there was the night of the rehearsal dinner, then camping—"

"I called this," Tara repeated. "Well, not the baby. Damn, Kate. You're having a baby?"

Kate couldn't help the smile and shrug. "Of all people, the CEO of Savvy Scheduler did not plan this."

Lucy stepped forward and extended her arms. Kate shook her head and held her hands out, silently telling her friend no.

"I can't do comfort right now," she explained. "I'm barely hanging on here and I just need to come to grips with this—"

Lucy wrapped her arms around Kate and that was

all it took for Kate to finally crumble. Tears fell, fear took hold, and soon Tara's arms were banding around them as well.

"It's going to be okay," Tara stated. "A baby is a wonderful blessing."

"What did Gray say?" Lucy asked, easing back slightly.

Kate sniffed and attempted to gather herself together. "He proposed," she whispered.

"That's great," Tara exclaimed. "I always thought you two would end up together."

Swiping her face with the back of her hand, Kate pulled in a shaky breath. "I turned him down."

Tara gripped her shoulder. "What?"

"I'm not settling," Kate explained. "I want to marry someone who loves me, who isn't marrying me because of some family pressure or a pregnancy."

Kate stepped back to get some space. She didn't want to cry about this, didn't want pity. She wanted to figure out what her next step should be and she needed to be logical about it.

Maneuvering around her friends, who continued to stare at her as if she'd break again, Kate went to the sofa and sank into the corner.

"He proposed before I told him about the baby," she explained. "He's got that offer to sell the bar and his father has been on him for years to settle down. Gray wants to move ahead with the deal and figured if we got married, maybe his dad wouldn't be so upset about losing Gallagher's. Then when I told him about the baby, well, he thinks it's only logical."

Tara sat on the edge of the accent chair across from the sofa. "What's logical is that you should tell him how you really feel so the two of you can move on."

"You do love him, right?" Lucy asked as she sat in the chair right next to Tara's hip. "I don't mean like you love us as your friends. I mean, you love Gray. I know you do or you never would've slept with him."

Kate couldn't deny it—she didn't want to. She was tired of the sneaking, the secrets, the emotions.

"I do," she whispered. "But it's irrelevant because he doesn't see me like that."

"Men are blind." Lucy reached over to pat Kate's knee. "Sometimes you have to bang them over the head in order for them to see the truth. You need to be honest with Gray. He should know how you feel."

Kate had put her love out there before. She'd had a ring on her finger and a dress in her closet, but that love—or what she'd thought was love—had been thrown back in her face.

She loved Gray more than she ever did Chris. Gray was…well, he was everything. How would she handle it if he rejected her? At least if she kept her feelings locked inside her heart, they could remain friends, raise the baby and not muddle up their relationship with one-sided love.

"How are you feeling, other than Gray?" Tara asked. "Physically, I mean. Have you been sick?"

"Gray made me potatoes and ham for breakfast and the smell woke me when my stomach started rolling. Sick doesn't begin to describe my mornings."

Lucy's eyes widened. "He made you breakfast? That's so sweet."

Kate laughed. "He's always taken care of me. That's not the problem."

"The key to any good relationship is communication," Tara stated, and the wistfulness in her tone had Kate turning her focus on her. "Trust me. You need to tell him how you feel."

Kate tucked her hair behind her ears and wondered what would be best. Baring her heart to Gray as to her true feelings or just waiting to see what happened? For all she knew, he would sell the bar, go on some grand adventure to find himself and then discover that he never wanted to return. Then what?

"I honestly don't know what to do," she muttered. "I don't want him to feel sorry for me or think I fell in love with him because of the pregnancy. I've loved him… I don't even know how long. Maybe forever, but I didn't realize it until recently."

Lucy grabbed Kate's hand. "Well, right now let's focus on you and this baby. I'm confident Gray will come around."

Kate wished she had Lucy's confidence and Tara's courage. But this was her life and this pregnancy was the biggest thing that had ever happened to her. And she didn't want to put her heart on the line again because she'd been right from the very beginning. She could lose Gray's friendship if all of this went wrong. Losing the one constant man in her life wasn't an option. Especially now that the same man would be needed as a constant for their baby.

Gray set the glass of sweet tea on the counter in front of Sam. The bar didn't open for another hour and Sam had stopped by after a long week at his new job. Gray admired the man for putting his family first, for selling his own company and humbling himself to get counseling before going to work for another construction company.

He'd helped himself but may never get his wife back. The harsh reality was a bitch to bear, Gray was sure. Sam was a great guy who'd made poor decisions.

"Are you really selling the bar?" Sam asked, gripping the frosted glass.

Gray flattened his palms on the rolled edge of the bar. "I am. I haven't contacted the guy from Knoxville yet, but I plan on calling Monday morning."

"What does your dad say about it?"

Gray didn't like to think of the disappointment he'd seen in his father's eyes. He knew his dad wanted to keep the bar in the family, but would ultimately support Gray no matter what.

The problem was, Gray wasn't a hundred percent sure what he wanted. He did know that the money from the sale would put him in a perfect spot to provide for Kate and the baby.

He hadn't mentioned the baby to his dad because that would've brought up a whole other set of issues…like the fact that she wouldn't marry him.

But he knew where her doubts were coming from. Kate had been left so shaken when her parents had passed. Then her fiancé had revealed his true colors and broken her heart. Gray never wanted her to question where her foundation was again. He knew she was scared with this pregnancy—hell, he was, too. But there was nothing he wouldn't do for her even if she refused to marry him.

"Dad isn't happy," Gray finally replied. "But he respects my decision. He'd like to see me settled down with a wife and a bunch of little Gallaghers running around and gearing up to pass this place to them."

Sam took a hearty drink of his tea and set the glass back down. "That's not what you want, I take it."

Gray gave a slight shrug, feeling something tug on his heart. "I don't know what I want, but has been on my mind."

Especially now.

"It's not for everyone, that's for sure." Sam slid his thumb over the condensation of his mug. "Tara is everything and when you find a love like that, it's worth fighting for. I really messed up, Gray. Don't learn from my mistakes."

Gray gritted his teeth and tried to sort through the thoughts scrolling through his head.

The most dominant thought was love. Love worth fighting for. He loved Kate. Hadn't he told her as much? They'd loved each other for years, so why was she so adamant about not marrying him? Wasn't any level of love a good basis for a marriage?

But she'd told him she wouldn't settle, that she wanted to be with a man who loved her the way a husband should love his wife.

He didn't even know what that meant. He thought she'd be happy with him, that they could be happy together. Obviously she had other expectations about her future.

"How are things with Tara?" Gray asked.

Sam shrugged. "Still the same. We get along for Marley and we're always civil, but it seems so shallow, you know? We just go through the days, same cycle, same fake smiles, like we're both not hurting."

Gray hated seeing his friends so torn. Yes, Sam had made mistakes, but he was human and he'd fought like hell to get clean and make up for the pain he'd caused.

Is this how Gray and Kate would be? Would they be moving through the days just living civilly and trying not to break? Would they bounce their child back and forth and pretend everything was okay?

And what would happen if Kate wanted to go on a date or brought a man home?

Jealousy spiraled through him at the mere thought of another man in Kate's life. Another man in their child's life.

Gray went about getting the bar ready to open. He chatted with his employees when they came in the back door and he welcomed the first customers who started to filter in. Sam remained on his stool, sipping his tea, then finally beer. Gray made sure to always keep an eye on his friend when he came in, and Sam usually limited his drinking to one or two beers. He seemed to be on the road to getting his life back under control.

Too bad Gray couldn't say the same.

Chapter Seventeen

"This was a mistake," Kate growled as Lucy practically dragged her inside the front door of Gallagher's. "A pregnant woman shouldn't be hanging out at the bar."

Lucy held onto her arm. "This is exactly where that pregnant lady should be when the man she loves is the owner. Besides, Tara is home with Marley tonight and Noah took Piper on a father-daughter date to the movies. I wanted to get out, so you're stuck with me."

Kate shouldn't be here. Then again, she shouldn't have put on her favorite dress and curled her hair, either. She didn't do those things for Gray. Absolutely not. She did them for herself because...

Fine. She did them for Gray because no matter how much she wished it, she couldn't just move on and forget her feelings for him. Pregnancy aside, Kate wanted Gray just as much as ever. Even if she hadn't been carrying his child, she would be completely in love with him.

For years she'd wanted a family of her own. She'd dreamed of it, in fact. Then she'd started her little business and focused on that after her world was rocked when Chris left. Now she was being given a second chance at a family, but Gray wasn't on board…not in the way she needed him to be.

Inside Gallagher's, an upbeat country song was blasting as several couples danced. The tables were full, except for one table right smack-dab in the middle of the floor. Fabulous. Why couldn't their usual corner booth be open? That real estate should always be on reserve for her.

Kate dropped to the hard wooden seat and hung her purse on the back. This was not ideal, not at all. Here she was, front and center of the bar, almost as if fate was mocking her.

A slow, twangy song filled the space and even more couples flooded to the dance floor.

"Fancy seeing you here."

Kate turned around, barely registering the cheesy line and her ex before he whisked her out of her seat and spun her toward the dance floor.

In a blur, she saw Lucy's shocked face.

"Chris, what in the world," she said, trying to

wriggle free of his grip on her hand. "I don't want to dance."

Banding an arm around her waist, he took her free hand in his and maneuvered them right into the midst of the dancers.

"Just one dance," he said, smiling down at her as if he had every right to hold her. "Surely you can give me three minutes to talk and then I'll leave you alone."

Kate didn't want to give him three seconds, let alone three minutes. She didn't get a chance to say anything because Chris was jerked from her and then Gray stood towering over him.

"You're Chris?" Gray asked, his body taut with tension.

Kate stepped forward and put her hand on his back. "Don't, Gray."

Ignoring her, he took a half step forward, causing Chris to shove at Gray. "I'm talking to Kate, if you don't mind."

"I actually do mind," Gray growled over the music. A crowd had formed around them.

"It's fine," Kate insisted. She didn't want an altercation.

"You heard the lady," Chris said with a smirk. "It's fine. Now go back to making drinks."

Kate didn't have time to react as Gray's fist drew back and landed right in the middle of Chris's face. Her ex stumbled back, landing on a table and upending another one.

Gray shook his hand out and Kate stepped around to stand in front of him, worried he'd go at Chris again. The last thing Gray needed was to get in a fight in his own bar. That wouldn't be good for business.

"Stop it," she demanded.

The look on his face was pure fury. Finally, he took his gaze from Chris and landed it on her. "Keep your boyfriend out of my bar."

Kate drew her brows in and dropped her hand. "What is wrong with you?"

"What the hell?"

Kate turned around to see some guy helping Chris up. The stranger turned his attention to Gray. "This is how you run a business?"

Gray moved around Kate and walked past Chris, the stranger and the crowd. Kate stared at his retreating back and was startled when a hand fell on her shoulder. She spun around to find Lucy.

"That was…territorial."

Kate shook her head. "What just happened?"

"I'd say your guy got jealous, but who was the other man who stepped in?"

Gray stalked back over to Chris and the other man. Kate watched, waiting and hoping there wasn't going to be another altercation.

"The bar isn't for sale." Gray stood directly in front of the two guys. Chris held his jaw, working it back and forth. "You two can get the hell out of here and don't come back."

Gray and Chris sparring wasn't something she thought she'd ever see. But no doubt about it, Chris wasn't going to win this fight no matter what he threatened.

"I'll sue you," Chris spouted. "My partner and I were going to give you a lot of money for this place."

"Sue me," Gray said, crossing his arms over his massive chest as if he didn't have a care in the world. "But leave."

He turned back around and went back to the bar. Kate watched as he started making drinks like his whole life hadn't just changed. Chris was a bastard, no doubt about it.

He'd wanted to sell the bar. He'd been pretty set on doing just that. What had changed his mind? He hadn't said a word to her. Between Gray's silence and Chris's betrayal, Kate wasn't sure how to feel, but pissed was a great starting point.

Then dread filled her. Had he done this because of the baby? Was he giving up what he truly wanted to make her happy? Because he'd done that with his father, when he'd taken over the bar after his tour of duty just to appease him. And here he was putting his own needs aside again. Kate intended to find out why.

Chris and his business partner turned and left, leaving many talking about what had just happened. Obviously the other guy was the one who'd made Gray the exorbitant offer.

"I can't believe he just hit him," Kate muttered.

Lucy laughed. "I recall him hitting another guy who got in your face several months ago."

Kate ran a hand through her hair as she met Gray's dark eyes across the bar. "At least he's consistent."

"Heard you made a little scene at the bar last night."

Gray rubbed his eyes and attempted to form a coherent sentence. His father had called way too early, knowing full well that Gray would still be asleep. The man had run the same bar for thirty years. He knew the routine.

"Nothing I couldn't handle."

Gray eased up in bed and leaned against the headboard because he knew his father didn't randomly call just to chat.

"Also heard you turned down the offer to sell."

Gray blew out a breath. Yeah. He had. That hadn't been an easy decision, but definitely the right one. The second he'd seen Kate in another man's arms, Gray had lost it. Then, on his way over, he'd heard Kate call the guy Chris and Gray nearly exploded. Okay, he did explode, but that guy deserved the punch—and more—for what he'd done years ago.

Kate was his family. Kate and their child was his family. The future had seemed so clear in that moment. All the times he'd waited for a sign, waited for some divine intervention to tell him what to do. But Kate and their family was everything. And he'd found that he wanted to continue that tradition with his child, boy or girl.

"I'm keeping the bar," Gray confirmed.

"Who changed your mind?" his dad asked.

Gray instantly pictured Kate. He couldn't help but smile though he was dead tired. He'd screwed up things with her. He'd legit botched up their relationship from the friendship to the intimacy. But he had a plan.

"I just realized nothing is missing from my life," Gray replied. "I'm staying here and Gallagher's will remain in the family."

"That was a lot of money to turn down, son."

Funny, but that didn't bother him anymore. "It was," he agreed. "Family means more."

Family meant *everything*.

He needed to tell his dad about the pregnancy, but he wanted to talk to Kate first. He had quite a bit to talk to her about, actually.

"I'm proud of you," his dad finally said. "Your grandfather would be, too, knowing you decided to stay in Stonerock, keep the tradition alive."

A lump formed in Gray's throat. "I wouldn't be anywhere else."

"Well, I guess I'll let you get back to sleep," his dad chuckled. "But Gray. Let's lay off the hitting. I know you have a thing for Kate, but control yourself."

His dad hung up before Gray could say anything about Kate or his self-control. He tossed his phone onto the rumpled sheet next to his hip. Raking his hands over his face, Gray attempted to sort his thoughts, his plans. Today he was taking back his life. Taking what he'd always wanted, but never knew he was missing.

And Kate wasn't going to get away again.

Chapter Eighteen

She hadn't seen Gray since the night before last. He'd punched Chris, turned down an enormous business deal and gone back to brooding.

Out of the blue, he'd texted this morning to tell her she'd left something at his apartment. There was no way she'd left anything there because she was meticulous about her stuff and knew where everything was.

Clearly he wanted her there for another reason. Kate found herself sipping her ginger ale and clutching a cracker as she mounted the outside back steps to the bar apartment.

Shoving the rest of the cracker in her mouth, she gripped the knob and eased the door open.

"Gray?" she called out as she stepped inside.

She'd never knocked before, so she didn't now, plus he knew she was coming.

Kate stepped into the living area and stopped short. The picture over the sofa was no longer the tacky *Dogs Playing Poker*. Tears pricked her eyes as she stepped closer to the image, one she'd seen so many times, but never like this.

A young Kate stared back at her. On either side of her in the portrait were her parents. All three smiling, not knowing what the future held. Kate had this exact picture in her bedroom.

"You like it?"

Kate was startled as Gray's easy question pulled her from the moment. Without turning, she nodded. Emotions formed heavy in her throat as her eyes burned with unshed tears.

"I remember that day so vividly," she told him, taking in every feature of her parents' faces. "We'd just gone for a picnic at one of the state parks. Then Dad took us on a small hike. My mom tripped on a rock and tore a hole in her tennis shoe. We laughed because she was always so clumsy."

She could still hear her mother's laugh—so sweet, almost wistful. "Not a day goes by that I don't miss them."

"They'd be proud of you."

Kate smiled as she turned to face Gray. "I hope so. I wonder what they'd think of me becoming a mother. Not having mine right now is…"

She blew out a breath and tried to gather her thoughts.

"I'm sure it's difficult," he told her as he remained in the doorway to the bedroom. "My mother passed when I was little, so I don't remember her. You're going to be a great mother and you've got those fond memories that will help."

She met his gaze, biting her bottom lip to cease the quivering.

"And you've got me," he added.

Kate blinked away the moisture and turned back to look at the picture. "Why is this hanging here?" she asked.

"This is your birthday present. It didn't come in on time, but I want you to have it."

This is what he'd done for her. For years he'd given her chocolate-covered strawberries, and this year had been no different. But he'd gone a step further and done something so thoughtful, so unique. Damn it, why did love have to be a one-way street with him?

"How did you get a copy?" she asked.

"Social media. I pulled it from one of your accounts and had it blown up on the canvas."

Crossing her arms, Kate turned her attention back to Gray. "If it's my birthday present, why is it hanging here?"

"Because you didn't like the other painting."

Confused, Kate shook her head. "I don't understand."

Gray pushed off the doorway and closed the distance between them. He stood directly in front of her, within touching distance, but didn't reach for her. As she studied the fine lines around his eyes, she realized he was tired. Had he not slept lately? Was he regretting his decision not to sell the bar?

"You and this baby are my priority now," he stated simply. "Not the bar, not moving and taking that money. Nothing else matters but my family."

What? Did he mean...

"I don't care where we take the picture I got you," he went on. "If you want to live here, we leave it here. You want to stay in your house, we hang it there. Our child will know your parents and I want to create a family with you."

"Gray," she whispered.

She dropped her face to her hands as another wave of emotions overcame her. He was only saying this to appease his dad, to make his father see that Gray was ready to settle down.

Kate swiped her face and met Gray's eyes. "We've been over this."

Now he did reach for her. Those large, strong hands framed her face. "No, we haven't, because we're about to have a whole new conversation. I need your undivided attention when I tell you I'm in love with you."

Kate's heart clenched. She stared up at him, gripped his wrists, and murmured, "You—you're in love with me? As in..."

"As in I want to make you my wife, not because of the baby and not because I'm staying here and keeping the bar." A ghost of a smile formed on his lips. "All these years I thought there was a void, but there wasn't. You were here all along and the only thing missing was having you even deeper in my life. That was the void. I need you, Kate. I know you'd be fine without me and we could share joint custody of our baby, but I want this life with you. I want this child and more with you."

Tears spilled and there was no way she could even think of holding them back. "You're serious?"

Gray laughed, then nipped at her lips. "You think I'd get rid of my dog picture for just anybody? I love you, Kate. I love this baby."

"But you were so angry the other night and I thought…"

"I wasn't angry with you," he assured her. "I was angry with that jerk who held you in his arms. I was angry with myself for being a dick to you, for not realizing sooner exactly how much you mean to me."

Gripping his wrists tighter, she so hoped he meant that. Every part of her wanted him to love her, to love this baby and to want to be a united family.

"Are you sure this isn't because of the baby?" she repeated.

"It's because of us," he stated, swiping the moisture from her cheeks. "If you weren't pregnant, I'd still be in love with you. I'd still want to spend my life with you."

"Spend your life with me?"

Gray let out a soft chuckle as he stepped back and dropped his hands. "You keep answering me with questions."

Kate watched as he went to the bedroom and came out a moment later holding something behind his back.

"I got something else for you."

Honestly, she wasn't sure how much more she could take. Between the photo and the declaration of love, she had more than she'd ever wanted.

Gray pulled out a thick book from behind his back. No. It wasn't a book at all.

Kate busted out laughing. "A planner?"

Gray got down on one knee and her breath caught in her throat. "Not just any planner, babe. Our life starts now. Marry me."

The front of the planner had a big gold heart on a white background. Gray opened the cover to reveal an attached satin ribbon to use for marking pages.

"Gray," she gasped.

Tied to the satin ribbon was a ring.

"I was just going to propose with the planner because I realize that's more important than jewelry to you," he joked. "But I hope you'll take this ring. It was my mother's. My dad saved it for me to give to the woman I love. There's nobody else I would ever give this ring to."

Kate's nausea chose that moment to make an appearance. She swayed on her feet, and Gray instantly came to his and wrapped an arm around her waist.

"I hope that's the baby and not my proposal," he said, guiding her to the couch.

"Definitely the baby," she told him.

He set the planner down on the old, antique trunk. "What can I get you?"

Kate closed her eyes, willing the dizziness to pass. "The ring on my finger, for starters."

She risked looking over at him and found him smiling, his eyes misting. "Are you going to cry?" she asked.

"Me? No. I don't cry." He sniffed as he untied the ring and held it up to her. "My dad said my mom loved pearls, but if you want a diamond or, hell... I don't know. I'll get anything, Kate. I just want you."

She held out her left hand. "And I want you and this ring that means so much to you."

Gray slid the ring onto her finger and let out a breath. "I so hoped this would fit."

Kate extended her arm and admired the ring. "It's perfect."

He pulled her into his arms. "We're perfect. I'm sorry I didn't see this before. When you said you needed me to love you like you deserve, I didn't get it."

Kate slid her arm around his abdomen and toed off her sandals. She propped her feet on the trunk and nestled deeper into his side.

"I've always loved you," he went on. "I even loved

you like a husband should love a wife, but it took a reality check for me to fully realize it."

"Was it Chris coming back to town?"

"Part of it," he replied, trailing his fingertips up and down her arm. "When you weren't here, I felt empty. Once we slept together that first time, everything changed. I wanted you more and more, not just for the sex, but because I felt alone without you."

Kate smiled and eased up. "Then you took me camping to seduce me."

A naughty grin spread across his face. "I took you camping to mark an item off your bucket list. The seducing was just a handy by-product."

His face sobered as he studied her. "I meant what I said before about helping you fulfill your list. Have you heard any more from the genealogy expert?"

"Not yet, but he's starting his research and that's a step in the right direction."

Gray kissed the tip of her nose. "What do you say we go pick out that dog you wanted? Sprout, right?"

Her eyes widened. "Right now?"

With a shrug, Gray sat up. "Why not? The local shelter is open."

Of course he'd want a shelter dog. As if the man couldn't be more perfect. She reached out and fisted his unruly hair in her hands, pulling his mouth down to hers.

"You're so perfect," she muttered against his lips. "Let's go get our Sprout."

"Want to get married, too?"

Kate stilled. "Today?"

"You still looking for something spontaneous for your list?"

The planner inside her started to have anxiety, but the woman who stared at this man wanted him to be hers in every single way.

"Don't worry about the perfect venue or the gown or flowers," he told her. "Marry me, Kate. Now. Today."

She let out a laugh, completely shocked at her response. "Let's do it."

Gray lifted her up into his arms and held her tight. There was no one else on earth who could make her want to ignore her plans and throw caution to the wind. But Gray made her want to live in the moment.

"Maybe I should write this in my planner," she told him.

He set her down on her feet and smiled as he reached down to flip the pages of the planner. "I already did. I had a feeling you'd say yes."

Kate glanced at the open pages. Her heart leaped in her chest at Gray's writing on today's date: Making Kate My Wife.

She smacked a kiss on his cheek. "I'm going to turn you into a personal planner after all."

"As long as you're mine, I'll make a thousand lists with you."

Epilogue

Sam stood outside his front door. Well, not *his* front door, since he and Tara had separated. Everyone thought their divorce was final and he'd never said otherwise. Tara had wanted the divorce, and he deserved all of her anger, but he'd never signed the papers. Sam Bailey never gave up and he sure as hell didn't intend to now—even when his entire world was slipping from his grasp.

He tapped his knuckles on the door—a door he'd installed when they'd bought the house only three years ago, a door he'd walked through thousands of times without thinking twice. Those days were gone. He'd severed his right to just walk in. At this point, he just hoped Tara talked to him.

The dead bolt flicked and Tara eased the door open, pulling her robe tighter around her chest.

"Sam, what are you doing here?"

She always looked gorgeous. Whether she wore her ratty old bathrobe or she had on a formfitting dress. His Tara was a complete knockout. Only she wasn't his anymore.

"Marley called me."

"What?"

"She said you'd been crying." He studied her face but didn't notice any traces of tears. "Everything okay?"

"I wasn't crying," she stated, but her swollen, red eyes gave her away. "Nothing for you to worry about. What else did she tell you?"

Sam swallowed. This wasn't the first time Marley had called him, trying to find a reason to get him to come over. He knew his little girl wanted her parents to live together again, but it just wasn't possible right now.

Even so, he and Tara had made it clear they would put Marley first at all times. They didn't want her to suffer any more than necessary. Keeping her happy, feeling secure, was top of their priority list.

"I'm fine." Tara licked her lips and raked a hand through her hair, then opened the door wider. "Do you want to come in and see her? She's getting ready for bed. Or I thought she was. I'm sorry. I had no idea she called you."

Again.

The word hovered between them because this wasn't the first time, and likely not the last. But Sam would come every single time if there was the slightest chance something was wrong with Tara.

"I shouldn't come in." Though he desperately wanted to. He wanted to walk in that door and tuck his daughter into bed and then go to his own room with his wife. "I don't want her to think she can keep doing this when there's nothing wrong."

But there was so much that was wrong. So much pain, so much heartache. All of it caused by his selfish desires, his addiction. An addiction he'd put ahead of his own family.

Tara glanced over her shoulder, then eased out the front door and closed it at her back. Sam adjusted his stance to make room for her. The glow of the porch lights illuminated her green eyes. It was those wide, expressive eyes that had initially drawn him to her.

"I know you're trying to move forward, to seek forgiveness or even more from me." She looked down to her clasped hands and shook her head. "But you can't keep leaving notes, Sam."

That's how he'd originally started to get her attention when he was serious about dating her. Stonerock was a small town, so they'd known each other for years, but something had shifted. He'd leave random notes asking her out and then, once they were together all the time, he'd leave little love notes. He'd done that for years, wanting her to know how special she was.

He'd messed up. There was no denying the facts. All he could do now was try to prove to her, to Marley that he was the man they needed him to be. No matter how long it took.

"I'm a patient man," he told her, fisting his hands at his sides because he wanted to reach out and touch her. He wanted to brush her hair back from her face and feel the silkiness of her skin once more. "I know I hurt you. I know I hurt Marley. But you know me, babe. I'm going to make this right."

"It's over," she whispered. "I don't want to keep dragging this out. What happened is in the past and we both need to move forward. It's not healthy, Sam."

"No, it's not," he agreed. "I'm starting over, Tara. I'm trying one day at a time."

"Maybe you should just sign the papers," she whispered through her emotion as she went back inside.

The door closed. The click of the lock seemed to echo in the dark of the night. But Sam couldn't give up. His family needed him.

He had every intention of proving to Tara that he could be a better man.

* * * * *

LET'S TALK
Romance

For exclusive extracts, competitions
and special offers, find us online:

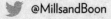 facebook.com/millsandboon

@MillsandBoon

@MillsandBoonUK

Get in touch on 01413 063232

For all the latest titles coming soon, visit
millsandboon.co.uk/nextmonth

MILLS & BOON

THE HEART OF ROMANCE

A ROMANCE FOR EVERY READER

ODERN

Prepare to be swept off your feet by sophisticated, sexy and seductive heroes, in some of the world's most glamourous and romantic locations, where power and passion collide.

STORICAL

Escape with historical heroes from time gone by. Whether your passion is for wicked Regency Rakes, muscled Vikings or rugged Highlanders, awaken the romance of the past.

EDICAL

Set your pulse racing with dedicated, delectable doctors in the high-pressure world of medicine, where emotions run high and passion, comfort and love are the best medicine.

ue Love

Celebrate true love with tender stories of heartfelt romance, from the rush of falling in love to the joy a new baby can bring, and a focus on the emotional heart of a relationship.

Desire

Indulge in secrets and scandal, intense drama and plenty of sizzling hot action with powerful and passionate heroes who have it all: wealth, status, good looks…everything but the right woman.

EROES

Experience all the excitement of a gripping thriller, with an intense romance at its heart. Resourceful, true-to-life women and strong, fearless men face danger and desire - a killer combination!

To see which titles are coming soon, please visit

millsandboon.co.uk/nextmonth

JOIN US ON SOCIAL MEDIA!

Stay up to date with our latest releases, author news and gossip, special offers and discounts, and all the behind-the-scenes action from Mills & Boon...

 @millsandboon

 @millsandboonuk

 facebook.com/millsandboon

 @millsandboonuk

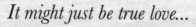

It might just be true love...

GET YOUR ROMANCE FIX!

Get the latest romance news,
exclusive author interviews, story
extracts and much more!

blog.millsandboon.co.uk